Praise for

Prize

"A profoundly moving and absolutely gripping novel about the choices women face—and the choices they are denied. I cannot recommend it highly enough."

—Elodie Harper, bestselling author of *The Wolf Den*

"Gorgeous. *Prize Wo*... ...portant message about wome... ...motherhood—took my breath aw... ...hinking about it."

—Jen... ...estselling author of *Ariadne*

"*Prize Women* is a serious, thoughtful, and epic journey into the trials of motherhood. . . . With her contrasting female characters, Lea interrogates the fight for female agency across class divides, a struggle that continues to this day. A fascinating snapshot of another time, perhaps not as far removed from our own as we might hope."

—Janice Hallett, bestselling author of *The Appeal* and *The Twyford Code*

"Masterful. Caroline Lea is a superb storyteller, and *Prize Women* deserves a huge readership. So good, I had to pull myself away."

—Elizabeth Macneal, bestselling author of *The Doll Factory* and *Circus of Wonders*

The Metal Heart

"The story of true innocents caught up in the machinery of war. Exquisitely researched, beautifully told, this tiny corner of Scotland came alive for me in all of my senses, and I found myself rooting for the central characters with all my heart."

—Mary Beth Keane, author of *Ask Again, Yes*

"A powerful Second World War love story. As tensions grow between the Italian POWs and the Orkney men, the scene is set for a dramatic reckoning. Lea writes beautifully of island life and love, and the sacrifices that both demand."

—*The Times* (London)

"Atmospheric, heart-wrenching, evocative; this is a gorgeously written story about the scars we carry with us, and how they can be overcome."

—Gytha Lodge, author of *Watching from the Dark* and *She Lies in Wait*

Glass Woman

"Gripped me in a cold fist. Beautiful."

—Sara Collins, author of *The Confessions of Frannie Langton*

"Piercing. . . . Devastating and revelatory."

—*New York Times Book Review*

"A fantastic, atmospheric debut."

—*The Times* (London)

"Memorable and compelling. A novel about what haunts us—and what should."

—Sarah Moss, author of *Ghost Wall*

"Lea crafts deeply intriguing characters while bringing to life their harsh landscape. Full of emotion, mystery, and suspense, this unique love story will keep readers guessing until the very end."

—*Booklist*

Prize Women

CAROLINE LEA

HARPER PERENNIAL

NEW YORK • LONDON • TORONTO • SYDNEY • NEW DELHI • AUCKLAND

For my sons, Arthur and Rupert.
And for Roger.

HARPER ● PERENNIAL

HarperCollins books may be purchased for educational, business, or sales promotional use. For information, please email the Special Markets Department at SPsales@harpercollins.com.

Originally published in the United Kingdom in 2023 by Michael Joseph, an imprint of Penguin Random House UK.

Image on page iv: Archives of Ontario. Series RG 22-305 York County Surrogate Court estate files file 55697 Charles Vance Millar.

FIRST HARPER PERENNIAL EDITION PUBLISHED 2023.

Library of Congress Cataloging-in-Publication Data has been applied for.

ISBN 978-0-06-324434-4 (pbk.)

23 24 25 26 27 LBC 5 4 3 2 1

Toronto Daily Star, November 1, 1926

Death of Charles Vance Millar

We regret to announce renowned lawyer Charles Vance Millar died unexpectedly yesterday at his desk, age seventy-two. The cause of his passing is believed to be heart failure. According to his associate, Mr. Charles Kemp, who was with him at the time, Mr. Millar had been intent on proving a point of law, and sprinted up three flights of stairs to his office, whereupon he was overcome by the sudden exertion.

High Jinks

A respected lawyer within the community, as well as the owner of racehorses and shares in the O'Keefe Brewery, Mr. Millar will be most widely remembered for his love of practical jokes, his favorite being to leave money on the sidewalk and conceal himself to watch while people picked up the dollar bills—an exercise which he called "an education in human nature."

The Last Laugh

Being unmarried and having no descendents, Mr. Millar had often claimed that he would leave his considerable fortune to the University of Toronto. However, we at this publication have been told, exclusively, that Mr. Millar's last wishes will bequeath his money to a variety of surprising sources: lifetime tenancy of his vacation home in Jamaica will be granted to three as yet anonymous colleagues, all of whom, we are told, are known to be sworn enemies of one another; Millar's shares in the Catholic O'Keefe brewery will be given to practicing Protestant ministers in Toronto; Millar's shares in the Ontario Jockey Club are to be given to two renowned anti-horse-racing advocates.

There are a number of other risible bequests, but perhaps the most surprising—and amusing—is that the remainder of Mr. Millar's considerable fortune is to be granted to the Toronto woman who bears the greatest number of children over the next ten years. No other details have yet been released, but we look forward to finding out more about this final outrageous practical joke from Toronto's favorite prankster.

Mr. Millar will be sadly missed, but this paper suspects his legacy will live on.

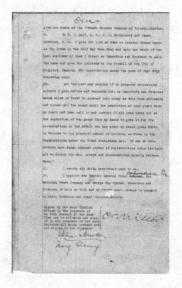

Prologue

Mae betrays Lily for the second time in a courtroom. It is October 20. It is the anniversary of Lily's son's death. A dull winter morning, the pale light seeping in through the high windows and gilding the spiraling dust motes so that, for a moment, the room is almost beautiful. Although this isn't what Lily is thinking as she sits, her hands clasped in her lap, answering the lawyer's final questions.

All around her, polished wood and winter furs; all around her, the smell of money—tobacco, coffee, leather, and cologne. It is the first time in weeks that Lily has been warm and she pulls her thin coat more closely around her shoulders.

Lily wonders how to answer the most recent question, only she can't remember what it is. Her attention must have wandered, because the lawyer isn't asking what they rehearsed. She was supposed to state only how many children she has, their names and ages. But the lawyer, the man employed by Mae to argue her case and Lily's, is talking about *morality* and *respectability*.

Outside, there will be frost. Streets away, where the leaky-roofed houses are crammed together, the mud will

1

be loosening on the paths, and Lily's children will be wrapping rags around their feet to keep out the cold while they stand in the bread line.

At the thought, her hands grip the plush velvet seat beneath her. She no longer tries to calculate how many meals she could make from selling even the cheapest chair in the courtroom.

The lawyer has been speaking loudly and at length about the amount of money at stake: hundreds of thousands of dollars to the mother who has had the most children in ten years. But, the lawyer explains to the court, puffing out his chest and pacing as he speaks—very specific criteria have to be fulfilled. As if the people watching don't already know, as if the Stork Derby hasn't been in every newspaper in Toronto for months.

"And," the lawyer says, "it is this court's task to ensure that the successful mother is a deserving, morally upright member of the community. That her representation of herself and her family is *honest*."

He talks on, his cheeks reddening as he warms to his theme. Lily's thoughts begin to drift again, to the children back at home and what she can possibly give them to eat; to her breasts, aching and heavy with milk from missed feeds.

There is a pause, and Lily becomes aware of the number of eyes fixed upon her, of the sniggers from the gallery. "I'm sorry, I didn't hear you," she says quickly, sitting up and trying to smile, to look appealing to the judge, to the people watching, to the reporters scribbling in their notebooks. Another titter from the gallery and this time the lawyer smiles, too, though he tries to hide the grin by stroking his mustache.

"I'm sorry," she repeats more loudly, smoothing her thin cotton skirt. "Could you say that again?"

The lawyer's smile widens. "Would you like me to word it differently, so that you can understand?"

More snickering from the gallery.

"Yes, please."

"I asked," the lawyer said, "what motivated you to come to Toronto? What made you leave Chatsworth and New Brunswick, your home? What made you leave your husband?"

Lily scans the courtroom to catch Mae's eye, but Mae is staring at her own hands, her posture a mirror of Lily's, knotting and unknotting her fingers. And Lily wonders why Mae won't look at her, why she won't meet her eye and somehow communicate the right answer. She wonders how the lawyer knows to ask her about Chatsworth when the only person who knows about that time is Mae.

High above, in the pallid sky, the sun disappears behind a cloud; the light in the courtroom dims. The golden dust motes vanish, as if something has snuffed them out.

part one

How can you frighten a man whose hunger is not only in his own cramped stomach, but in the wretched bellies of his children? You can't scare him—he has known a fear beyond every other.

John Steinbeck, *The Grapes of Wrath*

1

The weather has been odd all autumn: bright, cold days giving way to an open, star-stamped sky and the sensation of frigid air dropping from frozen space. Along the northern border of the small town of Chatsworth, the black surface of the Miramichi River roils.

It's hard to pinpoint the moment when something starts. Hard to identify the exact instant when the scales tip, when the hammer begins to fall, when the blade starts to swing downward. But later, when she thinks about it, Lily will remember the unseasonal ice that rimed the shores of the river for weeks; she'll recall the poor man whose thumb got jammed in the pulp-mill machinery when it froze; she'll think of the animals that skulked in from the dense forest all around—moose and foxes and even, it was rumored, a bear—creeping from the shelter of the trees to try to scrounge food from trash cans.

When she looks back on this time, Lily will see all of these things as warnings. Portents that everyone ignored.

But for now, Lily is in the cold kitchen plucking a chicken they cannot afford. Her fingers are frozen and she jiggles her legs to keep warm, trying to wrap her skirts around eight-year-old Matteo, playing silently with a train at her feet.

Tony isn't yet back from the paper mill. He will have gone to a tavern, as he has done nearly every night since the mill began laying people off. It is often Tony's friends who have been let go, and all the men are jumpy and angry, worried that they'll be next. When Tony staggers in, smelling of whiskey and other women, Lily often pretends to be asleep. But he'll poke her awake with his finger or his foot, and he'll sit on the bed, his weight dipping the mattress so that her body is thrown toward him.

"I don't understand," he'll say. "Business is booming everywhere, so why are they cutting men from jobs out here?"

"I don't know." And she doesn't, because it's true: everyone is making money. New taverns and shops are opening everywhere. Chatsworth sits on a large knuckle of land that juts out toward the Atlantic Ocean, as if pointing back toward Europe, where so many of its inhabitants and their ancestors first lived. In the summers, when the population doubles, tourists go boating in the river or take picnics into the forest, their faces flushed from drink as they call jokes to one another in their hard city accents and laugh, slurring.

Years ago, Tony used to take her on picnics in those dark pines. He'd lain next to her on a blanket and pointed at the towering trees. "See, look at these. These are money. Just growing out of this soil." And he'd dug his fingers into the earth and scattered soil along her arm, both of them laughing as she squirmed away from him.

His eyes were shadowed, his expression earnest as he'd told her, "Everyone wants wood for boats and paper and buildings. I'm going to have my own factory one day. I'll make us rich. I'll look after our children."

"Children?" She'd laughed. She wasn't yet twenty and had known him less than a month.

He'd raised his eyebrows and kissed her, saying *yes* against her lips, telling her that he wanted children with her dark hair and big eyes, telling her that they would have strong, brave boys and beautiful, gentle girls.

She'd loved this certainty about him. The cockiness, the almost-arrogance that helped him to ask for a raise at the factory, that kept him hopeful even after the miscarriages, even when the demand for wood went down and the factory first began laying men off. But seven years of disappointment have worked hard lines into Tony's face and a tension around his mouth, especially when he drinks.

"There's no chance for us here," he often grumbles, when he gets in from the taverns. "No hope for dumb dagos like us."

Lily flinches from the word *dago*, although she works hard not to show it. She keeps walking if she hears it whispered in the streets, and if people push in front of her at the bakery or the general store, then she knows enough to keep her smile fixed, to wait her turn, not to push back.

But it's harder to ignore the world outside when Tony brings it into their home.

"I think they've got it in for us," Tony will say. "The government doesn't care about the men who work in the factories and the paper mills. We don't matter."

"Of course you matter," she'll murmur, pretending to be half asleep, when every nerve in her body is alert, conscious of the tone of his voice, the twitching muscle in his jaw, the tightening of his hand on hers.

His breath will be sour with whiskey or rum. Since Prohibition, the taverns are only allowed to sell weak beer, or wine with a meal, but there's always a barman willing to fortify the ale with moonshine, for a price.

She mustn't ever appear to be frightened, or he will be angry. She mustn't contradict him too strongly, or he'll lose his temper and there will be no more sleep for anyone that night.

Afterward, he will be ashamed. He will hold her and kiss her; he will whisper tenderly into her hair. Sometimes he will weep, and look at her with such bewilderment that she will remember the man she married all over again. The man who never raised his voice or fist, who never sneered about himself, about her, as if he was cursing both of them.

She goes to the Catholic church on Brunswick Street every Sunday, but she is beginning to suspect that God heeds other people first, in the same way that Mrs. Griffin in the post office serves Canadians first—the people whose families sailed across from England hundreds of years ago. Then she serves Irish immigrants, then the very few Italians. And Lily assumes God has the same pecking order: why else would the older families have prayers answered so readily, with their big houses and their fancy cars and their healthy children?

Lily was two when her parents brought her across from the north of Italy, just after the turn of the century. She couldn't remember Italy, except, perhaps, a warmth in the sky and the richness of sunlight on orange stone walls, although maybe these things are memories that her parents gave her, stories about the homeland they missed. She had a slight accent still, mostly from her parents; it has grown stronger since her marriage to Tony. Tony, who grew up just outside Pisa and had been fiercely proud of this when she first met him.

"How can you call yourself an Italian," he'd demanded, "when you've never tasted a real tomato? These watery things do not count."

"I don't call myself an Italian," she'd said. "I call myself Liliana."

Earlier, after Mrs. Griffin had talked about the redundancies in the paper mill—after she'd spoken of the rumors that the owners were cutting down on workers, moving more of their business to the bigger cities to the west, Ottawa, Montréal, and Toronto, and transporting the trees there by rail, Lily had known: *Even if Tony keeps his job today, it won't be for long.* And then how would they afford the food on their table, the roof over their heads?

Their house is one in a long line, each sharing walls and noises—she knows her neighbors' sleep patterns; she hears their bickering and their reconciliations. This evening all the curtains are drawn even though it is not yet not quite—dark. Farther into town there are enormous mansions alive with candlelight, but her neighborhood is made of cramped buildings, with bad drainage and shared walls. Damp, and crumbling.

Lily sighs. Across the street, she catches glimmers of light behind an identical row of thinly curtained windows, shadows moving and laughter. In her imagination, her neighbors are nearly always dancing or laughing, or making love.

She pulls out the last of the feathers and puts the chicken into the pot with water. Roasted tastes better, but boiled with carrots and onions will last longer: she will be able to skim some of the fat from the broth and spread it on crackers for Matteo.

Matteo never complains that he is hungry. He rarely speaks at all, her only boy; his face crumples and she can see him rubbing his stomach, but he doesn't cry or moan. Her child has learned to make himself small and quiet and watchful.

"Why doesn't he *talk*?" Tony frequently demands.

But Tony's clenched fist creates its own language. It makes its own silences.

Matteo used to chatter all the time, when he was little. Then he talked only when Tony wasn't nearby. She last heard his voice a year ago.

With the chicken on the stove Lily has time—just—to take Matteo down to the river before Tony returns. Matteo loves it there. She kisses his soft cheek. And as she does so, there is a jolt, almost as if the earth beneath her feet has jumped. She blinks, stares at him.

"Did you feel that?" she asks.

He nods, his gaze wide and watchful behind the dark hair that is always messy, that always flops over his eyes. She leaves it longer than she should because he likes to hide behind it.

"Come on," she says brightly, shrugging away a sudden unease. "We've still time to get to the water."

Matteo smiles up at her. In his hand, he clutches the white, papery bark he strips from the silver birch trees. He loves to curl it around itself, using other sticks and pieces of wood to make masts and sails. Then he pushes his little boats out and watches them bob on the water, before they're lost farther downriver, as the banks widen and the river becomes tidal, the water cloudy with salt.

Lily has told Matteo that, if he builds a strong enough boat, it will sail downstream, out into the sea and be taken east.

"All the way to Europe," she says. "Perhaps even to Italy."

Lily feels her body relax and her lungs expand as they reach the bank. Matteo holds his boats tightly and she clutches his arm as he lowers the first curved piece of bark onto the river. He doesn't push it out far enough, and a rippling wave brings it straight back. Matteo grins, grabs the boat, and leans as far out as he can, so far that Lily can feel her hands straining to keep hold of him. "Careful!" she calls. But he gives the boats an almighty shove, all at once, and the fragile crafts skate out onto the water, one, two, three, four. And all of them are caught up in the current, carried toward the open sea.

Matteo gives a cry of excitement, and Lily, thrilled by his shout of happiness, picks him up and presses a kiss into the soft skin at the base of his neck, so that he squirms away, giggling.

She laughs too.

And then she feels it: another jolt. As if something has knocked into the ground below her feet.

Matteo's eyes widen.

"What was that?" Lily asks, thinking, absurdly, of the stories in these parts about a salmon that is rumored to swim in the waters, large enough, it is said, to swallow a child whole. The sky is darker now, the stars disappearing behind a rolling cloud bank, and Lily is suddenly aware of how alone they are, that no one knows they are here.

"We should go." She tries to keep her voice steady, not wanting to panic Matteo, but he isn't looking at her anymore. His gaze has slipped past her, out onto the black water, where his tiny boats are traveling *upstream*. Back toward them, as if pushed by some invisible, impossible hand.

"I don't . . ." Lily says, but the words die in her mouth, as a sudden swell of water rises over the bank, a wave soaking her boots, then receding before rising again.

She pulls Matteo to her, as she used to when he was much younger, ignoring the strain in her back, ignoring his struggle to be put down, ignoring his desire to run and fetch his boats.

As she turns back to the town, Lily notices that the stars have been obscured by thick swathes of cloud. Clouds tinged with orange, as if, somewhere, something is burning. She stands very still, listening. The night birds have fallen silent and, out of the stillness, a deer runs past, its hoofs clattering on the rocks. It stumbles but doesn't stop, and Lily can feel the panic emanating from the creature, can feel fear rising through her own body—some age-old animal instinct that something is wrong. Something has begun.

2

Lily grips Matteo's hand tightly as she hurries away from the river, pulling him along as they stumble back through the darkness, toward the lights of the town. Matteo slips and falls, but he doesn't cry out as he hits the ground. Lily stops, panic sluicing through her. He is unhurt, but his eyes are large and frightened. She kisses his forehead and attempts a smile; it feels like a fixed rictus. "It's nothing," she says, her voice too high-pitched. "Let's get back into the warmth."

Something sweeps through the air, almost brushing their heads, and they both jump.

"An owl," Lily says, her heart hammering. "Just an owl." But as its dark shape wings away toward the dense shadows of the forest, it gives a harsh cry, and Lily can't help thinking that this, too, like the deer, like the sudden clouds, is a portent of something awful.

"Come on," she gasps, and there is no keeping the fear from her voice now. That strange electricity in the air is building, the metallic tension that crackles just before a storm. Matteo must feel it too—he keeps pace with her, his mouth set in a thin, resolute line. She sees, for a moment, her own expression mirrored. It is the look that drives Tony crazy, but Lily feels a fierce pride. Her son will have to be obstinate to survive.

They hurry past the town hall, which is silent, and the paper mill—in darkness now. They avoid the direct route home, which would take them along the streets of bars and taverns, blaring lights and laughter, and turn instead to the road running past the Catholic hospital and the poorhouse.

Relief washes over her when she sees her little house, still cloistered in darkness. Tony is not yet home. She feels normality slipping back into itself, like a warm hand into a glove. Drawing a deep breath, she pushes Matteo inside, shutting the door behind them and leaning her forehead against the wood, listening to the thrum of her blood.

"Where have you been?"

Tony is sitting in the darkness, waiting.

Her stomach drops. Instinctively, she shoves Matteo behind her.

Tony stays in the chair, his face half lit by the sliver of moonlight stretching through the window. His arm rests on the table, which, she notices, she'd forgotten to wipe down before she left the house. His gaze is intense, his dark eyes shadowed. He is holding a glass: the room is pungent with the sweet, peaty smell of whiskey.

"You're early." Her voice is bright and strained. "I meant to clean the table. I'm sorry. Are you hungry? There's chicken in a pot on the"

"Where. Have. You. *Been?*" He taps his fingers on the dusty surface, emphasizing every word. He's always had strong hands. When they were first married, the rough rasp of his fingers against her breast used to make her shudder with desire.

"Where?" he whispers.

She tries to swallow, to think of something to say. She can't mention Matteo's boats, can't draw attention to him. Tony doesn't approve of Matteo playing, especially not if it draws Lily from the house. "I—I wanted to walk down to the river."

He stands, and she braces herself, but then he lurches and staggers slightly, before sitting back at the table, leaning his head on his hands. "I'm hungry." His voice is weary and, perhaps because of her relief, she feels a rush of tenderness.

She exhales. "Yes, sorry, of course. There's chicken in the pot. And bread. Do you want that? Or I can fry some cornbread—"

"Chicken."

She fetches a bowl, giving him a generous chunk of the chicken, along with four slices of bread and butter—the butter that was supposed to last the week, but never mind that now.

He eats hunching over, putting his arm protectively around the bowl.

She stands by the stove, watching him. Matteo hasn't moved from the door.

Tony pauses, mid-mouthful. "You're just going to watch me? Sit! Eat!" He gestures with his spoon, flashing his teeth. There is something . . . *off* in his movements. His smile too wide, his voice too loud.

18

She doesn't question him, fetching bowls for herself and Matteo. Like her, he will be too nervous to eat, the food like chalk in his mouth; like her, he will eat anyway, forcing himself to swallow. As she stirs the chicken broth, she can feel Tony's eyes on her face, moving over her body. She doesn't know when she developed this ability, this extra sense that tells her when he is watching her, what mood he is in. When she was young, she'd seen a farmer showing off his dog's obedience: it would run to him, would jump up and sit and roll over, all without the farmer saying a word. She'd thought they must be able to read each other's thoughts, that man and dog. The best of friends! She'd longed for such an animal herself.

Later, she saw the farmer walking home, saw him aim a swift, sharp kick at the animal's ribs; the dog jumped out of the way without the boot touching him, as if he'd sensed it coming.

Now, before Tony has laid down his spoon, she knows he will want more; she serves three brimming ladlefuls, more bread, the remaining butter. She wants to ask him what happened at the paper mill. She wants to know if he'd felt those strange skips in the land, if he'd noticed anything odd, if he'd felt, as she had, a sense of something dreadful approaching. But if she asks the wrong questions, she will make him angry. She spoons an extra piece of chicken into his bowl. When she places it in front of him, there is a moment when the corner of his mouth curls up. Again, she feels a relief that is almost affection.

He hadn't hit her after the first miscarriage. Or after the second. Or when Matteo was a sickly baby, howling all night. Or when he didn't babble or make any noises that might be speech. Tony didn't hit her, but he'd stopped talking to her. Stopped looking at her or smiling at her. He made love to her with his eyes closed, his face turned away.

Then he'd been overlooked for a promotion at work: a young Canadian-born man had been given the managerial role, while Tony had been relegated to the factory floor again. Lily had felt outraged. "But *why*? Why would they ignore you like that?"

His fist struck her across the face so quickly that she didn't have time to duck. She staggered and fell to the floor, cupping her hand over her throbbing cheek.

Tony had crouched next to her. "Oh, God, Liliana! I'm sorry. I'm so sorry." He helped her up, held a cold glass against her cheek, wrapped his arms around her and rocked her back and forth while she heard words rumbling through his chest, like the growl of far-off thunder. He hadn't meant to, he said, but she'd just made him so mad. It was the look on her face, you see. No man wants to be looked at like that by his wife. Like he's a worm or something. It just made him angry, that was all.

"Good woman," he says now. "This soup is good." And she feels a glow. And she knows that this will make whatever is coming even harder. Because something *is* coming— like the moment before a glass shatters. It has already been dropped; there will be no repairing it.

"A *whole* chicken?" he asks, looking toward the pan. His voice is still light, but she can sense other questions beneath this one: *How did we afford this? Why are you being wasteful with my money?*

"Mr. Murray let me have it cheaply," she lies. Murray has never sold anything for less than its full value, but Tony never goes into the butcher's, so there's no reason for him to disbelieve her. She stands; his eyes, gleaming, don't shift from her face. She feels heat creep over her chest—the telltale rise of blood.

At the end of the table, Matteo is chewing fast, his eyes fixed on his bowl.

As she leans across to clear Tony's dish, he slides his hand around over her skirt, to cup one of her buttocks, then squeezes—too hard. When she winces, he draws her in close to him, kisses her. She tastes ale and whiskey.

He pulls her into the little bedroom they share, barely bigger than the small bed. In the early days, Tony used to talk about the *fine house* he would buy one day. Now, he glares at the poky room as if the narrow walls are an accusation.

"Matteo, clear up," he says, without looking away from Lily. "Quietly, mind. No banging those pots."

And though Tony shuts the door as he pushes Lily onto the bed, she can't help listening to the muffled rattle of dishes in the bucket. Tony hitches up her skirt and pulls down his trousers, giving a groan that sounds torn between frustration and pain.

She bites the inside of her cheek, wraps her legs around him, and pulls him close to try to speed things along.

As Tony thrusts, Lily counts how much money they have for the rest of the week.

Not. Enough.

The crack on the ceiling has grown. The walls are yellowing. The thin curtains are torn from when Matteo used to pull himself up on them.

At the last moment, Tony turns toward her and she thinks he is going to kiss her. He recoils, groans, shudders, and collapses on top of her.

Afterward, when Tony is asleep, his trousers still around his knees, Lily stands, wipes herself off, and goes into the other room, where Matteo is lying on the mattress in the corner. He is pretending to sleep, his breathing light and shallow. As she rinses herself from the bucket, then empties the water outside the door, she sees him squint an eye open to examine her. He'll be looking for bruises, a limp, blood.

"Go to sleep," she scolds, knowing he will find comfort in her feigned irritation.

The tension eases from his body and he snaps his eyes shut.

He has always seemed ahead of his years: he walked at nine months and is a quick study at school—the other children tease him for being silent, wondering aloud if he can understand English at all, but the teachers praise his writing, his arithmetic. Lily taught him to read in the same way that she learned, from the scraps of newspapers and magazines stuffed into the window frames to keep out the drafts and used as paper for the outhouse, and she enjoys helping him to trace out letters in the dirt.

He must talk more, everyone says. But Lily sees the fear in his eyes when he is forced to say anything: the shadow of his father eclipses every request.

Now she puts the bucket quietly on the floor. Then gently, so as not to pretend-wake him from his pretend sleep, she pulls the blanket over his shoulders, kisses the pale, tender skin of his temple, and returns to bed.

She wakes to a pallid pre-dawn light. Tony is staring at her.

Nothing in his face changes when he takes her wrist and squeezes it so the bones crackle. She sucks breath into her lungs, instantly alert, instantly frozen, as if her body is balanced on a precipice and any movement she makes will risk plummeting downward.

"How did you know?" His voice is dangerously soft.

Her mind flickers back over the past evening, a trapped moth battering against the glass—how did she know *what*? The safest thing is to say nothing. The safest thing is to wait.

Will Matteo be awake yet?

"You went to the butcher's yesterday," Tony says.

She swallows, nods.

"You heard talk about men being laid off in the paper mill. You bought a chicken. You knew I'd lost my job, but you bought a *chicken*."

"I didn't know"

His hand tightens around her wrist. Pain like a burst of stars.

"Don't lie to me. You heard them talking. John Barry

said his wife saw you. But you bought that chicken. Throwing money away, trying to butter me up. Treating me like a child."

"I wanted to make you feel better."

"With a chicken?" He sounds amused, but she knows him too well to smile.

She looks again at the cracks in the walls, the yellowing paint, the torn curtains. "I'm sorry."

"For spending all my money? Or for taking my son out to avoid me."

"It wasn't to avoid you."

"Stop lying! You *knew*. You knew I'd lost my job, but you didn't say anything. Why?"

"I didn't know"

"Liar! You were trying to distract me. Like I'm a fool. Is that what you think? You think I'm stupid?"

"No!"

She can feel the pressure building around her wrist, the muscles in her arm burning as his grip tightens. And she realizes what he is doing. He has done this before: laid a trap for her. There is no way of her winning now, no way of avoiding this wave.

But there is a different tension too: the feeling she had yesterday, of something about to slip. She remembers the jerks she'd felt, as if the ground was jumping. The water in the river going the wrong way. The air tasting of iron.

She must leave, somehow; she must get away.

Twisting her arm free, she turns and darts through the door, toward Matteo, who is sitting up on the mattress, his eyes huge and terrified, just as Tony reaches her, drags her back, and punches her in the face.

An explosion in her skull, a high-pitched whine in her ears. She crouches on the floor, then lurches to her feet, trying to reach Matteo.

As she takes a step, the first real tremor shifts the walls and ripples through the floor, making Lily stagger toward Tony. She reaches out to steady herself against him, as if she wants to embrace him, as if his clenched fist isn't raised, as if her jaw isn't throbbing from where he has just backhanded her.

She doesn't immediately comprehend that the heaving of the floor and the shaking of the walls is an earthquake. At first, she thinks that her vision has changed, that Tony has jolted something loose in her brain, that rather than *knocking some sense into her*, as he's always promised to, he's slammed something *out* of her.

Tony's eyes are wide, furious, baffled, and for a moment, that's all Lily can see: the whites of her husband's eyes with their fine spidering of veins. Those eyes, red-rimmed with last night's drink, that tell her to *stand still and be quiet, woman.*

The shaking turns to rattling: pictures fall from the walls and, somewhere behind her, a glass shatters. On the mattress, Matteo cries out in alarm. She pushes Tony away, shoving his shoulders hard so that he staggers backward, into the wall. Grabbing Matteo, she pulls on his arm, crouching as she drags him under the table.

He is crying silently; she curls her body around his, shielding him. Waiting for Tony's hand on her shoulder.

Waiting for him to yank her away from their son and raise his fist again. Beneath her, the floor heaves and judders. She bites her tongue, tastes copper. There is an almighty crash as the shelves fall. Lily cries out, but the sound is lost in the grinding, groaning, scraping rattle of the world being shaken by its throat.

She squeezes her eyes shut, wraps her arms tighter around Matteo. How small he is. How fragile his bones. Something smashes near their heads; she covers his face with her hands.

Let it hit me, not him, she thinks. *Whatever it is, let it hit me.*

The shaking slows, the noise quietens, stops.

The stillness is so absolute, the silence so intense, that Lily thinks she has been crushed and killed. The roof has fallen in, she decides, or the walls have collapsed on top of her. She feels disconnected, floating. She thinks of the beliefs of the people who belong to this country, not the milk-skinned European immigrants, who think they own everything, but the native people, whom she rarely sees in the cities, and who are treated like dirt. They have a belief that when the body dies the spirit rises and travels westward, over the grassy prairies where it crosses a river and ascends a mountain into the spirit world. Perhaps the floating sensation she feels is part of that.

Then Matteo shifts in her arms and utters a tiny moan, and—*Oh, God, he's alive!* Somehow, miraculously, they are both still breathing, still able to move. She kisses his cheek, her lips leaving a bright bloodstain on his skin.

"Are you hurt?" she whispers. Her words sound loud in this newly silent world.

Speak to me, she thinks.

He shakes his head.

Idiota, Tony often calls him, grabbing him roughly by the shoulders, the collar, the ear, while Matteo stares at him in silence.

Tony!

Lily peers through the dust, across the room, to where she'd last seen her husband, to where she'd pushed him—hard. She can still feel the weight of him against her hands, can still picture the shock in his eyes as he'd stumbled into the wall.

He isn't there. Tony has gone. Disappeared.

The air is acrid, and thick with a swirling powder that fills her mouth and lungs. Lily coughs, wipes a sleeve across her eyes, then looks again. There is a pile of rubble on the floor and, somehow—Lily blinks—*somehow*, she can see *through the wall* to the trees outside, which slant at drunken angles. Slowly, she understands that the wall has collapsed and that the pile of bricks on the floor is all that remains.

It takes her longer to see Tony.

He is lying underneath the rubble, his hands splayed, as if he is reaching for something, or searching for help, or trying to escape. His skin looks oddly white, like the rest of the room. Lily rubs her eyes again, blinks. Gritty: the dust is settling over everything, draining it of color.

She turns Matteo so he cannot see his father.

"Stay here." She is surprised by the steadiness of her voice.

Everything inside her is shaking: blood, bones, heart. Every nerve quivering. The earthquake is within her now.

Slowly, she inches forward. Limbs aching. Taste of rust. She reaches out toward the inert hand on the floor. On his knuckles, beneath the white dust, she can just make out the blood from where his fist had struck her. She touches her jaw experimentally, runs her fingers over the bruise, swollen like a ripening plum. Through the blur of shock, she feels no pain.

She touches his knuckles. *Still warm.* Again she feels nothing, just the stunned reverberations that echo through her bones.

His face is pressed against the floor, eyes shut, mouth open. As she leans forward, he gives a wheezing groan.

She jumps back, as if he had reached out to grab her. He wheezes again, then coughs, and she realizes that the emptiness she'd felt—the hollow thud of nothingness when she'd looked at his broken body—had been relief. And that what she feels now that he is alive is panic.

She turns to Matteo, who is staring, his eyes terrified and trusting. She checks him for signs of damage: head, limbs, stomach all intact. No blood anywhere. His gaze flicks to his father on the floor, and when Tony wheezes again, Lily sees Matteo flinch, sees her own fear reflected.

For a moment everything slows: her heart pauses, her mind compresses, and she is breathless, waiting for a spun coin to land. Then, as if she has asked a question, Matteo nods quickly, once.

The coin clatters and Lily's heart thuds as she moves to the single, battered wooden chest. Quickly now, with a single purpose, she pulls out a bag, along with clothes and shoes, hers and Matteo's, everything she can find. She stuffs the lot into the bag in a jumble of material, not knowing if she has enough of everything, only knowing that she must move.

Quickly, quickly, quickly. Her heart pounds out the rhythm, echoed by her rapid breath: *Come on, come on, come on!*

Matteo puts a hand on her arm; she pauses. He holds both hands out. In one small palm is his wooden train, which he takes everywhere. In the other is a gold locket Lily's mother had given her when she died, ten years ago now, from the flu. It's her only jewelry, apart from her wedding ring.

"Good boy." She kisses his forehead.

Matteo looks toward the rubble, where his father is still lying facedown. Tony hasn't moved, but his groans have become louder and Matteo's expression is urgent. The doorway is blocked by fallen bricks and plaster: they will have to leave through the hole in the wall, clambering across the rubble and over Tony's body.

Fear tastes sour—or perhaps it is her blood still. Hard to tell.

They must leave now, before Tony moves, before another quake ripples through the little house, bringing more bricks down around their heads. She remembers Tony telling her about the earthquakes north of Pisa. Sometimes the aftershocks would go on for days.

Lifting Matteo over his father's body, she clambers over the rubble. As she steps past Tony, he stirs, hand twitching.

"Please."

Tony's eyes are open. He is staring right at her. He used to say that he would take her back to Italy one day. They would walk around the town of Moena in the north; they would find his aunts and uncles near Pisa. They would sit on the banks of the River Arno drinking red wine.

She draws a shaky breath, tries to speak.

"*Please*," he hisses.

The anger in his eyes—she recognizes the fury building there. If she releases him, if she scrabbles, bloody-fingered, through the rubble and lifts him from the wreckage, he will hit her. Again and again. He will hit Matteo. Everything will be as it always has been, only worse, because now he will know how much she hates him.

Hanging from the wall behind him is a solid piece of wood, one of the beams that forms part of the structure of the house. It is leaning over Tony's body. The only thing preventing it from falling is a twist of wire. Her brain trips and slips on the fact of the wire, on the position of the beam, on the bulk of Tony, half trapped under the bricks, but struggling to free himself.

He is still staring at her. Matteo, too, is gazing at her.

"Look and see if the street is clear," she says to Matteo.

As soon as he turns away, she reaches out, tugs. For a moment the wire catches on the end of the beam and she has to pull hard, has to strain, the wire cutting into her flesh.

It jolts loose and Lily steps backward.

The beam drops, cracking against Tony's skull. His body goes instantly slack, face inert, eyes closed. She can't see if he is breathing. And part of her wants to lift the beam off, to dig him out, to take him to the hospital because . . . *Dear God, what have I done?*

But the other part of her, the part of her that is a mother, turns to Matteo, who is momentarily frozen, his mouth slack with fear.

She puts her arms around him.

She steps over Tony, through the hole in the wall, into the street.

3

The street outside is pitted and rumpled—the cobbles like a badly made bed. Lily struggles to make sense of a world that looks both familiar and strange. There is the butcher's window, on the corner, only the glass has gone, and next to the carcasses that still swing in the open air, a ripped pipe spews water onto the road. Many of the neighboring houses have collapsed; those that remain half standing have gaping cracks in the walls and shattered windows. The road is covered with rubble, wood and glass, as though some beast has ripped through the town. Something crunches underneath Lily's shoe. When she lifts her foot, she finds the shattered mirror from a lady's dressing table. She averts her gaze from her splintered reflection, unwilling to meet her own eyes. She thinks of Tony, lying under the wreckage.

How long will it take before he stops breathing?

She remembers his fingers stroking her neck.

She remembers his hands around her throat.

She kisses Matteo's soft palm. He is crying soundlessly.

Other people are emerging from the surrounding houses, all of them pale, covered with the same white dust as she and Matteo. It is hard to tell who they are—everyone looks dazed, as though walking through some dark dream.

Far off, in the center of town, Lily can hear alarm bells and the chimes of churches ringing out a warning, although she doesn't know if people are pulling on the ropes or if the bells are simply swaying by themselves, as if whatever invisible hand has shaken the earth under their feet has also set the bells ringing.

In the distance, incongruously, she hears the howl of wolves.

I must be going mad. Wolf packs never come this close to the town.

Then she remembers the tiny zoo, which has become bigger and more popular over recent years, as more people from the surrounding towns have visited Chatsworth to boat on the river, play golf, and see wild creatures in cages. Lily wonders if the animals are loose. She imagines them prowling through the ruins of the hotels and taverns. She pictures them scavenging through the wreckage.

"Come on," she says to Matteo, her voice falsely cheerful. Her son is staring at everything, his face slack with shock. He has never been a boy to venture out alone, preferring to stay near to her and only go the short distance to the grocer's or butcher's—the sole trips Tony had permitted. The only place Matteo truly wanted to go to was the river, but if she went, Tony would glare and growl that she shouldn't be taking risks. He wanted to keep her safe, he said, because his own mother had been badly beaten in the street when his family first came to Canada.

Is it possible for anger to be passed from mother to child?

She hears a cry of "*Liliana!*" and she turns, sure it is Tony's voice, calling the name she used to have before he insisted that they become Lily and Tony, to blend in. It had made no difference.

It is not Tony calling, but a turkey vulture circling overhead, in search of meat.

"Quickly now!" Lily's voice is tight as she pulls on Matteo's arm and they begin to pick their way over the wreckage. There are more people on the streets now. Like ghosts emerging from a graveyard, they stir and stand upright. One woman is lifting bricks from an impossibly high mound of rubble and weeping, a high-pitched, repetitive sound, like an alarm bell. Lily wishes she could block it out. A vivid splash of blood stains the woman's neck and collar; Lily looks away, ignoring the twinge of guilt. She can't help anyone else: she must get her son safely away. Away from the risk of more quakes. Away from the memories of Tony and his body, and the stories it could tell.

Where can she take Matteo? Where will he be safe? Nowhere in this town: Tony is too well known from the paper mill and the bars. People will recognize her. They will ask where he is. They will discover that her husband is dead and that she is fleeing and . . . *Oh, God, what will they do?* She knows then that they won't be allowed to leave this ruined town: they will be made to stay in this place that pushes her to the back of lines, that never truly sees her, never wonders who she really is, what she really feels.

She smears brick dust across Matteo's cheeks, over the plaster dust, so that he is striped in red and white. "You look like a monster." She smiles, keeping her voice light, trying to reach him somehow through the shock that has gripped him. Matteo's teeth are chattering; his stare is fixed and glassy. She rubs the dust across her own face. "Now I'm a monster." She forces her grin wider.

His mouth creases. She pulls him close, cursing herself. He has enough to be afraid of, without imagining his mother as a beast. Although perhaps only a beast would leave her husband crushed beneath a wall.

How long until someone finds him? How long before they begin searching for her?

She thinks of the train tracks, the whole rail system that carries goods and people back and forth from here to the big cities to the west. She could live in Ottawa or Montréal, a thousand kilometers away. No one would know them there. No one would know what she had done.

She holds Matteo's shoulders, staring intently at his face. "We're getting a train. Just the two of us." She tests the weight of the coins in the pouch in her pocket. How much would two tickets cost? She closes her fist around it, hoping it is enough.

He opens his mouth and, for a moment, her heart lifts. He's going to speak. She waits.

A wind gusts pieces of paper through the air around them. A man shuffles past, a bloody gash across his cheek. Somewhere, in the distance, a woman screams.

Lily kisses her son's cheek, and they begin to pick their way through brick and wood and glass.

At the crossroads in the center of town, she stops amid the wreckage of broken wood and shattered bricks, the fractured shape of the monument for the men who died in the Great War. The statue of the man has cracked, so that only the legs and torso remain.

Pallid limbs stick out from under buildings. Lily tries not to look. As they pass what used to be the grocer's, Lily has to step over an outflung arm. The fingers are curled inward, as though their owner has tried to grasp something. Lily can hear a voice rasping, *Help me.*

She pauses mid-step.

Help me.

She is about to walk on, but Matteo tugs on her sleeve and stares at the mound of bricks, the smashed glass, the limp hand. The fingers twitch.

Matteo's face is pinched and he refuses to move. She looks over her shoulder, imagining Tony emerging from the rubble, rising from the dead, limping toward her. There are many figures in the street, bloody, dazed, stumbling, but none looks like Tony.

Lily crouches. "Hello?" she says.

On the fingers of the hand are two rings that she recognizes as belonging to the grocer's wife, Marie. Stern-faced, red-haired, and curt with customers, but she would always wink at Matteo. Once, she gave him a windfall apple that was too bruised to sell.

"Hello?" Lily calls, more quietly.

No reply, and those pale, ringed fingers lie unmoving.

Lily stays very still, aware of the rise and fall of her chest, the whoosh of her blood in her ears, aware of her son's small hand, hot and dry, in hers. Eventually, she forces herself to walk on, ignoring the rockfall in her stomach. Abandoning Tony had felt like freedom, an animal urge driving her away to safety. Leaving Marie's cooling body under a pile of broken bricks feels like smothering a part of herself. With each step, Lily is becoming someone else. She wipes brick dust from her tear-damp cheeks.

Monster, she'd joked to Matteo. She can't look at him as she tugs him on.

There is a rumbling and the ground shifts again beneath her feet. She pulls Matteo to her. He hunches down, his mouth stretched wide in a scream, although no sound emerges. She arcs her body over his. Bricks crash around them. The ground grinds against itself. Matteo reaches across her back. At first, she thinks he's balancing against her, and she holds him more tightly. But then he pulls her body closer. He's trying to shield her, too, trying to protect her.

"I'm here," she whispers, and she doesn't know if she's trying to reassure him or herself, doesn't know how he can possibly hear her above the clatter of bricks and the shatter of glass and the grating of metal, but she says it again and again, like a familiar song, like a shared heartbeat: "I'm here, I'm here, I'm here."

She counts in her head until the shaking stops. It's how she would retreat into herself when Tony hit her, trying to ignore the sting and thud of fists on flesh, trying to outlast the pain.

Sometimes Tony would be kind for months. He'd be affectionate with Matteo, tender with Lily. He'd walk over the golf course on his return from work, picking flowers. He'd say, *I am not perfect, but I love you.* And all that time, she would feel hope. And all that time, she would feel like she was kneeling beneath a raised blade, bare neck waiting. Every time he was ignored at work, or they hadn't enough money for new clothes, or she lost another baby, something would shut off in Tony's face. He wouldn't hit her for weeks, while she and Matteo tiptoed around him. Then she would say the wrong thing or look at him the wrong way. There are whole days she can't remember.

The shaking stops; she snaps herself out of the reverie. They must move.

She brushes Matteo down and checks him for cuts, but there are none. In answer to the unspoken question in his eyes, she shows him the unbroken skin of her arms and neck. "I'm fine," she says. He gives an adult nod, his child's lips trembling.

Lily has always loved this expression of his that tells her he understands her completely. The expression that tells her, although he is only eight, he knows somehow what she is thinking.

Perhaps he does because, without waiting for another word from her, he begins walking along the street in the direction of the station. She catches him up, barely seeing the glass at her feet or the shattered buildings that loom around her, like broken teeth; she hardly thinks of Tony lying under the rubble. All she knows is the warmth of her child walking next to her, trusting her. And of how, when the ground had shaken, her boy had put his hand across her back to shield her.

A few other people are wandering toward the station: confused or limping or bleeding. Despite the fierce, panicked energy that is driving her forward, toward the trains and freedom, Lily cannot help stopping to support people who need it, although she averts her eyes from the bodies lying still in the rubble. She pulls a young man upright; she grabs the arm of a shuffling gray-haired woman, encouraging the stranger to lean on her with every step.

"Have you seen my son?" the woman whispers, her voice hoarse. "My baby?" She looks old: any child of hers must be an adult. Her hair is matted with blood, her eyes unfocused.

"I'm sure you'll find him," Lily says. "Keep away from these walls—they don't look safe." And she holds the woman's arm. Not once does Lily let go of Matteo's hand.

By the time they near the station, they have formed a large, bedraggled group, stumbling forward together. Some weep. The gray-haired woman on Lily's arm keeps crying, "My son! My baby!"

The station building's walls are fissured but still standing. Lily's heart lifts and the feeling fades of Tony chasing them. Even though she knows he can't now, that he won't chase her ever again, still there is the echo in her head of his steps, his voice, the smack of his hand against her cheek. All of it fades because here is freedom. No one will find her and take her back to that house once she is on the train. No one will know that she has left her husband lying dead. That she let a piece of wood crack onto his skull. That every time she closes her eyes, she sees his head hitting the floor, hears the thud of it.

When Lily sees the tracks, it takes her a moment to understand.

The metal is twisted and buckled. At one point, the track dips into a hollow in the ground, before rising again, then curling in a half-circle, a large loop out to the side, so that it is suspended over a farmer's field. It looks like a sinuous metal snake, and though it still winds off into the distance, toward Québec City, Ottawa, Montréal, and Toronto, there is no hope that a train would be able to travel on this broken trail.

The crowd stops dead. A keening rises from them, a sound of such despair that it makes the hairs rise on the back of Lily's neck, until she realizes that she, too, is crying. She stands still, but the people around her continue to walk until they reach the tracks, then turn and begin to follow the warped metal.

"Stop!" Lily calls. "There won't be a train."

The woman with gray hair pauses, wipes her hand over her blood-darkened forehead. "Not yet. But maybe farther on. It can't all be like this."

And she limps to join the crowd of people who are returning to their loved ones in far-off cities, or else looking for somewhere safer than the wreckage of their town. Lily considers joining them, but she stares at the track, then back at Matteo. What if a train manages to travel along it, after all, and plows straight into the people? And what if someone finds Tony's body and discovers that she and Matteo have abandoned him, then hears that many people left on foot, following the rail lines? It must be a crime to leave her husband's body in the rubble, even if they don't suspect her of harming him. A policeman might hear that a group departed from the town along the train tracks, might trace her route all the way west.

Instead, she turns to the road, longer and dustier, but with more places to hide. In the distance, looming mountains. She thinks of the deep forest, the animals, the cold and rain and hunger. The wide arc of the sky, endless and unlidded.

The indecision, the terror, is paralyzing.

She closes her eyes and imagines Matteo growing up in this broken-down town. With the shadow of his dead father; with no hope of getting a good job; with children who will think of him as simple and stupid.

She thinks of her parents as they left Italy and sailed west in hope of a better life for themselves and for her. She thinks of the way Tony used to shout her down if she ever mentioned leaving, telling her she didn't understand anything about surviving in this world.

She lifts her chin, holds her son's hand tightly. They begin to walk west.

4

They have been walking for less than an hour when the pain begins. Lily recognizes the deep ache in her belly and back, the clamping squeeze of a hot fist around her midriff. The headache that has nagged at her since before the earthquake—since Tony hit her across the jaw—intensifies, turning into a thudding agony, hammering at her skull with every step. She slows, trying to place her feet more softly, trying to quell the rising nausea that washes through her.

This is how it has started every time. Once before Matteo, and then six times in the years since. Lily holds her stomach, picturing the warmth and darkness inside her body, trying to clench herself shut around this little thing, this little life that is trying to leave her before it has even begun. She's only missed two of her monthly cycles.

Stay, she thinks. *Stay and I'll keep you safe. I promise.*

Sunlight pierces the pines, casting harsh, angular shadows across the path. In the shade, she shivers. It hurts. Everything hurts and she is so very tired.

Matteo gazes at her, a question in his eyes.

A few others also walk along the path now, averting their gaze from her pain. Two carts trundle in the same direction, away from Chatsworth, and two family groups travel in a huddle.

"I'm fine," she says. She wipes her damp forehead, licks sweat from her upper lip. "I'm fine," she repeats. And she will be, if she can just keep walking.

The ground judders. The trees sway and creak and they both stop, waiting. Around them, the other people also freeze—some throw themselves to the ground. With each previous quake, Lily has crouched and clasped Matteo close, but she worries that if she hunches over now, she might not be able to stand again. So she stays rigid, bracing herself against the tremor, bracing herself against the rising tide of pain.

When Matteo was born, she'd been terrified of the compressing agony that had gripped her, the way her body didn't seem to belong to her. She'd gritted her teeth and clenched her fists and writhed, until the kindly midwife— tired-eyed from delivering two babies already that night— had grasped Lily's arm and said firmly, "Stop fighting."

The babies had come soon afterward: Matteo first, followed by a sister, whose skin was tinged blue and who never drew breath. Tony had held Lily's hand as she cried. He'd kissed her hair and held her face, his own eyes full of tears. "We'll have others," he'd said. "And we've got a fine strong boy. Look!"

Tony had adored the baby. He used to press his stubbled face against Matteo's infant belly, blowing hot air into his stomach so that Matteo giggled and Tony laughed too.

Tony. Lily can't help looking over her shoulder. Far

behind, the town is a sprawling blank. From this distance, she can't see the fallen buildings, the skein of tangled wires, the dislodged pipes gushing water into broken streets. From this distance, it looks peaceful. No way to know how many bodies are buried under rubble.

Another wave grips her and she groans. No one stops. Everyone has enough pain of their own without worrying about hers. Perhaps they have lost homes too. Or perhaps they are strangers, returning to their distant cities where they will tell stories about the earthquake to people who love them and sponge their wounds and hold them close. People who will, one day when they die, shut their eyes and say prayers over their bodies.

Tony will be trapped beneath that wall, his body cooling.

He used to make her tiny sculptures from scraps of metal he'd found in the boatyard on the way to the paper mill: long bolts with nuts attached became a bunch of metal flowers; a ripped piece of rusted iron was polished until it became the wing of a bird. But each time she lost a baby, Tony had become quieter and darker and freer with his fists. Drunk more often, stayed out later, brought home nothing but anger.

Pain rinses through her, making her gasp.

"I need to go into the trees," she says to Matteo, gesturing at the closely clustered pines.

Lips pinched in a tense line, he nods.

They have been walking down a dirt road, flanked by a wide, flat plain, studded with bushes. Beyond this scrub, the darkness of trees—tall pines stretching skyward.

What creatures shelter in those shadows? Lily imagines a bear, watching. She imagines a wolf's eyes upon her and stops. She won't walk in among the trees. The bushes provide scant cover, but it will have to do.

She squats and lifts her skirts, clenches her teeth and pretends to wipe herself.

Something warm and wet. She doesn't need to look to know that it is blood.

With a hissing exhalation, she tries to stand upright, but fails. Pain, like a hand opening and shutting in her abdomen, like a second heartbeat, squeezing the blood from her.

Once, when Matteo was young and she'd lost yet another baby, Tony had taken her to a doctor, at the cost of three weeks' wages. The doctor, a heavyset man, had curled his lips in distaste as he'd put something cold and metal inside her. While scrubbing his hands afterward, he'd kept his back to her and told Tony her womb was *incompetent*. He'd asked Tony if she was prone to being hysterical; he'd said she clearly had a *character incompatible with motherhood.*

Lily had listened numbly, her hands chill, her insides cold and cramping. The words had slid over her, as if her skin was made of glass. She'd felt hollow and distant, but also like the slightest pressure might crack her.

Hysterical, incompetent, incompatible with motherhood.

"I'm not," she'd wanted to say. "I have a child. He's perfect. It's when Tony hits me, you see. That's when it happens."

But then, she'd wondered, why did Tony hit her and

shout at her? Perhaps there really was something wrong with her. Perhaps that was what he sensed when he struck her. That wrongness. In the same way that the rich women who occasionally paid her to do their washing or sewing were careful, when they took the piles of clothes from her, not to allow their hands to touch hers. As if she was contagious or corrupt.

She has lost so many babies—six that she knows of, but likely more—that sometimes she wants to put a stop to it all, to this endless cycle of birth and death that grips her body without her control or consent. And she wonders if this thought alone makes her *incompatible with motherhood.*

Now, she looks at her son, her lovely dark-haired, dark-eyed boy, and she tries to stand again. Everyone else might have told her she is wrong, might think she's incompetent or hysterical, but not him. She's never heard him say it, but she knows he loves her. And she senses that love in the anxious half-smile he gives her now, as she struggles to stand, as she clenches her jaw and lurches upright.

The world pitches. Lily stumbles. She needs to lie down.

She can't lie down.

Water. She forgot to bring water. Sweat beads on her upper lip, on Matteo's forehead. The people who were walking along with them have moved ahead, so there is no one to ask. She will have to go back to the town, back to her collapsed house with its dark memories and Tony's body bleeding on the floor.

She crouches, clasping her stomach. Dimly, she's aware of Matteo's hand stroking her hair. She is scaring him. She tries to say, *It's all right. I'm all right.* All that emerges from between her gritted teeth is a ragged groaning. She looks up at him, forcing a smile, but her eyes drift to a bird circling high above the shadowed pines. A hawk, skimming across streams of light and air, wings scything through the bright expanse of sky. As she falls back, Lily feels like she is being watched by something ancient, as if God Himself is looking down on her.

The ground is cold. The chill creeps into her blood, into her bones.

Please, she says, or thinks, or hopes.

A rumbling, as if another earthquake is coming, but Lily understands that the earthquake is within her again, that she is the one who is shaking. Her teeth are chattering, her stomach twisting, and the rumbling is getting louder.

Lily looks up, and through the haze of tears, she sees a cart moving along the road. She forces herself to sit upright, tries to wave down the family in the cart: a man and a woman, with four small children. They are dark-haired and dark-eyed, too, and, for a moment, Lily's hope rises: they must be Italian. Perhaps they will help.

Or perhaps she is imagining them. She wants to ask Matteo if he sees them, but can't summon the words.

"*Aiutaci*," she tries to say. "Help us." The words emerge as a tattered rasp, and Lily realizes how frightening they must look, she and Matteo, with their dust-covered faces and their wild eyes.

The cart rolls onward, the bony horse's hoofs beating a steady tattoo in time with the thrumming in Lily's skull.

They will die here, she and her son. What was she thinking, risking his life in this way?

Then she hears a shout: "Help us!"

It's a voice she barely remembers, yet she recognizes it instantly. She opens her eyes.

"Help us!" Matteo's cry rings through her head, travels through her chest, throbbing alongside her heart. His voice is raspy, high-pitched with panic. "Please," he calls.

It is a sound irresistible to any mother. The cart stops. The people turn. The mother, the father, the children. Even the horse turns to look at them.

Lily waits, not daring to hope.

But next to her, Matteo says, "Thank you," and gives a shy grin.

Where does it come from? Lily wonders. *Where does this trust come from?*

As the family helps them into the cart, Lily tries to gasp her thanks, but the family looks wary and the woman holds up a hand. "You are ill? Something infectious?" she asks. Her face is tanned and deeply lined, her hair pulled back severely from her face. She has the heavy accent of the French Canadians from Québec.

"Not ill," Lily says. "A stomachache."

The woman gives Lily an appraising look. "You have been in the earthquake. You are hurt?"

"Not much, just . . . my stomach." She clenches her teeth through a cramp. "You were in the earthquake too?"

"In a field nearby. The house we were renting is gone. And there is looting now, in the town. It's not safe. Why are you traveling, if you are ill?"

Lily hesitates. "Like you . . . my house was destroyed. Now the looting . . ." She holds her breath.

The woman's eyes flick over Lily's and Matteo's torn clothes, their grubby faces, Lily's swollen jaw.

"Sit down."

She gestures at a space between the youngest children; the older two watch warily from the far end of the cart. Exhausted, Lily slumps. Matteo crouches next to her.

The woman says something to her husband in rapid French. The man grunts, then passes them a canteen of water. Lily lets Matteo drink first. He takes a sip, then offers it to her; she shakes her head, refusing the water until he has had enough.

The woman watches them. "You have a good boy," she says. "No husband?"

"He died. A long time ago . . ." Lily fixes her gaze on Matteo. He swallows, and she knows he understands. Somehow, this is worse than letting Tony die. She feels like she has made him agree to kill his father.

"Ah, I'm sorry for your loss," the woman says. "And you have lost your home now too. Brave boy."

Matteo stares at his shoes and gives a shuddering sigh. Lily feels a stab of guilt, but it is soon chased away by another cramping pain.

"Drink this." The woman presses a small bottle into Lily's hand. "You are too pale. This will help."

Unable to argue, Lily sips the sour, brackish liquid. Some sort of moonshine. It burns and she feels almost instantly lightheaded, but the woman is right: the pain eases.

"You often bleed badly?" the woman murmurs.

"Yes." She tries to sit up. Will the woman let her stay in the cart if she realizes that Lily might be losing a baby?

"Where are you traveling to?" the woman asks, turning to Matteo. He says nothing.

Lily wonders if she had dreamed his voice, or imagined it. Or perhaps he had spoken just that once and won't ever speak again.

"West," Lily says. "Far away. A fresh start."

"Ah," the woman says, and although she looks skeptical, she doesn't stop the cart. "We're going west, too—Jacques lost his job in Québec. We came out this way, looking for work in the paper mill, but there's nothing left. Now things will be worse for a long time." She gestures back toward the ruined town. "So we are going to Toronto. We have family who will help us there. And you?"

"Toronto also," Lily says, fixing her eyes upon Matteo, who looks pale.

Does Toronto sound frightening to you? A big, far-off city you've only seen on maps.

He's still staring at his scuffed boots, but as the cart creaks forward, he looks up. "My train," he says, his eyes bright with tears.

He must have dropped it back on the road, perhaps when he tried to help her up. They can't possibly go back.

"I'm sorry," she says.

She wants to hear him reply that it's all right, that he understands, that he loves her, or that he doesn't understand, not at all, that he hates her. She wants him to say anything, anything at all. She just wants him to keep talking.

But his cheeks are wet and he stares at his scuffed shoes. As the cart rolls onward, westward, away from everything they know, he says nothing at all.

Lily lies as still as she can, watching the light seep from the huge sky, imagining the clamped, cradling darkness inside her. She tries to picture something warm. She tries to hold on to something that might feel like safety.

5

Bathurst Road

The cart rolls on, rocking Lily gently. She drifts. The yellow moon emerges, hanging low in the sky, and still they don't stop. The children sleep while the man and woman take it in turns to drive the weary horse.

Matteo snores softly, then slumps sideways, his head pillowed in her lap. Whenever she wakes, she strokes the hair back from his forehead. Once, she is dimly aware of the woman leaning forward and examining her skirts. She must guess that it's more than Lily's monthlies, but she doesn't panic, doesn't force them to get out. Perhaps there really are good people in the world.

"You are lucky, I think," the woman murmurs. "It may start again, but the bleeding has stopped." Her voice, with its slight French accent, is matter-of-fact, but in the pale moonlight, her eyes are soft and understanding. "You have lost one before?"

Unable to speak past the tightness in her throat, Lily holds up her open hand, fingers splayed, along with her forefinger. *Six.*

The woman holds Lily's hand briefly between hers. "Three. I'm Thérèse. That's Jacques."

"Liliana. Lily. My son is Matteo."

Thérèse glances at her husband, who is stiff-backed, driving the cart. He appears not to be listening, but Thérèse still keeps her voice low. "I didn't want so many, but he wouldn't keep off me. Now I have these." She indicates her sleeping children.

"You're lucky."

"Lucky. Yes. But they are noisy and greedy." She grins. "Sometimes I threaten to give them sawdust." Her smile fades. "Being a mother is hard." She sighs. "Toronto will be better, I hope. My cousin owns a steelworks, so he will have a job for Jacques, and there are rooms for us to rent." She looks at Lily, her gaze sliding over her wedding ring.

"You have work in Toronto?"

Lily shakes her head.

"Family?"

"No," Lily says softly.

"You have nowhere to stay." It's not a question.

Lily knows the look on Thérèse's face should fill her with dread. She should be panicked at the thought of going to this unknown city with her child and no way of supporting herself. But even as the blood jolts through her veins, even as her thoughts scrabble, another feeling forms: an untethered sensation, as though she is a hot-air balloon, cut free from its ropes and sailing higher every moment. She thinks of her parents again. The fear they must have felt. The hope. The people they must have trusted.

She leans her head back and gazes up at the star-salted

sky. Somehow, the thought of all that space, and her smallness in it, is a comfort.

The morning brings an ache to every bone in her body. Her muscles feel filled with ground glass. Even her eyelids hurt. She moans, conscious of Thérèse's face close to hers, and a cold cloth on her forehead. She thinks of how the Québecois are generally disliked: they're said to be strange and aloof, with odd habits and traditions. It's widely known that they don't school their children properly, and if they come into any of the other towns or cities, they often keep away from anyone who doesn't speak their own language.

But as Lily feels the cool cloth on her skin again and again, she can sense Thérèse's compassion. How strange it is, she thinks, that we believe other people feel differently from us, just because their language is different. The same people who told her stories about the Québecois were the people who, if she walked into the grocer's, would whisper to each other before talking to her or, sometimes, would walk past her as if they hadn't seen her.

"Thank you," she murmurs.

"You have a fever," Thérèse says. "We will stop for the night in Bathurst, a small town north of Chatsworth. You know it?"

Lily shakes her head.

"After we have rested, you will feel better. Then we will get a train to Toronto."

"What? No!" Lily tries to sit up, but her head pulses. "You can't do that for me."

Thérèse grins. "We are not doing it just for *you*. The

horse is tired, so he is slow. Jacques will sell him in Bathurst. I have heard it's a busy place because of all the trains."

"You don't need to look after me."

Despite the ease she felt just a moment ago, it makes her suspicious, this extra kindness. Why would these strangers give up so much to keep her safe?

"We planned to get the train from Québec City, but that is five hundred kilometers west. You want to sit in this cart for five hundred kilometers?" Thérèse grins. "No, your derrière will be numb. This way, we will reach Toronto sooner. It is good—the children are tired, and Jacques."

Jacques says nothing. Lily can see only his back as he drives the horse onward, but she senses his disapproval, wants to protest again. But then she feels Matteo pressing his face into her neck. Very faintly, he whispers, "Please, Mama." She can hear exhaustion and fear in his voice—the voice that is both familiar and strange.

"I don't have money for the train fare as well as food," she says.

"Jacques can sell your necklace."

Perhaps this is it, Lily thinks. Perhaps they want to sell her things, make money from her. Suddenly she doesn't care, as long as she can get to Toronto, or somewhere else far away. She unclasps her mother's locket and holds it out to Thérèse, who puts it into her pocket.

They reach Bathurst by nightfall. It is a town not unlike Chatsworth, with rows of houses along the riverfront, a street full of new shops and taverns, and then, behind these, older houses stretching back toward a church and a town hall. The newer homes, big riverside properties, are all freshly painted.

Her stomach is throbbing still. Lily tries not to imagine what might be causing it. She tries not to think about the woman at the end of her street in Chatsworth, who developed a fever after her baby died inside her— or perhaps the fever had come first, Lily can't remember. It took a week for the woman to die. Lily tells herself this is just a fever, nothing to do with the baby. The baby is still alive. It must be.

She is barely awake when they reach the guesthouse, drifting in a dreamy, twilight state, where it is hard to remember anything.

So cold. Voices whispering. Hands lifting her. So hot. Flashes of light and darkness.

A mattress in a small dark room. A whitewashed wall. Thérèse's hand, gentle behind her head. "Sit up. Have a mouthful of broth. Drink this water."

Lily turns her head away from the bowl.

Thérèse scowls. "You will need strength for the train journey. And here—Jacques sold your necklace to buy your tickets, but there is some money left over." She holds out a handful of coins.

Lily feels guilty for ever having doubted her. And she drifts into syrupy sleep.

At some point, she stirs, hearing music and laughter.

The room is dark and she feels confused, her thoughts like drifting feathers. How much time has passed?

Matteo is asleep next to her. Around the room, she can just make out the vague, half moonlit shapes of Thérèse, Jacques, and their children on the bed.

A trumpet is playing somewhere. The clink of glasses. She creeps over to the window and pulls back the curtain.

In the glow of a lamp outside the guesthouse, a group of people stand, holding drinks and laughing. One man has a violin and another a saxophone. They play occasional notes or lines from songs Lily doesn't recognize, while the other men and women pair up and dance around one another in the street. The women's dresses glitter as they move; their teeth gleam as they laugh. Lily remembers what Tony always said: *Business is booming everywhere. All the world's getting richer and we're getting poorer.*

Lily crawls back to the mattress, allowing the music and laughter to lull her back to sleep, the words of the song circling in her mind: *Pack up all my care and woe. Here I go, singing low.*

6

Bathurst

The station is busy, with people chattering in groups, voices lively as they discuss the tremors, felt here but not strongly enough to wreak any damage.

"I heard people were killed in Chatsworth," one woman says in a strong American accent. "And there was a tidal wave after the earthquake, so folks drowned too. Can you imagine?" There is a hint of excitement in her voice, along with the horror.

Her companion leans in conspiratorially. "*I* heard there's some people upped and left after the looting, but the papers're saying the police're calling out for them to return, threatening to find them who's fled. It's not right, folk using this earthquake for gain."

Lily imagines Tony lying dead in her house, his body being freed by policemen, or neighbors, or perhaps the fire crew. A group of rescuers digging through the rubble, searching for her body or Matteo's. Perhaps a neighbor will have seen them leaving. Perhaps someone will say that they saw her walking west.

No one will care, she tells herself. *I didn't take anything that wasn't mine. They'll forget all about me. About us.* Still, when she sees a policeman standing in the corner of the station she finds herself squeezing Matteo's hand harder than she should. She forces herself to breathe evenly, tries to sound cheerful as she says, "A train! Isn't that exciting?"

They've never ridden the railways before, despite the busy station at Chatsworth. Other poor families saved up money over the year for a summer day trip, but Tony hadn't liked going anywhere outside the town, and somehow, even when he was at work and would never have known, she'd felt his presence, as if he was watching her, as if he'd sensed her disobedience. Her life had shrunk to fit inside his slowly closing fist.

Even now, looking at the train, she can still feel his gaze on her, can hear his voice.

"Where do you think you're going?"

She jumps and turns, but it's only Jacques, frowning because, without being aware of it, she has turned away, has begun walking from the train.

Thérèse takes her hand. "No need for fear. And don't gape you look like a half-wit." She chuckles to take the sting from her words, her steady gaze and kind face bringing Lily back to herself so that she manages to walk over to the train, manages to step up and inside, where it is warm and smells of leather.

"This is first-class," Thérèse says. "We'll need to keep walking."

They move down the carriage, Lily unable to stop herself from staring into the compartments they pass— little rooms, where people sit facing one another but not talking. So many of them must be strangers, although their legs are touching. A man stuffs tobacco into his pipe while the woman next to him, her body angled away from his, holds up a pocket mirror and powders her nose. In the next carriage, the people sit around a table, laughing while a man deals cards—even the women are playing, their faces bright and carefree. These must be city people: glossy and happy.

Third-class carriages have no leather seats, only wooden benches; no smell of perfume and fewer extravagant dresses; sounds of laughter replaced by the chatter and cries of children. Lily presses her back to the window, feeling sick as the train gives a whistle and a huge sigh, then jerks forward. A steady *clackety-clack*, like a frantic heartbeat; a moment of terror—the knowledge that they can't go back, that they are traveling west, that she really has abandoned the dead body of her husband— but then she sees Matteo's eyes, shining as he cranes his neck to stare out of the window.

He nudges her to point out an eagle, then gives a gasp of delight as the train picks up speed, rattling by trees and rolling hills, the landscape scrolling past faster than Lily has thought possible. Matteo holds her hand against his cheek; his face is almost unrecognizable, stretched into a wide smile that she hasn't seen in years and certainly not over the past few haunted days.

"Look, Mama!" He turns her palm over and kisses it.

And for this moment alone, it has all been worth it.

The journey takes two days, the landscape unfurling in a steady stream of trees and greenery, hills and fields.

They travel through small stations, where people wave at the passing carriages. Matteo and Lily wave back, and the tension in her muscles eases. They pass farms where children help their parents to guide a horse and plow. They pass the blank darkness of forest. Once, they see a cloud of birds, twisting and swirling in the air, like a dancing specter, and Matteo shouts, "I love them, Mama!" with such joy that Lily's eyes fill with tears.

Without thinking, she reaches for Thérèse's hand and whispers, "Thank you."

"Ah, yes, I summoned these birds for you." Thérèse laughs. "I'm glad you feel better."

They change trains in Québec City late at night, after crossing the river. The glow of the city lights and its roaring sounds are hidden behind the station walls. But as the train pulls out, Lily watches the well-lit buildings and bright streets become dingy, dark houses and shadowy roads. Even at a distance, poverty is glaring.

At the smaller stations, Jacques gets out to buy bread or fruit or nuts from the vendors. Sometimes he leans out of the window, passing over coins for meat pies, still hot from the oven. Lily tries to refuse and then, when Jacques still insists on giving her the pie, she offers him money, which he will not take.

"Thank you," she says. "Thank you."

He waves away her words and goes to sit with Thérèse. Lily notes the way he tenderly strokes his wife's hair to get her attention, then presses his lips against the nape of her neck. Thérèse swats him away impatiently, but she is smiling.

It is dark when they pass through Montréal. Lily watches the glow of the city lights, the warmth of its many lives, giving her a feeling of safety. Dawn breaks on the outskirts of Ottawa. The train slows as it approaches and Lily sees a movement near the edge of the forest, where the trees thin: a ghostly dog-like shape, which freezes, paw raised. Even from this distance, Lily can see the slope of its shoulders, can sense the heat in its gaze—wolves have yellow eyes, which, it is rumored, can see into your soul. The animal throws back its head and howls. Though Lily can't hear the rending cry, still the hairs on the back of her neck rise. She is a long way from home.

When she wakes again, the sky is fully light and her head feels clearer. The occasional clenching in her abdomen has faded. Thérèse is still watching her, as if she hasn't slept at all, and there is something narrow and assessing in her expression again.

"We are nearly there. What will you do? Where will you live?"

"Don't worry," Lily says, trying to hide her own anxiety. "I can find sewing work, I'm sure. And I have a little money I can use to rent rooms." The words feel strange, as if she is speaking some foreign language, the language of men, who talk of *rent* and *work*, and who say things like *Don't worry about it*. The same men who get drunk and brawl in the streets. They stagger home and beat their wives, then crouch in the corner sobbing and begging for forgiveness. And the next day, they walk out to work with a swagger in their step and a whistle on their lips.

Still, Lily repeats, "Don't worry. Please."

The green landscape is giving way to houses and, in the distance, a densely packed mass, which looks, at first, like a low-lying oddly shaped cloud bank, blocky and oblong. It glitters strangely in the morning sunlight and, as Lily cranes her neck and squints, the rectangular blocks resolve into buildings, impossibly tall, with windows and towers, some of them belching steam and smoke skyward.

"Toronto, *hoorra!*" the children cheer, clapping. Jacques shushes them, and Lily understands why: he is teaching his children to go through life hiding their accents, never drawing attention. He is trying to keep them safe. For once, the children ignore him, and continue chattering and giggling. Thérèse looks brighter, too, her eyes fixed on the sprawling mass ahead.

Lily puts her arm around Matteo. He huddles into her, his nervous expression mirroring her own alarm, which she must try to conceal from him. Because when they reach Toronto, they will be alone. And she hadn't truly realized the size of it, the enormity of what she has done by bringing Matteo here. And she has made a terrible mistake, and the city is huge, and how will they survive and where will they live and how on earth will she stop it from swallowing both of them?

Her plan had seemed simple: use her remaining money to find somewhere to live, then get some work repairing clothes. And yet, looking at the size and scale of the city, she might as well have set herself the task of climbing one of the tall buildings with her bare hands or learning to drive one of the motorcars that are gliding along the road next to the railway line.

She swallows, rubbing her thumb over Matteo's knuckles. "Don't worry."

A horn blares on the road alongside the train—another motorcar, the people in it waving. Looking at their sleek hair, their gleaming teeth, their colorful clothes, Lily feels as if she is entering another country.

As they draw closer to the city, the cacophony builds: horns and engines and voices shouting. She is used to quiet: the gentle bubbling of water on the stove, the tap of a single set of footsteps outside her door; the far-off blare of a train passing into the night, or the chime of the clock on Chatsworth's high street. She is used to the hush of the river in the dry season or the frantic roar when it floods. But even then it is a safe noise, its notes contained within the span of the riverbanks.

But these new sounds grow around her, blending and blurring into something solid and pulsating.

Lily's cheeks ache from smiling at Thérèse as if she is confident, grinning at Matteo as though this is all an adventure.

In the back of her mind, in time with the rickety clackety-clack of the train, the question, *What will I do? What will I do?*

Alongside the train, the dirt road turns to cobbles. They pass the first, smaller buildings and the noise and confusion surge: the hiss of steam, the shouts of street vendors, the thrum of engines. The air thickens with smells of sharp fuel and salted meat and yeasty bread and sour sweat, and, beneath it all, the rank stench of the gutters.

Two women walk past, laughing, their shoulders bare and gleaming. They blow a kiss at Jacques, and at Matteo, who blushes in confusion. Lily imagines she can smell their perfume. She wonders where they live, these women whose bright dresses make her think of butterflies, whose faces are garishly painted.

"That's one way to earn a living," Thérèse says. "But they don't last long. Poor girls."

Oh. Lily has never heard of women who sell their bodies being called *poor girls*. Tony used sometimes to speak sneeringly of *whores* or *puttane*.

A large vehicle swings past and the children shout in delight at the streetcar, which is bigger than Lily had expected. Everything is bigger and louder and brighter, and she feels a new wave of sickening panic.

The train pulls into the station and a whistle sounds.

"All change!" a guard shouts. A scrabble as everyone gathers bags and coats. Lily has just one small bag. The only thing that matters is Matteo's hand in hers. He presses his body against her hip.

The station is a rush of people, a tide of loud, shouting faces and heavy bodies that jostle against Lily, threatening to carry her along the way a river in flood will sweep away anything in its path. Thérèse grabs her arm, and Jacques puts Matteo and the other children in front of him. Together, they push their way to a horse and cart, where Jacques talks to the driver.

At first, he pretends not to understand Jacques's

accent, and then, when they finally agree on a price, Jacques scowls and digs out a handful of coins, which he counts into the man's palm. Lily sees, in Jacques's expression, the resignation she feels at the grocer's or the bakery, where she knows she is being charged more, or given less, simply because of her accent.

They climb in and the driver flicks the reins. Lily tries hard not to stare at the people hurrying along the busy streets, tries not to shrink from the traffic, the noise. Men in suits march with their heads down, striding out without looking left or right. The women with children by their sides hurry along, too, the children running to keep up. Vendors call out from street stalls, holding up fruit or roasted nuts or colorful candy. Thérèse's children gasp and point. Matteo's mouth hangs open, his eyes vivid as coins. Lily pulls him close.

The driver follows Jacques's directions, turning the cart down one side street after another, past half-constructed buildings and teams of men raising huge steel girders with ropes; past narrow lanes with washing crisscrossing from one house to another, and women calling from their windows; past the rear of factories, where great crates of goods are being unloaded from carts. Finally, they stop in front of a tall, narrow building.

Lily wonders whether she can ask Thérèse if they can sleep on their floor. Just for one night. Just until she can find a place of her own. But no. She owes these people too much already.

"Found it," Jacques says. It's the first time Lily's seen him truly smile.

Thérèse presses a kiss onto his cheek. "Clever man!" To Lily, she says, "He's been here only once, but he has the brain of an angry wife."

When Lily frowns in confusion, Thérèse's grin widens. "Like a wife badly treated, he remembers all things."

Lily helps the children to climb from the cart. Her muscles are stiff and painful, but the ache in her belly has gone. Her breasts are still sore and she can still taste the familiar metallic nausea . . . Perhaps she is pregnant still. But then, what will she do?

She swallows. One thing at a time.

Thérèse is taking the boxes and cases out of the cart. Lily searches her empty pockets—she should pay Thérèse. She pulls the wedding ring from her finger, a plain thin gold band. The skin under it is pale and feels almost raw. "Here." She holds it out on her open palm.

Thérèse stares at the ring, then raises her eyes to Lily's face. "You are not kneeling. And I am married already."

It takes Lily a moment to understand, but when she does, she laughs. The sound and the sensation feel strange, as if they don't quite belong to her. "I would like to pay you. I don't want to just leave. I can stitch clothes for you, mend—"

"Do you think I can't sew?" Thérèse looks mock-offended.

"No! I'm . . . good at sewing." She remembers her mother teaching her to stitch a perfect seam, how to cut the cloth so that the dress would fit a woman's body faultlessly, flattering her waist, while leaving room to expand if she became pregnant. She'd shown Lily how to make the finest lace, the tiny repetitive stitching that was like spinning gossamer, a sort of magic.

Before meeting Tony, Lily had wanted to make clothes and sell them, beautiful pieces, with delicate embroidery on the collar or cuffs, rather than the mass-produced stuff from the factories. But Tony had wanted her at home.

Thérèse says, "I'd be glad of your help. But let me help you first. Where will you sleep?"

"I'll find a room to rent," Lily says, with more certainty than she feels, not daring to hope that Thérèse might offer her floor.

"Where? You can find a bed tonight if you want to become a prostitute, but it will not be a safe bed. I will help you."

"I don't need—"

"You are stubborn and you are annoying me. Silly woman," Thérèse snaps, all traces of humor gone. "And *he* needs somewhere safe." She nods at Matteo. "Jacques's cousin or his wife may be able to help you. They will be here soon. It's nearly midday."

"I can't ask them."

"You asked *me*," Thérèse says, her eyes gleaming with amusement again.

"That was different."

"Why? Because you might have died? Because you *want* to be a prostitute? It is a hard life, I think. Hard work."

"Please stop talking about prostitutes."

"Then you must stop being so stubborn. I will introduce you . . ."

Thérèse stops talking and her gaze moves up the street. Lily sees a motorcar turning down the end of the cobbled road. It's so wide it can barely fit between the buildings. The thunder of the engine fills the space so that the bickering children turn to stare. When the engine stops, the whole street is filled with silence.

The car door opens. A woman emerges, her eyes covered with dark glasses, a thick fur spread across her shoulders and a cloche hat pulled over her blond hair. Her lips are bright red. "This," Thérèse says, "is Mae."

7

The lawyer doesn't drop his gaze as Lily stumbles to answer his questions. *Why did you leave Chatsworth? Why did you leave your husband?*

"I . . . There was an earthquake," she says. Her mouth is dry; she licks her lips. "My home was destroyed and my husband . . ." She swallows hard, remembering again the weight of the wood under her hand, the crack of the beam against his skull. The dull, hollow thud as his head hit the floor. She'd stepped over his body as brick dust settled on his skin.

What sort of woman steps over her husband's body? What sort of woman leaves strangers to bury the father of her child?

"Yes," the lawyer says, riffling through some papers, but not reading them. He doesn't need to read his notes, Lily understands, but this is an important part of the show. She remembers his earlier words: that part of this trial is about *morality*. That the court has decided that the money can be awarded only to a woman of *good character*.

The lawyer knows exactly what he is going to ask

70

next. And suddenly so does Lily. Her legs begin to tremble. She shuts her eyes for a moment, as if she is bracing herself against a fist, waiting for the impact.

The people in the courtroom can sense it too: the judge, the journalists, the members of the public crammed into the gallery and looking down on Lily. All of them lean forward. She can hear them shuffling, whispering. She can sense them craning their necks, can sense their eyes upon her. The other Stork Derby competitors have sat up, too, having slowly slumped into their seats as one piece of evidence after another has been brought out and examined, as one fact after another has been called into question. This case may be all over the newspapers, the amounts of money unimaginable, but the trial itself is long and laborious.

The only person in the courtroom not looking at Lily is Mae. She is still staring at her lap, her fingers worrying an invisible thread or speck of dirt on her skirt. Lily remembers sewing that skirt for her. Remembers the soft hush of the satin under her hands.

"So you left your husband?" the lawyer asks Lily.

Lily tries to steady her voice. "I . . . It was all so confusing. I was very frightened."

"You were *confused*?" The lawyer's eyebrows shoot up. He gives a false laugh, a little *ha* of derision. "I hardly think confusion is a good reason for running halfway across the country."

He's enjoying this, Lily thinks, loathing him. She waits for the accusation.

"And do you think you are a good mother, a *responsible*

wife and mother, given what you did"—more shuffling of papers—"given the desertion of your husband, given the risk you placed your son under? Are you a good woman?"

"No," Lily whispers, feeling the color spread over her chest and her neck. The judge will be able to see it, this telltale blush, which is part dread, part frustration. Men abandon their wives all the time, without ever being asked if they are "good." Being a good man can mean many things. To be a good woman means being an obedient wife and dutiful mother. A woman must help other people. A man helps himself.

"So," the lawyer says, "do you think such behavior merits the Stork Derby fortune? Do you think a woman who behaves in such a way should be awarded so much money?"

Lily sits silently.

"Could you answer aloud for the court?"

"I . . . I don't know."

"Let the court note Mrs. di Marco's suspect morals."

"Duly noted," the judge says. He looks weary. It has been a long day.

Lily feels raw, as though she has had a layer of skin removed.

"And you married again, I believe?"

"Yes."

"And had more children, obviously, with this *other* man?"

Lily nods.

"Aloud for the court."

"Yes."

"And have you lived anywhere else, other than with your new husband, since arriving in Toronto?"

"Yes." Lily's mind compresses.

"With whom?"

"With Mae . . . Mae Thébault."

"I see. And can you point out Mae Thébault to the court?"

Lily lifts a shaking hand and gestures at Mae, who finally looks up, finally meets her gaze.

"So," the lawyer says, "if you lived with Mrs. Thébault, then you would agree that she will be able to give an accurate representation of your character?"

"I . . . Yes," Lily says. She attempts to smile at Mae, although her facial muscles feel frozen and numb. Perhaps Mae hasn't told the lawyer everything after all. She will point out that this has been a mistake, that her lawyer is supposed to be protecting Lily, not interrogating her.

But the stare Mae gives Lily is blank. As if she is a stranger she has encountered in the street, begging for alms. As if there is nothing more between them than this held breath, this held moment in the crowded court.

8

Mae, Toronto, November 1926

When Mae wakes up that morning, she's already considering leaving. The decision rests in her chest, like a caught breath: every previous gasp of air has built up to this one, and its release is inevitable, although no one would ever guess. Leonard wouldn't have known what she was planning—even if he had been the sort of man to wonder how his wife felt.

Mae rises, as always, at five. The house is still quiet, still dark, the children asleep. Leonard is snoring softly next to her. She eases past the crib, so that Peter won't wake and cry for a feed, and she creeps downstairs, where the maid, Clara, has just finished raking out yesterday's ashes from all the fireplaces and laying new kindling. A small, slight girl, she glances up as Mae enters the room.

"Do you need anything?" Mae asks. Leonard tells her it's foolish for her to feel guilty at having help, but Mae can't stop herself.

As always, the maid looks uncomfortable as she says, "No, ma'am. Thank you, ma'am." She lights the big range in the kitchen and throws on an extra bag of coal, and Mae moves closer to the fire.

When she was young, before she met Leonard, became his typist and married into this moneyed life, coal had always been a luxury. Mae and her sisters had lived in the town of Oakville, to the west of Toronto. Their father's leg had been shot off in the war in Europe when Mae was ten, and something had gone awry with the pension he should have had. Mae's mother always said that the government had stolen it. There was never enough money, and the children spent much of their time begging for scraps or collecting fallen branches and driftwood. It had burned too quickly to heat the soup, let alone their small house—when they had a house. The insides of the windows were often frost-coated.

Now Mae is rich—or Leonard is rich, with money from the railways. Leonard's father was a self-made businessman, who had been born poor and toiled his way up through the steelworks, until he managed one of the largest factories in Toronto. He'd apprenticed Leonard in the factory at fifteen years old, encouraging his son to climb the ranks, just as he had.

Hard work makes a man, he'd always said, a mantra Leonard repeats, although sometimes wearily when he returns late from the factory, which he now owns. Still, after Mae's poor upbringing and a childhood spent shivering and hollow-bellied, it is a relief that her children always have enough.

She tries to imagine describing fullness to her mother and sisters, whom she hasn't seen in years, and who, she suspects, must have died on Oakville's streets long ago, because her efforts to track them down have come to nothing. There is no one left who knows her as she was as a child, so most of the time she can forget that the thin, frozen, frightened girl ever existed.

Nowadays, she feels warm all the time. It's a little like being numb. Sometimes she places her hand in a bucket of iced water, just so she'll feel something. Every time she puts coal on the fire, she holds her hands up to the flames, luxuriating in having heat for its own sake, not just for cooking. She doesn't let herself think about the cold that waits for her later, if she goes through with her plan, if she actually manages to leave.

The cook works around her, pouring oats and milk into a pan and saying, "Sorry, ma'am," when Mae bumps into her. She is big-armed and broad, like all of the cooks they have had. Is her name Anna or Annie or Ann? Mae used to learn the names of the staff, but they've all moved on quickly—Leonard says it's because Mae makes them uncomfortable by "lurking" and "interfering." The first cook had been very offended, he said, that Mae got up every morning to make breakfast. She should be spending the time with the children.

How can Mae explain to him that she would rather sweep out the grate or cook oats? She knows how to do those things well. Being a mother reminds her of that childhood game she used to play with string—what had it been called? Cat's basket? Cat's *cradle*, that was right. She used to play it by herself, and always ended up with her hands snarled in the string, which pinched at the ends of her fingers, turning them purple.

Leonard gets up next. She hears his footsteps on the

floorboards overhead, hears him knock against the crib, hears him swear as Peter begins to wail. "Mae," Leonard bellows down the stairs.

Her heart sinks. "I'm making the breakfast," she calls.

The cook purses her lips and positions herself in front of the pan.

"Mae! The baby's crying."

Mae sighs and trudges up the stairs, past the closed water closet—Leonard will stay in there for at least half an hour, until all the children are fed and dressed. They will have to troop into the cold to use the outside privy. Robert, her oldest, always complains bitterly about this.

Mae lifts each child out of bed and dresses them while they shiver. Alfred, who is five, has wet the bed, so she flannels him off next to the stove, then is about to remove the sheets to the laundry room to soak them, but the small maid silently takes them from her. Mae resists for a moment, then lets them go.

"Can I have more milk, Mama?" Robert says. He refuses to eat porridge, drinking glass after glass of milk instead.

"That's the last of the milk, Robert, and we can't afford more. Have some porridge instead."

There is enough money to buy more milk, of course. Enough money for her to throw away the milk and the saucepan, and to take the children out for eggs and toast, dripping with butter. But she can't stand the idea of the children growing up thinking that everything just *appears*. She worries that they'll be spoiled and snobbish. When she says as much to Leonard, he laughs and says, "Teach them to be grateful, then." As though teaching the children anything is easy.

Robert stares at her rebelliously. "I don't want porridge."

She turns away, jiggling the grumbling baby on her hip and wishing she could take the cloth from Cook's hands and wipe down the stove, while Cook deals with the children. Betsy, who is seven, says, "Is something wrong, Mama?"

"No, darling." Mae hates herself for letting her children see her unhappiness.

Leonard comes downstairs just as the children are finishing and eats his porridge in four large mouthfuls. He is big and blond, with an easy smile and broad shoulders. She remembers when she used to love looking at him—the shape of his silhouette picked out in the early-morning light as he climbed naked from their bed. But after they had had the children, she was always exhausted, not by the housework, which she wasn't allowed to do, but by the tug of so many little hands and so many voices, bickerings and wailings. Even the children's laughter made her feel tired. Sometimes she would ask to employ a nanny to help.

Leonard would frown. "But they adore you. Why would you want someone else to care for them? And what else would you do with your time?"

He wasn't trying to be unkind, but she understands what he means: she doesn't have any friends, really—none of the wives of his colleagues want to spend their afternoons *with Leonard's typist*. She doesn't play bridge or know how to ride a horse or do any of the things she is supposed to do.

Leonard often returns home hours after the children are asleep. She rouses herself to sit with him while he eats his evening meal, which he always devours with brisk efficiency, before leading her up to bed, where he makes love to her with the same brisk efficiency, then falls into a deep, slack-bodied sleep. She lies awake, until one of the children calls to her from the depths of a nightmare or needs a drink or is frightened by the dark. The next morning, the cycle begins again. Sometimes Leonard pauses between mouthfuls of food—or, once, during lovemaking—and says, *You're happy, aren't you? We're happy?* She nods. What other response is there? In truth, she barely looks at Leonard, barely has the energy to consider what happiness might feel like.

They'd met on the day she'd started as a typist at his father's steelworks. Mae was busy trying to hide the shabbiness of her shoes behind her desk, and talk like the other typists, although she knew she didn't fit in—at eighteen, she had stolen two dollars from a man's wallet and, rather than giving it to her mother for bread and milk, she had jumped onto the back of a horse-drawn cart and gone to Toronto, where she'd bought a nice dress and enrolled in a typing course and, by smiling as often and as widely as she could, had found a job. She had always meant to go back to Oakville, to take some money to her mother and sisters and to bring them to the city, but by the time she'd earned enough, she couldn't find them.

They'd moved on, the neighbor said, and good riddance. Mae had returned to Toronto, feeling orphaned and alone.

When she'd started at the company, Leonard was taking over the reins of the business and enjoying the power. He liked taking the typists and secretaries out for drinks and had a *reputation*. The other girls were mad for him, but Mae found his confidence intimidating. When he'd leaned across Mae's desk on her first day, she'd blushed and refused his offers of drinks and meals. The result of her shyness was that he'd become obsessed with taking her out, then obsessed with getting her into bed, although he didn't try to force her. Instead, he proposed. Mae hesitated for only a moment: for all his bluster, Leonard was kind and gentle, and offered an escape from her tiny, dirty rented rooms.

Five children later and Leonard is still calm, still kind. He isn't trying to be malicious when he ignores the children's cries or asks why she can't keep them quiet and entertained. He looks at her with baffled amusement when the children bicker and shout that they're bored, or when the milk is finished because Robert has drunk it all again.

Listening to their shrieks, Leonard says, "What's wrong with them now?" or "Deal with that, would you?"

Leonard has never tried to change a diaper or feed a baby or read a story to children who don't want to listen, let alone try to do all these things at once. When he tells her that she looks a bit peaky, she says, "I'm exhausted."

"Yes, I'm tired too. Busy week." And then he kisses

the top of her head and tells her he loves her, and Mae echoes the words back to him.

She does love him. He's not cruel. This is what Mae tells herself, time and again.

Now Leonard scrapes his porridge bowl. "Any chance of more milk? No? Never mind."

He grins at her and, for a moment, he looks like the handsome, carefree man who wooed her. Who whispered that he couldn't stop thinking about her. Before his father died of a heart attack and he took over the business fully and spent every waking moment at the office. Now, when he smiles, there are deep lines around his bloodshot eyes, even though she heard him snoring all night while she was up three times with the children.

She shouldn't keep count of such things. It only makes her angry.

She tries to return the smile, then turns back to spooning food into Alfred's mouth. Leonard stands behind her, strokes her arm, presses his lips to the back of her neck. He smells of cologne. Later, she will have to wash it off, or Peter will cry when she feeds him and Robert will wrinkle his nose and complain that *you smell funny.*

"You were up early this morning," he says.

"Alfred was crying. He'd wet the bed."

"Perhaps we can both go to bed earlier tonight." He runs his hands over her shoulders.

"Sarah is having nightmares, so I'll sit with her until she's asleep. I'll be late to bed."

"You can wake me when you come up," he says,

pressing himself against her, kissing her. He is gentle, as ever. He doesn't dictate, only ever asks.

It's not that she dislikes sleeping with him. Only that it feels like yet another demand, yet another person wanting something from her body. And, if she is unlucky, yet another baby.

She feels the familiar rising in her chest, the crushing compression, as if a giant hand is squeezing all the air from her lungs. She closes her eyes, draws a slow breath, then another. It doesn't help. The darkness still squats there, a cold, tentacled ache.

"I really would like . . ." she says. "Can we talk about—"

"Can we talk about what? What would you like?" He breathes into her hair. He's still pressed against her, oblivious to the children, who are clattering their spoons in their empty bowls and, no doubt, smearing the remnants of the porridge over their clothes and the table and each other's hair.

"I'd really like to talk about getting some help," she says. "With the children."

He freezes. His hands on her hips are suddenly still. "What's wrong? Are you ill?"

"No, it's just . . ."

"If you're ill, you should go to the doctor."

"I'm not ill."

"Then I don't understand why you need help. They're wonderful children and you're an excellent mother. Surely you should be enjoying it all." Again, his voice isn't unkind, but she can hear a touch of impatience, can hear the slight emphasis on *should*. She can hear the question that he won't ask, because they've argued about it before: why do *you* find this so hard when other women manage?

"Aren't you happy?" he asks. "You have help with the cooking and cleaning."

She keeps her back to him, grasping the table, and nods mechanically. Other women do manage everything, and she has no idea how. She doesn't know how they make it through each repetition of clothes-on-clothes-off, don't-shout, stop-hitting-your-sister, do-you-want-a-story, no-you-can't-have-candy, day after day. And each day, she feels she's doing something wrong, either being too strict or too lax, and never, ever loving them enough. She can't help thinking that, if she had a nanny to help, she'd at least be able to see how a woman *should* be a parent. And then she'd have time to think about something other than the children, and that she doesn't know how to be a good mother, that nothing she does ever feels right.

She swallows, dries her hands, turns to face Leonard. He is frowning, but his eyes slide from hers—he already has that distant look on his face. It's not that he doesn't care, but this is a minor distraction when he needs to be thinking about the day ahead at the factory. He needs to plan how much more steel will have to be bought to make the endless railway tracks. He has to decide whom to employ, whom to promote, whom to sack.

"I'd like to get a job," she says. "They're looking for women in the typing pool. I could get up to speed again, if I practiced."

His gaze sharpens and he takes her by the shoulders. "And who will look after our children while you're gone?"

"I thought . . . if we got help—"

"You don't need to get a job. We have enough money. And you like spending time with the children. They need their mother. My mother was always at home with me. I'm still thankful for that."

"I just want to do . . . something." *Something I'm good at.*

"You're too busy anyway," Leonard says. "You don't need a job as well—you'd be exhausted. It wouldn't be fair on the children."

She flushes and drops her gaze. The darkness inside her gut shifts. The hand around her chest tightens.

"I work so you don't have to. I like to take care of you." He kisses her forehead. "Would you like some extra money this week? Go buy yourself something special. You can wear it at the dinner party on Friday."

"Thank you," she says dully. She'd forgotten about the party, when she will have to host all of Leonard's friends—bankers, factory owners, company directors— and their beautiful wives.

In the garden, the wind gusts through the trees. A pine branch squeaks against the windowpane.

"We're very lucky," he says. "We mustn't forget that."

She hears the reprimand: don't forget how lucky you are. Remember to be happy.

He puts his coat on. "Don't forget my cousin Jacques is arriving today. They sent word ahead yesterday and someone should greet them, settle them in. I've told the driver to be ready after lunch."

Mae closes her eyes. She'll have to take all the children with her across town. They'll be hungry and grouchy. Peter hates cars and will cry all the way. Leonard sees her expression and says, "It won't take long. Chin up."

A fine spattering of rain hits the window.

When the doorbell sounds two hours later, Mae is trying to rock Peter to sleep, while Betsy and Sarah argue over a doll, and Robert is taking the coals out of the unlit fireplace while the maid, Clara, begs him to stop. Alfred is crying while trying to climb up her legs and calling, "Mama! Mama!"

"Just a minute, Alfred! Robert, stop that now. Girls, put that doll down."

The doorbell shrills.

"Will you stop it and be quiet!" Mae snaps at the children, brushing Alfred off her legs and snatching the coal roughly from Robert's hands. Both boys start howling, along with the girls, who have broken the doll. Even Clara takes a step back. Baby Peter, who has been woken by the doorbell and Mae's shout, begins to wail.

Mae fixes a smile on her face and is ready to greet the postman or the milkman or the grocer's boy but, instead, finds herself face-to-face with Leonard's sister, Millicent. As always, she is perfectly turned out, her blond hair sleek under her cloche hat, her skin flawlessly pale and her lips in an affected *moue* of surprise.

"Oh, my dear, *hello*! Leonard did say you were in a

mess, but I didn't expect . . ." Millicent gestures at the crying children, Mae's unruly hair, the shattered doll. She raises her arms and shrugs prettily. "Goodness! I thought I could watch the children when you go across to help your cousin—is that this afternoon? Leonard said—yes?"

Mae sighs. Jacques is Leonard and Millicent's cousin, not hers, but Millicent prefers not to involve herself with relatives who require support or assistance, and Mae can't find the energy to correct her. Millicent had spent quite some time in various "finishing schools," although it's never been clear to Mae why more than one finishing school would have been necessary. Millicent's time at these places has given her a large number of strong opinions and a great confidence in her own abilities. Leonard says, with long-suffering indulgence, that Millicent went to three finishing schools so that she can *finish everyone else off.*

"Yes," Mae says. "I'm going to help Jacques and Thérèse settle into their rooms. Leonard has given me some money to pass on, and I think Jacques has a job at the factory."

"Yes, yes," Millicent says. "Leonard always thinks of everything. Clever boy, always has been. You can go across after lunch. I was hoping we might find time for a little chat, but you don't look quite right."

Mae runs her fingers self-consciously through her hair.

"You've porridge on your cheek, my dear." Millicent laughs.

That bright, lighthearted giggle has always grated on Mae, but she forces herself to smile. "Come in, Millicent," she says, wiping her cheek and opening the door.

Millicent steps through, dodging Alfred's attempt at an embrace and sidestepping the pile of stones that Robert collected in the park yesterday. "Goodness!" she says again, staring at the children, who have stopped crying and are gaping at their glamorous aunt. "Leonard wasn't exaggerating. You really *are* in a mess. How do you manage it? I think I'd find it all terribly depressing. Now, don't mind me, I'm here to help free you from the shackles of domestic drudgery."

Millicent is active in the National Council of Women in Canada, and often tells Mae that she shouldn't spend her life weighed down by children. *Women*, she tells Mae, *should be free and liberated.* There is no talk, of course, about how some women might be freer than others.

Now she surveys the hallway and smiles brightly. "So, children, if you could amuse yourselves. Go on, run away and play. Your mother's just going upstairs to lie down. And"—she winks at the children—"if you're *very* good, I'll give you candy."

"Actually," says Mae, "they won't eat lunch if they stuff themselves, so I'd rather you didn't."

"Oh, *Lord*, Mae! Don't be such a stick-in-the-mud. A little candy is just what you need, isn't it, children?"

Against the children's shrieks of "Candy!" and Mae's vehement protests, Millicent has the children bundle up the bits of shattered doll and broken coal into a single grubby pile, which Clara gazes at in despair, then looks embarrassed when Mae tries to clear it up.

Millicent ushers Mae upstairs to her room. "Go and rest, dear. You look dreadful. Perhaps find yourself something nice to wear. That always cheers me up."

Upstairs, Mae opens her wardrobe and stares at the rows of neatly hung dresses, many of them still in their store wrappings. She should wear them with Leonard when she goes to the functions and parties with his work colleagues, but all the clothes feel like the trappings of another person's life—costumes for a capable wife and mother. Mae sits rigidly on the unmade bed, listening to the chaos from downstairs, and then the silence as each child's mouth is closed with their promised piece of candy. Some part of her worries about the children choking, but the other part of her can't seem to move.

A minute or so later, there is a gentle knock and Millicent peers around the door, her kohl-lined eyes widening as she takes in the rumpled bed, the open wardrobe, the unworn dresses.

"Oh dear. You poor thing."

Millicent sits on the bed next to Mae and takes her hand. Her fingers are warm, her skin is smooth and her fingernails are perfect. Next to her, Mae feels like a chap-skinned old woman, even though Millicent is five years her senior. Along with her involvement in the National Council of Women, Leonard's older sister is a perennial flapper girl, happily unmarried, childless, and merrily living off her half of the inheritance from Leonard's parents, along with the monthly allowance he sends her.

Mae has always thought of Millicent as selfish and loud and shallow, but now, looking at her clean hands, her smooth stockings, her perfectly ironed skirt, she is consumed with envy. What she wouldn't give to belong to Millicent's carefree life of parties and drinks and late nights, followed by days of lunching and listening to speeches about the rights of women. Instead, Mae feels like an impostor a bad actress making a poor job of some other woman's life.

As if reading her thoughts, Millicent says, "It's exhausting." Or perhaps she's talking about Mae's life—the sleepless nights, the bickering, the five screaming children.

"It is."

"Look, my dear. I'm not wearing the right clothes for . . ." She waves a manicured hand toward the messy bed. "And the maid can do that, surely. But perhaps I can tidy *you* up a little. That always makes me feel better, if I look more . . ." she narrows her eyes at Mae, ". . . alive. You just seem a little down in the dumps. A touch of the doldrums—everyone gets them. Especially with all this . . . anarchy. As I always say, a woman should be able to choose her own life, but you do seem to have made rather *a lot* of choices, and they're all very hungry and noisy." She winks at Mae, who finds herself suddenly close to tears at the touch of Millicent's hand—its tenderness and lack of demand.

"No sniffles now, my darling. So, powder. A little lipstick. See, I have one here. Turn your face this way."

And Millicent holds Mae's jaw as she paints her lips in the same scarlet shade that she is wearing, then brushes her nose with powder and runs a black pencil along her lower eyelids.

"There now," she says, holding a pocket mirror up to Mae's face. "Doesn't that feel better? You're so beautiful. This wonderful blond hair! And your skin is really rather good, you know, all things considered."

Mae stares at the face in the mirror: the tired blue eyes, lined in heavy black; the papery skin, creased with powder, and the lurid red lips. She thinks of how much she looks like her grandmother, after the undertaker had worked on her face to make her *presentable for the open coffin*. The thought is so ridiculous, so awful, that Mae giggles, and tears well in her eyes.

"Oh, Lord," Millicent says. "Please don't cry. I'm no good with the weepies. Besides, your makeup will run." She passes Mae a tissue. "People tell me it becomes easier over time. I have friends who seem to cope very well with children. Perhaps this is just a bad patch." She gives a glossy smile.

"Peter is crying," says Mae, and stands.

"Heavens, not *more* crying! No, I'll get him. You stay there."

Millicent taps from the room and down the stairs, and Mae listens to her lifting Peter and talking to him softly. She's probably telling him she's no good with *the weepies* but whatever she says seems to work, because when she brings Peter into the bedroom, he grins at Mae gummily and holds out his arms.

She pulls him close and he snuggles into her.

Millicent watches them, twirling the beads at her neck.

"Listen," she says. "Why don't you rest with baby Alfred up here and I'll watch the others?"

"This is Peter. Alfred is his brother."

"Yes, yes." Millicent's smile doesn't falter. "*Peter*. But when you breed at such a rate, my dear, you can hardly blame me for losing track. Now, you rest awhile."

Mae wants to shake her head but finds herself nodding and saying thank you. She struggles to hold back tears again as she puts Peter into his crib for a nap and lies down on the bed.

Millicent draws the curtains, blows an extravagant kiss, and softly shuts the door.

Mae remains rigid in the half-darkness, listening to Millicent's cheerful voice downstairs and the children's replies. No shouting, no arguments, no tears.

She imagines staying like this: distant from her children, but knowing they are safe and well. And for the first time in months, the clawing sensation in her chest loosens. It occurs to her that they would all be much happier without her dragging them down. Quietly, she eases herself up from the mattress and fetches a small case from under the bed. In it she puts underwear and some dresses, along with two cardigans.

Peter stirs in his sleep, reaching out for her. She takes his little hand and he relaxes back into a gentle, soft-mouthed snore. And she knows she can't do it—she can't possibly go somewhere else, live somewhere else in the world, knowing that her children are growing older without her, knowing they are slowly forgetting her, wondering where she is.

It wouldn't be fair to them. They would think it was their fault, and it isn't. Far better if something just . . . *happened* to her. She imagines Leonard giving them the news that Mama is gone, that she had an accident, and that she's not coming back, but that she'll always love them. They will cry, of course, but they'll recover. Millicent will help to look after them. Eventually, they will forget about her. Leonard will remarry and they'll have someone new to care for them. Someone who can cope with it all.

Women have the right to choose. Isn't that what Millicent says?

So Mae closes the suitcase, gets a pen and paper from the drawer, and writes two letters. One for Leonard, one for the children. Dry-eyed and resolute, she tucks both under Leonard's pillow so that Millicent won't find them when she comes to check on Peter.

She hides the half-packed suitcase, presses her lips against Peter's warm forehead, and then walks slowly down the stairs. With each step, she feels more able to breathe.

The children are sitting at the table, bickering over a box of dry crackers. Millicent is leafing through Mae's copy of the *Canadian Home Journal* that Leonard buys for her each quarter, and which Mae never has time to read.

"Goodness!" Millicent says. "This rag has a lot to say about cushions and pot roast. It reminds me of school. I've done my very best to forget as much of this as I can. Doesn't your brain turn to cabbage as soon as you read it?" The horror in Millicent's voice, along with Mae's increasing feeling of lightness, actually allows her to laugh.

"Darling," Millicent says, "it's wonderful to see you

looking happier. I can come once a week to help. Well, perhaps not *every* week, but I'll certainly visit more often."

"Thank you," Mae says. "And are you truly happy to stay for the afternoon, while I settle Jacques and Thérèse into their rooms?"

"Of course. Take as long as you like. Look, you can borrow my dark glasses and then no one will see those ugly circles under your eyes."

And Millicent ushers Mae out of the door, talking over her instructions on the whereabouts of the bread and ham for dinner, and the amount of milk Peter will need when he wakes.

It's only after Millicent has shut the door that Mae realizes she hasn't said goodbye to the children. She can't go back, not now. If she goes into that house she will never leave. She will go slowly mad. All of them will be boxed up in the same four walls forever, gradually drowning in the same poison. This way will be better. They will have fond memories of her. And eventually, everyone will be happier.

Mae feels almost serene as she gets into the car. When she gives the driver the address of the apartment, her voice is steady.

She looks out of the window as he drives through the city—the rapidly expanding city, full of new buildings and men shouting, laying down bricks and lengths of steel. And with every girder that is hoisted onto a growing building, with every length of steel track that is laid for the railway, the money in her husband's account is multiplying. And with every brick, every track, every dollar, she feels further away from him—from everything.

In Oakville, she used to lie on her back at night, staring up at the stars, tracing the paths and pictures of their swing across the sky. In Toronto, it's often hard to see the stars. The new buildings cut jagged shapes out of the skyline, and the lights from buildings and motorcars combine with the factory smoke to settle in a haze over the city. And there is never any silence. The hoots of cars and the cries of hawkers and, when she is at home, the voices of her children, their cries of *Mama! Mama!*, sometimes make her think of little birds, with their beaks open wide and their stomachs never full, no matter that they have more food and attention and distraction than she could have dreamed of when she was a child.

She is glad to be free of them.

She misses them already. She should tell the driver to turn around.

She closes her eyes as they drive over the Don River Bridge. She imagines the dark water, the chill of it on her skin. She tries to imagine the tug of it that could take her anywhere. It will be so quiet.

After she has left Jacques and Thérèse, she will send the driver home. She will say she is going for a walk. She will set off for the bridge alone.

Perhaps she dozes off, because the driver makes her jump when he says, "Here we are, ma'am."

And they are among the run-down dirty streets of Cabbagetown, where she knows that each apartment will be full of families with more children than hers.

She looks at the filthy buildings, the gape-mouthed windows, the lines of grubby laundry fluttering in the breeze. How do other women manage it? How can they bear it?

Millicent will manage, though. Leonard will employ a nanny. He will marry again. Will the children call the new woman *Mama*? Will Leonard tell her that Robert needs to have his back rubbed at night or he won't sleep? Will Leonard remember that Betsy can't stand the texture of egg whites, and if she's forced to eat them, she'll vomit onto her plate, then weep in apology?

Mae's knees are shaking. *It's for the best.*

"Wait here, please," Mae says, and climbs from the car.

"Mae!" Thérèse calls, and Mae lifts a hand in greeting.

It's a long time since she's seen Jacques and his wife, Thérèse, not since the birth of their first child. They are dusty with travel and they look older and thinner and more tired than she remembers them. She supposes she must look similarly terrible, then remembers Millicent's dark glasses and lipstick and realizes that she must appear rich and distant—terrible in a different way. She feels too awkward to speak, so is unprepared when Thérèse gestures toward a slender, anxious-looking woman with a child. Both of them look petrified, eyes downcast, hiding behind their dark hair.

"This is Mae," Thérèse says. "Mae, this is Lily."

Mae nods at the woman, who is staring at her now. It's rude, really, and Mae feels horribly self-conscious. This woman must think she's a carefree socialite, like Millicent, with no greater concern than the shape of her hat or what length of hem is in fashion this season. Mae wants to snap at the woman to stop gaping, but she is so thin and ragged that Mae can't bring herself to say anything at all. Besides, it doesn't matter what the stranger thinks of her. Soon, it won't matter what anyone thinks of her.

She gives Thérèse a quick embrace, Jacques, too, and wiggles her fingers at the shyly hiding children—another Millicent-like gesture.

"You look well," Thérèse says. "We must smell horrible after our travels, and here you are, so beautiful, Mae. You weren't always such an annoying woman."

Mae gives a genuine smile. She'd forgotten how much she likes Thérèse. "Millicent put lip rouge on me."

"Ah! Millicent. Is she well?"

"The same. Leonard told me to give you this." She presses the envelope of money into Thérèse's hand. "Will you—can you visit him, from time to time? I think he'd like the company." Thérèse's gaze sharpens and Mae is aware of having said too much.

"Are you going somewhere?"

"No, no. I—"

"Good. Then I have something to ask. Lily and Matteo have traveled from Chatsworth and need help." Thérèse leans in close. "Their house was destroyed and she is a widow."

"Oh, how sad." Mae tries to feel compassion, but has only an overwhelming desire to be gone from here, to be in the cold and the dark and the silence, where nothing can touch her and she can't harm anyone anymore.

"Very sad. Lily and Matteo will need somewhere to live in Toronto. She is good with children, has been kind to mine. She would make a good nanny, I think."

"Oh, I'm afraid I don't know anyone who is looking for—"

"I thought she could stay with you and help you."

"What?" Mae looks across at Lily. The other woman is gazing at her feet, her cheeks flushed. She gnaws her lower lip. The yellowing outline of a fading bruise stains her jaw.

"Just for a short while."

"I can't, Thérèse!" Mae hisses, turning her back on Lily and her dark-eyed child. They are both so thin and grimy. They remind Mae of her life in Oakville. Mae takes off her glasses and glares at Thérèse, whose smile doesn't falter.

"They'll be no trouble."

"How can you possibly think to offer—"

"Just for some days, a week. See how much she helps you. I promise, you won't regret this."

"I—I can't!" Mae feels as though she might be sick. The thought of having to return to her house, with the demands and noise, with this stranger as a "nanny"— she can't do it.

"Mae," Thérèse says. "They have nowhere else to go. I can't afford to feed them. You have that big house."

Mae is about to refuse again, when she feels a presence behind her. A heat, almost. She turns to find that Lily is standing there, trying to speak through her obvious fear.

"Please," she says. And her voice is soft, melodious, with a slight accent that Mae can't identify. "Please. If you can't take me, I understand. But can you take my boy, just for two days, and this money too? I will send more, as soon as I find work." She presses a grubby pouch of coins into Mae's hand; it still carries the warmth of her skin. Her face is rigid, and as her son hears her words he throws himself at her. She holds him close and kisses the top of his head.

Mae thinks of her children at home, waiting for her. Robert's quick laughter, Betsy's tight embrace. The kisses Alfred and Sarah press into her cheeks. The smell of the top of Peter's head, like a warm loaf of bread. And she watches Lily holding her child, the way she gathers him to her, both of them closing their eyes. She tries to remember the last time she embraced one of her children like that, as if they were the only thing that mattered in this world.

"All right," Mae says to Lily. "Follow me." And she knows that her voice, strangled by the tide of grief and anxiety, sounds aloof and haughty, but she can't help it.

When they stand staring at her, she inclines her head toward the car. "Get in."

9

Lily, Toronto, 1926

Lily hesitates. This woman reminds her of the wives she sometimes saw, waiting for their husbands outside the golf-course clubhouse in Chatsworth. Lily used to pass the golf club sometimes, when she walked with Matteo down toward the river. The women had stood in chattering huddles, their synchronized laughter like the chiming of delicate bells. Sometimes, without noticing, they blocked Lily's path and she had to say, "Excuse me, please," several times, before they finally moved, without ever looking at her, or glancing quickly, then away, as if the sight of her old shawl or Matteo's thinning shirt was somehow offensive.

Mae has the same expression now: she barely looks at Lily, and after glancing at Matteo once, she averts her eyes, as if pained. Lily wraps her arms more tightly around her son. How can this woman have children of her own, she wonders, when she regards Matteo with such distaste? She imagines Mae's children: they will have been showered with gifts but often ignored, and will be like the loud, demanding, arrogant broods of the tourists who had visited Chatsworth and complained because their ice cream was the wrong flavor.

She turns to Thérèse, who feels like the only person she can trust. Thérèse smiles and nods toward the car where Mae is standing, holding the door open, but still averting her gaze from Lily and Matteo. The stillness in Mae's face makes Lily think of a picture in a book that Tony had bought for her long ago from a traveling salesman. It was full of photographs and pictures from Italy, most of them hand-painted in garish colors. One of Lily's favorites was of a woman standing in a seashell, her long hair blowing in some unseen sea breeze. Underneath, Lily had traced *Venus*. There had been a remoteness in the beautiful woman's eyes, a sadness in her distant smile. Perhaps it is this which makes Lily think that Mae looks like the woman in the painting. Her hair, which is tightly pinned at the nape of her neck, is a similar shade to the bright golden yellow of the picture.

What must it be like, Lily wonders, to be so very beautiful? Everything must feel easy for her, the world laid out at her feet.

"Please hurry," Mae says, still not looking at Lily. Her voice is sharp, almost angry, although her expression remains distant.

Thérèse nods encouragingly at Lily, then gathers her into a quick, tight embrace.

"Thank you," Lily says to Thérèse and Jacques, aware that that isn't enough to convey the gratitude she feels. Still, when she turns to the car, she hesitates, and it is

Matteo who scrambles in, grinning shyly and waving for Lily to follow.

Mae gets in after them, and pulls the door shut. Lily tries not to jump at the loud noise, tries, for Matteo's sake, to smile and appear calm.

As the driver starts the engine, Lily sits forward in her seat, trying to touch the leather as little as possible with her hands, which feel filthy against the gleaming, polished surfaces. The leather is sleek and black and impossibly smooth—like water, she thinks. She has never been in a motorcar, has rarely even touched the outside of one. The engine is loud and thrums along with the pounding of her heart. Next to her, Matteo presses his nose against the window; he, too, sits bolt upright, but he seems more excited than scared. When he moves his face away from the glass, he leaves a greasy smudge. He wipes it off with his sleeve and gives the open beam she'd seen so rarely in Chatsworth.

On her other side, Mae sits impassively, fur pulled up around her mouth, eyes shaded by dark glasses. She could be glaring or sleeping—there is no way for Lily to know. Her throat is dry. The engine fumes are stifling, as if she's choking on something sharp. Is the heavy smoke poisonous? Lily squashes the thought: she can't ask a stranger such a ridiculous question. A stranger who has offered to take her in.

Mae's eyes had widened when Thérèse suggested Lily would make a good nanny: she'd removed her glasses and revealed bloodshot blue eyes, fierce with indignation—or,

Lily had wondered, was she drunk, despite it being early afternoon?

But Mae hasn't said a word since the driver started the engine, the heavy, throaty thrum that makes Lily think of the earthquake, of the tumbling wall, of the ringing inside her skull every time Tony had hit her.

Now Mae leans back against the leather—perhaps she really is sleeping. Lily feels sick but can't ask the driver to stop, so she holds on to the smooth seat, squeezing it until her knuckles ache and turn white. She closes her eyes.

"Thérèse tells me you like children. Says you were good with hers."

Lily opens her eyes. Mae is staring at her—Lily can see the faint movement of her eyelashes behind her dark glasses.

"Oh," Lily says. "Yes."

Thérèse had exaggerated. Lily had felt too awful and too terrified on the journey to say anything very much to Thérèse and Jacques's children. They had all blurred into a single nervous child. Other than when Thérèse had been speaking to her, the only person in the world who had existed for Lily while her body had been racked with pain, as the world had clamped shut around her, was Matteo.

Still, this woman is expecting her to be some sort of nanny, so she forces her face into a friendly expression. "Yes," she says, with more conviction. "I like children."

"I have five," Mae says, staring out of the window. "Five," she repeats softly, then puts a hand to her stomach. Lily recognizes the gesture and puts her own hand over the aching hollow in her own belly. Is the baby there, still?

The car lurches onto an enormous bridge, and Lily can't look down, can't think of the yawning void beneath the bridge, can't let herself imagine the river far below, the torrent roaring over the rocks, racing toward the sea. But Mae freezes, then turns—as if she's suddenly remembered something or seen someone she knows. She presses her face against the glass as Matteo had done when the car first started moving. Her red-painted lips almost touch the window and, as Lily watches, a tear rolls from under her dark glasses, traces a line across her powdered cheek, and splashes onto the fur around her neck.

Lily leans forward, wanting to put a hand on the woman's arm, to ask her what is wrong, to tell her that, whatever it is, it will be better soon, it *must* be better soon.

But then Mae turns to her and, before Lily can touch her, she says, "*Don't!*" She growls the word with such ferocity that Lily recoils, sitting back against the cold leather, turning from the furious expression in the stranger's eyes.

"I'm sorry. I didn't mean . . . But please don't touch me," Mae says, then unlatches the window and yanks it down, letting in a blast of cold air and fumes. The surge of noise is instant. Mae turns her face toward it, shutting Lily out.

Lily, relieved to break the tension between them, turns

to look out of the window too. Outside the car, the streets rush past unimaginably fast, a blur of buildings and people.

She looks up at the thin sliver of sky. She is so used to being surrounded by the huge expanse of blue that it's strange to see the sky cut off and divided, strange to have her gaze brought back to the busy streets and the sharp shapes of the buildings. Lily tries to take it all in: the women in short dresses and neat hats, the men on bicycles and behind the wheels of motorcars. Smells of smoke and meat cooking and river water and sewerage. Beneath it all, a deeper, more pungent smell: some grimy thing that is living, and breathing, something that is dying and rotting. The smell of the city itself, like some sticklebacked beast that is constantly sloughing off its own skin. Under the roar of streetcars and the rumble of buses, there is a constant buzzing in the air, as if the city is running on an unseen energy: a low, predatory rumble that makes Lily think of the wolves in the zoo back in Chatsworth.

From the corner of her eye, Lily watches Mae, watches the tension in her body as they pass over the bridge. As soon as they are out of sight of it, Mae relaxes, turns to Lily, and fixes her with a bright, brittle smile. "Nearly home," she says. And her painted red mouth is set in a thin line. And on her cheek, still, is the silvered path of a tear.

10

Mae, 1926

When she climbs from the car, Mae's legs are shaking. In the thrum of her blood, she feels it still: the pull of the river, the cold that had seemed to radiate from it as they crossed the bridge. What if she had asked the driver to stop? Again and again, she pictures herself climbing from the car up onto the side of the bridge.

The sudden drop.

The moment of lightness before she hits the cold water.

But the woman and the child had stared at her and she couldn't do it, not in front of these strangers. Perhaps later, at night, when the city is asleep. Perhaps tomorrow.

Mae braces herself against the side of the car, summoning the energy to go into the house. She can feel the woman, Lily, watching her, so she forces a stiff nod, thanks the driver, then pats the car to signal that he should drive to the back of the house to park. The gesture feels efficient and capable—something Millicent would do.

She turns her bright Millicent smile on Lily and the boy—Matthew is it?—who are huddled together on the sidewalk. The woman is stroking the boy's hair; he is leaning in to her. The gestures look utterly natural and entirely foreign. When had Mae last stroked Robert's hair?

Leonard won't like them being here. But Mae needs the help. And something in them had tugged at her: the way they stood, mother and son, with the whole city looming behind them, monstrous. Mae recognized a little of the woman's fear, her desperate need. And she felt, very briefly, ashamed of her own hopelessness. How could she feel lost when she had so much, while this woman was widowed, homeless, friendless, and yet still knew how to make her child feel safe and loved?

Now they are on the doorstep of her house—the house she is lucky to have, filled with healthy children, whom she is lucky to have—and her panic swells.

The door swings open and Millicent is standing there, still wearing her high-heeled shoes, which will have scratched the wooden floor. Her makeup is somehow still perfect, her hair immaculate.

"There you are!" She laughs. "I thought I heard a car. We've had *such* fun."

She is holding Peter with one arm and hugging Betsy to her with the other. "The cook and maid were being morose, so I sent them home. I've given the children more candy for dinner. They love it!"

"What about the ham?" Mae says, taking Peter, who snuggles into her. "I asked the cook to prepare a ham. It's the children's favorite."

"Oh, yes, I ate some of the ham—rather a lot, actually. It was *delicious*," says Millicent brightly. "Too good for the children. Which butcher do you use? I'll send my cook."

106

"Where did you go, Mama?" Betsy asks, her eyes tear-filled. "Robert hit me with a spoon. And I'm *hungry*."

There is a shriek from inside the house. Mae peers past Millicent. The hallway floor is covered with a mixture of the dirty and clean laundry, along with muddy footprints. Both older boys, their faces smeared with chocolate, are racing around, brandishing wooden spoons and hitting each other over the head. Sarah is crouched under the hallway table, covering her face with her hands. All the children's eyes are filled with a feral glitter. Mae's shouts at them to *stop* and *calm down* go unheeded.

"Candy!" Robert roars.

"I don't know where they get their energy," Millicent says placidly. "They haven't stopped."

"Thank you, Millicent," Mae says. "It's so kind of you, but I really must be—"

Millicent holds up a manicured hand. "Mae. I don't want to alarm you, but there are two . . . *people* standing just behind you. Now, come into the house quickly and I'll shut the door."

Mae turns. "Oh, no. These are Jacques's friends, who will be staying for a little while. Lily and Matthew."

"Matteo," Lily says quietly, and Mae hears, again, the slight accented lilt in her voice. And she notices, for the first time, how dark Lily's eyes are, how long her lashes. On her cheek, another faint shadow of an old bruise. Lily glances up and tries to smile, before looking nervously away, and Mae feels a rush of compassion.

"Come farther in, Lily," she says, "out of the cold."

Millicent leans in close to Mae, her eyes round. "Surely you're joking. What on earth will Leonard say?"

"Let me into the house, please, Millicent," Mae says wearily, beckoning Lily and Matteo to follow. They shuffle in nervously, stopping just inside the doorway, their mouths slightly open.

Mae is suddenly aware of the sweeping wooden staircase, the plush rugs, the electric lights. She sees, as if for the first time, the polished wooden table that Sarah is crouching under, and the telephone attached to the wall above it.

Alfred comes haring back along the hallway, pursued by Robert, who is still brandishing a spoon. Both boys yell in delight as their feet slip on the pile of laundry. Alfred stumbles and Robert pounces on him triumphantly, and begins hitting him over the head with the spoon handle. Alfred hollers.

Mae grabs the spoon from Robert, who gives an indignant wail. "I'm *drumming*!" He tries to snatch it back, and Mae finds herself holding it out of reach while her son tries to climb up her, pulling at her coat, then yanking her hair. "Give it *back*, Mama!"

Mae tries to keep her voice level. "Let go, Robert."

Millicent is laughing, hands clapped over her mouth. Peter begins to howl as his brother grabs his leg.

"Robert, for goodness' sake!" Mae says.

But Robert continues to struggle, puce-faced and snarling. He snatches the spoon from her, but then a hand reaches out and Lily takes the spoon.

"He needs a sharp slap," says Millicent.

"No!" Mae says, suddenly worried that Lily might take Millicent's advice as an instruction.

Robert tugs at the spoon, outraged, but Lily holds it firmly. She crouches next to him and looks him in the eye. "Let go," she says quietly, firmly. "You are hurting your mama."

He stares at her, then lets go of the spoon.

Lily nods. "Hitting hurts." Something in the seriousness of her tone stills him. "Good boy." She smiles and, very faintly, he smiles back, before running off again.

Even Millicent looks impressed. "Now, Mae, why can't you do that with him?"

Mae sighs. "I've never been very good at . . ." She indicates the children's retreating backs.

Lily turns to Mae. "You are a kind mother."

Mae shakes her head. "I feel like a very poor mother, I'm afraid."

"I feel like that too. Perhaps every mother does. You're a good mother."

Mae blinks. *A good mother?* No one has ever told her that. She remembers her own mother: poor, sad, and harried, always failing to conceal her simmering anger.

Mae has a sudden sense of being seen. It is as though, for the first time in many weeks, she can draw a full breath of air.

"Thank you," she murmurs.

Lily gives a quick, shy smile, which lights up her whole face.

*

Later, after Mae's older children have been put to bed, Millicent is "helping" Mae, Lily, and Matteo with dinner – "That ham needs finishing off," she says.

The bread feels like dust in Mae's mouth, but she forces herself to chew. Across the small kitchen table— there didn't seem to be any point in setting the large dining-room table—Lily and Matteo press together, still nervous and covered with dust from their journey. Mae wonders, suddenly, what on earth she is doing, bringing these strangers into her house alongside her children. But it is too late now: she would have to throw them out onto the street. She would have to force them out of her door, into the darkening night.

As if sensing her thoughts, Lily glances up and meets her eyes.

Silence.

Millicent holds up a hand. "Wait! I've remembered something." She begins searching through a pile of books and papers. "It's here *somewhere*."

Mae frowns, catches the same expression on Lily's face, and hides a smile.

"You don't have to stop eating," Mae mutters. Lily and Matteo have devoured slice after slice of bread and ham. The boy barely chews, swallowing so quickly that he gives himself hiccups, and Mae can see Lily trying to restrain herself from doing the same. She remembers that clawing, bone-deep hunger, which feels like it can never be satisfied—a hunger rooted in months of near-starvation, whose closest relative is cold.

"Aha!" Millicent waves the *Canadian Home Journal*. She

leans as far from Lily and Matteo as possible, turning her chair to make clear that she is talking to Mae. "When I was reading today, I saw this piece about the baby race. Of course, everyone's been talking about it for days. I thought it was just gossip, or some sort of elaborate hoax, but, no, it appears it's true."

"A baby . . . race?" Mae pictures Peter crawling alongside other infants, or in his baby carriage perhaps, being pushed.

"Yes! You must have heard about Charles Millar's baby race? Really, Mae, everyone's been talking about it at all the clubs and parties."

"I haven't felt like going to parties lately," Mae says quietly. She'd grown tired of getting dressed up in stiff, formal clothes, just for Leonard's friends to ignore her. When she'd first been married, they'd invited her to take afternoon tea with them, or go on shopping excursions, but she always seemed to say the wrong things and choose the wrong clothes. She'd seen them laughing behind their hands at her, calling her *the typist* and *the home help*.

"Having children is no excuse for missing parties, Mae. And missing parties is no excuse for ignorance. I thought you'd have heard of the baby race. It's quite disgusting. The Women's Council has been talking about it for weeks, although no one truly believed anyone would leave such a strange will."

"A will for . . . *babies*?"

Millicent leans forward, her eyes bright. "Charles Vance Millar was a *millionaire* and a real piece of work, by the sound of it—a devilish sense of humor. He died last year, but he has no heirs, so he left his money to strangers. He left shares in a brewery to some of the Prohibition League, and Jockey Club shares to some men who are absolutely against gambling. He left a house in Jamaica to four lawyer friends who *loathe* one another, but they all have to stay on the island at the same time if they want to use it." Millicent laughs.

Lily and Matteo stare. Mae tries to imagine how peculiar it must be for them, being tired and hungry and, from what she can see, almost penniless, yet listening to a discussion about a house in Jamaica. What will it matter to them if some rich lawyer has decided to write odd requests into his will?

Mae tries to smile. "He sounds . . . strange."

"Very." Millicent grins. "But wait for the strangest part! He left the rest of his fortune—*hundreds of thousands* of dollars—to the woman in Toronto who can have the most children in the ten years after his death. Every baby born between October 1926 and October 1936 will count. And the family who wins will be rich. Isn't that *disgusting*? A dead man *paying* women to have babies! Revolting!" She laughs.

But Mae can't laugh. She sits back in her chair. Upstairs, she can hear Robert and Alfred punching each other, and one of the girls sobbing quietly. Her limbs ache with a marrow-gnawing exhaustion. In her lap, Peter dozes and squirms, pulling her hair every time he moves. "Yes. Revolting. I suppose it is." Although Mae can't help thinking that, if women are going to have to have lots of children—and there's no avoiding it, really—then it might be nice for someone to give them some money. She tries to picture what she would do with hundreds of thousands of dollars of her own, without Leonard telling her which dresses to buy and which clubs to go to. When she imagines having that money to herself, all she can think of is silence. She would buy a moment of silence, somehow. Not the dark quiet of the bottom of the river but a moment of peace, staring up at a blank, open sky, when she knows that the children are safe and the nagging voices in her own mind have faded—voices that keep her awake at night, telling her she is a terrible mother, that she will never be a good one because she doesn't know how.

"It's appalling, forcing women to put their bodies through this. The article points out that some women can have almost a baby a year, if they really try, so nine or even ten children. And that's not accounting for twins. Can you imagine all those children?"

Mae thinks of her five, their noise and clamorous need. She tries to imagine *ten*. Good Lord, a woman with that many demands on her would deserve every penny of this strange man's inheritance.

"And, of course," Millicent sniffs, "it'll be the poorer women who try to get the money, having more babies when they can't afford them. As if there aren't enough starving children around the city already."

"What if they can't help having the children? Or if they want them," Lily asks quietly. She is looking down at the table and has moved slightly closer to Matteo. Her cheeks are flushed.

Millicent frowns, but doesn't turn to Lily as she says, "Whether women should be allowed to prevent pregnancy is a complicated issue, and I hope you don't expect to start discussing matters of *that* ilk over dinner. Nor do I think we should speculate over what individual women might want. The question is clearly a larger one, to do with society."

The faucet drips water into the sink. Matteo chews and swallows. Lily's cheeks are even pinker than before, but Mae can still see the fading outline of that bruise. She feels another rush of sympathy.

"But," Millicent continues, "as I said, it only includes children born from the end of October this year. And that's what made me think of you, Mae." Millicent gives a little laugh. "You like having children and you have this big house. You've got baby Alfred already."

"Peter—"

"Peter! Exactly. He would count toward your number."

Please don't joke about this, Mae thinks, looking across at Lily, who has clasped her hands together in her lap so hard that the bones show white.

"And," Millicent says, laughing, "the next one will be due before the summer, I'd say."

"The next one?" A chill descends over Mae.

Millicent blinks, then shoots a glance at Lily, who is still staring at her plate, as if she can't hear them, as if she is somewhere else entirely.

"I'm sorry," Millicent says, in a whisper that is too loud. "Should I not have said, in front of . . . ?" She inclines her head toward Lily and Matteo.

"I'm not—" Mae stops.

How could she have missed it? The exhaustion, the scraping anxiety, the churning nausea—even her plummeting mood. She hasn't been having her monthly cycle because of feeding Peter, so it hasn't occurred to her to count, or even to notice her own body very much. Tiredness is part of her existence. But she must be paler than normal, perhaps. She remembers Millicent painting her lips and powdering her face this morning. And the way she'd sipped at the tea Millicent had given her and tried not to retch . . .

Millicent might behave like a fool, but she's not stupid. Now she puts a cool hand on the back of Mae's neck. "I'm sorry, I shouldn't have said anything until you were ready to tell me. Listen, Leonard will be home from work soon and you'll have to explain . . . this." She gestures toward Lily and Matteo. "Why don't you go up and put the children to bed? They're making a terrible fuss still. I can hear them shouting about being hungry. I'm not sure how they can be, given the amount of candy they've eaten. Still, you'd better check."

Mae nods dazedly and stands. Millicent returns to leafing through her magazine, pointedly ignoring Lily and Matteo.

As Mae climbs the stairs toward her shouting children, shifting Peter on her hip, she feels a weight descending. All the bubbling fear finally slumps into a single point of terrified inevitability, which is growing with every passing minute. She stops, leans her head against the cool wall, kisses Peter's head. She thinks of Millicent's horror about the baby race, thinks of the poor women who will be desperate enough to try to have more children for money. She thinks about the women who have no choice in the matter.

A thud and a cry from upstairs.

Mae threatens and cajoles and bribes the children until they are quiet, then goes into the darkness of her own room, laying Peter in his crib, tugging the blankets tightly around him and resting her hand on his chest so he doesn't stir.

She sits on the bed, her hands pressed against her stomach. *Oh, God*, she thinks. *Oh, God, oh, God.*

She's never been one for praying. Perhaps now would be the time. What would she ask for? What could she possibly beg from God that wouldn't be sinful or selfish?

Freedom, she thinks, then shakes her head and covers her face with a hand. She presses her other hand hard against her stomach and lies back on the bed.

Something crackles under her head.

A moment of confusion and then she remembers: the notes! The letters she had written for Leonard and the children, still tucked under his pillow.

The scrape of a key in the front door.

Millicent's cry of "Leonard!"

Lily will be down there now, and Mae can't allow Millicent to introduce Lily to Leonard—goodness knows what she'd say. She gathers the letters quickly, screws them up, then hurries downstairs. On her way past the drawing room, she throws the balled-up paper into the embers glowing in the grate, then goes into the kitchen, where Leonard seems very large all of a sudden, staring at Lily, who looks terrified, her back pressed against the sideboard.

"Friends of yours, Millicent?" he asks doubtfully, eyeing Lily's and Matteo's clothes.

"Oh, *no!*" Millicent giggles, too loudly. "These are Mae's. Strays. She *found* them somewhere—"

"They're Jacques and Thérèse's friends," Mae interrupts. "They're new to the city. They need somewhere to stay. Thérèse asked me to help them."

"Well," Leonard says slowly, "if they're friends of Jacques's, then shouldn't *he* be the one to help?"

"Their rooms would be too cramped," Mae says, "and . . ." She looks at Lily, who seems to have shrunk at the sight of Leonard: her shoulders are hunched and she is staring at the floor. Matteo, too, is clearly frightened.

Again, Mae finds herself wondering what they've seen, what they've left behind. "Lily," she says, "just go through there." She points toward the drawing room. After Lily has shut the door, Mae takes a breath and fixes her gaze on Leonard. He is kind, she tells herself. He might be busy and detached and brusque sometimes, but he's always been kind. "They've nowhere to go. She needs somewhere to stay. And I need help with the children. I'm not . . . managing."

"Don't be ridiculous. We've been through this—just this morning, in fact. It's the best thing for children to be raised by their mother, like I was." And she knows he will be thinking that this is another of what he calls her *phases*, like when she worries that Robert is too rough with his younger siblings or that Betsy is too quiet.

"I need help," she says again, like an actor sticking stubbornly to a learned script.

"The children need you, not some . . . *stranger*." He takes her by the arms, holding her tight, as if that will convince her. He's always been physical, affectionate. She used to like it, before she had the children and felt that even his arm around her would eventually lead to yet another baby. He says, "You need to worry less. Stop getting worked up."

"I'm pregnant," Mae says softly.

She can't look at Leonard's face, but can feel the exchange of glances between him and Millicent. He lets go of her arm.

After a beat too long, he says, "That's marvelous!" and wraps her in a tight embrace. "You must be pleased, aren't you, Mae?" There's a begging note in his voice. He'd always wanted a big family and she can sense his desperation for her to be happy, his fear that she isn't.

She nods. "Of course." She leans her head against his shoulder, swallowing tears. The wool in his suit smells earthy: fresh air and freedom. Her throat aches with the effort of stifling a sob. Her lips brush the rough wool as she says, "Please let them stay. Just for a short while. They need help. And I've told them how kind you are, how generous."

He hesitates, then finally, woodenly, says, "All right."

While Millicent is putting ham scraps onto a plate for Leonard, telling him that there's very little left because, my *goodness*, those children can eat, Mae walks into the drawing room where Lily and Matteo are standing in the half-darkness near the window, holding hands.

They're always touching. Part of her is irritated by the way they clasp each other constantly. But the other part of her is filled with longing. There's such simple affection in the way Lily rests her fingers lightly on her son's shoulder or he leans his cheek against her. She can't remember the last time anyone touched her in a way that didn't feel like a demand or an instruction.

In Mae's stomach, a new pulse thuds. She clears her throat. "We're happy to have you here," she says. "Leonard too. There's a room in the attic you can share."

"Thank you," Lily says softly. Mae nods, and turns to go back to the kitchen, but feels, with a jolt of surprise, Lily's hand on her arm.

The other woman is holding something out to her.

"These had fallen out of the fire," Lily says. "I picked them up and . . . Are they yours?"

Paper. Sheets of paper, creased, half scorched and blackened from the glowing embers.

They have unfolded in the heat, not entirely but enough for some of the words to be easily visible: *I'm sorry . . . You're not to blame . . . Don't waste money on an expensive funeral.*

Mae flushes, wondering if Lily has seen them, knowing from one glance at her face that she has. The shame leaves her breathless, speechless.

"I didn't mean to look, but I couldn't help seeing . . ."

119

Her dark eyes are inscrutable, but Mae can see *something* there. Pity. Or understanding.

Mae swallows, tries to speak, but can't force words past the throbbing in her throat.

"You don't want these," Lily says firmly. "I'm going to burn them." And, slowly, she reaches out, brushes a tear from Mae's cheek, then rests a hand on her shoulder.

For the space of a minute, in the velvet darkness and stillness, Mae feels like this stranger's hand might be the only thing holding her upright.

11

November 1926

The house is full of strange noises at night. The clank of pipes, the slick shoulder of the wind pushing against the sealed windows, the sighs of small children shifting in their sleep. Lily lies in the attic with her arms around Matteo, trying to force her eyes to stay open through the burn of exhaustion. Matteo is deep under, his breathing easy, but Lily can't convince her body that this house is safe, even after three days.

Beneath the other sounds, from the room below hers, Lily can hear the rumble of a man snoring. Leonard's presence fills every room: his huge clothes, his loud voice, his expectation that everything will be just as he wants it. Even Mae jumps, sometimes, at the boom of his laughter.

The attic ceiling is painted white. Dark shadows of branches move across it in the moonlight. Lily stares at the patterns as they become a train, a horse and cart, a man's face, huge with rage—

She starts upright and Matteo stirs. She rubs her eyes and mentally lists the things she has learned since being here: how to find the quietest room in the house and take a moment, leaning her head against the wall to breathe; how to smile at Leonard, so that he doesn't mutter to Mae that she *seems surly*; how to ask Cook if she could please make a pot of tea; how to ignore Cook's scowl. Lily knows the heat of judgment and understands how to make herself invisible. She has never been around servants before; she will never be able to order them about. Their baffled looks and deliberate silences toward her make her feel intensely lonely. She knows how to set games for Mae's children in the big garden, and how to run them ragged, until they fall into an exhausted heap around Mae after dinner, and Mae looks up at Lily with her eyes full of wonder.

But Lily doesn't understand what to do when Mae says, *Thank you, you're marvelous!* She doesn't know what to say when Mae presents her with a pair of her own gloves, which look quite new to Lily, and are of red wool, still warm from Mae's hands. She doesn't know how to sit close to the fire in the evening, thawing her skin and watching the flames flicker over Mae's face. She doesn't understand how to bask in the heat, without the fear of getting burned. She doesn't know how to tell herself not to be afraid.

So she lies awake, in the snug attic, running her hand across the small mound of her belly, staring at shadows and telling herself to watch, to wait, to be ready.

December

Mae dresses carefully for the Christmas party. In the mirror, her face is as pale as ever, her blond hair swept back to show her cheekbones, her collarbones, which Leonard loves to run his fingers over. After the party, when they are alone, he will glide his hands across the silk of her new dress, sliding past the growing swell of her belly to cup her hipbones. She tries to keep herself slim through her pregnancies, although it is harder with Lily here: she gives Mae cookies and slices of hot buttered toast, looks at her with a serious expression and says firmly, "You must eat."

And the scolding tone in her voice feels, somehow, like being visible for the first time in years. Lily sees everything. She leaves weak tea and an oat cookie outside Mae's door to quell her morning nausea. She gives her glasses of milk for indigestion, almost before Mae has registered the pain. She must have been, Mae decides, a very attentive wife before her husband died.

Mae hasn't asked about him yet. She's waiting until the time feels right. She can hear Lily putting the children to bed, counting off fingers and toes with a song that makes all of them laugh. Mae had wondered if she might feel jealous of these moments, but instead all she feels is . . . *hollow*, somehow.

She buttons her dress—black with silver beading, too tight across her stomach, really—but struggles with the clasp of her strings of pearls.

"Leonard!" she calls. "I need help." Then she remembers, of course, that he is working late, that the driver will take her to the party alone and Leonard will join her after the dinner.

All those people staring at her. What will she talk to them about?

She swallows hard and pinches the bridge of her nose. Crying won't help anything.

"Mae?" Lily's voice is soft, and when Mae opens her eyes, Lily is standing hesitantly in the bedroom doorway.

"I'm fine," Mae says, more sharply than she intends. She puts the pearls on the dresser. "Go back to the children."

"They're all in bed. Can I help you?"

Again, Mae feels that clutch of loneliness. The children hadn't asked for her. They'd been happy with Lily's silly songs. *How do you do it?* Mae wants to demand, but she doesn't say anything because isn't this what she wanted?

"Can I help?" Lily asks again.

Unable to speak, Mae nods, watches Lily in the mirror as she walks across the bedroom, treading lightly, in that noiseless way of hers. She reminds Mae of a cat. Silent and elegant, she takes up so little space. Leonard sometimes seems to forget that she's there, but Mae is always aware of her.

Lily picks up the pearls and brushes cool fingers across the back of Mae's neck, so the stray hairs don't catch. She fastens the clasp, her gaze meeting Mae's in the mirror. "Beautiful," she murmurs.

That night, at the party with Leonard's friends pushing champagne glasses into her hand, and their wives asking about her *new Italian nanny*, and Leonard himself, putting his arm around Mae's waist and guiding her from one laughing group to another, all Mae can think about is Lily's cool touch as she fastened the necklace and the brush of breath against her skin.

Beautiful.

February 1927

Lily can't remember shopping for new clothes before: she'd always bought dresses from the thrift store and restitched the material into something that fitted her better, but Mae insists they will go to the clothing stores on King Street. "It will be fun," she says, smiling.

Lily can't imagine herself inside the shop, behind the polished glass, among the bright lights, like a thousand gleaming eyes. The women in there look polished, too, and Lily stops outside the door. "I'll stay here, with the children," she says, although there is a cold wind picking up and the children are shivering.

"Nonsense!" Mae says. "We'll all go in."

The bell tinkles as they enter the hushed shop with its smell of clean wool and expensive perfume. The children shuffle in behind Lily. Robert looks surly and nudges a pair of expensive-looking leather shoes with his toe.

"Now, children," Mae says, "you wait here while I look." She runs her fingers over a silk scarf and turns to Lily, her eyes lively. "This is such a treat, to pick my own things."

Lily frowns. "Don't you usually choose your clothes?"

"Goodness, no! I haven't had the time with the

children. Or the energy. Leonard usually has one of his secretaries pick some things for me. But now . . ." Her cheeks are flushed. "Thank you, Lily."

She half dances around the shop, holding dresses up to her body, smoothing the material over the mound of her stomach, pressing her face against a long wool cardigan. "I love that smell, don't you?"

Lily decides not to tell her that wool is treated with sheep fat and urine to make it waterproof.

Mae looks so much younger, her voice so light and full of laughter. Lily thinks back to the scorched letters she'd found in the grate the night she arrived. She can't imagine this woman writing them. She watches Mae flit from one item to the next, glowing, beautiful, adding scarves and dresses and skirts and gloves and stockings to the pile on the counter, while the shopgirl shoots anxious glances at Robert, who is rubbing dirty fingers over a white fur muffler.

"Leave that," Lily murmurs. "Not long now."

He pretends not to hear her, but Lily knows not to scold further: he will only make a scene, then pinch Matteo when she isn't looking.

The shopgirl glares at him and Lily drops her eyes, waiting to be told to leave. But then she looks back at Mae, who is humming happily under her breath as she adds more stockings to the pile. Lily draws herself up to her full height and forces herself to stare back at the shopgirl, who holds Lily's gaze for a moment, then looks away, her jaw tight as she picks up a newspaper from under the counter and begins leafing through it.

The headline reads:

MILLAR'S BABY RACE GETS OFF TO
A FLYING START:
THE GREAT STORK DERBY'S EARLY
CONTENDERS!

Lily can't read the article at this distance, but a few phrases in capitals stand out: THREE CHILDREN ALREADY! PLANS TO HAVE A DOZEN MORE!

Lily thinks back to what Millicent had said about this baby race, calling it *disgusting* but also laughing at the idea of women having babies for money. What Lily had wanted to say was that Millicent couldn't possibly understand that it was more complicated than a *disgusting joke*. That it might be possible to want a baby *and* dread it. That pregnancy wasn't always a choice. She rubs her hand over her own swollen stomach.

Then Mae is next to her, slightly breathless and smiling. In her hands is a beautiful rounded cloche hat, similar to the one that Mae herself wears, only a deep purple.

"For you!"

"Oh," Lily says. "I couldn't! You mustn't—"

"You can and I must. Do you like it?"

Lily nods as Mae pulls the hat lightly over her head, smoothing the hair back from Lily's face and laughing. Her breath smells of peppermint. "You look wonderful, Lily! Doesn't she?"

The shopgirl glances up from her newspaper and gives a grudging nod.

"Thank you." The words don't seem enough, but they're all Lily can manage. "Thank you."

April

It's easier putting the children to bed with Lily's songs and stories—even Robert seems calmer and sometimes sits near Lily, leaning toward her but not quite touching her. He rarely comes to Mae at all. She tries not to mind too much.

Tonight, Leonard will be late again and will have dinner in a restaurant with some colleagues before coming home.

Once the children are asleep, Mae and Lily tiptoe down to the kitchen, where Cook has left some plain white fish for them in a creamy sauce and some thick, dark ale.

Good for the baby, good for the blood.

Mae detests the pale fish and white sauce, and hates the ale, which tastes like cold gravy.

Instead, they take a loaf of bread and a pat of butter into the drawing room and sit on a blanket, spearing slice after slice of bread on the toasting fork and slathering the hot toast with butter, which melts and drips off their fingers.

"I love this," Lily breathes.

"Buttered toast? It's delicious," Mae agrees.

"Not just the toast. Everything!"

The toast is warm, the fire is warm. Mae closes her eyes, basking. Leonard still mostly ignores Lily or complains that she is "odd" and "too quiet." Mae doesn't see

Lily as either of these things, but then Lily is so different when Leonard's not here: she laughs openly and talks freely. Perhaps Mae herself is different too.

"Do you mind Leonard working late?" Lily asks, as if reading Mae's thoughts.

"I used to. The house is so big. It felt . . . empty."

"My house was small and it felt like that."

Mae leans forward and brushes a toast crumb from Lily's shoulder. Lily smiles at her, and for a moment, there is just this: her hand, Lily's shoulder, the fire.

May

Lily feels a pain in her back and a twisting in her abdomen for hours before the contractions become unbearable. By that time it is night, and in her attic room, she knows she must stay quiet so Matteo can sleep: she mustn't panic him. She exhales through her teeth and watches the shadows on the ceiling: tree, bud, bird. For the first time in months, she feels the wrench of loneliness, the awareness that she is trapped in her own body, unreachable.

She stands, paces, bends, counts, breathes.

Labor wasn't this bad with Matteo. Or perhaps it was, but there was a woman on their street in Chatsworth who helped with all the babies, for a fee, and she'd stayed with Lily throughout.

If she calls to Mae, will it wake the other children? Will it wake Leonard? She has watched the man press his lips to Mae's forehead and hold her as carefully as if she is a delicate glass vase. But she has also seen the flashes of impatience in his eyes when the children squeal or when Lily commands too much of Mae's attention.

She paces, leans against the bed frame, grips it, exhales, her knuckles white, her breath ragged. The beat of her blood in her skull, like a hand tapping on wood, like something asking to be let in or out.

And then the tapping grows louder and Lily forces herself to stagger to the door, to push back the latch.

Mae's face is drawn, her eyes full of fear. Under her nightdress, her own stomach is swollen, but she is not due for another month. "I heard you pacing. The doctor will be here soon."

Lily manages to rasp her thanks, lets Mae half rouse Matteo and usher him downstairs to the boys' bedroom, then allows Mae to lay her down in the bed, on her left side, and hold her hand. Mae counts out the time, tells her when to breathe, tells her not to push, not yet, to wait. Strokes her damp hair back from her forehead and whispers that it will be all right, that she's doing so well.

Lily closes her eyes, allowing Mae's voice and touch to tether her.

"Breathe now, that's right, my dear. I'm here. Breathe now."

June

Mae's labor is quick and sharp. A stab of pain in the night and Leonard calls the doctor immediately. Mae stays quiet—she doesn't want to wake Lily and her new twins by crying out. Still, Lily must sense it, somehow, and she is there, asking if she can help, despite the bawling of her month-old twins from the attic. Leonard ushers her away, and before he shuts the bedroom door, Mae catches sight of Lily's face, fear-tightened, and she remembers her own terror when she watched Lily give birth last month: the horror of seeing her in pain; the dread that she might lose her. The relief when her babies had finally arrived: the boy first, then the little girl two minutes later. Mae adores them.

The pain grips Mae again. She closes her eyes and the door slams shut.

August

Lily's eyes are gritty with exhaustion. Her bones ache. The twins, Luca and Julia, wake at different times throughout the night. Lily rises in a daze, barely noticing which baby she is feeding. Sometimes she hears faint crying from downstairs and knows that Mae will be rising to feed baby James. Mae, too, looks exhausted. Leonard is terse and complains at being woken. On many nights, he sleeps at the office, then returns brighter, more cheerful and louder. He strides into the kitchen and presses his rough face against Mae's neck.

"There's a dinner next Friday. All the wives will be there. I said you'd come."

Lily watches Mae's body stiffen. "Oh, I . . . I don't really feel—I'm so tired."

"Exactly! All this time in the house is wearing you down. It'll do you good to get out."

He waits until Mae nods, then kisses her again, very gently.

Lily looks away.

October

Mae is basking in the late-autumn sun, which turns the yellow leaves gold. As Lily picks weeds from the flower bed, she seems haloed in light.

"You're stealing the gardener's job," calls Mae.

Lily looks up, grins, then turns back to digging through the soil.

Mae closes her eyes, listening to the children bickering and playing somewhere in the house. When she opens her eyes again, Lily is there, her hands behind her back. "You've seemed sad today and I thought . . ." And from behind her back, she produces a single rose, its yellow petals almost crisp in the cold.

"Thank you." Mae knows the words sound wooden, but it's hard to speak when her vision has blurred and her throat aches.

Lily sits on the wooden bench next to her, laying the rose between them, and she waits, her breath hanging in clouds.

When she can speak, Mae finally says, "I'm pregnant again."

"So soon? I thought you didn't want—"

"I didn't. I don't. But Leonard likes . . ." Leonard likes sleeping with her and likes the idea of a big family. He calls them his *herd*, then shuts himself in his study or stays late at the office. Mae reaches for Lily's hand. "I'm so glad you're here."

April, 1928

No time to fetch the doctor for this birth. Lily presses against Mae's back to relieve the ache, grabs her hand, tells her to squeeze it hard. White knuckles, gritted teeth. Red wash of pain. Mae's pulse a jolting music under Lily's fingers. Their joined hands a rope, an anchor.

Baby Jane is born within an hour. Both women hold her, bloodied, weeping.

Lily's lips on Mae's forehead. "Hush. Hush. I'm here."

June

Lily lies awake in the attic, straining for the sounds of Mae moving around downstairs. Jane is a fretful baby and Mae looks hollow and brittle, with dark shadows under her eyes. In the time that Lily has lived in this house, she has grown used to the clanking of pipes and the cries that echo through the empty corridors at night; she has become accustomed to the shapes of branches that move across the attic ceiling in the moonlight—they no longer look monstrous, but like curved arms, beckoning her into a dark embrace. But while the house feels more like home, Lily feels increasingly restless—an itchy anxiety that keeps her awake, as she recounts conversations with Mae, the sound of Mae's laughter, the way Mae looks at her across the room, past Leonard and the playing children, as if there is some silent dialogue between them. Lily has never felt that before, with anyone. An unspoken, wordless communion, like an undercurrent, an undertow.

And now, at night, in the attic that has grown familiar, Lily aches, as if something is missing.

A scratching sound. A light tapping on her door. Lily tiptoes past Matteo and the twins and then, as if she has summoned her with her thoughts, Mae is standing outside her door, an open bottle of wine in one hand and an uncertain smile on her face. The moonlight reveals the shape of her still-swollen belly under her nightdress. She looks vulnerable and beautiful.

"Are you . . . What is it?"

"I can't sleep," Mae says. "Jane is asleep. Leonard is at the office still and I feel . . . I wondered if you would sit with me."

Lily's heart lifts. She looks over her shoulder to where Matteo is sleeping peacefully, the twins on the mattress next to him.

"We could go to the garden. I just want to feel . . . I want company. But if you're tired—"

"No!" Lily says, too quickly. "I'm not tired."

Under the moon, the garden is pearled with light, the grass damp between Lily's toes as she follows Mae, placing each foot where Mae's own feet have been, so that when she looks back, there is only one set of prints.

The wine is a warm and heavy red. Lily drinks, then passes the bottle to Mae. A light breeze lifts the hairs on Lily's arms. Mae shivers and moves closer, tucking her feet beneath Lily's legs.

"Where would you live," Mae asks, "if you could live anywhere in the world?"

It is a rich woman's question and Lily's first thought is *Somewhere warm and safe*, but the second is *Here. With you.*

She feels the heat in her cheeks, is glad of the darkness. "I haven't thought about it."

"I'd live somewhere quiet." Mae's voice is soft, her words wine-loosened. "Alone in a forest somewhere." She takes Lily's hand between her own. "Wouldn't you like to be somewhere alone?"

Unable to speak, Lily nods.

Mae leans her head against Lily's shoulder. "This is nice here. With you."

Lily can feel her heartbeat in her throat, or perhaps it is Mae's heartbeat, the warmth of her, the rise and fall of her chest.

Lily doesn't dare move.

Mae turns her face so that her cheek rests against Lily's collarbone. She can feel Mae smiling against her skin. Lily dips her head, so that her lips brush Mae's hair.

The tiny span of air between them is suddenly charged. Lily is aware of her every movement, the way Mae's breathing has fallen in time with her own, the flicker of Mae's eyelashes against her neck. Mae presses her lips to the base of Lily's throat. The lightest of kisses, but the sensation travels through Lily's body. If she moves her mouth downward, her lips will meet Mae's. If she lifts her hands, she will be able to cup Mae's face in her palms, pull her closer and then –

And then what?

A pulse in her chest, in her stomach, her throat, but Lily can't make herself move.

They sit very still, sharing the same cold air, the same warm breaths, their mouths inches apart.

"I wouldn't want to be alone," Mae whispers, so faintly that Lily thinks she might have imagined the words.

She brings her hand up to rest on Mae's cheek, feeling the heat there.

"Yes," Lily whispers. And she isn't sure what she means or what she wants. All she knows is that everything in her—the thrum of her blood, the beat of her breath, the rise of her flesh—wants to say *yes*.

Such a small word. An impossible word. A tiny sound, a whisper on an exhalation, which the night breeze carries up toward the cold stars, each point of light alone in the darkness.

August

For Lily's birthday, Mae waits until Leonard has gone up to bed and all the children are sleeping. Then she leads Lily into the drawing room. Buttered toast by the fire again, taking turns to hold the toasting fork and cut thick slices from the loaf. Mae gives Lily a small parcel, wrapped in brown paper. All day she has been aware of its weight in her pocket.

Lily's eyes widen as she unfolds the paper and sees a string of gleaming spheres on a delicate silver chain.

"Your pearls! I can't possibly—"

"I insist."

"But they're yours. What will Leonard say?"

"Perhaps . . . don't wear them when Leonard will see. I can keep them for you."

"When would I wear them at all?"

"Now. Here, I'll put them on you. Lean forward." And Mae brushes Lily's hair to one side, just as Lily had done for her nearly a year and a half ago. After she has fastened the catch, she settles the pearls upon Lily's collarbone. It is hard to gather air into her lungs.

"Beautiful," she breathes.

And then she looks up to see Leonard staring at them. She doesn't know how long he has been standing there, or what he could have heard, but his face is frozen and, as she watches, he turns away.

Later, in bed, in the darkness, he says, "I think Lily would be happy if we could find her somebody."

"What do you mean?" She feels suddenly nervous, suddenly sick.

"A man. Someone to be a father to those children. Get her out from under our feet."

Mae's chest is tight. "She's not under our—"

"I wasn't asking your opinion, Mae. I was telling you how things are for me. In my house."

"It's my house too!" Mae says, in a fierce growl that she doesn't recognize. And even though she knows he will be hurt and angry, even though she knows he won't speak to her tomorrow, she continues: "You can't just go and search the streets for a . . ." The word *husband* catches in her throat. ". . . for someone for Lily. You can't just decide for her."

"Neither can you," he says, his voice even. And she can hear him smiling as he says, "Besides, I don't have to search the streets. There's a man at work. I've told him all about Lily."

"You can't do that," she says, a sensation like cold water running through her.

He leans across and brushes dry lips across her forehead. "Good night, dear."

October

It has become an afternoon ritual of sorts. At least twice a week, before Leonard returns from work and the older children have slammed into the house from school, while the younger children are napping or resting, or at

138

least if they're not grizzling, Lily and Mae will sneak out to the bottom of the garden, arms laden with blankets. There is something deliciously freeing, Lily thinks, in sitting under the shade of the maple, its leaves flaming red and orange in the autumn sun, watching the house from a distance, imagining its homely safety, while next to her, Mae talks about how she'll ask Leonard for the money to change the drapes in Lily's attic room, or how she will persuade him to move to a bigger house—*one with more space for all of us*.

"What will Leonard think about that?" Lily asks. She has noticed, recently, the way Leonard looks at her when she is talking to Mae. There is something narrow and dark in his expression. Sometimes, when she walks into the room, he stands up and leaves.

"Oh, don't worry about Leonard," Mae says. "He's always at the office. The house is my responsibility."

Lily looks up. Mae has started saying things like this: that she can change things in the house because it's her job, or that she can ask Cook to make chicken pie for dinner, even though Leonard doesn't like it, because *we all love it*. Lily is glad to be included in this *we*, but when she sees the new hardness in Leonard's gaze, she feels as if she is balancing on a ledge, which is slowly crumbling.

Lily lays a light hand on Mae's arm. It is an anchor point, a reminder that she doesn't need to be frightened anymore. She is safe.

Voices from inside the house—a low male rumble. Both women look up, to see Leonard back early from work, walking into the garden, the smile on his face too wide. Behind him is another man, taller, broader, dark-haired.

Lily's stomach drops because *How can Tony be here?*

But then the man steps into the sunlight, her vision clears, and she sees that, although he has the same heavy brows and prominent nose as Tony, his expression is softer and, even from this distance, kinder.

Mae walks across the lawn to them, her gait oddly stilted, as if something has startled her, too; as though she is approaching something dangerous.

"You're home early," Mae says to Leonard, pointedly ignoring the other man, which is not like her.

"Ah, we had to shut a bit sooner than usual. Some wage cuts for some of the men and they were getting ornery. But Paolo here calmed them all down. So I thought I'd bring him home, introduce him to you and Lily." They approach Lily, still sitting at the end of the garden, and Paolo smiles and takes her hand. *"Piacere."*

Lily feels a sudden joy. It's so long since she's heard anyone speak Italian to her and there is such warmth in this stranger's greeting, such gentleness in his eyes, that she finds herself smiling at him. *"Piacere,"* she says softly, her own language like rich wine in her mouth.

Leonard says, "I thought we could give Paolo a nice meal tonight."

"It's chicken pie," Mae says, without blinking.

As they walk back into the house, Lily can feel Mae staring at her, but when Lily turns, barely able to suppress a smile, Mae's expression is shocked, as if she's seen something awful.

February

Mae is curled up on the chaise, pretending to be asleep when Lily comes to talk to her. Mae knows what is coming, has been able to sense it for weeks, like the threat of gray rain clouds over an already flooded city. Lily has been jumpy around her, has taken to speaking Mae's name, then trailing off, as if she wants to confess something.

When Mae looks up and says, "Yes?" keeping her tone remote, perhaps even slightly hostile, Lily always blushes and says, "It's nothing," or "Never mind," and the bright spots of color on her cheekbones and across her neck make Mae's chest ache.

Lily has a kind of beauty that isn't dependent on the right clothes or the cut of her hair or a flattering lip rouge. A month ago, Mae would have been able to say, quite naturally, "You're so beautiful," or "I miss you." But the words would feel wrong now, would hang between them awkwardly. Feeling Lily retreat from her, Mae has done the same. It is safer.

Still, when Lily comes into the drawing room and kneels next to the chaise, Mae knows that she can't avoid the conversation any longer. Leonard and Paolo are in the smoking room—Mae can hear their quiet laughter and the clink of ice in glasses. A toast, a celebration.

The urge to be sick is almost overwhelming. Mae keeps her breathing regular, hoping Lily will leave her, that she can delay this conversation yet again, that she can change this thing that is happening—that has, from the sound of the ice in the glasses, already happened.

"Mae," Lily whispers, and places a hand gently on her arm.

Mae doesn't move, focusing on the pressure of Lily's fingers, trying to ignore the burning in her throat, the pressure in her skull.

"Mae."

Lily's face is close to hers, her eyes brimming with happy tears as she says, "I have the most wonderful news."

And Mae nods blankly as Lily tells her that the wedding can happen within a month, that she knows it seems rushed, but Paolo is just so kind, so wonderful with the children.

"And I'm so happy, Mae. I was worried, before, that we would have to move away, that I would see less of you. But Leonard says that Paolo and I can stay in the old barn at the end of the garden. He says it has furniture from when his mother lived there, though it might be a bit dusty, but I don't mind that, not at all. Oh, say something, Mae. I'll still help you with the children, so you mustn't worry. Are you happy for me?"

Mae swallows. "Yes. I'm happy." Her voice doesn't wobble and her smile is steady, even though her face feels like it doesn't belong to her—like every muscle is attached to a string being tugged into place by someone else.

Later, a glass of champagne warming in her hand, Mae watches Paolo and Lily as they dance slowly to "Somebody's Lonely" on the gramophone.

Leonard leans against the mantel next to Mae, then kisses the corner of her mouth. She stays rigid, her eyes never leaving the dancing couple, never leaving Lily.

"Perfect result," Leonard says in a low voice. "A real win for both of them."

"It's not a horse race, Leonard."

He starts, and she knows her tone is too sharp, but she can't stop herself. "What right did you have to meddle? Lily was happy. She didn't need—" Her voice cracks as she gestures at Paolo, who is holding his arm out so that Lily can spin, laughing as she stumbles backward. He catches her, puts his arm around her waist.

"Everyone needs someone, Mae." Leonard sounds hurt; she can't meet his gaze.

Lily giggles. Paolo is whispering something into her ear. She rests her head on his shoulder.

"This is good, Mae," Leonard says. "This is the best thing for everyone."

Mae takes another gulp of champagne. It is warm now, flat and sour, and that is why her eyes are stinging suddenly; that is why she has to rush from the room to the little bathroom, where she leans her forehead against the cool tiles, fighting the urge to double over and vomit.

12

It is late now. Outside, the light is draining from the sky and the birds have fallen silent, intensifying the stillness inside the courtroom. Darkness has begun massing in the shadowy corners, hiding the scrolled oak leaves and the gold cherubs with their silent trumpets. The electric lights cast a muted glow, but not enough to pick out the faces of those in the gallery, just enough to reflect off their gleaming eyes. In the growing gloom, Lily hears every one of them take a breath.

The lawyer steps forward. He is smiling, but the dim electric bulbs overhead highlight his cheekbones, his nose, his chin, casting the rest of his face into skullish shadow.

"Can you describe the nature of your relationship with Mae Thébault?" His voice is gentle, easy, as if he has asked Lily this question before. As if she is prepared to answer it.

"She was my friend."

"Your *friend*?" He says the word sneeringly, seeming to imply—in the way he elongates the vowels and swallows the final sounds in a laugh—that everything about Lily, from her face to her accent to her obvious poverty,

144

would make friendship with a woman like Mae impossible. He turns to look over his shoulder at the gallery, as if sharing a joke.

And Lily wonders, but daren't ask, why this question is important. He is trying to cast further doubt on her morals. Of that she is sure, but she doesn't know what direction his questions will take, so she draws a breath and tries to keep her voice level. "She was my employer and my landlady. I was a nanny to her children." Lily's mouth is dry. She watches the lawyer's eyebrows rise, watches his face lift, his smile grow. He casts another glance at the gallery.

"But you were *friends*?" That word again. That sneer. That laughter.

"We are. We *are* friends."

Still, Mae doesn't look at Lily. She is picking at a loose thread on the skirt now, plucking at Lily's careful stitching.

"I see," the lawyer says. "But you don't live with Mae Thébault anymore?"

"No."

"Can you explain why? A difference of opinion, was it, that led you to leave? Differing moral standards?"

Lily bristles. "We had two big families. For one house, it was . . . it's a lot of children." This is at least part of the truth.

He nods and leans forward, as if she's said something fascinating.

"Exactly. A *lot* of children. And can you explain how you came to have so many? You, in particular, and from two different marriages. I'm aware that Mrs. Thébault has long had a big family, but your own large family is more recent and, if I might say so, quite *sudden*."

"Sudden?"

"You're aware, of course, that some women were dismissed as claimants to the fortune because they were *masquerading* as mothers of large families, and that some of the children were, in fact, not properly registered, possibly not actually theirs."

"All my children are mine." It seems a ridiculous statement to have to make. Lily is so tired.

The lawyer nods. "How did they come to pass, these children?"

Lily stares. "You want me to explain *how* I have children?"

Laughter from the gallery. And the lawyer himself chuckles, his eyes flashing, his face pink, his eyes hard. "No, no, I'm quite familiar with the . . . mechanics. I want to know *how* so many, so suddenly."

There is no answer to this, so Lily says nothing. The judge makes a note. She feels queasy.

"All those mouths to feed," the lawyer says musingly. "Where did you expect the money to come from? Or perhaps you didn't give that much thought. During the . . . mechanics."

Someone in the courtroom titters. Lily sits, staring at her hands. From the corner of her eye, she sees the judge make another note.

The lawyer leans farther forward, and the people in the gallery lean forward too.

The silence reminds Lily of a church. She'd never been much of a churchgoer before living with Mae, but they went together sometimes, taking the children with them—Lily had only been to Catholic services before, with their long sermons and focus on guilt. But Mae's Protestant services were shorter, with less talk of damnation. Mae wasn't particularly religious either, but it was somewhere for the children to be quiet, *somewhere to feel a sense of peace*, Mae said, and Lily agreed that churches made her feel something. A lifting of her spirits, or an awareness of a presence—someone or something watching her.

The courtroom gives her that feeling now. The lawyer is the priest, delivering his sermon, and Lily is powerless to change his words. But who is God? Is it the people in the gallery, who are watching her always? Or is God the judge, the man who will decide her fate?

No, Lily decides. God is the unseen imagined person outside the court. God is the cry of the newspapers, who will say they have seen inside her soul, who will claim to know her. God is the voice in the street that will judge her, after this. The voice that will condemn her. The same voice that assumes she must be immoral and lazy because she is poor and an immigrant; the same voice that assumes she can't read, can't write, can barely count.

"How so many children?" the lawyer asks again, and Lily jumps in her seat. "If, as you earlier claimed, you had lost some through miscarriage in your first marriage, how is it that this stopped so suddenly? How is it

that you were suddenly able to have one child per year—
or more?"

"I wanted the children." This is mostly true.

"You wanted *something*," the lawyer says.

Ribald laughter from the gallery.

"Perhaps—even more than making children—you
like getting money for them, eh? So much so that it might
be that you're claiming children as your own when they
don't belong to you, to cheat your way into getting the
money."

"No! I—"

"But you want the money, don't you? You need the
money desperately?"

There is no answer to this. Doesn't everyone want the
money? Doesn't everyone need to put food in their own
mouths, in their children's bellies? Clothes on their
backs, shoes on their feet? Doesn't everyone dream of
waking up warm, knowing where they will sleep
tonight?

"There's a name, you know, for women who cheat
others for money and get paid for spending time on
their backs."

"Now, now, that's quite unnecessary," the judge interrupts, though Lily sees him making another note. Suddenly she feels very cold.

"When did you first hear about the Stork Derby? Was
it after you had moved in with Mrs. Thébault? A respectable woman. A *wealthy* woman at the time, although sadly
since fallen on misfortune. And Mrs. Thébault sits in the
courtroom today, with a valid claim on Mr. Millar's

fortune. She's an honest woman, of good character. I wonder if you can say the same."

She stays silent. Mae's lawyer is picking her apart again, trying to paint her as immoral, as reckless, as deceitful, as unreliable. It must be Mae's doing. What has she told him?

"Was it . . ." the lawyer asks, very quietly, so that everyone in the court has to lean forward farther, so that Lily herself has to bend forward to hear him, has to hold her breath, has to sit absolutely still, ". . . was it before or after you tried to kill her son Robert?"

This change in tack throws Lily and she gapes. She had been braced to argue that the children are hers, that she is no less deserving of the money than any other woman, but she hadn't been prepared for this and she can't find the words to defend herself.

The judge scribbles something down.

"I didn't ever—I wouldn't! How can you say such a thing?" Lily shakes her head. The accusation is unthinkable. She's staring at Mae now, furiously, daring her to look up, to meet her eyes one more time. Mae doesn't move.

13

Lily

It is mid-morning on October 29, 1929.

When Lily looks back on this day, she will think of it as the point when everything changed. She has never heard of Wall Street and only vaguely knows about the stock market from headlines that shout about falling prices and paperboys on street corners who call warnings about people selling shares. There is no reason why suddenly plummeting share prices should affect Lily. There is no warning tremor in the earth, this time, to tell her that everything is about to collapse.

At this moment, she is walking across the grass, with the lake ahead of her, listening to the crunch of the cold grass beneath her boots.

When the paperboy had hollered that the lake was frozen in *October*, the children had all shrieked with delight and disbelief, and had begged to go and see it. Lily had been reluctant, but the idea of keeping the boys from trying to sneak out was too draining, so she'd grudgingly agreed. Mae had planned to come out with them, too, but she felt nauseated and looked pale.

She has been odd with Lily ever since she moved into the barn with Paolo.

"This doesn't change anything," Lily has said, time and again. "I'll still help with the children."

Every time Lily says this sort of thing, Mae looks away, pressing her lips into a thin line. At the small wedding ceremony, earlier in the year, she'd barely said a word, and had claimed to feel sick, so that she didn't have to dance.

Despite herself, Lily has felt hurt, and even slightly angry of late. "Don't you like Paolo?" she asks sometimes.

"Of course I do," Mae says tonelessly.

But there is some new distance between them . . . or not a distance, exactly. It is as if they are both underwater, where everything is blurred and sounds are distorted. If Lily were to reach out and try to put her hand on Mae's arm—a gesture that would have felt natural weeks earlier—she might find that Mae is too far away for her to touch.

Now Lily watches the boys running ahead of her, toward Lake Ontario. "Not too far!" she calls, but they ignore her. She calls again, and Matteo slows, but then Robert grabs his sleeve and pulls him to run faster. Lily tuts under her breath. Robert is tall for his age—at nine, he is a year younger than Matteo, who is as gentle as ever. Sometimes Lily sees terror on his face, just for a moment, when Robert hits him, and she knows he's thinking of Tony. She wants to tear Robert off her child and slap him across the face.

The urge is shameful.

Lily rarely thinks of Tony anymore. Paolo is so

different—so kind and softly spoken. Quick to laugh and gentle with the children, who all adore him. There is a reliability that gives Lily space to breathe. Her children are safe. She is safe. His love for her is simple and predictable and steady.

Ahead of the children, the ground drops away. Soil becomes a small sandy stretch that leads toward the lake. Today everything is coated in ice, right down to the water. Except ... there is no water. There is only ice, stretching out across the surface of the lake, the blackness of the water a distant dream beyond.

The boys run straight onto the frozen surface before Lily can stop them.

"Boys!" she calls. They don't hear her over their own cries of excitement or the crunch of their feet. Only the parts near the shore are solid, Lily sees. Farther out, the ice has formed large, ovular sheets, which grate and shift as the boys hop onto them.

Matteo's face is ecstatic. His arms fly up as he jumps onto the first sheet. Robert is ahead of him, Alfred just behind.

"Boys! Stop!"

Lily drops the girls' hands and begins to run. Her breath clouds the air in ragged puffs of panic. She pauses at the edge of the frozen lake.

She shouts again. Matteo halts, turns. Alfred, too, stops.

But Robert continues, jumping from one ice sheet to the next, yelling in delight as they shift under his weight. Above, the sky is gray and heavy with the threat of snow. Lily's words echo between land and water and clouds.

As Lily calls again, there is a crack like a splintering bone. Robert's hands fly up as the ice breaks beneath him. His body disappears.

"Robert!" Lily calls, and the children cry out, the girls screaming, but there is no reply.

She runs out onto the frozen lake, her feet slipping, the ice creaking beneath her. In her head, she is counting. *Five, six, seven.* How long can he survive in this cold water? Is he unconscious? *Nine, ten, eleven.*

She staggers past the two boys, who are stock-still, their faces bloodless and blank with panic.

Robert's head bobs to the surface. He draws a breath, but it is shallow. The water must be so cold around him—so cold he can't even scream. He locks eyes with Lily. It's the first time she can ever remember seeing him scared. His hands flail at the ice as he struggles to pull himself out. He heaves, lifting his head out of the water, then slides back.

"Stay there!" she calls pointlessly, as he sinks beneath the surface.

The ice won't hold her; she knows it. Matteo is calling at her to stop, to come back. She steps onto the next frozen plate.

Robert's brown glove scrabbles at the ice, slips, sinks. His head doesn't rise.

She begins counting again. His time beneath the water. *One, two, three . . .*

The gaps between the ice plates are bigger now, the cold water black between them.

Lily steps across the gap to the ice plate where she'd

last seen him. It pitches beneath her and she crouches instinctively, hunching low and staying very still, her heart hammering.

. . . four, five, six . . .

She can't see Robert's beige hat, his dark green coat, his brown gloves—there is no glimpse of color anywhere: everything, everything, is the bleached white of ice and the black of the water, as if every other shade has been scrubbed away by her dread.

She lies flat on her stomach, pulling her glove off, and slides her hand into the water, gasping at the cold. Nothing. There is nothing there. He must have sunk deeper. In a wave of horror, she pulls herself forward, putting her arm and shoulder into the freezing water. Her fingers brush against something, but she can't quite grip it.

Six. Six. She has been counting six for so many seconds. Her fingers slide over his hat—or is it his hair?

Six, she thinks dully, her mind scrambling. And she takes a lungful of air and then sinks her head and shoulders beneath the cold surface, reaching with both arms.

The water clamps around her skull.

Six.

She stretches out her arms, feeling for his raised hands and pulling. One hand, then the other. There is a moment when she feels herself slipping, when she feels the weight of their bodies balanced on the thin sheet of ice, when she is aware of the downward tug and the darkness that will take them both.

Six, she thinks.

And then she is free, her head breaking the surface,

her arms straining upward, pulling him to her, yanking him free of the water, dragging his wet, cold body close to hers.

She sits on the ice with her arms around him. His cheek is freezing against her chest, his lips are blue. He isn't breathing.

Panic is a dull, senseless ache as she claps him on the back.

He coughs and chokes, screwing up his eyes as he spits out water.

Then he cries. Not the smothered sobs of a nine-year-old but a full-throated animal howl of terror—wordless and ageless.

Lily holds him close and pats his back and, sitting on the ice with him cradled in her lap, she rocks him back and forth, her teeth chattering. "Hush," she says, pressing her lips to his cold forehead. "You're all right."

They shiver on the ice, and Lily pulls off Robert's sweater and shirt as Matteo crawls toward them, dragging Alfred's coat, which he puts around Robert's shoulders, taking his own off to drape it over Lily, pulling his hat down over her ears and rubbing at her arms. Robert's face is pale, but he stops crying. His nose is bleeding, the blood a shocking red against his pale skin.

After some time, she helps him to stand shakily. They pick a careful path back across the ice, his hand in hers. The other two boys, mute and open-mouthed, follow.

They walk home without talking, Lily pressing Robert's body against hers, trying to warm him. She cannot shake the noises: the crack of ice; the splashes; the cries; the silence. He is shuddering convulsively, blood dripping onto his collar from his nose. Her teeth chatter, ice feathering around her heart, inside her bones.

He grips her hand; his other arm is tightly wrapped around her waist.

When they arrive at the house, Mae is sitting at the kitchen table, leafing through a magazine. She calls a greeting without glancing up. Only when she is met with stillness does she close the magazine and turn to look at them. Her eyes scan their bedraggled hair, their shocked expressions; she pauses on Lily and Robert, soaked and shivering, rusty bloodstains drying on their sleeves and collars.

"What on *earth*? Robert!" She holds out her arms and he runs to her, weeping.

"What happened?" she asks him.

And he turns his face to Lily and says, "She let me go out on the ice. She watched me fall in. I nearly died."

Outside, in the massing darkness of early evening, the rain begins again, signaling the start of the thaw, the end of the magic of the early, unseasonal ice. Beyond the window, Lily watches the lid of night descending; in the glass, her reflection sharpens, until her face could be at the center of a photograph bought by some rich family. In the transparent image, she can imagine that she belongs in this room, in this house.

She can hear Mae in the drawing room, snapping the pages of a magazine. It is hours since she returned from the lake and the children are tucked up in bed, but Mae has been quiet and withdrawn.

"I'm sorry," Lily has said, two or three times, to Mae's stiff shoulders.

"Don't keep apologizing. I'm sure it wasn't your fault." But Mae doesn't seem sure. There's a wariness in her face, a watchfulness when she thinks Lily isn't looking. And Lily knows how she would feel, if someone had let Matteo fall through the ice. No matter whose fault it was, Lily knows whom she would blame.

"I'm so sorry," she says yet again. "It happened very quickly. He was only in for a moment. I really am sorry. I told him not to run out—"

"Please stop!" Mae snaps. She looks up and says, more gently, "Please. Stop. He's told me everything. I don't need to hear it again."

"But I'd like to tell you—"

"And I'd like to forget it ever happened." She smiles again, but it seems a quick, forced movement of her mouth. "I just feel –" Mae breaks off.

"Please, Mae. Please tell me what it is."

Only last month, Lily had sewn a ripped piece of lace on Mae's dress collar, the two of them standing in the drawing room while the children played upstairs. The skin of Mae's neck had been pale and warm under Lily's fingers; Lily had traced the line over her collarbone where the lace would sit, had watched Mae's skin flush at her touch.

But now, even Mae's neck—bare and rigid—looks

unfamiliar. *Where have you gone?* Lily wants to demand. *Come back, please.*

And then the key is in the door and Leonard comes home, bringing the icy air with him. Red-faced, eyes pouched with exhaustion, he doesn't greet Lily or kiss the back of Mae's neck in his usual way.

"Paolo will be working late today," he says quietly.

Lily nods. She is used to Leonard being big and bluff and loud. But today he slumps forward in the big arm-chair, resting his head in his hands. His eyes, staring at the grain of the polished wooden floorboards, are fixed.

For a moment, Lily thinks he must have heard about Robert. Someone must have told him, somehow, that the woman who is staying in his house, the woman who is acting as a nanny to his children, was responsible for letting one of them nearly drown. She imagines standing outside the house with Matteo and Paolo by her side, holding the eighteen-month-old twins close, with the snow spiraling from the star-salted sky.

Paolo's wages would be enough for them to rent some rooms in the poorer part of town, back where he used to live before he moved into the barn, but it would be a struggle. Only last week he'd told her how happy he felt now he didn't have to worry about money. How will she tell him that she has ruined it all?

She is about to explain, about to beg Leonard to let them stay, when he runs his hand over his face and looks at Mae.

"What is it?" she asks, still holding her magazine.

He swallows and licks his lips.

And then he begins to talk, in a halting, hesitating, flat voice, quite unlike his usual booming tone. He stares out of the window as he speaks, and he pulls his wedding ring on and off, squeezing the metal in his fist. His fingers are the color of bone.

He talks about the stock market in New York. He uses words like *drop* and *fall* and *collapse*. He uses the word *crash*.

As he speaks, Lily can't take her eyes from Mae's face, from the way that her body seems to shrink at Leonard's words. As if, as he talks about ticker-tape numbers and men plummeting from windows and bridges, dousing themselves in gasoline and flames, Mae herself is being pulled down into some inner darkness, where Lily will never be able to reach her.

Finally, Mae says very quietly, "What will this mean? For us?"

"We could lose everything." Leonard is still staring out of the window, still holding his wedding ring in his clenched fist, but it is Mae to whom Lily turns, Mae whose lip Lily sees trembling, who sinks down into a chair and places her head in her hands and—*Why isn't Leonard holding her?*

"The business?" Mae's voice is a whisper.

"Everything."

Tree branches rattle against the windows and a pipe clanks somewhere upstairs; there is a deep sigh, as if the house itself is groaning.

And Lily wants to reach out and put a hand on Mae's shaking shoulders, but it isn't her place to do that, not with Leonard here. Leonard, who is watching the quivering of the branches and who barely seems aware of Mae, or Lily, or anything outside his own body.

From outside the house, the sound of far-off shouts and a distant siren. Inside the drawing room, no one says a word. All Lily can hear is the echo of Leonard's voice in her mind: *fall, collapse, crash, everything.* All she can see is Mae, alone at the table, her hand pressed hard against her ribs, as if she is struggling to draw breath, as if something has sucked all the air from the room.

14

Mae begins bleeding in the middle of the night. A rush of warmth between her legs and, for a moment, she thinks she's lost control of her bladder. She has been pregnant for six months, has carried herself like a glass ornament, and still it is not enough. And she wonders if the child inside her has sensed the thoughts she has had, about wanting it all to stop—the spinning wheel that holds her body hostage for months at a time. When she'd spoken to Leonard about stopping the pregnancies, even though it's illegal to try, he'd shaken his head. "Don't be obscene."

Obscene. The same word the government uses. Obscene to prevent pregnancy. Natural for women's bodies to be stretched and broken again and again. Natural for women to convulse and bleed and risk their lives time after time.

She hasn't been sleeping as well since the night Leonard told her that their world was crumbling. She wakes often to find the bed cold and empty. He has cut back on the food allowance slightly, and forces the children to clear their plates, despite Robert's protests that peas are

161

disgusting. Last week, Robert had pretended to retch over his broccoli and Leonard had cuffed him around the back of the head, then continued to eat, ignoring the tears that welled in Robert's eyes.

Mae had sat, frozen. Leonard had never raised a finger to the children before. Across the table, Paolo had bowed his head and she'd seen Lily reach for Matteo's hand.

"You'll eat your food and be glad of it," Leonard muttered. "There are people starving." The words had reminded Mae of the cramped house in Oakville. The newspaper stuffed into the walls, which she'd rolled into tiny balls and chewed slowly, trying to soothe the ache in her empty stomach.

And it suddenly occurred to her that if *they* were losing money and cutting back, there was no way they could keep Lily and her family in the barn. If the factory went under, Paolo's wages would stop. Lily brought in a little money by altering dresses for some of the women Mae knew, but not enough to cover the cost of their food, particularly now that Matteo was growing so quickly. She imagined telling Lily that she would have to leave. The thought was so sickening that, for a moment, she had to put her fork down and take several deep breaths.

Leonard carried on eating, but Lily noticed immediately. "Are you all right?"

Mae blinked. Although she was used to how attuned Lily was to her moods, and although she was aware of every change in Lily's facial expression, it still sometimes took her by surprise that Lily could sense her distress before Mae knew she'd shown it.

"Of course," Mae said, falsely bright. "Just a headache." Not a complete lie.

"Here," Lily said. "Let me just . . ." And she leaned across and pressed her thumbs lightly at the point where the arch of Mae's brows met the bridge of her nose. The relief was instant, and Mae closed her eyes, feeling the pressure in her skull ease, feeling Lily's hands cradling her head.

When she opened her eyes again, Leonard, Paolo, and the children were all staring and Lily, pink-cheeked, had picked up her cutlery.

Mae couldn't taste anything and excused herself from the table to go and lock the bathroom door and lean unsteadily against it, pressing her own fingers to where Lily's had been, trying to feel it again: the pressure, the comfort, the safety.

Now, Leonard is snoring next to her and she sits up. Her immediate thought is how to change the bed linen without disturbing him, how to hide this from him until the morning. He's been frantic about the factory for the past two months, and even more so in the last few days, making long, expensive phone calls, hissing into the receiver, wearing a frightened expression she's never seen before. When he catches her watching, he flashes a quick smile. Then he returns to the bleak, empty expression that makes him look like a stranger.

At night, she hears the creaking of the boards in the study room as he paces up and down, up and down.

163

Toronto's streets are filling with sleepless men, who walk from one factory or office to the next, asking for work that no longer exists. They stand on street corners, their breath fogging the air in front of them, so that, as they multiply, it seems like some awful magician's trick where they appear, one by one, in a cloud of smoke.

The factory will last, Leonard tells her. It must last, although the demand for steel has fallen steeply as production grinds to a halt. So many of the rich investors have lost money—fortunes even—that vast building projects have been aborted. Half-finished structures sketch hollow outlines against the winter sky. There is a threat in the city's absence of noise: in place of the grinding, clanking machinery and the hum of life, the dark muttering of jobless men, and their flat, hopeless stares.

Leonard had fired some of the factory workers and brought in new men, bigger men, able to be both foremen and laborers. He'd hated to fire people: he worried about their families. "Still, better theirs than ours." He's always been so generous and caring that Mae has taken his kindness for granted. It's only now that she wonders whether he has been compassionate because everything had been easy for him: he grew up wealthy and handsome and adored.

She knows he has tried to call some of his friends, those born into a long line of money. They are always *indisposed*. Last week, when she was browsing hats she hadn't the money for, Mae saw Mrs. Thomson, smiled, and said hello. Mrs. Thomson had turned and walked in the other direction. Mae started mentioning it to Leonard, then thought better of it.

He looks exhausted and scared, his remoteness leaving Mae feeling cold. When she looks in the mirror, her haunted expression reminds her of her childhood in Oakville and the old terror threatens to swamp her.

So how can she wake him now? How can she disturb him? All this flashes through her head before she's fully awake, before she remembers that it won't be her bladder: she's six months pregnant. It will be her waters.

The thought feels like a missed step: she is suspended, just waiting for the shock of the fall.

It's too soon. The baby won't survive, can't possibly survive.

She reaches down and, although she doesn't want to look, she pushes back the sheets.

Blood. An oval-shaped red stain, spreading out from under her. The smell of it like hot metal in the sun. She recoils, puts her hand on Leonard's shoulder, shakes him.

"Leonard? Leonard! I'm bleeding."

He's awake immediately, his eyes wild, his mouth agape, as if she's said she's dying. "Where? Bleeding where? How?" he asks.

Unable to speak, she points to the sheets.

"I . . ." he says. "What should I do?"

"Fetch Lily."

He looks at the blood, then back at her face, and scrambles from the bed. A moment of hesitation in which she can almost hear his thoughts: how little he wants Lily in the house, caring for Mae like this; how much he simply wants to call for an ambulance, which they can ill afford.

"Get the doctor," she says. "But fetch Lily too."

She hears him cursing as he rushes down the stairs.

Mae, sitting in the bed in her own blood, listens to Leonard shouting into the telephone, then walking out of the back door and down the garden path toward the barn. She tries to steady her breathing by picturing him knocking, by imagining Lily stirring, then rushing into the house and up the stairs to help . . . But what can she do? The first pain clamps around Mae's gut, and there is another warm rush of blood from between her legs.

She begins to weep. Silently at first, not wanting to wake the children. And then, as she hears Lily coming up the stairs, as Lily comes into the room and puts her arms around her, Mae draws a great, shuddering breath and sobs.

When she was thirteen and found herself pregnant, Mae kept it to herself for the longest time, until her mama noticed her swelling breasts and the shape of her abdomen rising, like a new loaf, under her dress. They were living in the cellar beneath a boardinghouse then, among the pipes, which clanked and leaked, but it was better than freezing to death on the streets.

"Who've you been sleeping under, Mae?" Mama had demanded.

And Mae made up a name for him: Henry. And she made up a job for him: he was a sailor. Because she didn't want to tell Mama that there had been three of them in an alleyway. They had jumped on her when she was

166

walking home from school, and she hadn't known any of their names.

Henry had romanced her, she told Mama. He'd promised her the world before he disappeared. And Mama had stroked her hair and tutted. "You fool," she said. Her voice was gruff, but her hand was soft. And so Mae convinced herself, over time, that she'd fallen in love and been left. Jilted was better than ruined. A man who left you to sail away to other lands was better than three men who left you lying in an alley, blood soaking through your ripped drawers.

Mae had cried when she'd told her father, had cried when he hadn't spoken to her. She'd sobbed her way through labor, then held this tiny, warm thing in her arms. It was a miracle, this life she'd grown all by herself.

She called him Henry. After his papa.

When her own papa had wrenched the baby from her arms at two days old and taken him away, she'd wailed like the child she still was. It made no difference. Papa gave her baby to an orphanage. He wouldn't say which one. "Better like this," he said, not looking at her. "He never existed."

She still scans the faces of boys in crowds. He would be fifteen, her oldest boy. Older than she was when she birthed him. She tells herself he might have sailed away to other lands, like his papa.

She never lets herself cry for him.

The doctor pushes past Lily, palpates Mae's stomach, listens, examines the blood between her legs, and shakes his head. "Perfectly normal failed pregnancy," he says. "You'll bleed awhile is all. Distract yourself or sleep."

Distract myself?

Mae doesn't have the time or breath to voice her outrage through her agony, before Lily ushers the doctor from the room, then returns to the bedside and, squeezing Mae's arm, begins to describe the trees outside—the maple in the garden with its bright leaves.

"It's bare now, but they'll come again. The grass will come back, and the sun. This isn't forever. You'll see."

Mae listens to the lull of her voice, keeps her gaze fixed on Lily's mouth, gulping the words like air. "Don't leave me."

"I won't leave you."

It is hours before the birth is over—longer than her other labors. Lily holds her hand, wipes her face with a cold flannel, makes her take sips of water, puts an old sheet under her.

"You're doing so well," Lily says.

Mae grips her hand and closes her eyes, and she stays in the room, with the pain. She fights the drifting sleepiness that tugs at her, the drowsiness she feels she could so easily sink into, never to emerge again.

Pallid light is creeping into the room by the time the last racking spasm pushes something from her. She keeps her eyes shut, doesn't lift her head, stays absolutely still while Lily wraps the baby in a blanket and places it on Mae's chest.

It is barely longer than her splayed hand, its skin

translucent, its body the deep red of a heart. She is surprised by the weight of it on her chest, by the warmth of it.

It doesn't move, of course. It isn't breathing. Its face is still, tiny, perfect.

"What's wrong with it?" She runs her finger over its nose, its lips, its little chin.

Lily has tears in her eyes and shakes her head, kisses Mae's forehead, wrapping her arms around her. And Mae leans into Lily's embrace.

"I'm sorry," Mae says. And she doesn't know who she's apologizing to, or what it is she's done wrong, but it's the only word she can bring herself to say. She can't find the energy for *Why?* or *How?* or *What now?* So she says it again and again. "Sorry. I'm sorry."

"Hush," Lily says. "It's not your fault. Hush."

And Mae rests her head against Lily's chest, listening to the steady strumming of her heart, weeping, as if she herself is as defenseless as a newborn, as if only Lily can help her make sense of the world.

15

Lily, January 1930

Lily can't stop picturing the baby as she scrubs the blood from the sheets. She'd wanted to take Mae in her arms and tell her that all would be well. Of course she hadn't, because of course it wouldn't. Nothing will be quite the same again, but everything will continue anyway. Life will go on, a ghost child counting the years among them.

After Lily and Leonard have arranged for the body to be taken to the morgue, they sit across from each other at the kitchen table in the phantom pre-dawn glow, waiting for the children to wake. Soon, Lily will start breakfast, then scrub the floors—Leonard has had to let the cook and the maid go.

Upstairs, Mae is slumped in a drugged sleep. She's unlikely to wake any time soon, but still, Lily listens for her movements. She imagines creeping upstairs and tucking her body next to Mae's, falling asleep to the beat of her breathing.

Out in the barn, her children will be stirring. Paolo will take longer to wake: he sleeps with the sprawled-out abandon of a man unaccustomed to being dragged from sleep by a child's cry. Still, he won't ignore them if he wakes to find her gone: he will give the twins a cup of milk and a cracker each. He will try to talk to Matteo, and although her son likes him, he is still very quiet around this new man in their lives and watches him with the wary uncertainty of a wild animal.

Lily had felt like this, too, at first. On the first night that Paolo stayed, he'd rolled over in his sleep, his hand brushing against Lily's leg, and she had bolted upright, her heart hammering, filled with the urge to slap him, to claw at him, to grab the children from their beds and run.

Her breathing must have woken him—she saw his eyes glint in the half-darkness and, before she could speak, he whispered, "*Calmati, amore mio.*" And he took her hand, his touch gentle, then slid his fingers up her arm and rested his palm on her shoulder, tapping out a slow heartbeat until her breathing slowed and her pulse steadied.

From Matteo's bed, she heard a murmur: "Mama?" She could tell from his voice that he had woken with the same fear. But Paolo had called softly to him, had pulled back the covers so that Matteo could pad across the room and crawl into bed between them.

A few days later, Paolo started performing magic tricks to make Matteo laugh, pulling coins from his ears or producing flowers out of thin air.

"Where did you learn to do that?" Lily asked him, giggling.

"I lived on the street for some time. It is good to be quick with your hands," Paolo had said. There was a tautness in his smile and Lily didn't push for more.

She had told him little of Tony. Only that he'd been cruel, that he was dead. Paolo had nodded slowly, then kissed her cheek.

"He is the past now. He can't hurt you."

Lily can't talk to Mae about Paolo, can't explain the feeling of safety he gives her, how his kindness helps her to breathe, to imagine a future for her children. She keeps envisaging confessing all this to Mae, but each time, Lily pictures the way Mae will purse her lips, then turn away. The image feels like a slap.

"Do you trust him?" Mae has asked more than once. "Does he treat you well?"

And Lily's answer is always the same: "Yes. I do. Yes, he does. Yes."

Mae never asks if Lily loves Paolo. The question hangs between them in the silences.

Now, Leonard drinks his coffee too slowly. "I'll go into work early today," he says.

"Oh." She nods. She hadn't expected him to look after Mae, not really. But she had thought he might stay at home until she woke.

But perhaps Lily's face betrays something, because he says, "When she wakes, tell her I had to go in."

"Oh." It's difficult to know what to say: Leonard barely talks to her most days, and certainly never mentions work. This conversation feels oddly intimate. She wipes the clean sideboard again, scrubs at an invisible spot on the cupboard door.

"She knows there's been trouble at the factory,"

Leonard says, "so don't worry her with that. Just tell her I've had to go in."

"All right."

Lily imagines Leonard facing a crowd of shouting men. She imagines them trying to grapple with him. There's been trouble everywhere: riots in the streets, lines of shouting men outside the butcher's. On Yorke Street, a soup kitchen has been set up and families stand there all day, thin-faced and sallow-skinned, a hopeless anger in their eyes as they wait. Later, Lily will have to go out for bread. She will walk home quickly, her basket held close to her chest, and she will try not to catch the eye of any of the men who stand on street corners, their hands stuffed into their pockets, waiting for the day to end. She doesn't know where they sleep, these men; she tries not to think about it.

Over in Cabbagetown, Thérèse and Jacques are surviving only because Jacques has a job in Leonard's factory. Lily visits them once a month, sometimes with Mae and all the children, sometimes just with Matteo. Together, they eat whatever cake or cookie Lily has brought from Mae's house. Lily always finds a time when Thérèse is out of the room to tuck some notes Mae has given her into a drawer, and Thérèse pretends not to see. Although the last time Lily went, a week ago, she opened the cutlery drawer while Thérèse was boiling some water, and Thérèse said sharply, without turning, "Not today."

Lily pulled away her hand as if the drawer had scalded her. "Why?"

"I've no need of it today." Thérèse still didn't turn.

Her shoulders were rigid and thinner than Lily remembered.

Lily looked around at the bare shelves, the bottle of milk that was nearly empty. "Mae wants you to have it."

Thérèse turned then. "The factory is going bad. Leonard keeps Jacques on when many other men have lost their jobs. I can't take more money from them."

Lily thought guiltily about her space in the barn, about the meals and the other kindnesses that Mae and Leonard have extended to her. She looks after the children and helps around the house, and occasionally buys extra food if she earns money from her sewing, but she knows that without Mae's generosity she would never have survived in this city.

Now, in Mae's kitchen, she wonders if Leonard will have to let Jacques go, or if he will have to fire Paolo. She can't bring herself to ask. She doesn't understand the forces that are at work, taking everyone's money. It is as if, somewhere, a great plug has been yanked out and everything is slowly draining away.

She listens to the sound of the front door closing. The noise disturbs Jane from her nap, and Lily rushes upstairs. She holds the child to her chest, kisses the top of her head, and sways until the crying stops, but not before the other children have woken. Mae will sleep for hours until the drugs wear off, and in the meantime Lily will have to soothe six grumpy children.

As they troop down the stairs for breakfast, Lily feels a roiling in her stomach, a rising of the same queasiness she'd had when she'd been scrubbing the bloodied sheets. She's hungry, and though she would normally wait for the children to eat before serving herself, she puts Jane into her chair and feeds her at the same time as spooning porridge into her own mouth. It is too milky and her stomach churns, the nausea worsening.

Perhaps she's eaten something bad, she thinks, as she gags. She has no time to do anything other than turn to the sink, where she is repeatedly, violently sick.

"Are you all right?" Robert, uncharacteristically caring, suddenly sounds very young.

"Yes," she says, not turning to look at the children, to see their shocked faces. "I'm just tired."

And she is exhausted, she realizes, and not just this morning. She's felt utterly drained for a week now, her muscles heavy and aching.

Eyes watering, she leans forward, resting her head in her hands, and counts. Backward four weeks, then, with a growing sense of dismay, back further.

The sensation is unmistakable, really. How had she not noticed before? As she straightens, her queasiness all but gone now, she forces a bright smile for the children, then turns back to the sink and runs the water. In a minute, she will have to go out to the barn and wake her own children. She will have to tell Paolo that he must get to the factory. She will have to hope that Leonard has the money to keep him on. Sometime later, she will have to go upstairs and hold Mae while she cries, stroking the hair back from her forehead, feeling her grief as if it is her own. Later still, she will have to call the morgue and find out what to do about the poor dead baby. At some point, she will have to talk to Paolo. She will have to talk to Mae. She will have to tell them both.

But for now, all Lily has to do, once again, is rinse the sheets in the sink, until the rust-colored water runs clear.

16

Mae, April

Mae watches the way the material of Lily's dresses stretches tighter over her swelling stomach each passing day, and tries to feel pleased for her—she *is* pleased for Lily. And for Paolo. Of course she is.

"You need new clothes," she says, one evening, when Lily is sitting in the drawing room, a glass of water resting on the globe of her belly. "Your things look ridiculous." She had meant it to sound teasing, but she hears the sharpness in her tone, sees Lily's wounded expression.

"Ridiculous?"

Mae's smile feels plastered on. "Don't you have anything else?"

"We threw out the dresses I wore when I had the twins," Lily says. "And your things will be too small, I think."

"We'll have to visit the fabric store." Again, her tone is too harsh, but Mae thinks that if she softens her voice at all then she might weep.

"Stand up," she says in the same hard voice. Lily rises, her expression uncertain. Mae walks around her, assessing.

"Your arms are still slim," she says. "It's just tight around the middle when you stretch. Look." And she lifts Lily's right arm above her head, watching the way the material presses against her skin. Lily is all curves now, the smooth line of her neck sloping into the swell of her shoulder and breasts and the growing distension of her belly.

Lily looks down at the tight press of the material. "You're right, I need something bigger. All Paolo's money has been going on drapes and furniture. He's working so hard to make the barn homely."

Homely. Because her home is with Paolo now.

"I'll buy you some material," Mae says.

"Oh, I couldn't let you—"

"I want to." And this, Mae suddenly knows, is the truth.

"Thank you," Lily says, reaching for her arm, but Mae brushes past her and walks away, frightened that Lily will see the tears in her eyes.

There is a throbbing in Mae's stomach still, as she walks down the street to the fabric store, a heaviness in her breasts. Or perhaps it is just her imagination, her longing, her refusal to let go.

Sometimes she dreams that the baby is still alive, but that she has fallen asleep next to it and rolled on top of it. In her sleep, she is too tired to move, while being filled with panic at the thought of the baby's body under hers, the slow crush of the air from its lungs.

A boy. She'd looked beneath the sheet, before Lily

had taken him away. He'd had her mouth, the shape of Leonard's closed eyes. Elliot, she'd called him. Sometimes she says the name out loud to herself in the dark when she's sure she's alone. But not now. Now, Lily is walking next to her. It is early, still dark. A pale moon hangs above the horizon, like a thin paring of a fingernail.

Mae has no fingernails to speak of at the moment—she's chewed them all off.

She knows that Lily looks at her with concern when she picks at her food. Often, after the children are in bed, Lily will bring Mae the tiny pieces of curled pastry that she knows she loves, sprinkled with sugar and baked until crisp. If Mae refuses them, Lily will insist that she made them for herself and will sit next to Mae on the chaise or the bed or the floor, wherever Mae is huddled, and will talk to her about her day and the children and Paolo, filling the air with light chatter and nibbling cookies until, at some point, Lily will make Mae laugh, in spite of herself, and Mae will sit up and eat one of the cookies, then two; then, as if her body has suddenly remembered how to feel hunger, she will eat the rest while Lily watches, smiling.

There are these moments still when they are alone.

Two weeks ago, she had walked into the kitchen and had seen Lily standing in front of the sink, Paolo behind her. Lily's head was thrown back as Paolo kissed her neck and moved his hands across her breasts.

Mae had gone into her bedroom and shut the door, trying not to picture Paolo's large hands, hearing again and again Lily's gasp as Paolo kissed her.

179

Mae could imagine marching back downstairs into the kitchen and telling Lily that she should be hanging out the washing, or finishing the ironing, or preparing lunch. Everyone's life is harder without help in the house, and it's Lily's job to fill that space. She could hear herself saying the words, but couldn't make herself move.

She wants Lily to be happy, but she can't stand the way she looks at Paolo. It makes Mae feel so lonely.

Lately, Mae's mind skitters from one idea to another—she can't seem to gather her thoughts. She sees faces in the soap scum when she washes herself, thinks that the bubbles look like the curve of lips or the arch of a back. She hears words in the moan of the wind down the chimney and wonders if, somehow, she can hear the noises that Lily and Paolo make in the barn at night, while Leonard sleeps turned away from her, his back like a wall.

Mae thinks back to a year earlier, when she and Leonard had stood as witnesses for Lily and Paolo's marriage in the small Catholic church on East Street. The service had been long, with much kneeling. Mae had tried not to cry. The children had been bored and restless, until Paolo dug into his suit pocket and pulled out little almond cookies wrapped in paper—one for each of Lily's children and for Mae's too. How had he thought of such a thing? How had he afforded them? When had Leonard ever done something similar? Lily had caught Mae's eye, as if she couldn't believe her luck. Mae had tried to return the smile.

Lily and Paolo had gazed at each other throughout the priest's droning. Mae had looked instead at the carvings of Christ being crucified. His face, as blood dripped from His holy hands, peaceful.

Just a few hours before the wedding, Lily had been fretting about the roughness of her chapped hands. "I'll look like a washerwoman."

Mae retrieved a tiny pot of expensive hand cream that Leonard had given her years ago. It was from a store in New York, a gift that seemed too special to use.

Lily tried to refuse it. "You've done so much for me already."

"Please. I'd like to give it to you." And, suddenly nervous, Mae reached for Lily's hand and begun rubbing the cream into her reddened fingers.

Lily didn't look at her. "I thought you were angry with me."

"Why?" But Mae knew why. *I miss you*, she wanted to say. But instead, she said, "You're imagining things."

A sudden stumble over a broken cobble wrenches Mae into the present. Millicent is looking after the children—*all* of the children, including Lily's. She'd volunteered the afternoon before, when she'd found Mae standing next to a pile of smashed plates in the kitchen, making no effort to clear up the shards. She was staring out of the window toward the barn.

"Why don't you go out for an hour or so, Mae?" Millicent had asked, her eyes large and blue and a little frightened. "Go and do something *fun*."

"*Fun?*" Mae had said faintly, as if it was a foreign word. And she found herself thinking of the time, months ago, when she was still pregnant. Leonard and Paolo were both working late and a tree branch had been tapping against the living-room window, driving Mae to distraction. Lily had fetched Leonard's saw from the tool shed and begun sawing at the wood, cursing the tree and laughing when the pine needles hit her in the face. Mae had laughed, too, holding the branch steady until Lily had sawn it off and held it aloft like a trophy, staggering under its weight, then embracing Mae in celebration. Both of them had smelled of pine sap all evening, sitting on each other's feet to keep them warm.

"Yes, fun!" Millicent had smiled. "A drink in the Royal York Hotel—have you been inside yet? It's so extravagant. You'll love it. And I'm happy to pay, if you're short."

Finished less than a year ago, the Royal York is the tallest building in the Commonwealth. Mae knows that it is Millicent's favorite destination for *being seen*. But the idea of sitting in the bar and drinking—while the factory was in danger and people were starving—seemed so ridiculous that Mae began to laugh. With the shards of smashed crockery around her ankles, and baby Jane crawling over the floor to reach them, Mae laughed and laughed until tears welled in her eyes.

"What's *wrong*, my dear?" Millicent asked.

Mae had shaken her head, still laughing. How could she explain the way her life had constricted? That she missed the evenings spent with just her and Lily, who was becoming more of a stranger with every passing day. That her stomach ached around a phantom memory. That Leonard barely looked at her now. That her skin burned with the longing to be touched.

She couldn't say any of it, so she laughed.

And now they are walking on the frosty street. Mae has some of this week's specially saved housekeeping money in her purse. She grips it, imagining how happy Lily will be with the material for a new dress. Perhaps it'll ease the silence between them.

The buildings look grimmer by the day, with more and more storefronts boarded up, covered with scrawled messages in black paint—angry expletives and threats against the government that make Mae avert her eyes. She has the feeling, sometimes, that they are on the lip of some gigantic mouth—that the warning signs are there, but everyone is ignoring them and soon it will be too late.

The newspaper sellers are restocking their stands, pasting today's headlines onto their boards: BABY RACE WINNER WILL TAKE HUNDREDS OF THOUSANDS!

Mae doesn't normally read beyond the headlines, but Millicent keeps lecturing both her and Lily on the scandal of *that rich lawyer's will*. She seems to derive a perverse pleasure from loudly declaring how *strange* it is that women choose to *shackle* themselves to children and a life of *drudgery*. Such exhorting has increased since Mae's *mishap with the last one*, which is how Millicent refers to the stillborn baby. It is difficult to know how to explain to Millicent the conflicting forces that tug at Mae—that must tug at so many women: she doesn't want more children, but she has no choice. Her heart and her battered body are bound to child after child. And every one of them, wanted or not, she adores.

"Honestly," Millicent recently intoned, "there are people breeding like dogs. Those poor women, having one baby after another. One woman has had *four* children in the last *four* years. Can you imagine?"

One popular opinion of the Stork Derby—which Millicent shares—is that it is *outrageous*. Although her disgust seems to apply particularly to poor women. The women, Mae thinks, who truly need the money from the will.

Lily's reply to Millicent's indignation was lost in the shrieking of children running down the hallway. All Mae could catch was Lily's final remark: "Having children is not so simple." Mae had tried not to hold her hand over her empty stomach, but the room was suddenly airless. Lily had placed a hand lightly on Mae's shoulder. Mae had frozen, not knowing what the touch meant, not daring to move.

On the way to the fabric store, they pass another billboard shouting, *Baby Race!*

And Mae finds her eyes filling with sudden tears, sees that her pace has slowed, that she's staring at the board and the boy who is stacking the papers.

Lily squeezes her arm. "Keep walking," she says softly, and Mae does, feeling an emptiness that isn't quite rage, isn't quite grief, some emotion that sits deep within her. A feeling without a name. Why would it have one? Women aren't the ones who name things—even the children's names had been Leonard's decision. So her feeling is nameless, as if it doesn't exist.

There should be a special word for the grief—the ripping, listless guilt that a woman feels—after the loss of a child. But there is no word for it at all, just silence. No one even talks about the baby. Everyone behaves as though it had never lived at all. Everyone except Lily, who asks Mae how she is and looks at her with such tenderness that Mae sometimes feels like howling. It makes Lily seem like the place where she keeps her grief and the place where she finds her comfort. And yet even that is bound by Paolo's presence and Leonard's watchful gaze. These men, who come and go as they please, who think what they want and say what they think, while the women lose themselves in pregnancies and raising children. At home, she is always a wife and a mother. Only with Lily is she something else. Only with Lily does she sometimes catch a glimpse of who she might be.

The fabric store looks closed from a distance, but as they draw closer, Mae sees a dim glow from the back room. Many of the shop owners keep the lamps dim now and the temperature low, hoarding the light.

Mae stops outside the door. "I'll wait here." Because, suddenly, she can't stand choosing material for the dress that will allow Lily's body to swell with Paolo's child. She can't stand gazing at the swathes of fabric while Lily is measured, can't stand the thought of hearing Lily talk about Paolo: how kind he is, how happy she is.

"Will you be all right?" Lily looks anxiously at Mae's face.

Mae forces a stiff nod, then turns her back on Lily as she walks into the store, the bell tinkling overhead. As the sky pinks and pales, the street around Mae lightens into focus and the gray, grainy shapes on corners and in doorways resolve into the bodies of men, hunched under mounds of blankets.

Mae shifts uneasily: she might not read the newspapers, but Millicent tells stories about people being set upon by vagrants. Newly unemployed and homeless, there are more men on the streets all the time. They are hungry, cold, and if the stories are to be believed, they are violent.

Mae remembers being seven or eight, walking home from the bakery with her mother, the loaf of bread clutched close to her chest, still warm from the oven. They rarely had enough money for a fresh loaf and usually had to wait for the cheap, stale bread at the end of the day. A man had stopped in front of her. Thin, with sores on his face and hands, he had smiled at Mae with yellowing teeth. "Give me the bread, sweetheart."

She'd shaken her head—the bread was supposed to last them two days.

The man had pulled out a knife. Mae's mother had screamed, snatched the bread from Mae, dropped it, and grabbed her hand so they could run.

Now, the streets are full of thin, dirty, desperate men. Mae counts the heaps of blankets—eight on this street alone. Her mouth is dry.

Slowly, a sharp, cold band of light creeps across the ragged, dirty bundles, and one by one, they sit up and stretch, blinking blearily at the winter sun.

Fearful of making eye contact, Mae tries to watch the men without looking at them directly, and as they stand upright, she sees that some of the covers conceal a number of people, of all different heights.

Families. Men and women and children, all curled up under a single blanket against the cold.

A wrench of shame. But she doesn't feel any less afraid as one of the men—no more than five meters away—turns to her.

"Spare a penny, can you, sweetheart?" he rasps.

She shakes her head and watches him gather a small child into his arms. There is no mother that she can see.

He continues to gaze at her imploringly.

"Can't you go to the soup kitchen?" she asks eventually.

His cold stare travels over her clothes, her expensive hat, her polished boots.

He coughs. "What does a rich bitch like you know about soup kitchens? You haven't any idea."

His eyes are full of such burning defiance that she can't gaze back, has to look at the cold wet cobbles, has to turn toward the fabric store, pushing to get inside, away from his scornful stare, away from the emptiness in his child's expression.

But before she can hide in the warmth and safety of the shop, the door is pulled back and Lily rushes out, her face set, and strides down the street.

"Wait!" Mae follows, slipping on the cobbles, ignoring the shouts of the angry man, the muted cries of his child.

"Lily, wait!" she calls, but Lily keeps walking.

"Please stop," Mae says, grabbing Lily's arm. "What happened?"

Lily averts her eyes from Mae. "It doesn't matter."

"What's wrong? Where's the material?"

Lily mutters something, which Mae doesn't hear.

"Say that again."

"She wouldn't serve me," Lily says, her jaw hard, her mouth trembling.

"Oh," Mae says, momentarily lost for words. "There must . . . There's been a mistake."

"No mistake," Lily says. "She said she hadn't any material for my sort."

"*Your sort?*" Mae frowns. "What does that mean?"

"It means my face. My accent. It means me." Lily's mouth is quivering again and her eyes shine, but she doesn't cry. "She said her husband lost his job to an Italian. Her children are going hungry because of *my sort.*"

Mae blinks. "But you're not Italian," she says. "Not really."

"What do you mean? Of course I am."

"But you're not like . . . them," Mae says, thinking of the penniless Italian men she's seen around the city in recent months, the hunger in their eyes. She looks at the softness of Lily's face, the curve of her lips—her gentleness. Lily wouldn't hurt anyone, ever. There's no reason for people to think badly of her—the thought that anyone might fills Mae with a protective rage.

"You're nothing like them at all. Wait here, I'll tell Mrs. Petit. I'll explain that you're my friend. You're nothing like the Italians she's thinking of . . . You're the best person I know and beautiful."

Instantly, she knows that, somehow, she has misunderstood. Somehow, she has said the wrong thing. And she wants to apologize, because the wounded fury in Lily's expression is dreadful. Mae knows that Lily must have seen something in her eyes, must have heard the longing in her voice. And for a moment, Lily's expression reminds her of the vagrant's: the contempt on his face when he'd said, *You haven't any idea.*

All the way home, Mae struggles to think of something to say that could explain what she meant, how she feels. But there is something closed off in Lily's face. When Mae asks if she should go back herself and get the cloth, Lily says quietly, "If you like," her voice tight and polite, as though she has chosen her words carefully. Mae wants to beg her forgiveness, but is frightened to look at Lily again, is terrified of the appalled expression she'd glimpsed for an instant.

So they walk in silence, as if they don't know each other. As if they've never met.

part two

This will is necessarily uncommon and
capricious because I have no dependents or near
relations and no duty rests upon me to leave any
property at my death and what I do leave is
proof of my folly in gathering and retaining
more than I required in my lifetime.

The Last Will and Testament
of Charles Vance Millar

17

Courtroom 2B, October 1937

The courtroom is dark-cornered, lamplit, deeply shad-owed, the air hushed, still filled with the silence of that held breath. The lawyer stands frozen, mid-stride; the judge sits with his head cocked to one side, like a sight-hound, watching, listening. Lily sits listening too. Be-cause they are not waiting for her answer this time, but for movement from outside the courtroom. Beyond the door, on the streets, in the massing darkness, a crowd is gathering. Along with the journalists, photographers, and gossipmongers are protesters, at least three differ-ent groups.

A small faction declares the Stork Derby to be a "dis-gusting display of excess" and would like proceedings to be stopped, Millar's will to be contested. Another group wants the money to be shared between all the women in Toronto who have more than five children, regardless of how rich or poor they are. The final protesters, from what Lily has seen as she has gone into the courtroom each morning, are mostly women, who are arguing that contraception should be made widely available, and that women should have more choice in whether they have children.

Lily admires the idea, but there's something so ... *privileged* in the protest. It's almost laughable, although not at all funny: the idea of all women having a choice. It's a rich women's campaign.

A pebble pings against the window and everyone in the courtroom jumps. Lily can hear the police outside, bellowing at the crowds to disperse, and can hear shouting: the words *money-grabbers* and *whores* filter through the hubbub. And, over it all, she can hear the chants of *Make it stop! Make it stop!* The voices of the women who want other women to insist on using "protection," even though contraception has been illegal for more than forty years.

To Lily, it feels like yet another responsibility: women are told that they can have babies—they *should* have babies, in fact—but they must make sure they don't have too many. And Lily wants to roar at all those people outside, and at all the people inside, who are staring at her and at Mae and at all the other Stork Derby mothers. She wants to ask them if they've ever thought about how impossible it might be for some women to insist on *contraception.* She wants to ask how some women could possibly begin to ask their husbands to use anything to stop a pregnancy, and what would happen if their husbands refused.

She saw a woman this morning, waving a placard that read *Take back control!* Lily had wanted to grab her by the shoulders and say, *I've never had any control. None of us have.*

The very idea of *choice* feels like a torturous dream, where she is trying to hold on to something that doesn't exist—except that people keep telling her it does. *Take it!* they say. *Grasp it!* Only she can't see or even imagine the shapeless, formless thing that they want her to have.

She is so tired of it all: the guilt, the blame, the expectation, the responsibility. There is no right way to be a mother, it seems. No right way to be a woman.

She fights to hold back tears. She bites the inside of her cheek. She counts every baby she loved and wanted, once they arrived. And she wishes that every one of them had been a choice. And the wishing, too, feels like torture.

And all the while, the people outside the courtroom, who are fighting for her rights, shout and jostle and chant and hurl stones.

Lily looks across and meets Mae's eyes. Mae mouths something, which might be *I believe you.* But watching her, Lily reads it as *I'm like you.* And she feels a moment of connection with Mae again, the invisible thread of expectation and guilt binding them together, holding them alongside all the other women in the courtroom, and all the women outside, even those who don't understand. Lily closes her eyes and listens to the chanting and shouts. She listens to the words beneath the anger, and she hears it, again and again.

I'm like you. I'm like you.

18

Mae, May 1930

There is a new smell in the city. Even with the car windows shut, Mae can detect it. Above the usual aromas of horses and engine fumes and baking bread, over the dankness of the river and the billowing swirls of smoke and smog, there is the stink of something rotting. It is a sickroom stench, which reminds Mae of when, at age nine, she had been sent to say goodbye to her dying grandfather. As she bent forward to press her lips to the papery skin on his forehead, she caught a scent that reminded her of mold and meat gone bad. And this is the aroma that hangs over the city now, as Mae sits in the back of the hired car on the way to Cabbagetown to see Thérèse.

They have left the children in the care of the neighbor's girl, Bertha—thin and pale-eyed, with skin the color of day-old milk. Her parents' house is as grand as Mae's, but she hadn't objected when Mae had offered to pay her to watch the children.

Mae inhales. Like the city, the seats of the hired car have a strange odor; the driver's skin is gray and waxy, as if he spends all his daylight hours inside the car, as if everything, everywhere is slowly decomposing. Leonard had had to let their own driver go last year and Mae loathes hailing a cab in the street, hates the dread that creeps over her skin at getting into a strange car with an unknown man.

Still, it is easier with Lily alongside her. It helps Mae to feel tethered, as if she is a kite being buffeted by the wind. Only Lily's hand holding the string stops her from being swept skyward. Like Mae, Lily is staring out of the car window, and the shocked expression on her face must mirror Mae's own. The whole of Toronto is crumbling, it seems: the ragged incisors of half-finished buildings cast strange, spiked shadows over the streets. The sidewalks, once so clean, are littered with old newspapers and the gleam of glass from smashed bottles. But it is the people that fill Mae with dismay. Where have they come from, these grubby ghosts, who haunt every corner and seem to multiply every night? Mae watches a group of men, huddled around a trash-can fire. Their clothes are drab and dirty, but as the car draws closer, Mae can see the fine cut of their ruined coats, the expensive leather of their battered shoes.

"How is it possible," Mae murmurs, "to lose everything so quickly?"

"I don't know. I've never had anything to lose before."

They seem to share so many thoughts, so that they can have a wordless conversation with only a raised eyebrow or a smile across a busy room. And now Mae hears the echo of her own fear in Lily's voice: she's never had this much to lose either. She had always imagined that wealth was like a shield, an impenetrable barrier made of cars and clothes and home help and a home itself—a solid structure. But now, it seems, all that can disappear overnight, and as soon as it does, you become a different person. You become a gray, shapeless, faceless figure, crouched around a trash-can fire. People fear you, and you fear everything.

"I can't go back there," Mae says. She feels Lily take her hand and hold it between her own. And, for a moment, it is both easier and harder to breathe. How is it possible for someone to make you feel entirely safe and utterly terrified?

They haven't talked about what happened after the fabric store. Mae wants to say that she is sorry, that she hadn't meant to hurt Lily, that she will keep her thoughts to herself. But she worries that anything she says will be the wrong thing.

She grips Lily's hand more tightly and runs her other hand over her stomach. It is still flat, especially as Leonard has given her less money to buy food lately, but Mae's cycle is more than a week late. In the past, pregnancies have always made her feel hopeful: however exhausting she finds motherhood, being pregnant, wanted or not, has always given her a strange sense of euphoria, along with the sickness and tiredness. But this time, her body feels heavy and the exhaustion is overwhelming. When Leonard had wanted to sleep with her, she'd pushed him away, told him she was too tired. He'd seemed to think this was a challenge and had kissed her neck until she'd relented.

"It's too soon for another baby," she'd gasped.

"Don't worry," he'd said, as though he could control such things.

In the past, she has asked him if he might wear a prophylactic, but he looked at her with a faint revulsion and told her that it was *unnatural* and, *frankly, uncomfortable.*

She had wanted to ask how comfortable he thought labor was.

She can feel Lily's eyes upon her, watching her hand on her stomach. Mae considers saying, *Have you ever regretted having your children?* But the question is unspeakable, and Mae's own answer is difficult to put into words: she has never regretted having them, has never wished them away. But sometimes she imagines what her life might have been without them.

A gust of wind blows a sheet of newspaper across the windshield. The driver curses and tries to reach it, the car lurching to one side as he half leans out of the window and grabs at the fluttering newssheet. The headlines scream:

JOBLESS JEOPARDY!
RIOTOUS RABBLES!

On the facing page, an advertisement for the new talkie, *A Lady to Love*, which shows a smiling Vilma Bánky, with her smooth, pale hair and white teeth gleaming. Underneath her picture, another headline: *Stork Derby: Threats of Riots Rise.*

Over the past year, Mae has caught snatches of information about the lawyer's outlandish will; some months ago, there was talk of Charles Millar's distant relatives trying, unsuccessfully, to challenge his wishes. Now the government is discussing whether the will can be legal when it is so "morally reprehensible," which has led to some riots, as the newspapers stoke outrage at the government "taking money from the people." The stuffy men in charge consider it "indecent" to pay women to have children.

She opens her mouth to ask Lily what she thinks about it all, but, again, it feels unsayable. She feels she knows Lily completely, and sometimes that she doesn't know her at all: that along with the closeness and wordless understanding between them, there is a fragile filament of connection, which exists in the same way as a dream does upon waking. Mae worries that if she tries to describe it, it will melt into the air.

Nearer to Cabbagetown, the streets narrow, the shadows thicken. A group of children jump in a puddle in the middle of the road. The driver grunts and leans on his horn. The children, who can't be more than ten years old, turn and make obscene gestures. One throws a stone, which clunks against the side of the car.

"Animals," the driver says, his mushroomy skin darkening. "And look at the mothers—just washing their clothes in buckets of filthy water and letting the children run wild. This is what keeps our prisons full."

Mae inhales sharply so she can't snap a reply. She fixes her gaze on the back of the driver's head, the carefully pressed collar of his shirt. Does he have children? Does his wife let them play in the streets while she irons his shirts? If Mae focuses on these things, she won't be dragged back into memories.

Still, she can't help but see the flickering flames from a metal barrel; she can imagine the shadowy fingers surrounding it, their hands scorching in the heat. She remembers standing so close to the fire that her skin pinked and the smoke curled in her lungs, giving her a cough every winter.

She's taken back to the smells in the alley: the stench of piss, the sour reek of whiskey on the men's breath, the bitter smell of old soil as they pressed her face into the dirt.

She rubs at her knees, where there are faint scars still.

When she glances up at Lily, she's staring out of her window, watching the groups of children. Some look up as the car passes and try to chase after it, their bare feet slapping against the cold ground; they soon fall behind. Lily turns to watch them out of the back window.

"I have some coins," she says. "We should stop."

Mae swallows nervously. "Let's keep going."

"It will only take a moment."

"I don't want to stop." Mae grips her knees.

"Mae, please. Look how thin they are."

"I don't want to." But she can't help it. The fire in the barrel flickers. The four men standing around it glance up at the car. Mae can feel their eyes on her. Her knees ache.

"If I stop here, I'm not waiting," says the driver. "It's not safe."

"No." Mae can hardly gasp out the words. "Please drive on."

She senses Lily's disappointment, her disbelief. She

knows Lily must think of her as cold and uncaring. She must think she doesn't understand.

Mae considers telling her everything she understands. About the hunger that clenches so hard your body doesn't recognize food and you bring it back up onto the sidewalk; about the fear that won't let you sleep, even if you have a bed indoors for one night, because your mind is listening to the noises outside in the darkness, where you'll be sleeping tomorrow; about the days that break, one after another, relentless drowning waves.

She wants to tell her about working her way into the typing pool at Leonard's father's factory: about the careful way she dresses and the slow way she eats, like a person who has never known starvation; she wants to tell Lily about the vowels she consciously rounds out, even now, terrified that some inflection of her old voice will creep through and expose her. She wants to tell Lily that seeing the people on the street reminds her of a part of herself that she has hidden, some hungry, angry specter, long buried.

She wants to reach across the car and take Lily's hand and hold it, as if it can secure her in this moment, as if Lily can tug her out from that dark alleyway and the men's weight and the blood running down her legs.

Mae wants to tell Lily everything. But even if she could find the words, what then? How would she tell Lily that right now, more than anything, she wants to hold her and be held by her? She can't explain to Lily that the only time she has felt entirely safe was in her garden, dozing on Lily's shoulder, lulled by the steady pulse of her breathing.

19

Lily, May 1930

The closer they get to Cabbagetown, the more shocked Lily feels: since they last visited Thérèse, nearly two months ago, the number of dead-eyed men and women on the streets has multiplied. Every one of them looks thin and tired and cold. Blank-faced children stand on the sidewalk, as if half asleep, or else they shout and throw stones at the car, then stare after it, their shoulders slumped, their bodies seeming small and defeated. Lily is reminded of the people she saw stumbling around after the earthquake, the way they had scanned the roads and the sky, as if looking for help, as if hoping for the hand of God to reach down and pluck them from this sudden hell.

These lost, displaced people feel, suddenly, like Lily's people. She is nervous of asking Mae for money: she has already given Lily so much, and there is a strange tension between them sometimes—a feeling of closeness and distance that Lily can't describe. Now Mae is perfectly groomed, but she looks terrified as she watches the homeless children running after the car.

"We should give them something," Lily says.

"I don't want to stop," Mae says, her face pale, her lips

bloodless. Lily considers reaching across to take Mae's hand and tell her that she is safe, that all will be well. But Mae's expression is distant, as though she is somewhere else entirely, as though she is remembering something awful.

What have you seen? Lily thinks. She knows that Mae wasn't rich before meeting Leonard, but that would give her more sympathy for these poor people, surely.

Lily suddenly pictures her mother, Maria, who had never been rich but had always had money and time for people who had less than her. She'd arrived in Miramichi on a boat from Naples in 1898. She'd grown up fast and left home early, boarding a ship going west as soon as she could escape her parents, who'd insisted she marry a local boy. Nimble-fingered and gregarious, Maria had tried to find work as a seamstress for the rich ladies in their big houses, but one door after another had been slammed in her face.

The only thing that saved her from the street was meeting Giuseppe, Lily's father. Originally from a village within sight of Florence, he, too, had wanted to escape family ties. Maria was seduced by his quick smile and his willingness to put his regular salary toward buying her meals. She fell pregnant quickly and they married just as quickly, to save people talking.

They were never rich: everything was hand-to-mouth. Meals were often based around fried cornmeal; clothes were patched, passed down, and repurposed. But every time anyone asked Maria for money, she gave it to them. She would carry wrapped cornmeal cookies in her pocket so that, if a child stopped her in the street and she didn't have any coins, she could give them something.

"Please, Mae. I'd like to stop the car."

Mae won't meet her eye but continues staring at her hands, then rubbing her knees, a strange gesture, as though she's trying to scrub her own skin, as though she thinks that even looking at these poor people, even thinking about stopping the car and helping them, has somehow made her unclean.

The driver swears and slows the car. Another group of men ahead, half blocking the road. Some of them are carrying sticks and they move with an easy, coiled menace that reminds Lily of Tony.

The driver pulls over to the sidewalk and brakes hard, throwing both women forward.

"I can't take you any farther," he says, looking straight ahead at the group of men, who have turned to stare, their gaze predatory. Lily feels the hairs rise on the back of her neck. Some age-old animal instinct makes her want to tell the driver to turn for home.

"Please," Mae says, in a small voice Lily has never heard before. "Can you go—"

"I can't go anywhere except back to the depot, ma'am. You can get out and walk here, or you can try to get another cab. But I can tell you now that every driver I know will be locking his car away tonight. The best thing you can do is find somewhere inside and barricade the door."

Lily feels the same electrified current in the air as before the earthquake, feels the same urge to get inside, somewhere safe. It will take them hours to walk home from the city center.

She turns to Mae. "We can walk to Thérèse's rooms in five minutes."

Mae shakes her head. "I can't . . ."

Lily rests her hands on Mae's shoulders. "We can. But we have to go now. These men won't hurt us." She tries to keep her voice certain and clear. "They're not angry with us."

Mae's hands are unsteady; her jaw is pulsing.

Lily swallows the dread, as she used to every time she faced Tony. Every time she thought he might lash out at her, there was a moment when she braced herself, when she promised herself that she would survive. She takes Mae's hand. "I won't let go."

Shivering, Mae climbs from the car and stands alongside Lily.

"The trick," Lily says, "is to walk as though you're not afraid. Walk quickly. Don't look at them. They don't want to hurt you." She doesn't know if this is true, but the thought makes her voice stronger. "Focus your eyes on the ground," Lily says. "And start to walk."

Beneath their feet, the sidewalk is dusty. As well as the articles about the Stork Derby and the riots, the newspapers talk of a worsening drought. They talk of crops failing to the west on the plains, and to the south, over the border in America. They talk of the land being like a giant swirling bowl, where the winds whip up clouds of dust, stripping the earth of its skin and shedding it miles away. The open sky arches off beyond the cramped streets of Cabbagetown, with its ramshackle houses and dirty streets, beyond the high buildings, some half built and abandoned, standing open to the sunlight like parched mouths.

If Lily just looks up at the sky, without seeing the buildings or listening to the hubbub of the street, she could be anywhere. She could be back in Chatsworth, with Matteo by her side and the twins cradled inside her.

The dust beneath Lily's feet could have come from anywhere. She likes the idea of being carried away to settle where nobody knows your name or where you're from. Paolo offers her safety; she loves his steadiness, his unquestioning adoration. But there is a freedom in thinking that she could be swept away to somewhere else, with the children—that she would find a way to survive, somehow.

Although how would she live without Mae?

Lily closes her eyes at a wave of nausea.

"What's wrong?" Mae asks, her face tight with terror, but so clearly trying to stay calm for Lily. "You don't look well."

"I'm all right," Lily lies. It is a strange feeling, this mixture of honesty and deception, all for the good of the other person. Both of them terrified, both of them pretending.

They walk side by side, heads down, until they are past the group of men, until they can no longer feel the eyes on them, weighing value, worth, and risk. The wind carries a distant sound, like a crowd of people shouting or chanting. They grip arms as they walk on wordlessly, matching stride for stride, breath for breath. Lily feels as though, all around her, the city is crumbling away or being ripped apart. The only solid thing, at this moment, is Mae's arm in hers, the warmth of Mae's body next to hers, the need to comfort her and keep her safe.

20

Mae

As she knocks on Thérèse's door, Mae blinks back tears of relief. She wants to explain because she knows that her fear must make her seem skittish, even melodramatic, like Millicent. But then she turns to glance at Lily, who is gazing at her, as if she understands.

"You're safe now."

Mae nods. Where does she find the strength?

Thérèse is opening the door and Mae forces a bright smile.

"At last!" Thérèse says. "We were worried."

"So were we." Lily presses Thérèse in a quick embrace. Once they are sitting down with water and some dry crackers Thérèse has produced, Mae feels she can breathe more easily.

"I had no idea things were so bad. It was . . . frightening," Mae says.

"Ah, yes! The Stork Derby has given us all something to yell about," Thérèse says. "Listen!"

And Mae hears it still: the sound of a crowd chanting. "I don't understand. Isn't the will just a rich man's joke?"

"Yes," Lily adds. "It's not serious, surely?"

"The papers have made a song and dance, and now everyone has an opinion on it. They've got people laying bets on who will win."

Mae frowns. "But it ends in 1936. They're betting on something six years away."

Lily says quietly, "Perhaps it's just something for people to hope for."

"More babies?" Thérèse says drily, nodding at her children, who are elbowing each other in the ribs. "It will be men placing the bets then, while the women do the hard work."

All of them laugh quietly, a little guiltily. Mae can't meet their eyes. It's not that she doesn't want this baby. She's just so very tired. "So the problem is that the Derby is immoral? Or so the government says."

Thérèse snorts. "What right do these rich men have to decide what's moral? As if women would have children for money. I'd like to see one of those stuck-up bastards pregnant, see how easy it is. I'd march myself, if it wasn't for the police turning things so nasty."

"You wouldn't." Lily laughs.

"I would! The government has no right to take money that should be going to some poor woman. Having babies is hard work and keeping them safe is harder still."

Lily rubs her swollen stomach, her face suddenly sad, and, for a moment, the presence of Mae's lost, silent baby is as loud in the room as the cries and shouts of Thérèse's living children.

Thérèse smiles at Lily, and Mae can hear the forced

brightness in her voice. "By the size of your belly, you're having twins again. You'll be earning that money yourself if you carry on."

Lily grins back at her. "Maybe I should be marching."

Outside, the shouts of the crowd grow louder. Mae can hear the drumming of hundreds of feet stamping across the big road at the bottom of Thérèse's street.

Thérèse rubs her eyes. "They will gather in the square near here. The police like to block off the roads to the better parts of the city so that they can talk about the problems of people in Cabbagetown and how poor people spend their time angry and rioting."

Mae bites her lip, thinking back to just how many times she's seen newspaper headlines about the poor areas in the city saying exactly this sort of thing.

"You can stay here until the police have bashed enough jobless men over the head," Thérèse says wearily. Lily gives Thérèse's shoulder a sympathetic squeeze.

Mae turns away from them, wishing she had paid the driver extra and begged him to return. With the car, they might have gotten through the crowd. Then again, if the mood had turned ugly, they could have been stuck in the car.

"We can't stay here," Mae says. "What about the children?"

Lily sighs. "Bertha will do her best." But she doesn't look certain. "We could try to walk back."

As if there isn't chanting and shouting from the end of the street, as if she can't hear the far-off sound of alarm bells and the cries of *Police*, followed by curses, Lily walks out of the front door. Where does she find such bravery?

"Lily, wait! You can't!" Mae grabs her arm, but Lily shakes her off.

Mae forces herself to follow.

In the street, the noises are louder, seem closer. And at the end of the road, within throwing distance, hundreds of men are gathered. Mae can see a few women and children among them, but the crowd is mostly men. Some are in ragged clothes, some are in overalls, and some are in smart business suits, as if they have just this minute stepped away from their banking job and will return to work straight after the protest, although Mae knows that banks and businesses everywhere are closing. It's not just the factories, not just the steelworks. She thinks of Leonard, who looks thinner and grayer by the day, as if the pressure of everything is shrinking him. She's become used to watching the muscles jump in his jaw as he reads the paper, before pushing his breakfast away, uneaten, to scribble down numbers and figures. But Leonard's desperation is nothing compared to the anger she can see in these men and women, voices and fists raised as they march.

"We should go back inside," Lily says, but Mae can't move, her mind back in the alleyway. The men telling her to lie still. And outside the alleyway, the shouts and catcalls of a drunken crowd. If they noticed what was happening to her, they ignored it. Or perhaps they thought she wanted it. Whatever the crowd thought, their shouts and laughter made Mae feel invisible, as if the men's thrusts were making her disappear into the dirt.

Sour acid rises in her throat. Dimly, she is aware of Lily tugging on her hand, but it is as if she is underwater and Lily is calling her from the land. Within the depths, Mae cannot fathom which way to turn.

"Mae! Come inside. Please!"

Lily pulls sharply on Mae's hand, so that Mae stumbles forward and Lily puts her arms around her, stopping her from falling.

And then they are back in the doorway, and Lily is leaning Mae against the wood and saying, "I'm here. It's all right. They're not coming this way."

Mae can feel Lily's hands on her face. They are wet, although she doesn't know when she began weeping.

"I don't want –" Mae gasps.

"All right." Lily wraps her arms around Mae and holds her tight. "All right." And she pats a hand on Mae's back, in time to a slow, steady heartbeat. Mae feels the rhythm travel through her, feels her breath and her pulse falling into time with it. And, slowly, she puts her own arms around Lily's waist, feeling the rise and fall of her breath, feeling the vibration of her words, which thrum through both of them.

"It's all right," Lily says. "We're all right."

It is a long time before Mae stops shaking, a long time before they can go back inside.

21

Lily

The marching and shouting continue for the next hour. Then there's the sound of police whistles, followed by smashing glass, and, far off, something that could be gunfire.

Thérèse's children flinch at every noise, as does Mae. Lily is aware of each movement of her body—she can sense Mae's anxiety, can sense Mae watching her.

"Jacques won't come home tonight," Thérèse says in the late afternoon. "And if there is unrest elsewhere then perhaps Leonard and Paolo will stay at the factory too."

Lily looks around at the cramped little rooms, which Thérèse has made pretty with embroidery on the curtains. Everything is small and pristine, but next to the harsh sounds outside, the rooms feel insubstantial, the walls flimsy. They remind Lily of a doll's house she had seen in the window of an expensive shop in Chatsworth. She had liked to stare at it, but the old man who owned the shop always noticed her, would come to stand in the doorway, arms folded across his thin chest, until Lily had moved on.

Now, Lily imagines how it must feel to be alone in this

house with your frightened children, trying to shield them from the noises outside.

"Would you like us to stay?" she asks, and both Thérèse and Mae look at her with gratitude and relief.

There is another crash from the street. Everyone jumps. Mae pales. With her eyes shut she looks, for a moment, like a waxwork doll, perfect and breakable.

"I have an idea," Lily says to the children. "When my children can't sleep, I tell them the story of Prunella and the witch. Would you like to hear that story? It ends happily. Mae, you know it too. You can do the voices."

When Lily first moved in, she was shocked to find that Mae didn't tell stories to her children. "No wonder Robert won't sleep," Lily had said. "We'll tell him a story every night. He'll soon settle."

Mae was skeptical, but after the second night, when Robert let Lily sit on the side of his bed, and even hold his hand while telling the story, then drifting into sleep, Mae became convinced.

"Of course it works," Lily had said. "Didn't your mother tell you stories when you were young?"

Mae had looked blank.

Since then, Mae has learned all the Italian folk tales that Lily tells the children. Before Paolo, she would often plead with Lily to come into the children's rooms at night, where she would listen to Lily's stories of kings and princes, farmers and witches. Sometimes, she joins in with the voices, but for the most part she has always sat and listened, seeming as enthralled as the children.

Now Lily begins the story about the little girl who had

214

taken a plum from a tree every day, not knowing that the tree belonged to a witch.

When she reaches the speaking parts, Lily looks to Mae. "Come, Mae, this is you."

Mae hesitates, before quietly repeating the first line of the speech. "Ah! You little thief! I have caught you at last. Now you will have to pay for your misdeeds!"

By the time they reach the end, with Prunella defeating the witch and marrying the witch's son and living happily ever after, the children have crowded around Lily's feet, even Louis, who is too old for fairy tales, really, and they cheer.

Thérèse mouths, *Thank you*, at Lily.

She looks across the room at Mae, who is smiling, and Lily feels warmth travel through her.

Darkness falls. There are screams from outside and feet pounding past the door.

The children still look anxious, and as the noises rise, Thérèse decides that it's time for bed. She bundles all the children into her room and tells Lily and Mae that they will have to sleep on the chaise, next to the kitchen table.

"I can give you my bed," she says, "but you would have to take all the children in with you. And the little one has sharp elbows." She tickles her youngest's neck and he giggles. A little boy of two, with dark curls and a gap-toothed grin, he reminds Lily of Matteo at the same age and she feels a flicker of fear. Will her children be safe at home with Bertha? None of the riots or unrest over the past month has ever touched their quiet part of the city, but Matteo and the twins will worry when she doesn't return. And Paolo: where will he be?

Mae says she is anxious about her youngest too. Betsy and Sarah will be helping Bertha, but it still feels wrong to be so far from the little ones. Thérèse is right, though: the risk of going out is too great, with the whistles of the police and cracks of gunfire growing closer.

Thérèse ushers the children to bed, leaving blankets for Lily and Mae. Then she gives them a final tired embrace, goes into the bedroom, and closes the door.

The silence is broken only by the noises from outside.

Finally, Mae says, "You take the chaise. I don't think I'll sleep anyway."

In the lamplight, Mae's features are soft, her eyes large.

The crash of glass smashing in the street. Mae looks nervous, but then a man shouts and both of them jump, looking at each other with sudden understanding.

And in that moment, Lily reaches out and takes Mae's hand. "No one will hurt you."

Outside, the sounds swell and surge, closer now. More shouts. Crash of metal. Thud of fist. Crack of bone. And the long, drawn-out howl of a man when pain has stripped him down to his animal self.

Lily doesn't know when she decides to quench the lamp, when she decides to crouch under the table. She only knows that Mae is next to her, their bodies trembling. The sliver of light between the drawn curtains throws shadows onto the wall. Something that might be a raised fist thumps into something that might be a head.

A man screams again; another roars.

Inside, Mae and Lily press against each other. Comfort of warmth. Comfort of skin.

In the light from the window, Lily can see the gleam of Mae's eyes, watching her. Each waiting for the other to move. A single, shared breath between them. Inside, the stillness. Outside, the uproar. Inside each woman's chest, the unsteady countdown toward some unraveling. Toward something irreversible.

Eventually, the sounds fade and the velvet of darkness settles again. Lily's arm around Mae's back; Mae's arms around her neck. Neither one moves.

"Are you all right?" Mae's face is so close to Lily's that she feels the words as well as hears them.

The question is more than *Are you scared?* It is a question about their arms and their breath and the silence. A question about what will happen in the next moment, and then the one after that, and all the moments to follow.

"Yes," Lily says, and she hears Mae swallow, hears her draw a breath.

Her leg still warm against Lily's.

One breath, two, three. Mae's face close enough for Lily to feel the heat of her skin.

There is an energy in the air that she doesn't understand, yet also feels she knows. Recognizes, and wants. It's dizzying.

It's like speaking a word in a language you never knew existed and suddenly finding you understand the dialect, recognize it, without ever having learned the words. That you have known them all along.

And Lily moves, or Mae moves, or they both move toward each other, closing the final space between them, the final inch, which feels like a chasm, and then, as their lips touch, feels like no distance at all.

The shock of skin on skin leaves them breathless.

For a brief moment Lily worries that Mae will flinch and push away. But then Mae leans in to kiss her again.

And, more than the shock of it, there is some feeling of relief. As if she has been slowly drowning for years, and suddenly Mae's lips are breathing life into her, pulling her up from the depths, out of the dark water and into fresh, cool air.

Some part of her body takes over, without thought, as if, like breathing, some part of her has always understood how natural her arms would feel around Mae. Now that she is holding her, she can't understand why she hadn't embraced her every moment, from the first day they had met.

Long ago, the summer after she had first arrived in Toronto, Millicent had looked after the children one morning, while Mae took Lily to Lake Ontario. Lily had loved the size of it, the way it stretched off into something unknown, the way the flat surface concealed dark, mysterious depths. Lily had never set foot in the seas near Chatsworth, but Mae brought swimming dresses for them and persuaded Lily to clothe herself in the strange, clinging garment. Mae walked out into the water, beckoning Lily to follow. At first Lily was terrified, but Mae had taken her hand and they had floated for a moment on their backs, side by side, fingers touching.

Gazing up at the sky, Lily had felt weightless. It was as though she was suddenly free of her body, while also trusting it, for the first time.

Early the next morning, Lily lies awake, Mae's head pillowed on her shoulder, her hair fanning out over Lily's chest. Gently, so as not to wake her, Lily presses her lips to the soft, pale skin where her golden hair is parted.

It is Sunday and the streets outside are quiet now. Lily sits up, easing herself from under Mae's sleeping body before tucking the blanket around Mae, pulling the cover over her legs. She looks out at the soft sunlight, filtering onto the cobbles, and can't believe that those same streets were filled with shouting, angry, frightened men.

Everything about last night has the vagueness of a dream, a blur of images and sensations. She glances at Mae, whose face is still relaxed in sleep, her hair fanned across her bare skin. Lily considers kissing her, but suddenly she doesn't feel brave enough.

In Thérèse's bedroom, she can hear the children stirring, and she pulls her own dress on, waking Mae by stroking her arm. Mae's eyelids flutter and, as she focuses, Lily sees the same mixture of doubt and disbelief reflected, just for a moment, and feels worried. Then Mae tugs on her hand and kisses her lightly, pulls on her dress, and embraces her. The rightness of it, like cool water.

They separate just as the children come running into the kitchen. Louis rushes past the women, fetching the water jug and going outside to the street pump before Thérèse emerges from the bedroom.

Thérèse stretches and yawns. "As if the street wasn't bad enough, I had the children clambering over me all night. Like trying to sleep in a basket of puppies."

Every time Lily glances up, Mae is looking toward one of the children. Her cheeks are pink and she must sense Lily gazing at her, because the blush spreads across her throat. She is smiling.

Later, they walk out onto the quiet streets and hail a car to drive them back to Mae's home, past piles of burning wood and buildings covered with angry black letters, past the soup kitchen line, where many of the men sport makeshift bandages and bruised faces. Yesterday, all this would have terrified Mae and worried Lily, but today Lily's whole body feels lit up from within. At one point, both she and Mae begin laughing, for no real reason. The driver glances back at them, looks at the desolate streets around him, and shakes his head.

When they reach the house, Mae taps lightly on Lily's leg and gives a rueful half-grin.

Lily knows what she means: they must pretend now.

For the first time, Lily thinks of Paolo and feels shame. He is a good man, utterly kind and dependable and gentle. He has never made her cry out in passion. He has never made her forget every other thought. They have never looked at each other and had a wordless conversation. She has never caught his gaze and felt her stomach drop. She has never felt that he knows and understands her.

Mae is right. They must pretend.

The house is in chaos: Bertha looks harried as Leonard rushes to Mae's side, Paolo close behind him. The children clutch at the women's skirts, telling tales and asking for more food.

"Thank Heaven you're safe!" Leonard says to Mae. "We were stuck in the factory and then we got back this morning and you weren't here. I've been worried sick."

Paolo wraps his arms around Lily. "I wanted to come find you, but—"

"The police insisted everyone must stay inside. They were out cracking skulls." Leonard winces, as if the police had hit him, and puts his hand around Mae's waist. She stands stiffly, as if she hasn't noticed, and he lets his hand drop.

Lily kisses Matteo's cheek, hugs the twins, and inclines her head to indicate that they should go through to the kitchen, away from Leonard's loud voice and his heavy arm, now resting behind Mae's neck, his fingers rubbing away tension. Again, she doesn't respond. Lily can't watch.

"I've missed you," she says to Matteo.

He nods. "Me too."

"Were you happy here, with Bertha?"

He frowns. "She forgot to butter the bread, so I helped her make the sandwiches." He rubs his nose, then says, more quietly, "She said it was foreign immigrants rioting. She said they don't belong here."

"Bertha is wrong," Lily says.

"Are *we* foreign immigrants?" He looks worried.

"We're Italian and Canadian and that's something very special, my love. You know two languages, *si*?"

"*Sì.*" He smiles, and Lily makes a mental note to tell Bertha to keep her views to herself.

Paolo ruffles Matteo's hair. "Good boy." Then he pulls both Matteo and Lily in close, pressing his stubbled face against Lily's cheek. "Nothing to worry about. We're all safe."

Over Paolo's shoulder, Lily catches Mae's eye. Leonard's hands are around her waist now, and Lily has to look away.

"You didn't see any trouble then?" Leonard asks.

"None," Mae says, her voice a little too high-pitched, a little strained.

Leonard pulls her to him. As he kisses her, Lily sees Mae stiffen, very slightly, and turn her head, so that his lips brush her cheek. "I'm just going to see the children," she says, too brightly, and sweeps past Lily on her way from the room.

Lily follows and catches Mae's arm as they walk through the door into the kitchen. "I wanted to say—"

Mae looks down at Lily's hand. "We have to be careful."

The longing Lily feels for her is almost painful. She takes a step toward Mae, who opens her arms and embraces her. They stand together for a moment, not daring to move. Then she feels Mae shift, feels Mae's lips against her jaw, her neck, then, very gently, her mouth. She kisses Mae softly, her hands in her hair. It is a kiss of reassurance, a promise, a moment of steadiness as they cling to each other.

A floorboard creaks. Both of them turn.

Leonard is standing in the doorway, staring. Finally, "What's this?"

"Nothing," they say, almost at the same time. Lily stumbles away from Mae, iced water trickling down her spine.

"Lily," Mae says, her voice tight, "I think you should take Paolo and talk to him in the barn. Be careful."

Lily understands instantly what Mae means. She must try to tell Paolo what has happened just now, must find the words to explain this away, somehow, must be *careful*.

She keeps her gaze fixed on the floor as she walks past Leonard, who is still staring at Mae. And, for a moment, Lily wants to stand next to Mae, wants to take her hand and tell Leonard to stop glaring so, because this doesn't concern him. This fragile, precious thing belongs to her and it belongs to Mae. It's nothing to do with him.

But of course it is, because Mae's body belongs to him, just as Lily's belongs to Paolo.

Lily pushes open the outside door, gulping in the fresh, cool air as she tries not to cry. She finds Paolo, smiles at him mechanically as they walk back to the barn, but tells him nothing of what has happened—how can she when she barely understands it? She has heard the word *love* before, has even said it, to Tony and to Paolo. But this is something different from the gratitude she feels for Paolo's steady kindness. This is something more.

Later, when she has avoided telling Paolo anything, and when neither Mae nor Leonard has come out to find her, Lily returns to the house, dry-mouthed. She needs to find Mae.

The house is a bright blaze of light against the shadows of the garden. Lily stands on the damp grass for a moment, hoping to see Mae at one of the windows. There is a rustling behind her, but when she turns, no one is hidden in the bushes or the bower at the end of the garden where she and Mae had sat and drunk wine together. Where Mae had pressed her lips lightly against the pulse at Lily's throat.

Lily creeps into the kitchen quietly, hoping that Mae might be waiting there for her. But instead Leonard is sitting at the table.

"Leonard, I . . ."

She must tell him it was nothing. She must convince him it meant nothing.

Words stick in her mouth. She can't tell him that what he saw was nothing, because it feels like everything.

"Where is Mae?" she asks.

"My wife is very upset."

Lily hears the emphasis on *my wife*. "Is she . . . Does she . . ."

Is she crying? Does she regret what happened? What has she told you?

Finally, Lily manages to say, "Can I see her?"

Leonard gives a sharp bark of laughter. "Not a good idea. You seduced her, Lily. You made her do . . . unnatural things."

Unnatural things. She thinks of the warmth of Mae's mouth, the softness of her skin, the ease of it all. And more than that: Mae's hand in hers, her eyes on hers—the understanding between them. Each sensation and every moment had felt like the most natural thing Lily had known.

Leonard is watching her, waiting for a denial. Lily says nothing. Her heart batters at the cage of her ribs.

"I think you should leave."

"What?" Lily croaks.

"You should leave now. All of you."

"But—but we haven't anywhere to go."

"I'm afraid that's not my concern."

"Where is she? Let me see her." That ice-water sensation again, through her veins. Lily begins to shake. Mae can't have agreed to this, can't possibly want this.

Suddenly Leonard looks tired. "She doesn't want to see you. You should go now."

"Please," Lily says, thinking of Paolo and the children, who are playing together in the barn, who have no idea of how their lives are changing at this moment, who will not survive the cold and the riots.

Lily sees movement at the top of the stairs and Mae is standing there, her face flushed and damp. She clings to the banister for support.

"Please, Mae," Lily says. "Please."

Mae walks down two steps. Then, as if her legs won't hold her anymore, she sits down. She says nothing, only shakes her head.

"Please," Lily gasps, her voice cracking, her own eyes filling with tears.

As if she hasn't heard Lily, as if Lily no longer exists, Mae stands unsteadily, turns, and walks away.

22

Mr. Donovan is the lawyer's name: he is sharp-suited and spectacled, with a habit of rubbing his right ear after he has asked Lily a question. He has red hair and pinkish skin, so that, as the late-evening sun illuminates the courtroom, it brightens his face and renders his ears almost translucent. Lily cannot take her eyes from them and has to ask him to repeat his question.

"Are you perhaps hard of hearing, Mrs. di Marco? Or is it a translator you need?"

Titters from around the courtroom, and Mr. Donovan looks smug, straightening the handkerchief in his jacket pocket, which, throughout every day of the court case, has always been perfectly pleated, has always matched his tie. Lily imagines Mrs. Donovan at home, laying out his clothes the night before—his matching tie and handkerchief, which she will have carefully ironed and folded. Do they have children? Does Mrs. Donovan stay up late into the night, ironing and folding, or does she rise early? Does she place his slippers, just so, by the side of the bed, so that his pinkish feet never have to touch the cold floor?

Lily feels a sharp distaste for this red-faced man with his mouse-like ears, his quick, harsh laughter, and his questions that are not really asking anything, but are telling the court and the judge and the journalists that Lily is stupid, that she is foreign, that she is not to be trusted.

Outside, still, the faint shouts of the rioters who have been moved on. Those people who all want their voices to be heard, even when it doesn't concern them. Those people who are so full of opinions, when it is Lily's life and future at stake. Lily swallows the surge of frustration, tries to keep her voice cool. She leans forward, enunciating slowly and clearly.

"I can hear perfectly, thank you. And I don't need a translator. But you have asked a lot of questions."

"Ah, yes, I see. It must be confusing. Let me go more slowly for you. Mrs. di Marco, I asked about the father of your children."

Lily pauses. She can feel the eyes of everyone in the court upon her, can sense their held breath. This, she realizes, is the case that Mae has helped build against her, painting Lily as a woman of loose morals—promiscuous. Like all *immigrant* women.

Well, she won't have it. She *won't*.

She raises her chin, looks him in the eye.

"I was married to my first husband when I lived in Chatsworth. I had three children with him." *Three surviving children. Six miscarriages and stillbirths.* "A beam fell on him during the earthquake," she says. She remembers his body sprawled out under those stones of the collapsed wall. She remembers the shudder of his breath.

The wet-fish open and close of his mouth. She remembers the beam that had cracked his skull. She doesn't remember her hand releasing it.

"And?" asks the lawyer.

"And," Lily says, deliberately quietly, "I married again."

"And had six more children. Over how long?"

"Nine years."

"You have been . . . *busy*." He smirks.

Laughter from the court. Lily flushes, forces a tight smile.

"But children from different marriages," Mr. Donovan says, "are not necessarily valid in the eyes of the Church."

"This is not a church," Lily says, before she can stop herself. There is tutting from around the court. Mr. Donovan glares.

Lily, you fool.

She'd promised herself she wouldn't answer back in court. She wouldn't give them the pleasure of labeling her a hysterical woman. All those ideas they have about the angry poor, never asking why they might be furious.

It is impossible to be calm and polite now: the lawyer's words make her feel dirty, when he questions whether her children—her flesh and blood—are *valid*.

Mr. Donovan leans forward, his pale eyes blinking behind his spectacles. "They are not legitimate in the eyes of this *court*. And how can you be entitled to anything for illegitimate issue? Bastard children are not recognized."

Illegitimate. Bastards.

Lily grips the sides of her chair until her hands ache.

"My children . . ." Her voice shakes. She stops, clears her throat. "My children are *not* bastards."

"This is not a fish market for you to argue, Mrs. di Marco. You must answer my questions with facts. This court does not care for your opinion. Now let us move on. You left Mrs. Thébault's house in 1930. Is that correct?"

Lily nods.

"Answer aloud for the court, please."

"Yes," Lily says cautiously.

"And when did you decide to become involved in the so-called Stork Derby?"

Lily frowns. Why does it matter when she first realized she might qualify for the money?

"Was it," he asks, "when you first discovered that the newspapers would pay for pictures of big families—even pay for them to have meals in public? Was that when you decided that having more children might be of benefit?"

"Why does that matter?" Lily snaps.

The lawyer raises his eyebrows at her tone. "I think it will matter to the court."

"Why?"

"Answer the question, please."

"It doesn't matter when I first realized that I qualified."

"Was it when a reporter knocked on your door, offering you money?"

"Isn't that the same for the others? Why is that important?"

Only Lily knows that it is. Lily understands that, to discredit her with the judge, with the journalists and everyone who is following the story, this man must prove her claim is invalid in every possible way; he must make her sound mercenary and calculating, so that the judge will have no choice but to dismiss her claim, so that no one will protest on her behalf.

He stares at her, waiting. Unblinking, with his pink-rimmed eyes.

Lily keeps her voice steady. Calmly, with perfect grace, she turns toward the judge.

"In 1935. I thought I might qualify for the money in 1935."

23

Mae, October 1935

Mae lies quietly, listening to the sounds of the house around her. It has taken her a long time to become used to this new, smaller, older place. There are cracks in the walls and, if the wind blows strongly, the whole building seems to creak and groan, as if it is some living creature in pain.

These were the noises that used to haunt Mae when they first moved here in 1932, once renting out the old barn in the big house wasn't bringing in enough money.

Leonard had come home from work one day, put his head into his hands. Mae knew what he was going to say, though she made him say it anyway.

"I have to sell the company."

Leonard's steel business went for a laughable price to a large man with millions in the bank, who'd smiled sympathetically as he signed the paperwork and had patted Leonard on the shoulder, telling him, "It's not your fault. Lots of small-time guys are selling." And then he'd tucked the signed papers under his arm and walked out of the room, holding their livelihood in his fat hands. He'd left Leonard shrunken, defeated. When Mae remembers that moment, it's as if she can see Leonard aging: his posture stooping, his hair graying, his mouth fixing into a grim, bloodless line.

She'd rubbed his back, feeling him shake, but the gesture seemed mechanical. Sometimes, when he put his arms around her, the memories would come back unbidden. Mae sitting on the stairs. Lily pleading with her. The fear and betrayal in Lily's voice.

She wished she'd been able to lie to Leonard. She wished she'd been able to shrug off his fury, his angry questions. *What were you doing? Did she force you into this?*

Instead, she had looked steadily at him. "I love her."

Of course he wanted Lily out of the house. Of course he threatened to take the children from Mae if she saw her again. Of course he told her she wasn't to speak to Lily.

Every night, when she wakes, Mae wishes she had lied.

So when it's not the groaning of the house that has woken her, it's often Leonard. His limbs begin to twitch, like a dog's when it dreams of pursuing a rabbit, before he cries out. A full-throated yell, which wakes the children and travels through the thin walls into the house next door, so that Mr. Schwartz bangs on the wall with his fist and Mrs. Schwartz glares at Mae the next morning as she's hanging the threadbare sheets on the outside line.

Mae has trained herself to wake as soon as Leonard begins trembling. She watches him in the darkness, resenting him, willing him to be quiet so she can sleep. She can't wake him too quickly—on the few occasions she's tried, he's wept, like a child in the grip of a night terror. By day, his behavior is odd, full of strange new habits: he has grown out his beard and his hair hangs lank and greasy over his temples. There is a sour animal smell to him, as though he has been sleeping in his clothes. He refuses to bathe for weeks at a time, saying he will drown himself in the bath. Mae has hidden the sharp knives.

She doesn't criticize his drinking, though they can't afford it. If she questions him, his face crumples and he sobs, pulling her close and saying, *I'm sorry, Mae. I've let you down. I'm sorry. I'm such a failure.* She pities him and is repulsed by him. She often sends the children upstairs so they won't have to see the desperation on his face. Or the revulsion on hers.

Tonight Mae wakes just as Leonard begins to tremble; she immediately takes one of his hands and squeezes it hard. Next to their bed, baby Michael sleeps in the crib; she prays he won't wake, or he will take hours to settle, wanting to be fed, which will leave her nauseated with exhaustion. And she can't be sick tomorrow because she has to take all the children to the Stork Derby tea, run by the *Ottawa Citizen*, the *Toronto Daily Star,* and at least three other newspapers.

It had been just after baby Michael's birth that a journalist and photographer had knocked on her door, asking how many children she'd had since 1926 and telling her she was in with a chance of winning Charles Vance Millar's fortune, and would she take a dollar to put a picture of her and her kids in the paper?

It won't be until October 1936 that Mae can submit

233

all her paperwork to the court, but the journalists tell her she stands a good chance of winning. In the meantime they are willing to pay for her picture and the papers are happy to put on Stork Derby teas and parties, where members of the public can come and gawk as she and the children eat.

The younger children are still excited, but the older ones have become bored of the relentless focus: the photographs, the interviews, the jokes at school. Betsy endures it all with an anxious fixed smile, encouraging her siblings to try to do the same, but the other older children are withdrawn around the journalists. Robert, especially, has taken to avoiding the events when he can. Her eldest says that he feels like *a zoo animal*. Last time they had their picture taken, he'd pretended to pick fleas from Michael's hair until Mae snapped at him to stop.

At sixteen, he's vocal in speaking out against the Stork Derby anyway, doesn't try to hide the fact that he thinks it's gut-churning that his parents are always having babies. He complains of headaches, says that the flashes of the cameras set off *awful lights in my brain*. He's taken to lying down for hours afterward, his hand across his eyes.

Sometimes, Mae lets him stay away from the reporters, but not today. Today, food and drink will be provided, and she needs the children to eat as much as possible to make the cans in the cupboards last longer.

Leonard jolts again, crying out. The room is dark, but Mae knows that his face will be twisted into a rictus, as if he's witnessing, in his dreams, some act of horrible violence. She has tried asking him what he dreams of, in the hope that it might make him sleep more quietly so that she can rest, but his eyes slide from hers as he tells her he can't remember, not really.

Sometimes she feels glad that he is unhappy.

On the rail lines to the west, and on the roads that spread eastward, men who are jobless and on poor relief have been shipped to camps where they dig highways and clear the path for railroad tracks. They are paid a pittance to send home to their families, but at least they're not rioting. At least they're not sitting at home, making dark comments about the pointlessness of it all.

When she'd mentioned the relief work to Leonard, he'd looked at her as though she'd suggested murder, then shut himself in their bedroom. From behind the door, she could hear his panicked breathing.

Mae worries about the strain on the children. She worries when she can't afford meat—some weeks, it feels as though they live off stale bread and old potatoes. She worries about the older boys and how they will find work. And what it will do to them to grow up without a job, without prospects, without hope. Only Robert has had a job offered to him—he will start next month at the post office and is keen to distance himself from all the Stork Derby *nonsense*. Mae hangs on to it as a glimmer of hope.

Leonard writhes and gives a strangled shout through gritted teeth. She strokes his hair, like she does with Donald, who is four, when he has a nightmare. She tries to quash the distaste she feels at having to soothe a grown man as if he were a baby: this is hard for all of them, so why is he the only one who is allowed to collapse? Why does she have to remain strong?

"Hush," she says without feeling. "You're safe." Although she doesn't know if he is. She doesn't know if any of them are safe. The sale of the big house has given them some money, but it's not enough. Not enough to last if this depression goes on, if he can't find work.

Sometimes, she visits Thérèse, who still lives in Cabbagetown, though Jacques is working at one of the government relief camps.

"I miss him," Thérèse once said. "Even though he used to get under my feet all the time."

"Was he . . . sad?" Mae asked.

"Of course. We're all sad."

"But was he . . . Did he shut himself away? Refuse to talk to you?"

Thérèse reached over and patted Mae's hand. "Leonard will get better. He's lost so much."

So have I, Mae thought. Out loud, she said, "Everything has changed for everyone. I didn't think it would get so bad. Even with the riots . . ." She trailed off, remembering.

"I saw Lily at the market," Thérèse said. "Have you seen her?"

Mae shook her head, struggling to speak. Finally, "Is she well?"

"She is struggling, like all of us. I'm sure she would like to see you again. Such a shame you fell out. Did you ever find out why she left? She won't tell me anything."

Mae froze, aware of Thérèse watching her, considering. Then the children rushed into the room, and Mae had time to swallow the pain in her throat and blink back the heat from her eyes.

A spill of moonlight on the wall shivers as the draft through the cracked windows stirs the curtains. In his cot, Michael grumbles, still hungry, but doesn't wake.

Next door, she hears David, who is three, cry out in his sleep. She is about to go to him, but then she hears footsteps padding across the hallway. The soft sound of singing quiets the cries. Betsy is such a good girl.

Mae lies still, listening, as Leonard's breathing settles. She watches the moonlight on the wall fade, watches the shadows brighten, watches the room sharpen into focus as the pale sun rises.

By the time baby Michael stirs fully and begins to squeal for his morning feed, she's already put the diapers in to soak, cleared the grate, swept the floors, and set the porridge on the stove to boil.

Betsy and Sarah bring down the younger children: they've put six-year-old Jane's hair in bunches, and have scrubbed Donald's and David's cheeks. Both boys are usually full of mischief, but the girls must have threatened them into submission, because they sit to eat their porridge.

Mae's had to make it with water this morning, adding only a splash of milk for the children and Leonard. She will eat the pan scrapings herself, to stop the morning nausea, and then suck a pebble. It's an old trick that Mrs. Schwartz from next door had told her.

"Here," Mrs. Schwartz had said. "Tuck this into your

cheek whenever you feel sick or hungry. It doesn't always work, but it's better than nothing."

That was in the days when Mrs. Schwartz used to speak to her—when they first moved in and they had some money to spare from the house sale still, and Leonard had hopes of getting a job, so would still talk to people. Now, Mae suspects, her neighbors think her withdrawn or strange. But she has so little energy for chatter.

Mae ladles the porridge into bowls and calls the older boys for breakfast, lifting Michael into his high chair. Alfred, Peter, and James come clattering into the kitchen and begin hungrily shoveling porridge into their mouths, wincing at the heat, but not slowing.

Leonard doesn't come down, and neither does Robert.

"He has another headache," Betsy says. She's grown into a tall, serious girl of fifteen, with the beginnings of frown lines etched between her eyes. She wants to be a nurse, she tells her mother often. Mae doesn't argue. It's good to dream.

"Robert!" Mae calls up the small staircase. "Robert?"
No reply.

Mae runs up the stairs, taking care to miss the third step where the wood is rotting, and knocks on the door of the room Robert shares with his younger brothers, all of them piled in together.

"Robert?"
She pushes on the door. Robert is lying on his bed, his arm across his eyes. The room smells bitter.

"I don't want to," he mumbles from under his arm. He's in his nightclothes still, the thin blankets pulled up to his chin.

"You really should," Mae says gently. It's so hard to know how to talk to her prickly oldest child, her boy who is nearly a man, who will be finishing his education in a matter of months and is eager to escape it all, to start work. Some of the schools have shut, unable to afford to pay the teachers, so her children are lucky, she tells them. None of them like the huge classes, and the older children complain that the lessons are too easy. Robert loathes everything about it.

"Come on, Robert. There's porridge downstairs."

"Not hungry," he grunts.

"You need to eat."

He opens one eye and glares at her balefully. Some days he will be remote like this, reminding her so strongly of Leonard at his worst that it's hard for her to challenge him; it's hard not to feel abandoned by her own child. The distance between them is agony. Other days, if Leonard is being particularly morose and distant, Robert will be affectionate, putting his arms around her, offering to fetch water from the street pump or sweep the outside step and *Please, just sit down and rest, Mama.*

But whatever mood he is in today, however much of a *headache* he has, he must be there for the news reporters. It doesn't matter that he's too old to count in the Derby. They like to have pictures of huge families for their readers—the sight of all those children sells papers, and Mae can't help hoping that public opinion will somehow work in her favor—that if everyone expects her to win she will stand more of a chance.

She pats his thigh. "Come on, up!"

He sighs and begins to rouse as she walks back down the rickety stairs. The door to Leonard's room is shut. She decides to leave him to sleep. Often, if he's in this sort of mood, it's easier to manage their eleven children by herself.

Once the children have all been put into their smartest clothes, they set off together, down through Cabbage-town, past Thérèse's house, although they don't have time to stop, and to the green near the center of the city, where the tea is being held.

Mae keeps the younger children close as they walk along the dusty streets. All along the road there are houses with their windows smashed in or cracked—who can afford to repair the glass in this area? At the end of their street there is a clearing that used to be a park full of greenery. Now it is a dusty wasteland, covered with makeshift houses cobbled together from old wooden boxes and sheets of rusting metal. Crude tents have been made from once-white sheets strung across ropes; grubby children in tattered clothes peep from behind them, watching Mae and her family pass. Behind the filthy children stand exhausted women and defeated-looking men.

Mae remembers when she'd have felt terrified at being so close to these people. Now she feels only pity.

As they near the center of the city, there are fewer

fractured windows and crumbling houses, and more derelict buildings. Half finished, they remind Mae of the pictures she has seen of bomb-blasted France and Belgium after the war. There's a grayness to everything. A coldness. Among the wreckage, families have fashioned pieces of steel or boxes into makeshift houses. There's something ghostly about these people, as if they are as fleeting as their flimsy homes. As if they might dissolve or vanish and no one would really notice.

Mae and the children round the corner to the park. Inside a roped-off area, tables stand laden with sandwiches and cakes. Pots of tea and jugs of fruit juice wait invitingly for the children, who rush forward with exclamations of glee.

At the sound of Mae's family a few reporters turn and begin taking photographs. A small crowd gathers. One family is there already, a gaggle of dark-haired children stuffing sandwiches into their mouths while their mother berates them, her back to Mae. And though she hasn't seen her in five years, though her hair is cut shorter and she is wearing a hat, Mae would recognize her anywhere. Would recognize the tone she uses with the children, which is warm, even as she scolds them. She would recognize the lilt of her voice, the curve of her neck.

Lily.

24

Lily, October 1935

In the hours before dawn, when light is still as elusive as the sleep that Lily can't recapture, her tiny home makes her think of a cave. She stares up at the low ceiling, its cracks and stains hidden by the darkness, and listens to the children breathing around her, counting their exhalations. There is an empty space on the mattress next to her, where Paolo sleeps when he returns from digging roads out to the west—it pays a pittance but is the only work he can find.

Lily reaches out and brushes her fingers over the sheet. She misses the warmth of his bulk, the steadiness of his breath, the way he feels as solid as a rockface, even when everything else has crumbled and collapsed.

On the single chair, beyond the mattresses where the children sleep, is a pile of other people's mending, which usually earns them enough money for food and coal. Lily's fingers are raw from needle pricks and her eyes ache from sewing in the dim glow from the small fire.

First light glances through the curtains, brushing golden fingers over the grubby wall and, for a moment, it is all beautiful: the huddle of her children's bodies, her breath misting the air above her face, the gradual stirrings of sounds on the street outside.

It will get better, Paolo always says. In these quiet moments, holding her palms up to catch the golden dust motes, which vanish as soon as she touches them, Lily can almost believe it.

Footsteps on the street outside, low voices—male—and the bang of a fist on the door break the spell. Lily sits upright, buttoning her coat to the neck for warmth. Who could it be at this hour? Could Paolo have forgotten to send rent money to the landlord?

The paint on the door is cracked and peeling over the flimsy wood, and she pulls cautiously on the handle, always fearful that the rickety thing will come off its hinges. On the street outside are two men, one holding a notepad, the other a camera.

They must have the wrong house. What are they doing on these dirty streets in their smart suits and polished shoes? The area is called Skid Row: a mess of crumbling houses and wind-battered tarpaulins, which shelter whole families. On the corner is the rusty skeleton of a burned-out car, where ragged children play in daylight hours.

But it is too early for that. Too early for men to be knocking on Lily's door for any reason—even for unpaid rent. She waits for them to apologize, so that she can close the door and climb beneath the layers of blankets before the cold air wakes the children. On the mattress, her youngest babies sleep with their hands touching. Marcello and Angelo, twin boys, born eight months earlier. She is pregnant again, due in December, and exhausted.

"Mrs. di Marco?" the man with the notepad asks, his smile full of too-white teeth.

"Who are you?" She pitches her voice low, as Paolo has taught her—she mustn't seem scared of people. She must appear strong. Squaring her shoulders, she fixes her face in a frown.

The man removes his hat and tucks his notepad under his arm.

"I'm sorry, Mrs. di Marco. Your neighbors said last night that we could find you here, but it was late. We didn't want to scare you, so we came back early to be sure of catching you."

The wind blows a tin can along the street and gusts past her into the small room. Behind her, Lily hears the children stirring; one of the twins gives a sharp cry.

"I don't know you," she snaps, pushing on the door, nearly shutting it.

Both men move forward at once, and the man with the camera says, "Wait! We're sorry. We should explain. Please wait." He has thick glasses. Behind the lenses, his eyes are pink and vulnerable. His smile is less wolfish than the other man's, his voice softer.

"We're from the *Globe* and we'd like to talk to you about your children."

Marcello begins to cry, throwing his arms up against the cold.

"How would you like to be rich?" the man asks.

"I . . . What do you mean?" She is struck by the absurd thought that these men want to *buy* her children or sell photographs of them. "Leave me alone." Lily steps back and shuts the door, leaning against it.

She can hear the men's voices through the thin wood. "Please, Mrs. di Marco. We just want to talk to you. It's about the Stork Derby. You know, the baby race. You must have heard of it."

Lily says nothing, holding her breath. The Stork Derby has been in the newspapers more and more. She doesn't have the money for the papers herself, or the time to read, but she sees the billboards announcing *NEW ENTRANTS!* and has heard the paperboys shouting about the amounts. *Hundreds of thousands of dollars.* People are betting on the winners.

The babies are still crying, and the other children are sitting up, rubbing their eyes, their faces pale.

"What's wrong, Mama?" asks Julia.

The voice from behind the door again, softer now: "We'd like to pay you if you let us take some photographs of you with your children. You have seven children, don't you?"

Eight. Lily thinks of Matteo, who is digging roads out west with Paolo. And she thinks of the baby born without breath in 1933: Ana. A tiny name for the tiny life cut short.

"You could be in with a chance at the money, Mrs. di Marco," the man says. "And you can come to all the events. Just next week, there's a picnic for all the Stork Derby families. Food and drink. We've hired a band. It'll be like a big party. And we can give you a dollar for your photograph right now."

Lily looks at her children's thin faces, at the pile of

245

mending that will earn her pennies, at the grubby sheets and the cracks in the ceiling.

She opens the door.

Lily holds her head high as she walks the children to the picnic. She is wearing her best coat, stretched tight across her pregnant belly, and some old shoes that had once been Mae's, and she feels like a stranger, as though she has never lived on these grubby streets. She has to quell a smile at the stares and whispers of the women on Skid Row, as they watch her picking her way around the puddles and piles of manure.

"You show them, Lily!" a gray-haired woman calls. There has been excitement in the street ever since the reporters knocked on her door last week. Everyone is convinced she's going to win, even though there is a year before anything will be decided. Lily's sewing work has doubled, with people peering into her little rooms, asking to see the children, as they pass Lily their ripped skirts and torn trousers. Some bring gifts: new hairpins; a napkin embroidered with flowers; a cardigan for the babies.

"Remember us when you're rich," they say. And though they laugh, Lily can sense the seriousness of the request, the feeling that she carries some sort of glamour that can somehow lift the whole street from the dirt.

She had spent some of the reporter's money on a huge red blanket, which she drapes across the children's legs. The brightness of the color brings warmth to their skin and they look, for a moment, rich and healthy.

It had been strange seeing her own face staring back

at her from yesterday morning's newspaper: she'd sent Julia out early to buy a copy with some of the money the reporters had given them. The children had pored over their picture, laughing at how rigid and frightened they all looked, giggling at the way baby Angelo seemed to be scowling at the camera. The neighbors had knocked on the door all day, wanting to see the photograph, pressing their fingers to the pages until the ink smudged.

Walking to the picnic, her expensive shoes clipping the cobbles, Lily can't remember the last time she felt so . . . *light*. Mrs. Holt, from three doors down, had loaned her an old baby carriage, which everyone had smartened up, scrubbing the material and scraping off the rust. Julia is pushing the babies in it now, and the movement has lulled them to sleep.

She can see the crowds before she gets close to the picnic lawn: a hubbub of chatter and excited laughter from the men, women, and children gathered around the green. Some are in shabby, well-patched clothes, but others wear expensive dresses and business suits—a reminder that not everyone has lost money these last years. As Lily apologizes, squeezing through the crush of bodies, people turn and notice her, then the children.

"That's Mrs. di Marco," someone whispers.

"The new one. You must have seen her in yesterday's paper."

"Look at those kids. She's got seven—do you count seven? And she's pregnant again."

Three photographers push their way through the crowd, the bulbs of the cameras flaring and popping.

"Do you think she'll have more? Hey! Mrs. di Marco! How many more babies do you want?"

Lily feels herself blush.

As she nears the green, a band strikes up a rousing march and the crowd begins to clap along and cheer, moving to one side to allow Lily through. Ahead of her, the musicians are on a tall bandstand, trumpets gleaming in the sun.

In the center of the lawn, long trestle tables are weighted down with food and drink—the children squeal as they see the piles of sandwiches with chicken or beef and lettuce, along with biscuits and gravy, hot bread rolls, warm apple pies, cakes dripping with syrup and bowls of apples and pears. The whole spectacle is surrounded by yellow rubber balloons, which dip and bob in the breeze.

Lily feels tears sting her eyes. If Paolo were here, she would clutch his hand. She would lean in close to him and she would whisper, "We were right."

And he would kiss her cheek and say, "We are right."

Right to have the children. Right to hope for more. Right, even though, for so long after Mae and Leonard had thrown them out, everything had been wrong. As they'd trudged along the road away from the house, clutching their belongings close, the children's lips trembling in the cold, Paolo had asked, "What's happening, Lily?"

She had fixed her gaze on the road ahead, on the shadows, on the slanting rain. "I don't know."

"Please tell me. Why are they making us leave?"

"I don't *know*." The savagery in her voice had made him flinch and fall silent. He hadn't asked again, but over the years, she'd felt Paolo staring at her sometimes, wondering. And the weight of his doubt had cast a shadow over them—over everything he did. She saw his hesitation before he touched her, when he told her he loved her and waited for her to say the words in return.

She always said them, but it felt the same as saying, *I like the strength of your hands*, or *I like how kind you are to all of us.*

I love you meant many things when she said it to Paolo. But it never meant what it should. It never meant, *I need you.*

He sensed her distance and tried to fill it with his gentle embraces, with his acts of kindness. "We shouldn't have more children," he'd said sometimes. "You're so busy all the time. I want to make you happy."

"You do," she always replied. Which was the truth and a lie.

Even if it had been easy to prevent babies, even if it hadn't been illegal, Lily couldn't imagine it. She'd lost too many pregnancies to try to stop them. And perhaps part of her hoped that each child would bring them closer.

Of course they hadn't.

But now this: the band, the crowd, the sunlight, the laden tables. The feeling of standing taller, of filling her lungs with air, filling her body with light, with hope.

A hand taps her on the shoulder. She turns, ready to smile at one of the reporters, ready to pose for photos, to tell them that she is thankful, so thankful for all of this.

"Lily?"

For a moment, everything seems to pause: the breeze drops, the music fades, the bars of golden sunlight dim. The crowd recedes, their chatter and laughter silenced, and the only voice Lily can hear, the only face she can see . . . The only person on that lawn is Mae.

It's been five years and Mae looks entirely different. Her blond hair has been badly cut; her face is lined and slightly tanned, when she always used to take pride in being able to keep her porcelain skin out of the sun. She isn't wearing powder or kohl; her clothes look shabby, her shoes scuffed, and there are shiny patches of wear on her coat. Even her eyes are different: Mae had always had something fierce in her expression, a challenge in her blue gaze. But now, as she smiles nervously at Lily, she looks tired and defeated.

For a moment, Lily cannot speak. Seeing Mae brings back all the old hurt and anger, the confusion at being forced into the street and cut out of Mae's life. But alongside that, she feels a momentary longing to put her arms around Mae, to hold her close, to feel the beat of her heart. She keeps her hands at her sides.

"What are you doing here?" she asks, attempting to keep her voice level.

"How lovely to see you," Mae says stiffly, in the tone she used to reserve for Leonard's work parties. "You look well."

"I'm . . ." But even as she attempts to form a reply, Lily has to make herself pause, take a steadying breath. There are too many things she wants to say: that of course she doesn't look *well*; that she cannot possibly look *well*, since Mae allowed Leonard to throw her out into the cold. And she is hungry and her children are hungry and baby Ana—poor baby Ana—probably died because Lily couldn't afford to eat properly. She wants to take Mae by the shoulders and shake her until her teeth rattle. She wants to hold her and weep. She wants to be lying on a blanket in Mae's big garden, beneath the maple tree, her head pillowed on Mae's stomach, dozing to the echo of her breathing, the hum of her words.

"Are you . . . ?" *Are you happy? Where do you live now? Do you ever think of me? Why did you let him force me out?*

"Why are you here?" Lily finally asks, lamely.

"I was going to ask the same. Are you part of . . . all this?" She gestures at the reporters, the crowd, the balloons, the band.

"Yes. I only realized that I . . . I haven't been following it. Reporters found me last week," Lily says. "And you?"

"They knocked on my door a month ago. Michael, my youngest, means . . . Well, I have seven children who qualify. How many do you—"

"I had twins in February and, yes, I have seven also."

"Twins *again*? Congratulations. And is Paolo . . . ?"

Working on digging a relief road that leads to nowhere, Lily thinks. "Paolo has a job just outside the city. And . . . how is Leonard?" She forces herself to say his name.

"Oh, Leonard doesn't feel well today, or he'd have come along."

Mae avoids mention of Leonard's job, Lily notices, but

251

from her changed appearance and the children's thread-bare clothes, Lily guesses that Leonard must have lost the factory. *Good!* she thinks, and immediately feels ashamed of the spiteful twist of pleasure she has from imagining them losing everything, sleeping on the street, standing in the breadline. Although she's never seen Mae waiting there. Perhaps she sends Robert or Betsy or Sarah.

Lily glances at them, these older children, whom she knows so well, but barely recognizes now. Betsy looks similar, she supposes—still with an anxious crease between her brows. She gives Lily a half-smile, which Lily returns.

It is the change in Robert that shocks Lily: he is tall and thin, much taller and thinner than she remembers, and he has the beginnings of downy hair on his upper lip. With his direct, unflinching gaze, he reminds Lily of Leonard—or as if Leonard has given him advice on how he should behave—a feeling that only grows stronger when he takes her hand and holds it. Then he seems suddenly unsure of what to do and, after squeezing it too hard, he drops it again and backs awkwardly away—suddenly a boy again.

"He's starting work for the postal service next month," says Mae, smiling with pride. "An old friend of Leonard's arranged it. He doesn't really want to be here. He thinks it's all a sham."

"I suppose it is," Lily says, although she can only think how much Matteo would love a real job, how much he would enjoy the food and the music and the celebratory atmosphere today. But he is digging roads in the dust bowl for pennies.

"Well," Mae says into the silence, "I suppose we should sit down."

As Mae settles into the chair next to her, Lily sees the dip at Mae's collarbone as she inhales—she's wearing bulky clothes, Lily realizes, but she's thin too: her skin is stretched white over the bones in her hands. She looks breakable.

They eat without talking to each other for some time, each pausing to tend their children. Lily is glad of the distraction. It allows her to catch her breath.

But Mae has always been good at pretending: all those business dinners with Leonard's colleagues long ago had taught her to put on a wide false smile and speak with ease. "So," she says brightly, placing sandwiches on her children's plates, "what do you know about the other families?"

"Nothing, really," Lily says. "I haven't much time for reading the papers."

Lily wonders if the newspaper reporters have printed Mae's picture; she wonders if Mae feels the same strange mixture of shyness and hope that she does—the sudden sense that her life might matter to someone now, that she might be able to change it for the better. But perhaps Mae has always felt she could do that—she'd married Leonard, after all. She'd picked Lily up and then discarded her. What must it be like, to have that sort of power?

Maybe it's similar to what Lily had felt when they'd taken her photograph. "You'll be famous," the journalist had told her. "Everyone in Toronto will know who you are."

Now she sits with Mae and watches the other families arrive, watches the reporters taking pictures of the other mothers with their children. They seem used to the media attention and don't flinch as the camera bulbs flash, but smile and walk toward the picnic tables—at least four other couples and so many children between them. Lily stops counting at fifty. A crowd of curious members of the public has grown around the tables, too, with people pushing at the rope for a chance to get closer to the families.

"That's Mr. and Mrs. Timmins," Mae whispers, pointing to a thin, well-dressed couple to their right, who are barely touching the food. "They've twenty-three children."

"Twenty-*three*?" Lily hisses.

Mae nods. "Only seven for the Stork Derby, though, so they're not ahead of me—of us. And that other couple is Mr. and Mrs. Green. Though she has a job in a shop anyway, and he's earning good money as a carpenter, so they don't need to win like we do."

Lily can smell the rose scent of the expensive oil Mae always wears. She blinks away an unexpected heat behind her eyelids. "What about the last family?"

"Sixteen children, seven of them qualify. The whole family is very religious, and they have made a great fuss over whether to enter the race at all. The mother, Mrs. Devon, has been saying to reporters that she thinks the competition is immoral because it's forcing women to have more babies. I don't know why she says that when she's happy to have so many herself."

Mae laughs, and in that moment, she reminds Lily of Millicent, who is comfortable enough to have all sorts of high-and-mighty ideals without ever having to dirty her hands. But then surely Millicent must be affected by Leonard's loss of money too. Lily wonders if she's still flirting with the Women's Council during the day and cocktail parties at night. She wonders if Millicent is still rich enough to think the Stork Derby is *disgusting*.

Still, Lily keeps her smile fixed because she's aware of the crowds, of the reporters, and of the fragile thread that suddenly links her to Mae, after so long.

"And that man," says Mae, pointing to a thin, gray-haired figure on the edge of the crowd, "is Mr. Mackenzie King, who might be our next prime minister. He's promising to create more jobs and more houses. Mind you, Mr. Bennett, the current prime minister, is promising the same."

"Who will you vote for?" asks Lily.

Mae shrugs. "They're the same man in different clothes—does it matter?"

Lily laughs and Mae joins her, holding her gaze.

"Watch out, Mama," Robert blurts out, too loudly. "Here comes another photographer." He is leaning too far toward them and his gaze is slightly unfocused, as if he is drunk.

Mae's expression is worried. "He hates all this," she mutters to Lily. "He thinks it's a sham and he loathes the cameras."

"Oh, let's see that smile again!" cries the photographer. "Two of the competing mothers laughing together. I gotta get a picture. Look this way, ladies, and say, 'Stork Derby.'"

"Stork Derby," Lily says mechanically, as Mae chimes, "Stork Derby," and smiles. She's wearing lipstick, Lily notices. Who can afford lipstick, these days?

The bulb flashes, and Lily imagines the grainy photo that will appear in tomorrow's newspaper. Mae's bright halo of hair next to Lily's dark head. Somehow, the thought is like being stripped of a layer of skin. And it's partly that people will look at the two of them together and be drawn to Mae's beauty, her wide smile—perhaps they will think, just from looking at them, that Lily is less deserving of the money. Then this new hope that Lily feels, this *lightness*, will be snuffed out forever.

But it's also that Mae herself will see it. That she will hold up a picture of Lily's face, next to hers, and she will see the difference between them more clearly than ever.

At the moment the photographer's bulb flashes again, two things happen: in Lily's lap, Alessandro cries out and flings himself backward, wailing. So Lily's attention is upon him when there is a *crash* from across the table and Robert falls to the floor, cracking his head against a chair. He lies on the ground, his limbs trembling, his jaw working, his lips slowly turning blue.

Mae leaps up and runs to his side, trying to hold on to his arms, stroking his face.

"Robert!" she cries. "Robert, what's wrong? Get up, Robert!"

He shakes, his eyes rolling back in his head. Lily is frozen, holding Alessandro.

The photographers stand back. One lifts his camera to take a picture, but the others shout at him to *Stop, you goddamn fool!*

Lily gives Alessandro to Betsy, rushes to Mae's side, and crouches next to Robert. His shaking has stopped and he is lying quite still. A dark ribbon of blood trickles from his mouth, down his chin. His eyelids flutter then and he seems to come back to himself, staring up at Lily and at Mae, his eyes slightly glazed, as if he has just woken from a deep sleep.

"What's wrong, Mama?" he says to Mae. His voice sounds very young.

Instinctively, Lily reaches out to take his hand, but Mae bats her away. "Don't touch him!" She wears the fierce, savage expression of a mother who would do anything at all to protect her child.

Another camera bulb pops, capturing the moment: the fallen child, the two women, one reaching out, the other with teeth bared in something close to a snarl.

And as she looks at the reporters crowding around them, Lily feels the last shreds of her earlier hope fading. Instead, there is the sensation of something having slipped. Something precious has cracked, while nobody was looking. There is a crushing feeling in the air, like a gathering thunderstorm, which is just about to break.

25

Mae, October 1935

Mae doesn't remember the discussion between the journalists about where Robert should be taken. She doesn't recall crying out for help in getting him to a doctor, or pushing everyone away from him, shielding his body with her own while the camera bulbs crack and shatter around her.

"Ma'am," one of the reporters says, his eyes kind, "move away, please. Let us carry him for you."

She watches as two of the reporters lift Robert between them and take him just across the road to the large hospital, with its dark wooden walls and its smells of bleached floors and antiseptic. She's been there before, and so has Robert—when he was two years old and fell on a rusty nail, cutting his arm open; and when he was nine, the day after he fell through the ice and Mae wanted the doctor to look him over. She has brought the other children here at various points, too, but not for the past five years, not since they moved to Cabbagetown. In that time, she's used the local midwives for advice on the babies and asked for Thérèse's help when the older children have been sick. She has kept wounds clean and has

258

prayed that God will keep infection and illness away. But it seems that the poorer she has become, the less God has listened. The children have spent all winter with rattling chests and pale brows. Mae has sponged their hot limbs with cool water, but she has stopped praying, afraid that, if the children don't recover, she'll lose God as well as everything else.

But now, following the men carrying her son into the hospital, watching the way his limbs hang loosely, the way his head lolls and his eyes roll, she prays.

Please, God, please. I'll give anything. Please.

The warmth of the hospital envelops her. The dark wood feels like the security of a familiar embrace, and when a white-coated doctor rushes over to the reporters and asks what's wrong with their friend, Mae begins to breathe more easily. But then the reporters indicate Mae and, when the doctor looks at her, in her old coat and scuffed shoes, his expression changes.

"Do you have medical insurance?" he asks.

Mae shakes her head. It wasn't something they'd needed when Leonard could afford the bills, and then, after they'd moved out of the big house, if the subject of insurance came up, Leonard would always scowl. "Highway robbery, that's what it is."

"But what if we need to pay—"

"Then we'll find a way of paying." He'd said this with some of his old confidence: the self-assurance of a man who had grown up with money and had always been able to afford to live.

"But *how*?"

He'd glared from the armchair where he spent his days and evenings, barely moving. "Have you ever paid a bill, Mae? In your life? Have you made a single business transaction, ever? Put money in the bank?" He speaks in the harsh tone that comes so easily to him now—the impatience she'd rarely seen before he lost the business, but which now seems to be a part of every conversation.

She shook her head, biting on the inside of her cheek to stem the tears that threatened.

"Then don't ask how it's done. Just trust that I'll do it."

Now, looking at the crease between the doctor's brows, at the way his expression becomes slightly pained when she says she has no insurance, a low hum of dread begins in Mae's ears, like a warning she can't quite hear, although she knows it is serious.

The doctor looks at Robert, then back at Mae. She smiles tremulously, hoping that the lipstick she'd put on this morning is still in place—the last scrapings of the lipstick she used to wear when they lived in the big house. She hopes he can smell the final drops of her rosewater scent.

"Please," she begs. The doctor's eyes flick over her. She can see him making some internal calculation. She continues to smile, hopelessly, until one of the reporters positions himself between her and the doctor.

"The paper will pay for some tests," he says, "if you can find time for an interview. An exclusive."

"Yes," Mae says. "Yes, please."

The doctor sighs. "I can run some tests. Maybe an X-ray." When she frowns, he explains, "A picture that will allow me to see his brain. I will have to drill a small hole into his skull and inject some air to allow me to see the brain. A procedure called pneumoencephalography." He lingers over the long word.

"A *hole* in his *skull*? You can't! That will kill him."

"I assure you, it's quite safe, in the right hands." He flexes his own large pair, as if that will reassure her. "I'm afraid it's necessary, if we are to discover what caused him to collapse. He had a fit, you say? And he's had headaches?"

She nods. "Will it"—she swallows—"will it hurt him?" *His brain*, she thinks. *There's something wrong with his brain.*

"I'll do my very best."

My very best to what? But she can't make herself ask more, can't do anything except slump on a chair, her body folding in on itself. It is an effort for her to sit upright.

Two hours later, the doctor asks her to come into his office.

Robert is lying on a bed, sleeping after his X-ray, his head bandaged. When the doctor calls her, Mae is counting her son's breaths, watching the steady rise and fall of his chest as she used to when he was a baby.

"Mrs. Thébault? Follow me." The doctor's face is blank, giving nothing away.

Her heart clenches in her chest.

"Sit down," the doctor says. His office is full of paperwork. There is an expensive chair, covered with soft brown leather, which she sits on. Beneath it is a beautiful Persian rug of the type she used to have in the old house. Books line the shelves, and the walls are crowded with certificates. Dr. Cooper, as he's introduced himself, makes some notes on a pad of paper, then looks up. The expression on his face is obscure, and unreadable, but at the same time, it tells her something. It tells her that she doesn't want him to speak, that she wants to stand and leave and run back to Robert's side and gather him to her chest, putting her body over his, shielding him from whatever this stranger is going to say, from whatever these words will do to him.

The doctor clears his throat. The light is coming in low through the window, making them both squint, but Mae is glad, because it's a distraction, the pain of the light in her eyes.

Something in her is ready for this moment—has been preparing for it since the first time she held Robert in her arms and looked into his eyes and knew she would die for this perfect little stranger.

"I'm afraid," the doctor says, "that the situation doesn't appear hopeful."

And suddenly she is not ready. She only thinks that she's been readying herself, as if by imagining all the awful things that might happen to her child, she can protect him. But she hasn't been able to imagine this: the roaring of her own blood in her ears that makes it almost impossible to hear the doctor's words. The way that her attention shifts back to the light, to the way it gleams on the lone spiderweb in the corner of the window, to the way it shines through the leaves of the plant on the sill, casting strange, shifting shadows across the doctor's face as he continues to speak but she can't make sense of what he is saying.

And through the booming of the blood in her ears, she hears the word *tumor*. She hears more words, some of which she knows, some she doesn't: *prognosis, treatment, limitations, excision, risks, morbidity*.

She wants to be sick. Her body feels separate from her thoughts. There is a tingling in her fingers and a roiling in her gut, as if her body has understood something she hasn't, as if it knows something she doesn't. Her thoughts feel like trapped butterflies banging against glass.

"Please can you repeat that? Please?" As if manners can save her son.

And he does. And he tells her what can be done. And he tells her how much it will cost. And he tells her about the chances of failure. He tells her what failure would mean.

She nods and leans forward and breathes. The light is still coming in through the window. The spiderweb is still in the corner of the room. The plant still casts its shadows.

And she vomits all over her scuffed shoes, all over the doctor's expensive rug.

The doctor says he will allow Robert to stay in the hospital for one night, paid for by the *Globe*. He frowns sympathetically at her and advises her to ask her husband about *payment decisions*. As if Leonard might be able to conjure the money from somewhere, she thinks bitterly.

Perhaps she can go to another hospital, get another doctor's opinion. But the doctor seems to read her thoughts: "I'm afraid we're the only hospital that provides this sort of treatment. The pathway in other hospitals tends to err toward reducing the patient's pain."

Mae's brain catches on the idea: reducing pain is positive, surely. But then she grasps what he means: other hospitals simply allow the patients to . . .

She can't think it.

She goes in to see Robert, who is still sleeping. She strokes her hand across the bandage on his head and kisses his cheek, inhaling the scent of him. It is so long since he has allowed her to do this—he always pushes her away or squirms out of her grip, or rolls his eyes. And suddenly she wants him to do exactly that. She kisses his cheek again and again, willing him to wake and protest.

He sleeps on, his chest rising and falling. And as the young nurse asks her if she could please leave now, because the patient needs to rest, Mae walks away from her son, a ripping sensation in her gut, as if something physical links them, as if the cord that bound them together for a moment after he was born stretches between them still.

When she arrives home, Leonard is still sitting in his chair, an empty whiskey bottle at his feet, his big blond features blurred with drink. The children were collected from the picnic by the neighbor, Mrs. Schwartz. They ask after Robert and she tells them that he is resting in the hospital and will be home tomorrow. She butters bread and gives them some of yesterday's beef broth, which is waiting on the stove. Normally she would take a bowl to Leonard, but she can't make herself look at him.

Eventually, she hears his footsteps shuffling through to the kitchen. She doesn't stir from scrubbing the pot in the bucket. The water is cold and the beef fat congeals on her hands. Her stomach turns and she almost vomits again. Her eyes water.

She doesn't look up at Leonard.

"How are we going to afford the hospital stay?" he asks. His voice is toneless and empty, with none of the gentleness of the man she married. She misses her husband, the man who used to hold her and tell her that all would be well.

She scrubs harder.

"How?" he says. "You should bring him home."

"Clear your plates and go upstairs," she says to the children. They do so wordlessly, their faces worried. Betsy pats her shoulder as she passes.

When the door is shut, Mae hisses, "I will *not* bring him home. They're letting him stay tonight because the newspaper paid. But he needs surgery and we can't afford that because we don't have health insurance."

He blinks. "Health insurance is robbery."

"Our son dying is robbery." Her voice cracks. She grits her teeth. "Not being able to afford the surgery is robbery. And he'll be in so much pain, the doctor said." She can't stop the tears now. She scrubs the pot hard, the wire brush scraping the skin from her hand, although she doesn't feel it. She feels nothing, nothing. And yet she can't stop crying.

Leonard kneels on the floor next to her. "They said he'll . . . Robert will . . ."

He can't say it either. She nods. He takes her hands, gentle. A glimpse of the man she recognizes in his bloodshot blue eyes.

When she can speak again, she says, "I told him—the doctor—about the Stork Derby. And he said he could . . . He might do the surgery if we can talk to the newspapers about what he's doing. I suppose it would help his reputation. It would . . . advertise the hospital, he said." The thought is sickening, but Mae understands: the hospitals need money, too, and fewer people can pay for health care these days.

Leonard's expression brightens. "So, he would treat Robert for free?"

She shakes her head. "It would be a loan."

"For how long? I don't know when I'll get a job, and the relief work pays pennies."

She looks at him and takes a breath. "The Stork Derby. If we can win the money, we'll be able to pay it all back. Even if the surgery doesn't work, we'll be able to give Robert whatever . . . care he needs."

The next day, Mae waits until Leonard is dozing in the armchair and the children are all outside, and she digs through her clothes chest. For a moment she thinks the necklace must have gone, that one of the children must have found it or Leonard must have sold it. Then her hand closes around the cold, hard beads and she draws out the string of pearls she'd given to Lily five years earlier.

It's her last piece of jewelry and she rarely allows herself to look at it. Occasionally, when she knows she's alone, she'll sit on the bed and press the pearls against her lips, remembering them warm against Lily's skin. Now she tucks them into her pocket and walks to the pawn shop. She tries not to look at the necklace as she passes it over to the pawnbroker, tries not to feel the weight of it leaving her hand.

The bundle of notes she gets in exchange seems impossibly large, enough to feed the family for months. But not enough for Robert's operation and the drugs he will need to stop his fits.

Instead, she takes the money to Carson and Sons, the big lawyer's office on King Street. And she tells the lawyer there, ginger-haired and spectacled, that she needs to win the Stork Derby. She knows, she tells him, that there are other mothers who have as many children as she does, but she also knows there is talk of the case going to court, of having to submit paperwork to a judge, who will decide which mother has a valid claim, which mother deserves the money.

"And I need to win," Mae explains. "I need that money. But I can't afford to pay you for long. Not unless I win."

At first, he sits back in his leather armchair and laughs. Then, when he sees she is serious, when she shows him the money in her purse, he leans forward. "*How* many children did you say you have?"

"Seven that can be counted. And another on the way." She strokes her stomach. "I have older children too."

She pushes away the thought of Robert, curled up in his bed, his face creased in pain, in spite of the drugs they've given him. With the bandage around his head, he reminds her of the men who had returned from war when she was just a girl. They had sat on the street corners in Oakville, with their missing limbs and bandaged heads, and they had looked entirely hopeless.

The lawyer takes out a thin cigar, trims the end, lights it, and exhales a long, slow stream of acrid smoke.

"It's an interesting proposition," he says. "And I suppose we could approach it from the position of morality—there's lots of talk about morals and respectability around this. Various groups are saying women shouldn't be breeding children they can't afford, that they should be preventing pregnancies and so on."

Mae swallows, then nods.

"And how many other families are in the race? The stories in the papers change every day."

"Four, I think. At the moment. Well, four with a chance of winning."

"I see." He exhales more smoke. "And the other mothers might have more children, too, so you won't necessarily be the front-runner. Unless you're cooking up triplets in there. You must have room for a litter by now."

He laughs and she forces herself to laugh with him, to smile through the revulsion she feels for this smug man, his cigars and his crass jokes about her body.

Then he grows serious. "Our job," he says, "is to prove that the other women's claims are *less* valid, that they're not moral, not *respectable* citizens. Not deserving.

The judge who's sitting on this case comes from old money and he has those old-money values—won't like the idea of the slums filling up with all these children." The lawyer's own mouth twists in distaste.

She blinks. She had come to the lawyer with the hope that he would make sure all her papers were correct, that he might argue her case in front of a judge. She hadn't thought about casting doubt on the claims of the other mothers, questioning their morality, their respectability.

Could she really do that to another woman?

Mae thinks of Robert. The sweat on his forehead. The way his eyes had rolled back in his head and his limbs had gone slack. The blood that had trickled down his chin.

She remembers the baby she'd held in her arms, the boy whose hand she'd clutched between hers, the child whose scraped knees she'd wiped. She would gladly offer up her own life for his, except her life is not the payment. Some other woman's good name hangs in the balance.

"So," the lawyer says, "as long as you're respectable and moral yourself—and you seem it, pretty and so on—I can start thinking about how to present the other women. If you can find out anything yourself, that would be helpful. Can you do that?"

She remembers the doctor's words. *Prognosis, treatment. Slim chance.*

"Yes. Yes, I can."

26

Courtroom 2B, 1937

The hour is late. The sun has dropped and the golden light in the courtroom windows has been replaced by a shifting gloom. Shadows creep up the walls. When the court attendants light more lamps, the walls become brighter, but the shadows still squat on the floor, and Lily, exhausted as she is, finds herself transfixed by them, as if they are scuttling toward her, like rats, intent on nibbling at her toes. She would like to jump up and run, but the courtroom is already set against her for her "lack of morals." They don't need to believe her mad too.

There are no rats. They're in your head, she tells herself. *Just in your head.*

But lately so much has been in her head. Lately it's been hard to know what to believe.

The lawyer is pacing back and forth, watching her watch the shadows. There is a glint in his eyes, or a reflection of the lamplight from his glasses, it is hard to tell. Either way, it makes him look predatory and she has to suppress a shudder as she waits for his next question.

"I want to ask," the lawyer says, "about the children you lost."

270

Lost? "Pardon?"

"Forgive me—I should be more direct. You had children who died, did you not?"

It is like a punch to the stomach. "Yes." It is all she can say.

"How many?"

One before Matteo, then six more. And he'd had a twin. But he isn't asking about those. Those babies mean nothing to him, mean nothing to anyone in the courtroom. He means baby Ana, who was stillborn in 1933, between Alessandro and Elena. And there was baby Sebastian, who had lived only a matter of weeks and then died of a fever.

"Two," she whispers.

"Speak up. How many?"

"Two." Her eyes burn. Her throat aches. "Sebastian and Ana." It feels important to say their names, even though her voice fractures.

"I see. One was stillborn?"

She nods.

"Speak up."

"Yes. Ana." Lily looks at Mae, who has tears on her cheeks. How can she allow her to be questioned like this? She knows what it's like to hold your baby in your arms after it has stopped breathing. To wonder if it ever breathed at all. To wonder if you could have done something differently. To wonder why you hadn't known, because surely a mother's job is to sense such things. Mae understands all of this.

The lawyer clears his throat and passes Lily the

handkerchief from his pocket, then turns away while she dabs at her cheeks.

"And can I ask if the stillborn child's birth was registered?" he says.

She pauses in wiping her eyes. "Of course. She had to be registered so she could be . . . So we could have a proper funeral."

Paolo had carried the box close to his chest, cradling it. Lily had felt her legs might give way.

"And," the lawyer says, "you are including this baby in the number counted for your claim to the will?"

"Of course," Lily says again. How could she forget her? Ana had been born with a head of black hair. Her little mouth had been firm, but it was so like her own mouth, so like Matteo's, that she could imagine it stretched into a smile. What would her voice have sounded like? "Of course I have counted her."

"Ah," the lawyer says. "Well. That is unfortunate. You see, for the purpose of the will, stillborn children will not be counted."

"What?" How can this be? There has been no talk in the newspapers of stillborn children being disregarded. She thinks of Mae's dead child, whom she had helped deliver. And then she does the calculations and realizes that Mae hasn't counted that baby. Or perhaps his birth hadn't ever been registered—he'd been so little: Mae had been only six months pregnant.

"For the purpose of the will—"

"I heard you. But that's—that's not fair!"

"Calm yourself, please, Mrs. di Marco." His reaction is

instant, and the judge sits up. Too late, she sees she's behaving as he hoped she would: he wants to provoke her so that the judge will believe she is quick to anger, immoral, undeserving of the money. But she can't hold back the words.

"You're saying she doesn't count as if—as if she wasn't a person. It isn't right. It's heartless."

"I'm sorry," the lawyer says, his face impassive. Lily balls his handkerchief into her fist, refusing to cry.

"So," the lawyer continues, "I'm afraid there is also a problem regarding your other child, who died of fever. There is the question of whether his birth was correctly registered, whether he should count."

Whether he should count. Those are the lawyer's words. She stares in disbelief.

"Sebastian," Lily says faintly. "His birth was registered too. And he was three weeks old."

"I can't find him in the city records."

"But he was registered. He was."

The lawyer spreads his hands. "I'm sure you think he was. But I'm afraid . . ." He gestures at a file in front of him. "I'm afraid we have only your word for his existence. And the newspaper story, of course. But, as I'm sure this court will agree, they're hardly the same as registration papers."

Again, Lily looks at Mae, who is still staring at the floor. And as Lily follows her gaze, it seems that the shadows really are moving toward her, really are swarming around her ankles.

She closes her eyes. Sebastian.

27

Lily, December 1935

Lily sleeps lightly during these cold days and colder nights. The children huddle close to her, and to one another on the floor. Earlier in the month, she had done enough sewing work to be able to buy a large roll-up mattress. It is thin and worn and stained, lumpy with the indentations made by other bodies over the years, but it is warmer and more comfortable than the floor.

Last time he returned from the relief camp, a week ago, Paolo had spent some of his money on a crib for Sebastian.

"He will be better on the mattress next to me," Lily had protested. "I don't see why he should have his own bed—he's too small to be the favorite!"

"I'm worried one of the bigger children might push him out in the night or roll onto him. He'll do better with his own space." Paolo took Lily's face in his hands. "I want to look after you. You do so much. Let me do this."

Lily had kissed his rough cheek. At times like this, she wished she could love him more—or perhaps not more but differently. She couldn't imagine her life without

Paolo's steady kindness and yet, even though she missed him when he was gone, she didn't pine for him. She didn't long for him.

She never dreamed about falling asleep to the rhythm of his breathing.

Knowing that he might catch sight of her picture in the newspaper from the Stork Derby tea, Lily had mentioned seeing Mae, keeping her voice light, her eyes fixed on her darning. She'd felt him sit up straight next to her, had felt him studying her face as he asked about Mae, about Leonard, about the children.

"We didn't talk," Lily had lied, tugging on the needle. "The photographer put us together and told us to smile." She could feel the color creeping into her cheeks and hoped he wouldn't notice in the dim lamplight.

He sighed heavily, took her fingers, and laced his own through them. "I love you," he said. She could feel the rough calluses from the shovel. They worked eighteen hours a day at the relief camp, but Paolo never complained to her.

"I love you too," she whispered.

He hadn't asked about Mae again.

Sebastian is a good baby: he cries only if he wants feeding or if he becomes very tired, but he feeds quickly and easily, and then Lily can give him to one of the older children to burp, before they put him back in his crib, where he soon settles to sleep. Or, if he cannot settle, they rock him in their arms and sing to him until he drifts off.

Paolo has gone back to dig the roads to the north. He will return by the end of the month, he says. Both of them had hoped that, when Mr. Mackenzie King won the October election, things would change for the better, but nothing seems to be different.

"I don't want to leave you," Paolo says.

Lily assures him, as ever, that she doesn't mind, that she understands, that she will miss him, that she will wait for him.

"I'm so lucky," he says into her hair. "I'll think of you every day."

She nods, unable to speak. He deserves so much more, so much better than her.

"Look what I've found," he says, pulling a twist of sugar wrapped in paper from Elena's ear. All of the children clap in delight and fight over the grains of sugar. He takes a few and sprinkles them onto Lily's tongue.

So sweet.

He puts his arm around Lily, presses his lips to her forehead, her eyelids, her mouth. "You really think we could win the Stork Derby money?"

"I do."

Mid-December, near to Christmas. The children are excited because she's promised she will try to get a chicken one day for dinner.

They are taking longer and longer to go to sleep at night—even the oldest twins, who are usually the most responsible, keep asking where she will get the chicken from, how she will cook it, what they will eat with it, will Papa be home. Question after question, and it is nearly midnight by the time all the children are asleep, and Lily herself drifts off.

She wakes almost an hour later. Sebastian is restless, so she picks him up, feeds him and rocks him, then settles him back in his crib before falling into a heavy sleep herself on the mattress on the floor.

It can't be more than half an hour later when he wakes again. His cry seems louder than normal, high-pitched and indignant. Again, Lily feeds him and soothes him, then puts him back in his crib.

She wishes Paolo was here. He would pick Sebastian up and sleep with him laid across his broad chest.

It seems she has barely closed her eyes when Sebastian begins crying again—a full-throated roar that she hasn't heard from him before. The other children fidget and grumble in their sleep, and Lily tuts. What on earth can be wrong with the baby? She stands, puts her hands in the crib to scoop him up. And, in the dim light of the embers from the fire, sees a dark shadow move over the baby's face. At the same time, she touches something soft and damp and furry.

A rat!

She screams and grabs Sebastian, who is still screaming himself. The other children are immediately awake, and she shouts at them to stand up, to move, to get off the floor because there are rats.

All the children begin crying at once, flapping their

arms and running on the spot, but none of them manages to get off the floor until she tells them to stand on the table or chair, and then the older ones do, helping the younger children to climb up, while Lily holds Sebastian, who is still howling. With a trembling hand, she manages to light a taper from the embers of the fire, then a candle.

His face is bleeding from at least three rat bites, and he has another on his arm.

Lily gasps and nearly drops the candle, but manages to steady her voice enough to tell the older twins to fetch a bucket of water and a cloth. And she sponges the blood away while Sebastian screams and screams and screams.

For the rest of that night, the whole family huddles on the table together. No one sleeps. Julia, who is eight and trying to be grown-up, rubs at Sebastian's back and puts her arm around her younger sisters, Katerina and Elena. Luca stares moodily at the floor, brandishing a stick. His hand is shaking. Lily loves her children even more for these touches of bravery.

Sebastian cries until he exhausts himself, dozes, then wakes to cry some more. Lily holds him and tries to feed him, but he wails and squirms and will not suck. In desperation, she tries squeezing milk from her breast into his mouth, but he simply chokes, then vomits, and continues to cry.

In the pale gray light of morning, Lily examines the cuts on Sebastian's face and arms: they are livid and the area around them is puffy. When she presses her fingers lightly against them, Sebastian roars. His brow is hot. His whole body burns.

"He needs a doctor," Lily says aloud. But she knows, she *knows*—and her thoughts stutter—that it is too late. Rat-bite fever. She'd watched her own younger brother die from it.

"Will Sebastian be all right?" Katerina asks. She is five and her eyes are wide and terrified as she strokes her baby brother's hot head.

"Of course he will," Lily says, clamping her jaw around the tears.

A doctor will not be able to do anything, will be expensive, but she has to try.

She tells Julia to fetch Mrs. Palumbi from along the street. "I'm going to take your brother to a hospital," she says.

Julia's eyes are dark and fearful, but she nods and leaves immediately. Lily begins to run in the opposite direction: the nearest hospital is nearly half an hour away. Sebastian cries all the way.

When she arrives, sweating and half crying, she shows the duty nurse her crying baby. "He needs a doctor."

The nurse looks at him: his face is puffed up and bloodied, and his cry has become strange and wheezing. She takes a step back. Her eyes travel over the blood on his nightgown, and on Lily's own nightgown, which she hasn't bothered to change. "Everyone here needs a doctor." She indicates the line of people waiting, all of whom are eyeing Lily and Sebastian. Some of them mutter to each other.

"Please," Lily says. "Oh, God, please help me."

"No need for blasphemy, ma'am. Go sit and wait your turn," says the nurse.

By the time the doctor sees them, hours later, Sebastian has stopped crying. His eyes are closed and his skin is burning. Occasionally, he gives a strange shudder and a little moan. His breathing is fast and light.

"You should have brought him straightaway," the doctor says.

"I did," Lily replies, thinking guiltily of the hours when she'd sat on the table with the other children, waiting for morning.

"I'm sorry," the doctor says. "There's nothing to be done." He looks at the shock and desperation on Lily's face and adds, "You can wait in a private room until . . ." He averts his eyes from hers, then says, "And I won't charge you. As there was no treatment."

He looks at her expectantly and, on some automatic impulse, Lily says, "Thank you."

Afterward those words will haunt her almost as much as the doctor's impassive tone, his weary face. She won't be able to recall Sebastian's face at all. She won't remember the pitch of his cries or the heat of his skin or the weight of his body in her arms. She won't be able to recall when it was exactly that he made no noise at all anymore.

The next morning, they are all woken by a banging on the door. It is a reporter, with a pad and a photographer.

They want to take pictures of the crib where the *Stork Derby Baby* died so tragically.

Lily shuts the door and pulls the thin layer of material over the cracked windows, but she can hear the reporter shouting, "Do you still have rats, Mrs. di Marco? Are you concerned for your other children? Do you blame yourself for this?

"Come on, Mrs. di Marco! Our readers will want to hear your side of the story. Such a tragedy—they'll be rooting for you to win now."

Lily closes her eyes and gives a shuddering sigh, then fastens her coat and steps out into the cold. As the camera bulbs flare and pop, she gazes directly into the light, as if she can somehow stare past the camera to look back at the people who will see her picture—as if she can reach out to them, somehow, and tell them she *has* to win this money now. How else will they survive?

She thanks the photographer for the dollar he gives her. Then she buys two rat traps. The children are scared and grieving, but they give a weak cheer every time the rat trap snaps.

Lily watches them and promises herself that she will do anything—anything at all—to make sure she wins that money.

In the numb days that follow, she sends word to Paolo with one of the men from the street who is due to travel north to the relief camp. Before the Wall Street crash, Emmet had worked as a foreman on one of the building sites in the city center that now stands abandoned.

"Tell Paolo to come home," she says to Emmet. "But don't tell him what's happened. I'll wait until I see him. I don't want him to blame himself."

"I'll have to tell Paolo something," Emmet says, "or he'll imagine worse."

What could be worse? Lily thinks.

He must understand her expression, because he says gently, "He'll imagine it's you."

It is me, Lily thinks. *Part of me is gone too.* And maybe no one in the world can imagine what this might feel like. Except, perhaps, Mae.

But she must find out where she lives. Dry-mouthed, hollow with grief, Lily walks to Thérèse's house in Cabbagetown. She hasn't seen her since before Sebastian's death and, as she trudges across the rain-slicked streets, she resolves to keep her visit short. She will ask Thérèse where Mae lives now and then she will leave.

When Thérèse sees Lily, she ushers her children outside to play in the rain, then gathers her into a tight embrace. "Come here. I'm so sorry."

And as Thérèse holds her close, Lily feels a swelling tide of grief. She weeps until her eyes swell, until she is exhausted, until she can barely speak. Thérèse wraps a blanket around her legs and brings her a small glass of some foul-tasting moonshine, which loosens Lily's thoughts and helps to steady her breathing.

"I read all about it," Thérèse says. "Have you seen what they printed?"

Lily shakes her head. "I couldn't bear to look."

"They made it sound an awful place. Skid Row, your rooms, all the children crammed in."

"It is awful." But even as Lily says it, she thinks of the neighbors who have given her food and clothes, who have looked after the children. Mrs. Palumbi is watching them right now. The kindness of these people, whose lives are just as difficult as hers.

"If you haven't seen the papers you won't have read about Mae and Robert?"

Lily shakes her head. "He collapsed at the picnic, but I haven't seen them since."

And then Thérèse shows her the newspaper. Robert's face stares out at her, gaunt and dull-eyed, next to a picture of Mae, whose smile is rigid. Beneath the photograph, the headline reads *STORK DERBY MOTHER'S STRUGGLE*. The article says that Mae, a *devoted and beautiful Stork Derby hopeful*, has been devastated by the illness of her oldest son, Robert.

"A brain tumor?" Lily says, forcing the words past the tears that threaten to overwhelm her again.

Thérèse's face is somber. "He's having operations and treatment, but they don't know . . ."

The silence is filled with the unspeakable words. Lily folds the paper and pushes it away from her, but she can't get the phrases out of her mind: *Pregnant Mrs. Thébault desperately needs the Stork Derby fortune to save her child's life. Let us hope that the judge who decides the outcome will take pity on her and on her son.*

"A judge?" Lily says finally. "I thought the money would just go to the woman with the most children."

"I don't understand either, but Mae says it's all being decided by a judge. To make sure no one is cheating, I think. Mae knows more than I do about it."

"I should go and see her," Lily says.

"You should. I don't know what you fell out about, but this is more important. Here's her address."

Lily takes the piece of paper from Thérèse and tries to gather the courage to visit Mae.

Mae, who desperately needs the money because otherwise Robert will die.

In the days that follow, a cold wind sweeps across from the west, bringing a dust cloud so thick it blocks out the sunlight. Since the droughts have dried the crops, the land is parched and the soil is often swept up in the strong winds, but Lily has never known it so bad. Three days of choking darkness. There is no hope of visiting Mae. The dust makes their food gritty, makes the air feel suffocating, as though it's burning their lungs. All of them cough, all the time, and the children's faces are gray with dirt.

At night, she dreams that the barren, cursed land is making its way into their blood, into their bones, infecting them all. She wakes, grasping at air, searching for Sebastian's little body, trying to dig him out of the dirt, then lies in the darkness, weeping.

On the third night, she dreams that Paolo is coming back to her. In her dream, there is a river he must cross and he is swimming through the water, which keeps closing over his head.

She wakes with churning dread in the pit of her stomach, waiting for the knock at the door. She doesn't know how she knows, yet she does.

And when Emmet raps his knuckles on the door and falls to his knees, she doesn't feel the shock of it, as much as the inevitability. Everything is unraveling around her.

Paolo had left the camp as soon as Emmet had told him the news, in spite of the dust storm, in spite of the winds and the temperatures on the plains. They had told him not to go, had begged him not to leave, but he had wanted to get home. To Lily, Emmet said, "He couldn't stand the thought of you being alone and in pain. I told him he should wait. But he wanted to see you, to hold you."

They'd found Paolo's body halfway between the camp and Toronto. He was buried up to the waist. His nose and mouth had been full of dust. He must have drowned in it.

Emmet's voice breaks a little as he tells her this, and all Lily can think is that he must be thirsty. She hears Emmet's words, but they feel like wasps, buzzing around her head, circling—she can't understand exactly what he is trying to say. How could dust kill a man?

"The children are asleep," she says softly. "Would you like a glass of water?"

And then her body folds under her—not a faint, exactly, but more as if her muscles have suddenly stopped working and she collapses to the floor, banging her head.

Emmet curses and pulls out a handkerchief, which he presses against her bloodied temple.

"I'm all right," Lily says reflexively. "I'm all right." She can't stop saying it, even though she knows it isn't true. Even though it feels as if something has disappeared inside her, as though, where her lungs should be, and her stomach and her heart, there is a gaping, empty space.

How will we live now? How will we pay the rent? How will I buy food?

"I have to tell the children," she says, knowing it will destroy them, imagining their incomprehension, their disbelief. They are already in shock about Sebastian. How can she kill their papa for them too?

She can't. She won't. Not now. Not yet. She will sit on her doorstep for a while longer, holding a handkerchief against her head and wrapping her other arm around her body as she tries to hold herself together, tries to find something to hold on to.

28

Mae, January 1936

Most nights Mae sleeps on the floor next to Robert's bed, as she used to when he was a baby and wouldn't settle. Leonard used to tell her that she should just leave him to cry, but Mae had often crept into his cold room and pulled his warm little body close to hers, rocking him until he was drowsy, then placing him gently back in his crib. She would wake in the morning, cramped, lying on the floor, her hand squeezed through the wooden bars, resting on his chest.

Now, all these years later, she lies on the bare floorboards in the boys' room in a different house, listening to Robert's breathing. If she concentrates hard enough, she thinks, she might be able to help him to recover. She takes to sitting up, staring at him, watching his rib cage rise and fall. She imagines the inside of his skull, the tumor growing in his brain, and she wills it to shrink.

The doctor wants to operate, but it is a risk, and there's the matter of the money. Mae has assured him that they will be able to pay in a year, as soon as the Stork Derby fortune comes through.

Leonard says the man must be a charlatan: *He simply*

wants his share of whatever we have in return for . . . what? For
slicing into our boy's skull? No, Mae, no.

Even when she begs, when she weeps, Leonard won't give his permission, in spite of the increasing pain Robert has: the nausea, the headaches, the fits that make him fall to the floor. She cradles his head as he shakes, while the other children cower against the walls, staring. When the fit passes, Robert's eyelids flutter and open.

"What happened?"

He takes hours to come back to her fully, and each time more of him slips away, as if he is losing part of himself in the darkness of the fit. His smile, his ability to laugh at a joke, it's all being stripped from him, bit by bit. A slow peeling of everything he is. Sometimes, when he first wakes, he seems not to recognize her at all.

There is no hope of him taking on the job at the post office. They've given it to someone else.

"Perhaps," she says to him, "after the operation, you will be able to get a different job."

But Leonard's reluctance has influenced Robert too: whenever Lily mentions the surgery, Robert scowls. "I'm not letting them cut my head open," he says, or "It won't work. Just let me die in peace."

One morning in January, he takes longer to wake than usual, then seems drowsy and confused as he walks downstairs. He catches sight of himself in the mirror and says, "God. Betsy looks terrible."

Mae laughs, humoring him, but then she sees he is serious: he doesn't recognize his own face.

"Leonard!" she calls, forgetting that he has gone down

to the dock to see if he can find any work. There won't be any—even the young, burly men are struggling. Leonard is sad and thin and he smells of yesterday's whiskey. He will be home within an hour, surly and silent, and he will drink until he falls asleep in the chair.

Robert is almost at the bottom of the stairs when his foot catches on the broken third step, the one they all know to avoid. He stumbles and goes down, hitting his head. Immediately, his limbs begin to shake. Mae cries out and holds him, calling his name as he writhes and trembles. It is not a long fit, but afterward his eyes don't open. He lies still, so still that, for a moment, her heart lurches with the horror that he might be dying. His breathing is quick and shallow.

"Fetch the doctor!" Mae calls to Betsy, who nods and runs out of the door, even though Mae knows they can't afford to pay another doctor, that a house call will do no good at all, that she needs to take Robert to the hospital and beg the doctor there again to please, *please* save her son, to assure him that she will be able to pay, that she will win the money, because she is pregnant again.

Robert stirs and looks at her.

"We're going to the hospital," she says. "You're having the operation."

Robert blinks, which she takes as agreement. Then he says, "You're a funny-looking woman. Who are you?"

She calls down the street for Betsy to come back, tells her to watch the younger children, to keep them inside.

Betsy's face is tight with anxiety. "What shall I tell Papa when he comes home?"

"You tell him . . ." Mae starts, then sees the terror in Betsy's eyes. "You don't tell him anything. You wait for me to come home. You say you don't know where I've gone, that I didn't tell you."

Betsy swallows and nods. Mae strokes her cheek. Her anxious daughter, who is petrified of everything, who is so desperate to take care of everyone, for them to be well and happy: this must all seem like a nightmare to her. Her younger sister Sarah, who is braver and angrier, holds Betsy's hand. "We will be all right, Mama." But she looks scared too.

Mae had wanted to give her children a different childhood from the one she'd had. She hadn't wanted them to know what fear was, hadn't wanted them to know anything but happiness, even when she had been short-tempered with them: it had been a feeling born of frustration—that she was giving them more than she had ever had yet they still weren't happy enough. But it seems to her, looking back, that they'd never been happy, even when they'd had money. And she wonders what on earth she has done wrong.

Mae helps Robert to his feet and together they walk along the street, with him leaning heavily on her arm. His gait is shambling, she notices, and a bruise is forming on his forehead.

"Did you hurt your leg when you fell?"

He stares down at it, as if it doesn't belong to him. Then he looks frightened and, without any trace of his usual sarcasm, he says, "I don't know. I can't feel it."

A cold horror seeps into her, but she forces herself

to sound brisk and unconcerned. "Let's get to the hospital."

They near the main road out of Cabbagetown and a streetcar sweeps past. Mae has thirty cents in her purse. At the next stop, she holds up her hand and the streetcar pulls up.

The driver looks at Mae and then at Robert. "We don't take drunks."

"He's not drunk! He's just a child and he's ill."

Robert sways and mutters, "Tell the man he looks like a potato."

The driver doesn't hear, but his gaze takes in the bruise on Robert's head and his weak leg, then their scruffy clothes and Mae's wild hair—she hasn't had time to put on a hat, or gloves, and both she and Robert are shivering. She is dressed in a coat of Leonard's, one he rarely wears as it's too big for him, given all the weight he's lost. She must look ridiculous, possibly mad.

"Please," Mae says. "I have the money."

The driver nods reluctantly and lets them on. When she tries to give him the money, he waves her away.

"Thank you," she gasps, close to tears.

Robert slumps into a seat, closing his eyes and leaning his head against the window. The other passengers edge away from them, as if worried they might catch something.

Mae takes off her cardigan and wedges it under Robert's neck. She is wearing a thin shirt underneath and she sees a man in an oversized coat and flat cap staring at her chest. He raises his eyebrows. She looks away. When she glances over, he is still staring at her, and has opened his coat and angled his body toward her, so that she can see the swell in his trousers. She crosses her arms over her chest and the man laughs.

She spends the rest of the journey looking past Robert's sleeping face, out of the window. The city is ramshackle and grubby. Late last year the prime minister, Mr. Bennett, had given speeches on the radio about *social reform*, talking about how he would make things better for the workingman, just as Roosevelt's New Deal had in the US. Along with her neighbors, Mae had gathered around the single radio in the street—owned by elderly Mr. Rosenberg, who often gave people news updates in return for bread or milk—and listened to Mr. Bennett promising health insurance and welfare relief and better working conditions. Mae had voted for Bennett, and had wept when he'd lost to Mackenzie King. It didn't seem to matter who was in power: nothing changed.

The streetcar reaches its stop, and Mae helps Robert to his feet. He seems sleepy and disoriented as he shuffles slowly to the door. When Mae walks past the man who had stared, he presses himself against her. She ignores him, her skin crawling, and helps Robert step down onto the sidewalk outside the hospital.

Once inside, the doctor presents her with paper after paper; they ask for money she doesn't have; they ensure that she won't take legal action *in case of death*. The risks of the operation are endless: *death, permanent disability, loss of sight, hearing, and other senses, loss of speech, impotence, coma.*

Mae picks up the pen.

"You'll need your husband's permission to sign," the doctor says. "His signature."

Mae shakes her head. "He's at . . . work. I've sent my daughter with a message, but he may not get it. He won't be home for hours and it will take him too long to get here. Robert needs the surgery now, doesn't he?"

The doctor nods grimly.

"Please," Mae says. "Please help him. My husband would agree, I know it."

The doctor sighs and nods.

She signs everything. She kisses Robert's forehead—he is too ill even to squirm away.

"I don't want to leave him," she says to the nurse, a red-haired woman with kind eyes.

"Course you don't," says the nurse in a strong Irish accent. "But how about you come with me and I'll get you a nice cup of tea? That's right, this way. Wave to your boy. He'll be right as rain."

She imprints his face upon her mind. And she lets the nurse lead her away.

To distract herself, she leafs through some of the newspapers. There are headlines about yet more terrible dust storms to the north and the west; there are stories about the drop in employment—more than one in three men is out of work. There are promises from the new prime minister, who speaks about moderate reform and slow change (which means no change at all). And there is a section on the Stork Derby.

There is a piece about Mr. and Mrs. Timmins, who are shown standing in a stiff line with their twenty-three children, seven of them valid for the competition. Mr. and Mrs. Green also have seven valid children. They both lost their jobs in the last month, and are desperate to win the contest. The very religious Mr. and Mrs. Devon, who have six children in the race, are shown in close-up, unsmiling and condemning the immorality of women breeding for money. They are only entering to donate the winnings to the Church, they claim.

It is the picture at the bottom of the page that holds Mae's attention: her own face and Lily's, as they sit behind a table of food at the picnic, their children around them. There is Robert, his eyes closed against the flash of the camera bulb. Had it started already, his first fit? Or was it just about to begin? Was this the last moment of his normal life, or had it started months before, when he seemed so irritable and withdrawn and made rude comments, then complained about the camera flashes giving him headaches?

Mae runs her finger over his grainy face and then over Lily's. She has been avoiding Lily ever since she spoke to the lawyer.

"This race is going to be about more than the woman who has the most babies," he'd said. "The government already put in a clause saying that the money can only go to a married woman. And there's a lot of talk about respectability, correctly registered births, and so on."

"But I can't just ask these women to tell me everything about themselves," Mae said.

"Sure you can. Make friends with them," he'd said. "Find out what you can. Everyone has secrets."

And Mae knew the easiest way to ensure that one mother at least was out of the race. She knows so much about Lily that would help the lawyer to cast doubt on her character, her respectability.

But she can't possibly do it, can't possibly take away Lily's chance of a share in the money. So, when she wasn't caring for Robert, Mae had tried to meet with some of the other Stork Derby mothers, asking about their marriages, their children. She'd found out nothing of any use; the women had been wary of her, despite Mae's best efforts to dress up for the wealthier families, and to wear her oldest clothes for the families who, like Lily's, had next to nothing. Mr. and Mrs. Devon had refused to talk to her about the competition at all, telling her that they were *praying for her soul.* Mrs. Timmins had looked exhausted but insisted on giving Mae an oat cookie. *You must be hungry*, she'd said, while her twenty-three children shouted in the background, the older ones chasing the younger, swiping at them as they ran. And Mr. and Mrs. Green had been too busy working to talk to Mae.

"You can find out something about *one* of them, surely," the lawyer had said, his pink ears darkening in frustration, his mouth a thin line.

"I can't." She'd shrugged helplessly. She wouldn't do that to Lily. She couldn't.

"Come on, Mrs. Thébault. You need this money for your boy. And I need to get paid, like everyone else."

Now Mae drops the newspaper into her lap and presses her fingers against her temples.

She thinks of Robert lying cold and alone in the hospital bed. What wouldn't she do to save her child?

She closes her eyes so that she can't see the newsprint of Lily's face staring out at her.

And she remembers. The glow of moonlight through the curtains. Lily's breath against her ear. It had set an ache and a longing in Mae that has never left. She would settle for Lily's hand on her arm, or for the sound of her laughter, or to be able to talk to her and listen to her, as she used to. It was different from the feeling she had with Leonard, where she knew she was supposed to love him and where some force of duty and gratitude bound her to him. But his touch was demanding: he wanted to possess her body, to move her like a jointed doll, to own her somehow. With Lily, every touch had felt like a question they were both asking, neither of them sure of the answer.

When Mae opens her eyes, she sees the article in the corner of the page: TRAUMATIZED STORK DERBY MOTHER REFUSES TO DISCUSS BABY TRAGEDY!

With growing horror, Mae reads about Lily standing silently in front of the photographers after her youngest baby died of rat-bite fever. The reporter talks about the *terrible poverty* in the area where Lily lives *in filth and squalor. We must pity her, this flower who has been cast into society's refuse heap and yet still remains strong. Surely Mr. Millar's fortune should be awarded to just such a woman, who not only leads the race with the number of children she has, but also with the measure of fortitude she has shown.*

Mae drops the paper, runs to the restroom, and vomits again and again. When she straightens, she stares at her glassy-eyed face in the mirror.

She sinks to the cold tiled floor and wraps her arms around herself, leaning her head forward onto her knees and trying to breathe slowly. Her need to be held is a physical ache. And yet it is not her needs that matter now. It is the needs of her children. Their chance at life. Their hopes and their happiness are all within Mae's grasp.

29

Lily, January 1936

Lily rises early each morning, before the children have stirred, brushes her hair and wipes her face, then pinches color into her cheeks to fetch water from the pump. There is comfort in the churning wheel of everyday tasks, but it is more than that: at least one morning a week, there will be a reporter or a photographer waiting near the pump or at the end of the street. They like to take pictures of her next to the burned-out car or as she struggles with the bucket of water.

"How do you feel, Mrs. di Marco?" asks a reporter with a thick black mustache. "Our readers are worried about you."

"I am well," says Lily. "It's my children I worry about." This is both the truth and a lie: she is not well at all—is desperate, hollow, restless, exhausted—but she is more worried for the children.

"Oh, listen to that selflessness!" the reporter declares. "Our readers will love that. They call you the Lily of Skid Row. They're all rooting for you to win. What do you think of that?"

Lily shrugs and tries to smile. "Thank you. Thank them. I must return to my children."

"Such modesty, such strength," he says, watching her lift the bucket.

And although Lily knows that his compliments must be false, as she walks past five or six other women also on their way to the pump, she can't help feeling some solace in the support of so many readers: *They're all rooting for you . . . the Lily of Skid Row.* She repeats the words under her breath, like a charm or a prayer. Along with the faith that this gives her, there is another sort of lightness: that people might see her picture in the paper, going about her everyday tasks, and might think her *strong* and *selfless.* It is a strange mirror and, for a moment, the uprush of hope makes Lily dizzy.

She is almost smiling as she nears her door when she sees a slight figure wearing an oversized man's coat and a badly knitted woolen cap. Reporters are not usually so scruffy, but perhaps he works for one of the small magazines. Still, Lily really doesn't have time to talk to anyone else this morning.

"I'm sorry," she calls. "I'm too busy to talk today. Perhaps a photograph tomorrow."

The figure turns and Lily drops the bucket.

Mae.

Water sloshes over her feet, but she barely feels it.

"What are you doing here? How did you know where I—"

"Thérèse," Mae says. Her face is bare of makeup and her smile looks strained.

The wind whips dust and leaves around Lily's face, and perhaps that is why her eyes are burning; perhaps that is why it is suddenly hard to gather breath into her lungs.

"I read about Paolo," Mae says, not meeting Lily's gaze. "I'm so sorry. And your baby. You must feel—"

"Thank you," Lily says quickly, because after she's wanted Mae's understanding for so long it is suddenly too much. She feels skinless, stripped, raw. With difficulty, she says, "I heard about Robert too. I'm so very—"

"Thank you," Mae says, just as quickly, looking at her feet. "They're doing the operation now. On his brain." Her voice is barely audible above the wind and they are both shivering. "Is Matteo still working at the relief camp?"

"No, thank God." After Paolo's funeral, Lily had begged him to stay with her. It wasn't just the awful conditions that scared her: it was the rumors of riots and marches and strikes, along with the huge protest in Regina last year, when policemen had dispersed the hungry, angry men by shooting into the crowd.

"I couldn't risk losing him," Lily says, then sees the anguish pass over Mae's face.

"Of course." Her voice is wooden and she shivers again.

"You could come inside," Lily says.

"Not today. But I wondered . . ." Mae hesitates, her expression haunted. "The reporters like you. They make you sound very . . . Well, you are brave. And I wondered if you would let me have my picture taken with you sometimes?"

"With me?" Lily feels her chest constrict. She'd thought that Mae had come to see her, that she missed her, perhaps. But it seems that all she wants is a way of getting into the newspapers.

"Or if you don't want to see me, perhaps you could mention me to the reporters."

"I don't know . . ."

"Or could you mention Robert? It's just that it must help your case, surely, to have your story in the paper. Everyone feels so sorry for you and that will help him, us . . ." She trails off miserably, looking as if she might weep, and it is as if the past five years haven't happened, as if Lily is standing in Mae's back garden, sensing her loneliness, her sadness, longing to comfort her.

"Of course," Lily says. "Of course I can mention you to the reporters."

"Thank you," Mae says, and she moves closer, reaches out, and lays her fingers lightly on Lily's arm.

Lily freezes, her blood a drum. There is the faintest scent of Mae's rose perfume, but she smells of the woolen coat, too, of the foggy outside air. Lily wants to embrace her, but she also wants to go into her house and shut the door against the cold, the wind, the confusion. It is the same as the way she loves to stare at Lake Ontario, feels its pull, knows its moods and how it changes in different weather, yet is fearful that its undertow could subsume her in a moment.

"I'm sorry," Mae whispers. "For . . . everything." She squeezes Lily's hand. Her fingers are cold. "I'm glad to see you."

Lily nods, unable to speak. She thinks of all the times she has pictured Mae's face, imagined her saying those words.

"I would like to see you again," Mae says. "I would like . . ." She trails off, seeming suddenly awkward and vulnerable in her huge man's coat.

Barely trusting her voice, Lily says, "I would like that. Very much."

"I've missed you," Mae whispers. "I have to go back to the hospital now."

Then she pulls up her collar against the wind and turns away.

Lily rights the empty bucket and goes into the house, leaning her head against the doorframe, watching Mae walk through the mist, listening to the tap of her shoes against the cobbles. The fog seems to envelop her and, in the shadows, a shape is moving. Lily almost calls Mae back. She'll tell her that it isn't safe to walk out alone. She'll tell Mae that she can stay until the fog clears. But the words stop in her throat, and she closes her door on the shifting shadows.

She can still feel Mae's hand in hers.

The scent of roses.

Lily sighs, rubs her hands over her face.

A knock at the door and Lily's heart lifts. Mae can stay until the weather clears. She will talk to her, ask her about everything that has happened over these past years.

She will ask, *Did you ever think of me?* Perhaps she will admit, *I thought of you all the time.* Perhaps she will fall asleep with her head resting on Mae's chest, listening to the pulse of her breath, the echo of her heart.

As Lily walks to the door, there is another hard knock. The familiarity in its rhythm stirs some memory. It doesn't sound like Mae. Absurdly, she thinks, *It's Paolo!* Somehow, the tale of his death was a mistake. It was some other man who drowned in that dust storm, some other man who left a widow and eight fatherless children.

She opens the door and that breeze scours in again, the wind burning her face, making her squint, so that it takes a moment for the shape of the man in the doorway to resolve itself into someone she knows.

It can't be.

Her stomach plummets.

"Liliana," he says. "Aren't you going to say hello?"

Tony.

30

Mae, late January 1936

It is the day after Robert's operation and Mae huddles close to the frosted glass, hoarding the dawn light, although there is no warmth in it. She has slept badly, listening to Leonard snore alongside her. In sleep, he looks smaller, his flesh drawn back over his bones, his face skullish. She can barely see the handsome man she married in this shrunken figure, who looks like a discarded puppet. He hadn't even been angry when she told him she'd taken Robert to the hospital. His face had been blank with rage and panic as she told him about the surgery: that the doctor said he thought he'd removed all of the tumor.

She tries to imagine Robert after his operation, sitting up, talking, laughing. He loves maple syrup—she will use some of this week's shopping money to buy him some. But she can't imagine him healthy and eating. Every time she thinks of him, she pictures the inside of his skull, although she doesn't know what she would see. Only blackness when she closes her eyes. How will he ever recover? How will any of them?

Except they will. The past years have taught her how

much her body can survive, how much her mind can withstand. She continues to eat and sleep and breathe and talk and smile, even when something inside her has crumbled. Her chest feels hollow but her heart still beats.

Now she turns from the window and pulls on her thick, shapeless dress, her worn stockings, her old cardigan, and goes down to make breakfast. She likes this hour in the morning, the brief slice of time before anyone else has woken, before there is any pull on her thoughts.

Lily had seemed the same in so many ways—the familiar weight of her hand, the watchfulness in her dark eyes. But at the same time, Mae had felt the change in her: the hesitation when she'd asked Lily to mention her to the reporters, the new strength in her gaze.

The idea of telling the lawyer anything at all about Lily is unbearable. But if Mae can get the newspapers to support her as they've been supporting Lily, if they hear of Robert's desperate situation, and understand how much Mae needs the money, they'll begin to champion her too. If the public think she deserves the money, perhaps, when it is time for the court to decide on the winner, the judge will look kindly on her.

It occurs to Mae that, on her way to the hospital, she could pass by the *Globe* offices on King Street. She might see if she could have her picture taken—perhaps outside Robert's room, looking tragic but stoic. She imagines the judge opening his newspaper at breakfast tomorrow, seeing her picture, reading about her and thinking how deserving she is of the money.

She tells Betsy to look after the younger children, puts

on a dark green hat that she usually keeps in a box for best, pinches color into her cheeks, then sets off toward the newspaper offices.

The streets are cold, the smell of something rotting in the air, but Mae has grown used to ignoring it all: the huddled shapes in the doorways, the people who call, asking if she can spare a penny.

Near the *Globe* offices, the roads are busier, with hawkers yelling the prices on some slightly shriveled apples and paperboys waving today's edition. Mae has no money to pay for a copy, but catches sight of Lily's face staring out from the front page: *FLOWER OF THE SLUMS*.

Mae can't name the emotion she feels: something between panic and despair. Of course Lily will win the money; of course she deserves it. She has been through so much and Mae can see, in her steady gaze, the old fragility and strength—how could the public not love her? How will the judge deny her?

Mae hesitates outside the *Globe* offices, then turns away and nearly trips over someone standing behind her.

"Sorry," she says. And then she looks at the woman and has the reeling sensation that somehow she is imagining Lily—or that by seeing her picture and thinking of her, she has somehow invoked the living, breathing woman. "Lily? What are you doing?"

"Why are you here?" Lily looks over her shoulder and both ways along the street. She is breathing hard and sweat glimmers on her upper lip.

"I came to . . ." Mae shakes her head. "It doesn't

matter. What's wrong? What is it?" She imagines one of the children is ill, or that, somehow, Lily may have sensed something of her plan to talk to the reporters about Robert. But, no, that's ridiculous.

"I didn't know where else to go. I thought he wasn't going to leave or that he might follow me. Mrs. Palumbi is looking after the children so they're safe."

"Who? Who wouldn't know? Who would be following you? Lily, you're frightening me."

Lily's pupils are large and she looks left and right again, even though the street is full of its usual bustle, with no one paying any attention to the two women.

"Tony," she says. "My husband."

Mae says nothing. What can she mean? Is she unwell? Has Mae misheard, or . . . ?

Her face must be blank, because Lily says slowly, "Tony came to find me. He tracked me down."

Mae brings both hands to her mouth. "But you said he was dead."

"He was. At least, I thought he was." Lily swallows. "Honestly, I hoped he was."

"I don't understand."

"He survived the earthquake. Some people dug him out."

Mae takes a moment to absorb this. Lily looks so frightened; she mustn't add to that. She keeps her voice calm. "And how has he found you?"

"He's been looking for me for years, asking people about me everywhere he went, moving from city to city. And then he saw the story in the papers."

Oh, God. The Stork Derby.

"Does he want you back? Are the children really safe?" Mae has heard enough about Tony to know that he's dangerous—has sensed enough, in Lily's fear-filled reactions, the way she cowers at the first sign of anger.

"I think so, for now. But . . ." Lily's mouth trembles. "Oh, Mae! I just want him to leave us alone."

"You could go to the police?"

"What would I tell them? That he used to hit me, years ago, and that I left him for dead? They wouldn't give me a chance to explain, even if they believed me."

Mae wants to put her arms around Lily. She wants to say that perhaps he will leave her alone, after all, but she understands, with a sinking dread, that of course he won't. He will have read the newspaper articles and he will know exactly what Lily is worth.

"He has a job in a lumberyard and he's renting some rooms near Skid Row. He says he wants to see me again. But I thought if I came here, and I talked to the reporters and told them what had happened—how he used to treat me—they might be able to write about it. They might give me a chance to explain everything properly. I thought, once everyone knows how cruel he is, he wouldn't dare to touch me. He couldn't hurt any of us then. People have been so kind to me—the reporters have been so kind. They wouldn't let him hurt me."

"No!" Mae says. "You can't tell the reporters that your first husband is alive. That would mean that your marriage to Paolo wasn't . . . real. It would mean that your children are . . ." Mae can't bring herself to say the word, but it hangs between them still. She draws a steadying breath. "Think about the Stork Derby. Unmarried mothers can't win."

"I don't care about that now!" Lily's voice is savage, her eyes wild. "I don't care about the money. I care about being safe."

Mae catches her hand, holds it between her own. "The money would make you safe." She watches as some of the tension eases from Lily's face, and she hates herself for the flicker of resentment she feels. On the next street, in a hospital bed, her oldest son may be dying.

"What should I do, Mae?" Lily asks. "How can I make him leave me alone?"

"I think," Mae says slowly, "that you mustn't let him come to your house again. You mustn't let him find you alone. If he wants to see you, try to meet him in a tavern. Somewhere busy and noisy, where there will be plenty of people to see you. Tell him you don't want to see him, you don't need him. It will be harder for him to . . . He won't be able to hurt you in front of so many people."

Lily shudders. "I don't think he'll ever let us go." Her expression is haunted. "He always gets what he wants."

31

Lily, late January 1936

Lake Ontario is dark and cold tonight, with a crust of ice at the edges. Lily walks quickly along the road next to the lake, the echo of her footsteps bouncing off the water, so that she keeps looking over her shoulder, breath tight in her chest, to see who is following her.

She has never before been to the bar where she has agreed to meet Tony. It is one of the lakeside taverns, which, before the Crash, would have been a favorite haunt for the rich factory owners and steel magnates. Leonard used to go there, Mae had said, and it was a place that was always busy.

"There will be no chance of you being caught alone with Tony," she'd said. "And it's not one of those back-street dives either—there will be people in the area, so you'll be safe if he tries to follow when you leave."

Mae is right: the surrounding streets are busy. The closer Lily gets to the center of town, and the area that used to be full of fancy bars overlooking the lake, the more people she sees. But they are not the well-dressed people Lily had imagined: women in low-cut dresses lean against cracked walls, their eyes dull as they watch her hurry by. They huddle close together, shivering, until a man walks past. Then they throw their heads back and force a smile. The men ignore them, or shout at them, or grab at them, laughing, whole groups of them sometimes clustered around one woman, jeering and pawing at her before moving on. Only occasionally will a man nod and step closer to the woman, then follow her inside one of the buildings.

A young woman, whose breasts are half bared, calls to Lily, a word she doesn't hear but the meaning is clear. Lily shakes her head. She hasn't a penny on her, or she'd give it gladly, expecting nothing in return. The woman—no more than a girl really—shouts a curse after her, and Lily pauses, wanting to explain that the fancy clothes she is wearing are old ones of Mae's. She wants to tell the girl that she would be glad to give her money, just to get her out of the cold. The girl's bare arms are thin and bruised and there is a bald patch on her scalp where her hair has been ripped out—or perhaps it is a scar.

"What are *you* looking at?" the girl demands. "It costs money to look. You have to pay me or keep walking."

The girl has dark hair and eyes and, although she has no accent, something about her tells Lily that her parents are Italian.

"*Non ti faro del male,*" Lily murmurs. I won't hurt you.

There is a slight softening in the girl's face for a moment, or maybe Lily imagines it. Then her gaze flicks to the people walking nearby, who may have overheard, and her expression hardens. "Don't talk your dago language at me!"

Some of the men nearby look up, their expressions sharp, like dogs on the hunt. Lily mutters an apology to the girl and keeps walking.

Dago. It's a word that comes from America, just across the lake, and she rarely hears it; only Tony used to say it. Still, it stings more than it should—what does it matter what word the girl used when people often look at Lily with eyes that carry the same message? *You're not like me. You don't belong here.* But it does matter. Because the girl had understood her. The girl had recognized something in Lily, then turned away.

As she nears the bar, Lily blinks back tears. She can't worry about the girl or the names she's been called. She has to look for Tony. In her mind, she rehearses the words Mae had told her to say.

Don't make him angry, Mae had advised. *And make sure you stay near other people.* Lily reminds herself to sit close to the bar.

The place is crowded and smoky, the atmosphere thick with chatter and laughter, but Lily sees Tony almost immediately. He is waiting near the door, his expression wary and shuttered, as if he isn't expecting her to come. When he sees her, he lifts his hand, his expression brightening. For a moment, he looks friendly and handsome, and she remembers how he was when they first met. Before he lost his job. Before she lost the babies. Before the beatings began.

But she is wary, waiting for his anger—the anger he must feel, surely, after she left him for dead.

Still, her face returns his smile, even as something inside her flinches, bracing for what is to come.

"Sit," he says. And then, when she hesitates, he says it more forcefully: "Sit."

She sits and he is quiet, his eyes moving over her face, her hair, her clothes. "Still beautiful," he says softly.

She waits. He rarely used to tell her she was beautiful, and she remembers how often his kindness used to be a way of lulling her.

She remembers Mae's warning, to let other people see them, and she glances around the bar, trying to see if anyone is watching. "Thank you," she says carefully, still waiting.

"I know you will expect me to be angry. I felt angry for a long time. You left me for dead. You took my son."

"I'm sorry," she croaks.

"My leg was broken and I had to wait until someone came to free me. It was agony. I still have a limp when I walk and it hurts in the cold."

She watches the muscles in his arms, in his shoulders; she watches his hands and his eyes. Her own body responds just as it used to: if needed, she would be ready to run in an instant. Without directly looking, she tries to gauge whether anyone is listening, whether anyone would be close enough to help her—she wonders whether anyone would even try.

But then she forces herself to breathe. He wouldn't attack her in a bar. Mae was right to tell her to meet him in a place that is so crowded. Her mouth is too dry for speech, but Tony is waiting, his head cocked to one side. He reminds her of the men out in the street, the ones who had looked at both the prostitute and Lily with expectant eyes, like hunting hounds, biding their time.

"I'm sorry," she rasps. "I didn't know you were still . . . I thought you were dead. I was so frightened. I'm sorry."

He holds up a hand. "I was angry. For a long time. But now . . . you are so beautiful."

That word again, and the way his eyes flick over her body, so that she wants to cover herself up.

"I'm sorry," she says again, weakly.

"You married another man." A muscle pulses in his jaw.

"I thought you were dead. I'm sorry, Tony. I am." She keeps saying sorry in the hope that it will placate him— it's an old habit, of begging forgiveness, as if the words can shield her from his fists.

He relaxes slightly and sighs. "I've missed you. And we can forgive each other, I hope." He leans in closer, across the table, and she has to force herself to stay still, not to arch away from him.

She doesn't know how she should respond to this, so she says nothing.

"I know," he drops his voice, "that I was a bad husband. I treated you badly."

Her fingers are tingling. There is a feeling of unreality about everything. She nods, a slight inclination of her head, wary that anything more will set him off.

"I am a different man now. I don't drink often."

She thinks of the alcohol she'd smelled on his breath

at her house, and as if sensing her thoughts, he says, "I needed courage to visit you, so I had two drinks after work. Just two!" He holds up two fingers. "See, I have work now! A good job!" His voice is bright, everything an exclamation.

He calls over the barman, who brings a bottle of whiskey, as if Tony had asked for it—perhaps he did, before Lily arrived. Even though Prohibition is just a memory, bottles of whiskey aren't often sold in bars unless you have money to bribe the barman. He tips a generous measure into a glass and pushes it toward Lily, then pours some for himself.

"And tonight I can have two drinks because I am celebrating finding my wife."

Something in her stomach plummets and she thinks of Paolo, lying dead in the dust storm. Paolo, who had lost his job but never hit her; Paolo, who had been so kind, who had never hurt her, but had looked at her, sometimes, with such sadness, the silence of the secret heavy between them. Perhaps, she thinks, she has caused this somehow. Perhaps something in her causes perfectly good, generous men to change, to become sad or angry, or to lash out at her.

She sips the whiskey. It burns and she squints.

Tony laughs. "The first mouthful is the worst. Try again."

So she does, and he drinks, too, then refills their glasses. A warmth spreads through her. She can't remember when she last ate.

The music blares around them. Her head swims. She drinks.

Tony puts his glass down and takes her hand. "I'm sorry for all my mistakes," he says. "I want to make things better. I want to be a father to the children—to *all* of them," he adds quickly, as she begins to interject.

And then he reaches into his pocket and pulls out three tin soldiers. "For the children," he says. "I've asked the grocer's boy to deliver some vegetables tomorrow too. I don't want the children to be hungry. I can have food delivered to you whenever you need it."

"Thank you," she whispers. And she wonders what he really wants. She can't believe he could have changed so dramatically.

"It hurts me," he says, "to see you so poor. You are thin, Lily. And the children—Matteo was sleeping, but I saw my son. His face was bony. But so grown-up, a man now."

"I didn't know you'd seen him." And she means, *I didn't know you'd recognized him.*

"I think you should talk to him before I meet him. Tell him I'm sorry. I want to be a good father to him. He needs a father. They all do. I can buy them food and clothes. I can look after all of you."

She finds herself nodding, despite the worry that gnaws in her gut, despite the anxious voice that tells her this can't be Tony—this *can't* be real.

Someone drops a glass somewhere, and people cheer.

The whiskey loosens her thoughts slightly, allows her to say, "You said you saw my picture in the newspaper."

"I was so happy!" he says. "I didn't believe it at first. Your beautiful face with all these children and such a strange story, this *Stork Derby*." His face looks almost contemptuous as he says it. "But you don't need to worry about that anymore. I can give the children everything they want. And you. I will look after all of you."

She swallows. He is talking as though it is already decided that they will be a family again, that he will provide for the children. Part of her wants to stand and walk out of the tavern, to run away. "You don't have to look after us," she says quietly.

"I want to!" he says. "The children are hungry. You are hungry. Let me give you food. I want to be a good husband."

His smile is too wide and he is talking too loudly, or perhaps it's the whiskey confusing her, or the noise of the band that has just started playing a slow version of a song from last year about a man dancing with a woman.

Tony sings softly along.

"Heaven. I'm in heaven."

He smiles at her and she can't help smiling in return. He's never sung to her before.

Encouraged by her smile, he places his hands on the table and moves his fingers together in pairs, as if they're dancing. She laughs and he joins in, then takes her hands in his and looks into her eyes. "I want you. I want to be a family. This other man—you talked about him last night—he is gone."

"Paolo." She wants to add, *My husband*, but she can see the muscle pulsing in Tony's jaw again.

"This . . . *Paolo*." Tony stretches out the vowels. "He

317

would want his children to be safe? He would want them to have food?"

She nods, unable to speak.

He squeezes her fingers and brushes the tear from her cheek—she hadn't even realized she was crying.

"Don't cry," he says, and pushes the glass toward her.

She drinks.

The band plays another song.

Tony talks. He refills her glass. She finds herself laughing again, although she doesn't know why.

She drinks.

He strokes her hand. Runs his fingers up her arm. When a man makes a lewd comment, Tony calls, "Be quiet, this is my wife!"

And, for some reason, Lily finds this absurdly funny, although she must begin crying again at some point, because suddenly they are outside and it is cold and Tony is holding her face in his hands and wiping the tears from her cheeks, then kissing them away, his lips gentle and warm.

Afterward she won't be able to recall the walk to Tony's rooms, except occasional flashes of moments when she stumbled and he grabbed her arm and steadied her. She won't be able to remember how they came to be standing in an alleyway, kissing, with her back pressed against the wall, although she will recall the thought she has, in that moment, of the thin-faced, dark-haired prostitute with the bruised arms and the haunted, hunted look in her eyes. Lily won't recall how they reached Tony's rooms, although she will remember the way he shushed her, whispering that the landlady didn't like him to bring back lady guests. She will remember thinking, Oh, and feeling a strange spiral of jealousy. And then she will think of Mae, and Mae's warmth, and how kissing her had felt as easy as breathing fresh air after years of being underwater. She will remember that Tony's stubble scratched her face.

She won't recollect the door to his room or how they came to be lying on the bed. She will remember the sensation of the bed under her—the softness of it. She will think of her children at home, sleeping on the hard, worn mattress and the pile of blankets.

She won't remember agreeing to let Tony take off her stockings and hitch up her skirts, won't remember allowing it, though she won't remember protesting either—and surely if she'd protested she would have remembered. She is almost sure.

She will remember the inevitability of it. Like the moment when a swung pendulum begins its return, or the moment when a dropped glass, although it is still whole as it falls through the air, is doomed to shatter and, once broken, is impossible to repair.

32

Mae, February 1936

"I've lit the stove for you, Robert," Mae calls, then listens to him lurching to his feet and walking unsteadily into the kitchen. He stops often to lean against the wall and his face has a grayish, mushroomy pallor. But the doctor has told her she mustn't help him to walk all the time: she must allow him to try, to fail and to fall. His face and limbs are covered with bruises, but he gives a lopsided smile when he sees the glowing stove and the chair pulled up close to it.

She scavenges wood where she can, going out early each morning to collect fallen branches from around the trees near the lake. It burns quickly, but at least, while it's lit, Robert is quiet and smiling.

When she first brought him back from the hospital, she had been hopeful, as had the doctors: the tumor had been smaller than they'd expected, and although his speech was a little slurred and his balance was off, they were optimistic about him recovering. Mae had felt briefly as though the world was bathed in light: everything had been worthwhile, and everything would be well.

Three weeks after the operation, Robert was able to walk around the house by himself, feed himself and hold a halting conversation. She kept waiting for him to say something harshly funny. Two weeks later he was talking to her all day, following her from room to room, chattering nonstop. He'd never been much of a talker, and certainly never to her. His speech was strange and he fixated on odd things, often repeating himself, but still, he was obviously better than he had been. Even Leonard, who had been silently furious when he first knew that Mae had taken Robert in for his operation, seemed to have forgiven her. Mae felt that this recovery should be properly celebrated.

Knowing she shouldn't waste money, she had nevertheless sold a skirt that had been expensive new but was too big for her now and, leaving Leonard at home, had taken the children to the movie theater to see *Top Hat*. The show was last year's, so the tickets were cheap, but they all sat perfectly still, entranced. She looked down the row of seats at their lit-up faces. They were all smiling, apart from Robert, who was sleeping, but that didn't matter: nothing else mattered because this moment was perfect.

Heaven, sang the actor, Fred Astaire. *I'm in heaven.*

Mae hummed the tune as she walked from the theater, her arm across Robert's shoulders.

They had been halfway home from the movie theater, the children dancing and singing their way through the crowds of shabby-coated men while Robert shambled next to Mae, his arm through hers, still talking about the movie—though he'd dozed on and off, barely seen any of it—and talking about the men on the street and what they were wearing, and the noise of the streetcar that had just roared past. His chatter didn't stop, and the pace of his speech was growing faster, Mae realized, more frantic. For the first time, she worried that this might not be recovery. She let herself understand that this felt like something else.

She stopped in the street, calling to the other children to wait. "Are you all right, Robert?"

But his gaze wasn't on her: it followed some man behind her. She glanced back to see him—a stranger wearing expensive clothes, with a woman on his arm, who was equally well-dressed.

"Look at the pretty lady," Robert called, the words of a young child but in his nearly-man's bass voice.

"Come here, pretty lady," Robert said, while Mae tried to shush him. The older children covered their mouths with their hands; the younger ones giggled.

"Robert's silly," said Jane, who was seven.

And then Robert had leaned forward and grabbed the woman's sleeve.

Before Mae could reach out or cry out or pull Robert away, the man had swung around and punched him in the face. Robert fell to the ground, smacking his head against the cobbles. The children screamed and Mae screamed, too, trying to lift Robert up, stroking his face as he blinked in confusion.

"Control your brats," the man snarled, then took the

woman's arm and marched away, calling that the city was full of *thieves and vagrants*.

Robert's head was bleeding and he stared at Mae and his sisters as though he didn't recognize them. She, Betsy, and Sarah helped him to his feet, while Alfred and Peter held the younger children back and calmed them. Robert walked home between them, without saying a word, blood dripping down his face onto his shirt.

In the weeks that followed, his behavior continued to change. He rarely spoke, unless it was about the man who had punched him: Robert threatened to track him down, to kill him. Gone was the sweet boy who chattered and helped her to hang the laundry. Robert was moody and aggressive with all of them, even with his father. Leonard was barely speaking to Mae as it was, but this cemented them into silence.

And then the fits started again. Night after night, they were roused from sleep by Robert's whole body shaking, by him falling from his bed or hitting his head. In desperation, Mae went to the hospital to see the doctor; he listened to her account of events, and shook his head gravely. "I'm afraid that a blow to the head, so soon after the trauma of the operation, may well have damaged his brain further, slowing his recovery. And now the fits will be worsening the situation, making his brain deteriorate more."

"So . . . he'll always be like this? Is there nothing to be done?"

"Well, there's phenobarbital, but it's not cheap."

"I'll take it," Mae had said. She signed more papers, putting her name to more bills she couldn't pay.

Now she lies awake, every night, waiting for Robert to fit. The medication makes him sleepy, but at least he is no longer aggressive. She buys more, on credit, signing away a future she can't imagine anyway. She doesn't know what she will do if she doesn't win the Stork Derby money— she will never be able to repay the doctor. She's gambling, she knows. Perhaps he's gambling too. Perhaps he has a sickly wife at home, or a sickly child, and even he can't pay the bills, and he's taking whatever chances he can.

Mae doesn't ask. Other people's worries don't matter. Only Robert matters.

One morning she is woken by a repeated tapping. She jumps out of bed and pads into Robert's room, ready to hold him while he shakes, ready to feed him another pill. But his room is dark and quiet, apart from the steady sound of his breathing. Mae goes into the other room, where all the other children have taken to sleeping since Robert's fits started—it terrifies them to wake and find him shaking on the floor, or that his face is a mask of blood because he is chewing his own tongue.

They are sprawled together on the floor, her younger children, and, in the dim light, she can't make out one child from another, but none of them is knocking or tapping. David and Donald, ages four and five, are sucking their thumbs, and Annette, who is just two, is frowning in her sleep and snoring softly, but there is no other noise from the children.

Mae listens again: the sound is coming from downstairs.

She rushes down and opens the door.

"Lily!" Mae says, feeling a wrench of remorse—caught up in everything with Robert, she has barely thought about Lily. She had seen her only once, the day after her evening with Tony.

Lily had said that Tony wasn't as she remembered him, that he had been kind and considerate.

"Are you sure?" Mae had asked. "Is he . . . safe? Was he really kind to you?"

"I"—Lily had blushed—"I drank a little too much, so I don't remember everything." Then her face had brightened. "He gave me some candy for the children, and he dropped in a parcel of fruit this morning. *Oranges*, Mae. You should have seen their faces. And he says he's going to bring a parcel of meat and vegetables every evening."

"And he won't hurt you?"

"The children are *full*, Mae. They're not hungry. They're sleeping. Earlier, I heard them laugh."

Mae had taken her hands, which were cold. "Are you sure this is what you want?"

"What choice do I have?"

"You have a choice! Of course you do."

"No," Lily had said sadly. "I don't have the same choices as you. You own this house. Your children aren't starving. People don't refuse to serve you because your accent is wrong."

Mae's stomach had twisted. Was Lily right? Was her life really so much harder, all the time? It was impossible to imagine how she lived like that.

"I'm sorry," Mae had said.

"No," Lily had said. "I'm sorry. I shouldn't have snapped." She'd reached out and laced her fingers through Mae's, then stroked Mae's forefinger with her thumb. "I know you're worried."

"Please don't let him hurt you."

"Does it really matter, as long as the children are happy?"

But now Lily is standing on her doorstep, her face pale, her mouth tense as if she's holding back tears.

"I'm pregnant."

Mae swallows an acidic taste, crushing the image of Lily in a man's arms, Lily with her head thrown back, Lily kissing him, beneath him.

"Congratulations," she manages.

But Lily is trembling, Mae realizes. "What's wrong?"

Without saying a word, Lily pulls back her sleeve to show long, ugly brown marks, which Mae takes at first for dirt, but then sees, with horror, are bruises. She gasps and gathers Lily into her arms. "Oh, God."

Lily's words are muffled by Mae's shoulder and Mae can feel her shaking.

"Yesterday, he said I was rude to him. He grabbed me and—" She breaks down into silent sobs.

"Oh, love." Mae holds her close, trembling herself

now. Lily's body feels so small, so fragile. "Oh, love," she says. "You can't stay with him. Can't you make him leave?"

"I'm so tired of not knowing what to do, Mae. Everything feels wrong. I can't leave him, but he's going to keep hitting me. What if I lose the baby?"

"Hush." Mae strokes her hair. "You're not going to lose it." She holds Lily close and says, "You can come here to stay. Until it's born. The children too."

Lily shakes her head. "You don't have room. And what about Leonard?"

"I'll make room. And I'll talk to Leonard." Mae is sure Leonard wouldn't let Lily into the house, but she can't stand the thought of Lily going back to that monster.

"Leonard wouldn't let me live here," Lily says. "Have you told him you've seen me again?"

Mae swallows and shakes her head. It's an admission of guilt. An admission of all that she feels for Lily.

Lily shakes her head. "Even if Leonard would let me stay, Tony won't let me leave," she says. "He'd be so angry. He'd find us and he'd . . . I don't know what he'd do to me."

"Then we'll call the police."

Lily looks at her with an expression Mae has never seen. "And what would *they* do? They don't care about us."

Mae thinks back to Robert being punched in the street, thinks about the policeman who'd walked past without stopping. And she realizes that Lily is right. People without money matter less, somehow.

After Lily has gone, with a promise to return the next

day to tell Mae what has happened, and assuring Mae that she will bring the children to her if she becomes scared, Mae stands in the kitchen, shaking. Outside, the noise goes on just as before: the wind buffets the old windows. The house creaks. A spill of sunlight gilds the rain-wet cobbles for a moment, before the clouds gather again.

She needs that Stork Derby money. Lily needs it too. If Lily had the money, she could leave Tony. She would be safe, her children would be safe.

But Mae needs every penny for Robert. *"Oh, God,"* she whispers. Upstairs, her child may be dying. Upstairs, her other children are hungry, are scared. Mae herself is hungry and scared and tired.

And, at this moment, Lily is walking across the city, back to a man who will hurt her. She will stay with him to keep her children safe. She will let him break her body to keep her children from starving.

Mae puts her face into her hands. She counts to ten. She wipes the tears from her cheeks with her palms.

Mae hears Lily's words, as if they are her own thoughts: *What choice do I have?*

Neither of them has a choice. It is as if everything they do has been set out long ago, laid down in the laws of this country, by the hands of the men who built the statues and wrote the rules and made the histories. They are all in the grip of an enormous wave, which is nothing to do with their choices. All their choices end in the same way. All they can do is hold on and hope to survive.

33

Courtroom 2B, 1937

By the time Lily finishes describing Sebastian's death, she is shaking, acid in her mouth. Outside, rain hammers on the courtroom roof. In Lily's mind, the drumming turns into the repetitive thrumming of her child's faltering heart. The wails of the wind sound like his fading cries and she cannot *stand* the way that the ghouls in the gallery are gazing at her in horrified dread—as if watching her pain makes their own lives seem somehow more bearable.

She's filled with a hot, shapeless fury. She wants to shake each and every one of these people. She wants to howl her rage at the smug lawyer, at the judge, who glances at the courtroom clock and yawns.

The lawyer clears his throat. "You look . . . *angry*, Mrs. di Marco."

"I'm not angry," she whispers. Her throat hurts with the effort of speaking quietly.

"Do we need to call a recess for you to compose yourself?"

She looks down and sees that her hands are clenched into fists in her lap, and that her nails have dug into her palms, that she has scratched her wrists. Bloodstains bloom on her sleeves.

"No," she says. Then, more loudly, "No."

"These will be my very *final* questions, I promise." He smiles, as though sharing a joke, and she vaguely recalls that he has made this promise twice before, although she can't understand why she is supposed to find this amusing.

"I must ask more," says the lawyer, "about the *fathers* of your children."

Lily waits. She is too angry to be agreeable now. If he wants her to answer him, then he should ask a question.

He shifts uncomfortably under her flat gaze, and from the corner of her eye, Lily sees a man in the gallery whisper something to the fellow sitting next to him. One snorts with laughter, the sound echoing off the wood-paneled walls.

I don't care, she thinks. She bites the inside of her cheek. If she opens her mouth, she will scream.

"We've discussed," the lawyer says, "that your children have *multiple* fathers."

She swallows. "Two."

Yesterday, when Lily had first been called to the stand, Tony had snapped at the lawyer twice, telling him to use a more respectful tone to a lady, saying he was just trying to blacken an Italian woman's good name. It was when he warned the lawyer, quite clearly, that he'd better steer clear of dark alleyways that the judge had asked for Tony to be removed from court or he would be charged with contempt.

At the time, Lily's face had burned and she'd wondered what effect Tony's behavior would have on the judge's decision, but now, with the lawyer asking her about Paolo, she is glad Tony is at home so she doesn't have to talk about Paolo in front of him—doesn't have to explain herself, yet again, seeing the skepticism on his face, the rage behind his eyes.

"So, some of your children are illegitimate," the lawyer says.

"No!" She's been through this already, but she forces herself to speak calmly. "I believed my first husband to be dead when I came to Toronto. I married again, but my second husband died. Then I discovered my first husband had survived the earthquake after all. We had two more children."

"A *history* of dead husbands, then," the lawyer says with a sly smile, and there is low laughter from the gallery. "Forgive me," he says in the casual, smirking way that men ask for forgiveness when they don't believe they've done anything wrong.

"And we've discussed," he continues, "that the law considers the children from your second marriage illegitimate since your first husband was still alive?"

"No," Lily repeats sharply. "I was *married* to Paolo. I thought Tony was dead."

"But he was alive. Without you knowing, which is strange in itself."

Lily's mouth is dry. "I *told* you—I left Chatsworth after the earthquake. I truly thought he couldn't have survived. I was scared. I wanted to keep my son safe."

"Ah! So you *abandoned* your husband, leaving him for dead?"

The hairs rise on the back of Lily's neck. Does he know, or sense, somehow, what she did to Tony? Lily tries to think if she'd ever mentioned the beam to Mae. She doesn't think so, but there is a sharpness in the lawyer's gaze.

"You must have been grieving?"

"I *was* grieving," Lily says through gritted teeth.

"Yet you remarried. And your second '*husband*'—how long was he dead before you returned to your first husband?"

Lily can't answer. There's a pressure in her chest.

Paolo, she thinks, and the grief is like a rockfall. She knows this lawyer will never understand—that no one will ever understand why she allowed Tony to return so easily. To make someone understand, she would have to starve them, then give them nine famished children to look after. She would have to place them in a dangerous neighborhood, where everyone is poor and desperate, and where the houses are infested with vermin. She would have to remove every last scrap of hope from their lives, and then she would have to offer them the faintest chance of survival, in the form of a man who might well hurt them, might well beat them, but probably won't kill them.

"How long?" the lawyer asks again.

"One month," Lily whispers, and she flinches at the intake of breath from around the court. The other Stork Derby mothers shake their heads in disapproval and Mae stares down at her skirt.

"One month," the lawyer says, "and you expect us to consider that your second marriage was valid? In the eyes of the law, it is invalid in any case, but one *month* gives you scant ground for arguing that you were truly grieving a lost husband."

"I was—"

"Is it possible, perhaps, that you were pursuing the Stork Derby money and you needed a man to get you with child? Might that also explain why you married your second 'husband' so eagerly?" In the front row, the religious Mrs. Timmins is nodding with fervor, as if she is listening to an enthusiastic preacher.

"And," the lawyer continues, "might that explain why you so willingly returned to your first husband? Because you viewed these *liaisons* as a means of accessing money?"

How can she answer that? How can this man, this rich, smug man, ever comprehend what it means to do something wrong "willingly?" How can he ever understand that *willingly* is a word that comes with money and that, for some people, choice has a price attached?

"I would suggest," says the lawyer, "that your motives are rather less pure than you would have us imagine. I would suggest to the court that *wife* and *mother* have been easy labels for you to implement in order to get what you want."

And he believes this, she sees. He believes that she is less than him. Because she is a woman, and because she is poor, and because she is foreign, she cannot possibly have the same feelings or longings that any other person has. She cannot be motivated by love. In his mind, she must be driven by need, by greed, by want.

"No," she whispers. Her head throbs.

"So you were able to leave your husband, declare him dead, then marry again, while living a life of luxury in

Mrs. Thébault's house. Then, when you needed to have more children in order to win Mr. Millar's fortune, you welcomed your first husband back."

"No!" she gasps again, but it is as if she is underwater, as if no one can hear the word bubbling from her lips.

The lawyer waves his papers at her. "Admit it: you've gone from one man to another, doing whatever suited you at the time, manipulating your way into getting other people's money."

"I didn't!" Lily is standing now, although she doesn't remember getting to her feet.

"Sit down."

"No. I want to speak to the judge in private." If only, she thinks, she can talk to the judge alone, without the lawyer's awful repeated questions, then she will be able to make him see that none of this is true.

"Sit down."

"I will not sit down! I want a recess. I want to be able to talk to the judge." Her voice is trembling, but she stands tall, gripping her skirt, refusing to drop her gaze. She can feel the eyes of the court on her, can feel their mixture of excitement and disgust as they whisper to one another.

The lawyer points the papers at her. "You can't speak to the judge in private. You can sit down and answer the questions, like all the other mothers."

"I won't! I won't answer any more of your questions. You keep asking the same thing and you're wrong. You're wrong!" Rage surges through Lily, driving her down from her platform and toward the lawyer, who falters and takes a step back—almost, she thinks, as if he is afraid of her. She feels a swell of triumph as she snatches the papers from his hands and rips them in half, letting the pieces fall to the courtroom floor.

The next moments are a blur. Around her, men leap to their feet, shouting. The lawyer's face is a frozen rictus of shock, and for a moment, before the whistle blows, before the court guards surge forward to grab her hands and pin them behind her back, before she falls to her knees and cries out in pain, Lily understands the rage that causes people to strike out. She has a glimpse of the hot anger that would enable her to rip into a man's skin to save herself, to save her children.

The court guards are strong and rough, their breath hot against her neck as they press her cheek into the cold wooden floor.

From somewhere, far away, she hears a man's voice— the lawyer's? It's hard to tell—shout that she should be locked up for this.

The courtroom falls silent and she hears the judge sigh heavily. "Send her home. No purpose in paying for her to sit in a cell overnight."

But she can hear the contempt in his voice and she knows that there is no chance now that he will believe anything she says. There is no chance that he will give her the money. She will have to go home to Tony. She will have to continue counting out the days of her life, feeling the chill of death's shadow every time he glares at her, every time he raises his fist.

In that moment, she knows it is hopeless. All this has been for nothing. She is lost.

34

Lily, September 1936

The twins are born in the early hours of one September morning, when it is still dark. It is too soon for them to arrive, but the labor won't be stopped. The contractions start just after midnight, and within two hours, Lily knows she needs help: the urge to push rips through her, but the babies aren't coming.

The children are still asleep, but Tony runs to fetch the midwife. When he can't find her, he comes back and waits outside the front door. Lily tries to labor quietly, but she's terrified because Tony is so close. His rage is like a constant storm on the horizon. Most of the time, he doesn't even need to hit her, doesn't need to hurt her. The slightest change in his tone or expression is enough to make her cringe. Her contractions slow and almost stop. She can hear him pacing outside, hear him clearing his throat. She can hear him drumming his fingers on the thin wood of the door, and each sound makes her insides curdle. But how can she tell Tony to step away from the tiny house, without him becoming angry and refusing to leave?

Increasingly, as Lily has become bigger, he has been

turning his rage on Matteo. Tony might bruise Lily's arms; he might, if he is really furious, deliver a swift, downward blow to her thigh. But he never truly hits her and he never touches her abdomen. Instead, he strikes Matteo. Sometimes, it is a casual backhand across the face, but more often it's a full-fisted punch to the stomach or chest. Lily never sees this happen. Instead, Tony will say to Matteo, "Let's walk."

When Matteo refuses, Tony's eyes will widen and he'll say, more slowly, "Let's walk, son."

Lily tries to stop him, but he brushes her off. If she shouts at Tony, or protests, then Tony hits him harder. When her son returns, he is often hunched over, but he always puts his arms around Lily and whispers, "It wasn't so bad today. Truly." Then he goes and rinses his face at the outdoor pump so she won't have to see the amount of blood in the bucket.

She knows it's selfish to want her son to stay. She tells him to leave often, but every time he shakes his head, she feels a wash of relief. Her mind scrabbles constantly for a way for them to escape. She can't force Matteo to go: he would refuse and Tony would punish her—or, worse, find Matteo and hurt him. She can't afford to feed the children properly without the money Tony provides. And she can't leave with the children. How can she take them away from food and shelter, into the streets, to be tracked down and brought back by Tony?

He doesn't mention the Stork Derby often, but she knows he must be thinking of it, when he says things like *When we have more money*, or *When we have a bigger house*, and *When I don't have to work all the time*.

Throughout this pregnancy, he has laid his head on her stomach every night—sometimes when her arms are still stinging with fresh bruises—and he has talked to the babies, saying, *Your papa can't wait to see you. You will make your papa so happy.*

Lily has stared at the handprints on her skin and tried to fight her nausea.

It has been hours and still the babies aren't coming. Her contractions have slowed and weakened even more—the pain is intense but nothing changes or shifts. She remembers Matteo's dead twin sister. Lily had always wondered if it was the long labor that had killed her: would she have lived, if only she'd been delivered sooner?

"Matteo," Lily calls softly. He is awake and up instantly; she can see his shadow moving behind the curtain around the bed. She dabs at her forehead with the blankets and tries to hide the sweat stains across her chest and under her arms.

He peeps around the curtain but keeps his eyes averted. "Mama?"

"The babies are stuck, I think," she gasps, trying to keep her voice calm and level, trying to hide her pain.

His eyes widen and, for a moment, she sees the terror of losing her on his face.

"Nothing's going to hurt me," she says through gritted teeth. "But I need you to send your father to look for the midwife again."

He hesitates. She sees his face tighten. Then he nods. "Okay, Mama."

She can feel another contraction rising. Soon she won't be able to talk, and seeing her in pain will frighten him. Quickly she says, "I'll be fine, my love. Watch your brothers and sisters. Perhaps take them outside, so they don't hear . . ."

He nods, brushes his lips over her forehead.

She hears his voice outside, pitched lower than usual, to hide his fear. She hears Tony's gruff response and then his footsteps receding.

She hears Matteo waking the other children, taking them outside, his voice warm and level.

She draws deep breaths. The next contraction is stronger. The next one stronger still. They build like waves, like a river current, sweeping her along.

By the time the midwife arrives, Lily is halfway through birthing the second baby. The first, a boy, had cried as soon as he was born.

The second baby is another boy. He doesn't breathe. The midwife clears his mouth and turns him on his front. The baby spits up a mouthful of fluid, hiccups, and cries.

Tony comes in, his face bright. He kisses her cheek, her hair, her mouth. "Nine babies," he says. "We have *nine babies*." And he kisses her again.

"Twelve," she whispers, thinking of her other children, the ones no one else seems to remember or speak of.

Tony watches her expression and says, "We have nine *living* children and eleven children who matter."

"Matteo matters."

"Not for that man's money he doesn't. Oh, don't look like *that*, woman. The boy *matters*. You can hardly forget he's there, with his smart mouth and his insolent face."

Through the gap in the curtain, Lily sees Matteo pushing the door open. She hears him kicking the wall as he walks past. Part of her is terrified that he won't come back, but the other part of her knows, with a sense of dread, that he will always return, no matter the risk.

For the next week, Tony is loud and boisterous, radiating raucous contentment. He laughs and struts as he shows off the babies to reporters. He holds them up proudly, a twin cradled in each arm and the other children clustered around him—at a wary distance, beyond the reach of his fists out of habit, even though he couldn't possibly hurt them with all the reporters watching and while holding the twins.

But after a week of sleepless nights and drawn-out days of repeated crying from the babies and whining from the younger children and sulkiness from the older ones, including Matteo, Tony snaps. It is the middle of the night, but he smashes the chair against the stove and threatens to beat them all. Then he kicks out the front door so that it dangles from its hinges and he marches off into the cold darkness, leaving them cowering in a room open to the elements.

The next morning, before it is fully light, Lily leaves the children with Mrs. Palumbi—apart from the youngest twins, whom she ties in a fabric sling—and she goes to see Mae. Mae who had continued to visit Lily through-out her pregnancy, and as her own stomach swelled. Mae who says, time and again, *I wish I could help you leave*, but never criticizes Lily for staying.

Mae's youngest child had been born just last month—a thin, sickly girl who will barely suckle and seems to grow scrawnier by the day, but it has delighted Lily to hold her warm little body against her chest, watching the relief on Mae's face that someone else is taking the burden, if only for a moment.

"At first I didn't realize I was pregnant again," Mae had admitted to Lily, when the baby was born too early and too small. "I was barely eating and I thought I was tired be-cause of . . ." And she'd indicated with her hand, a gesture that took in the house, the children, Robert, Leonard.

Tony doesn't like Lily going to see Mae. He thinks she's a snob, and Lily should stay in the house with the children. Or, he says, she can talk to the other women on the street when she's at the water pump. Isn't that enough?

And Lily does talk to them: about the weather, the price of food, the children. But she doesn't speak about Tony, about how she longs to leave him. What would they be able to tell her? They have unemployed hus-bands, too, and more children than they can feed. They have had dead babies and have been beaten by men and spat at in the street by strangers who don't like the sight of their poverty. They will understand Lily's despair, be-cause it is like their own. They will expect her to endure it, because they, too, have no choice.

But Mae? Mae will listen to Lily with horror. Her eyes

will harden with fury when she sees the bruises on Lily's arms or when she hears her talking about what a brute Tony is with the children. Lily doesn't need someone to understand her pain, to know it as their own: she needs someone to be angry on her behalf, because she is too tired to feel rage.

When she opens the door, Mae looks weary, but she coos over the twins, both fast asleep in the sling.

Mae's own children are upstairs and Lily can hear them running around. Leonard is in the small sitting room. When Lily peeps around the door, she thinks he is sleeping until she sees that his eyes are open, but he is sitting absolutely still, staring at the wall. She can hardly believe that this shrunken, dull-faced stranger is Mae's rich, confident, handsome husband. It doesn't seem possible.

"He's been trying to get a job," Mae murmurs, "to pay the bills for Robert. But no one will have him. Sometimes he sits there all day, without saying a word." And she shrugs. "The children try to stay away from him."

Lily wonders if her life would be easier if her children had an upstairs to escape to from Tony. No, she decides. He'd just follow them, a splintered chair leg in one hand.

There are lines at the corners of Mae's eyes and around her mouth. Lily's never noticed them before, or perhaps they are new, like the streaks of gray in Mae's blond hair. Still, she's so beautiful—and it's not her skin or hair or eyes. It's something within her as she scrubs the work surface, pausing occasionally to brush her hair back from her face. Lily feels a rush of tenderness and she rests a hand lightly on Mae's back.

Mae stops scrubbing for a moment and leans backward slightly, so that some of her weight is resting on Lily's hand. Lily can feel the outline of her spine, the delicate cage of her ribs, and, inside it, her heart's flutter.

In the sling, one of the twins shifts and gives a little cry. Mae swallows and begins to scrub again and Lily lets her hand fall back to her side.

"I saw the pictures in the paper yesterday," Mae says, a new tension in her voice. "You're in the lead for the Stork Derby now. Nine living children and . . . your other two."

"I haven't thought about it," Lily lies. Because she thinks about it so much. At night, she lies awake, imagining the freedom that money would bring.

Mae looks at her sharply. "You know the other mothers all have lawyers."

"And you," Lily says softly. "You have a lawyer."

Mae gives a tight nod. She doesn't meet Lily's eyes.

"Well," Lily says, "I can't afford a lawyer. I don't know how these other women are managing it."

"I think some of the lawyers are working for free, hoping to get the money afterward."

"And what will they do if they don't win?"

Mae pauses, then continues scrubbing the side, her back to Lily. "What does Tony plan for the money?"

Lily picks up a cloth, begins to help by wiping up after Mae has scrubbed. "It won't be Tony's money. It will be mine." She tries to imagine it: enough money to buy a house with a walled garden and an iron gate and an oak door too heavy to be kicked from its hinges. Enough money to pay a man to stand outside the locked gate and tell Tony that he can't touch her, can't touch the children.

Mae stops scrubbing and stares at Lily. "Do you really believe he won't take it, if you win?"

"It's what the will says. The money goes to the mother."

They work in silence.

"Do you . . ." Mae hesitates. ". . . do you ever think how strange it is, being paid to have children?"

"I'd have had the children anyway," Lily says quickly, before she can allow herself to think of how keen Tony was on her becoming pregnant, on how she hadn't wanted it, but then hadn't had a choice.

"I think that too," Mae says. "But when I found I was pregnant, I was so happy and I think—I think it was because of the money. And there must be other women who are desperate for money so they've had babies, but not enough to win. And the women who have babies but don't want them, not really, but then they're stuck with this . . ." She gestures with the cloth.

"Cleaning?"

"Cooking and cleaning and feeding and everything. I was scrubbing the floor last week and I felt as though I could see myself from the outside and—I didn't know who I was. I felt like everything that was me was . . . *separate*, somehow. I'm not making any sense, am I?" Mae says. She sounds exhausted, and she holds Lily's gaze, then looks away.

But Lily knows what she means. She's had the same feeling sometimes. That her desires and hopes are somehow outside her own body, and that her body doesn't belong to her. Her body belongs to Tony and it belongs to her children and it belongs to the journalists and the dead lawyer and the people who are betting on the outcome, cheering and cursing the women as if they are horses flagging at the end of a long race.

There's a silence as they both rinse the cloths in the bucket. Their heads bump as they lean forward; they smile and apologize. But there's a stirring unease in Lily's chest. Mae is right about Tony: he won't let her have the money. He's already building up debt at the tavern and has bought some new shoes and a suit on credit.

Mae drops her cloth, pushes the hair from her forehead. "I think you should talk to my lawyer."

"I can't afford—"

"I can. I've been pawning clothes and jewelry for months. The lawyer will work on credit until the winnings come through."

"You don't need to do that for me."

Mae turns to her. "I do. I know you *think* you won't need a lawyer, but everyone else will have one. What if they fight for the money to be split, somehow, and you don't have anyone to speak for you? If you talk to my lawyer, I can pay him, but he can argue for both of us. Please, Lily. Please let me do this for you. I want to make up for . . . hurting you."

Lily pauses. This is the closest Mae has come to talking about everything that happened six years ago. Her eyes are wide and honest. Lily feels the faintest flicker of hope.

"All right," she says. "I'll talk to your lawyer."

35

The day after she is thrown from the court, Lily arrives early, planning to plead to be allowed back in. She will apologize; she will beg the judge's forgiveness. But when she arrives, the doors are unlocked; the journalists and photographers are waiting for her.

"How're you feeling today, Mrs. di Marco?"

"Are you still angry with your lawyer?"

"Do you plan to confront him again?"

She stops before the courtroom doors, but the journalists push her forward.

"Don't you worry about staying outside," one of the photographers says. "You go right on in. Our editor knows the judge. But don't let that stop you giving your lawyer hell." He winks at her and the other journalists laugh.

Lily attempts to smile, her thoughts fuzzy. All this time, she'd hoped that the journalists were on her side, that people were rooting for her to win. But now she sees that it doesn't matter to these men who wins. They only want the best story.

"Can we have a quote from you?" one says.

She stares at him. "I don't think so. I don't have anything to say to you people."

Around her, the camera bulbs burst and shatter. She turns away.

She pauses in the doorway, aware that this morning will decide the rest of her life. She can't imagine the outcome without feeling that she is going to vomit. It is as if she is waiting in front of an executioner. Blindfolded and baffled, she has no idea when the blade will fall or if the blow will miss her entirely.

She can't let herself imagine Tony's reaction if she doesn't win. Every time she has tried to picture it, she can conjure only a dull blank. And yet she can't imagine being rich either—her dreams of being free of him have faded. What does it mean, that she can't conceive of a future? Is it a premonition? She has never been superstitious before, but now everything seems portentous: the expression on the judge's face, the whispers from the gallery, the hopeful smiles from the other Stork Derby parents—everything is a sign and none of them is good.

A broad-chested court officer catches Lily's eye. She can see him remembering the previous day, wondering if she is allowed in. He looks across to one of the other officers, a red-faced man, who scowls, then points for Lily to go and sit with the other Stork Derby mothers and fathers, along with their lawyers.

Mae sits apart, alone. Leonard hasn't come to court at all, and she looks small, vulnerable, and lonely.

Lily can't bring herself to go near her.

Mae had watched Lily being ripped apart by her lawyer and hadn't said a word, hadn't even attempted to contradict him or to tell him to leave Lily alone. Had this been Mae's plan from the beginning? To draw Lily close, persuade her to tell all of her secrets, then allow the lawyer to use them to make Lily seem immoral and undeserving?

Lily, who has the most children. Without her, Mae and the other mothers are tied for the lead.

"Sit, Mrs. di Marco," the judge says, indicating the seat next to Mae.

Lily stays standing, aware that every eye is on her, aware that the journalists are scribbling, aware that Mae herself is looking at Lily pleadingly, mouthing, "I'm sorry," and then, more audibly, "I'm sorry, Lily."

"The hell you are," Lily snarls. It's not an expression she's used before and it's satisfying to sound like someone else—like an angry man in the street. It makes her feel strong. It allows her to ignore her dry mouth, her shaking legs, her nausea.

The judge rubs his forehead and sighs impatiently. "Mrs. di Marco, please sit down."

"I'm not sitting near that woman."

"You'll sit where you're told or you'll leave my court."

Mae moves across so there is more room on the bench. Eyeing her balefully, Lily sits as far away from her as possible.

It is hard to gather breath in her lungs. When she left the children this morning, they all looked hopeful. Hopeful and thin. She promised to bring home candy for them. How can she afford candy if she doesn't win? It's a foolish worry, but Lily's thoughts snag on it again and again: she imagines the children's disappointment.

It is easier than imagining Tony's rage.

In front of them is the lawyer, with his oiled hair and his silk tie and his expensive shirt. He turns and gives Mae a quick, reassuring grin. She remains blank-faced, but it's enough to make Lily wish for the strength to stand up and leave.

On the other side of the court, the rest of the Stork Derby mothers are whispering to one another excitedly—even religious Mrs. Timmins looks bright-eyed as she waits for the verdict. They all have nine children who can be counted. Lily doesn't know if her children *count* anymore. It's an awful thought that, as far as this court is concerned, some of her children might not be valid, might not be recognized, might as well not exist.

The judge tells everyone to stand. Lily wishes, suddenly, that she hadn't come. There is no hiding from the truth anymore. She can't pretend to be hopeful. Now, at this final moment, she can allow herself to wish that she'd done it all differently, that she'd never come to this court, that she'd never spoken to the journalists, that she'd never heard of the Stork Derby. She can allow herself to acknowledge that this has all been for nothing.

She knows the outcome, knows what it must be. It was decided the moment Tony returned into her life. Or perhaps it was decided the moment she met Mae. Or perhaps it was decided long before that, before she had the power to make decisions, years ago, when her parents sailed across oceans to live in a country where everyone would look at them as something other than people.

Mae tries to take her hand, but Lily shakes her off.

The judge clears his throat. "This is the strangest case I've ever presided over. It's been called an unedifying shambles and a racket, and I'm inclined to agree. A disgusting display. Listening to how women have been breeding like rabbits to make money. Well, it's shameful. The last thing this country needs is more children living on our streets."

All the Stork Derby mothers look chastened. Mrs. Timmins glares, but none of the women protest—they know their voices wouldn't be heeded.

It wasn't to make money, Lily wants to tell him. *I love my children.*

And she wishes, in that moment, to be a man. If she were a man, she would be in charge of her own body. She would have a voice that could be heard. She would be able to act on her desires without being called *disgusting*. She would belong to herself, and she wouldn't be sitting in a court, waiting for a stranger to pass judgment upon her simply for having *too many* children.

She draws a shuddering breath.

"Still," the judge continues, as the families shift uncomfortably, "I suspect a great deal of the money has been promised to your lawyers. And, as you'll all have bills to pay, I suppose I should move on to the verdict."

The families sit up. Mae holds her breath. Lily feels a chill creep into her fingers. She knows what to expect, yet she can't help hoping.

Her heartbeat thrums in her ears.

"The money," says the judge, "is to be divided between four families, who will each receive one hundred and ten thousand dollars."

It's an impossible amount, an unimaginable sum. Lily, too, is holding her breath now. But the judge had said *four* of the families, and there are five sitting here.

"A remaining payment of ten thousand dollars is to be made to one family that I consider was the unfortunate victim of a misfiling of registration paperwork."

Lily's heart lifts. They must have found Ana's missing paperwork, Sebastian's too. She closes her eyes, imagining her babies, whom the lawyer had accused her of inventing. Tony had been convinced that someone had deliberately hidden the paperwork because they were Italian. Now, she allows herself to imagine telling him that he was wrong, then packing cases for herself and the children and leaving. She imagines him grabbing her arm. She will tell him to let her go, and if he doesn't, she will call a policeman to help and he will listen because suddenly her voice will matter.

The judge continues: "All the families awarded government relief money will have to repay it."

It is difficult to remember how much relief money Paolo and Matteo had sent home in the years that they worked in the camps. It hadn't seemed much at the time, certainly not enough to feed the children properly, but it must have added up over the weeks.

"Now," the judge says, "to the particulars. For those with nine children: Mrs. Green, Mrs. Timmins, Mrs. Devon, and Mrs. Thébault . . ." The judge pauses, looks over his glasses at them. ". . . the sum of one hundred and ten thousand dollars."

The families squeal and cheer. One of the mothers stands, then sits down, fanning herself as if she fears she might faint. There are whoops from the gallery above and even the judge smiles. Mae's lawyer turns again, takes her hand, and shakes it. But Mae is sitting very still, her face frozen in an expression not of joy or celebration but of relief.

Lily can't move. She thinks of the other sum the judge mentioned. *Ten thousand dollars.* Life-changing, still. She will be able to escape Tony, somehow. Without it, she will be lost. Without it, she will have to stay with Tony for the rest of her life.

She waits.

The judge waits, too, watching the commotion. When everyone is looking at him once again, he says, "And the sum of ten thousand dollars is to be awarded, as I said, to a mother who suffered from the disadvantage of the registration paperwork being lost for two of her children, meaning that while she may claim to have ten children, I am only able to consider eight of them as truly valid."

Lily blinks. She has Matteo and eleven other children, including Ana and Sebastian—but maybe he hasn't considered Ana. Still, he must have changed his mind about her marriages, about some of her children being considered illegitimate. She inhales. She imagines a bigger house. She imagines each child having a bed to sleep in. She imagines them being able to eat meat every day, oranges every day, able to laugh without being told to keep quiet, able to play. Lily will be able to sleep at night, without wondering whether Tony will climb into bed drunk, demanding sex, or whether he will lose his temper over some imagined slight and knock her head against the wall.

Lily draws a deep breath, listening to the judge.

"The mother submitted her claim without the direct aid of a lawyer in this court, and all the paperwork has been privately investigated and validated. The mother who is to be awarded the ten thousand dollars was adamant that she wanted to escape the media limelight that has made this such a *tasteless* ordeal."

Lily can't make sense of what he is saying. She doesn't remember submitting paperwork to the judge, but perhaps Mae's lawyer did so on her behalf without telling her. Perhaps his humiliating interrogation was all some awful sham. Again, Mae reaches across to grab her fingers. Lily is too nervous to move. She can almost taste the oranges. It is as if the judge is presenting her not with money but with time. Years and years, he is offering her. He's giving her life.

She tries not to smile too widely.

"So," the judge says, "the ten thousand dollars is to be awarded to Mrs. Kent."

Kent? Lily repeats it to herself under her breath once, and then again, louder. "Kent?"

It is a collection of sounds, not a name she can attach to anyone. This woman hasn't been mentioned in the newspapers—how can she have filed her paperwork without the journalists finding out about it? And yet there was never any need to go through the papers, Lily realizes. It was all a waste of time—all that energy spent talking to the newspapermen and having her photograph printed, having people talking about her. There was never any need to have strangers supporting her, hoping for her to win.

Three people had mattered: the lawyer, the judge, and the man who is eleven years dead and had started it all.

Dimly, Lily is aware of the reporters in the gallery murmuring and scribbling notes, their voices sharp with resentment.

She stares at the judge, watching his lips move, and she can't understand how he can do this. How can he be so calm, when his decision will take her freedom, her children's happiness, the food from their bellies? How can he be so calm, when his words are cutting the thread of her life short?

Where will Tony leave her? The thought is clear, as if she is thinking about someone else's body being hauled into the street or dumped in a ditch. And she reasons, again, quite calmly, that her body was never really hers to begin with. It has always belonged to someone else.

She hardly hears the roar in the courtroom, is hardly aware of Mae saying something again and again. Lily's vision darkens and she leans forward, trying not to vomit.

The court swings on some unseen axis, and a hand steadies her—Mrs. Timmins, she sees, when she looks up. Her face is bright; she is suddenly a rich woman, but all the same, she looks worried as she helps Lily to sit upright.

She blinks, counting her breaths. What will happen to her children after she is gone?

"What about Mrs. di Marco?" a journalist shouts from the gallery. And Lily is glad that Tony isn't here. He would have hurled himself at Mae's lawyer or at the judge himself, fists flying.

"Yeah, what about Mrs. di Marco?" another voice demands.

The judge doesn't answer, and suddenly Lily can't help herself.

She struggles to her feet, her breath loud in her ears. "What about me?" she asks. He still doesn't answer, so she calls it again, shouting the words so that they ring through the courtroom.

"What about me? What about my children? You don't understand! They'll starve. And I have nine valid children, eleven if you can find the papers for the babies. My children still deserve something." Her breath comes in sobbing gasps. "Please," she whispers.

The judge has been putting away his papers, but he pauses and looks down at Lily. "Mrs. di Marco," he says, "we have spent days discussing *you* and *your children*. As has already been stated, at least half of your offspring are illegitimate."

"No!" Lily calls. "No, they're not. My second marriage was legal. I had no idea Tony was still alive. And we need this money. There must be something for us."

"Furthermore," the judge says, as if he can't hear a

word she is saying, "furthermore, your behavior and demeanor in this court have left much to be desired. As Mrs. Thébault's lawyer emphasized, this court emphasized that this court made the decision to award the money to mothers of good character. As for your husband, he is lucky not to have been imprisoned for contempt—as, frankly, are you. I cannot say that your conduct, or his, gave me any confidence that you deserved the money, or that it would be a wise investment of the inheritance."

Investment? He is speaking as though it is his money, as though he is able to use it, as rich men use their assets and investments, expecting a return on them.

And Lily sees that, like Charles Millar, who started all of this, the judge is a man who lives in a world where everything belongs to him, not just money but other people's fates, their hopes, their lives. He can gamble with them as he likes. And for him, Lily is too risky. As far as he is concerned, she and her children are not likely to give a strong return on his stake.

Lily lives in a world where she has nothing to invest except herself. And soon she won't even have that. She feels her own body, suddenly, as impossibly light. As if she is a husk that will be blown away in the wind as soon as the court doors open.

Through all of this, Mae has said nothing. She hasn't spoken up in Lily's defense, hasn't protested at all. As they rise from their seats, she tries to catch hold of Lily's hand, but, once again, Lily pulls away.

"You can't go back to him," Mae says, her voice urgent.

Lily whirls on her and hisses, "I don't have a *choice*."

"Everyone has a choice." But Mae's voice is weak, her tone uncertain.

"*You* have a choice. But some of us don't. This was my one choice and you've stolen it. You've stolen my children's choices too."

Lily is sobbing now, and Mae's face is a mask of horror. "Lily," she says, "I didn't want—"

"Yes. You did."

"Please. I can help you get away from him."

"I don't want your help," Lily says, aware of the way her voice is echoing in the courtroom, aware of the people who are staring at them and whispering. She knows they will be telling stories about her—to each other and to the journalists. She will be the mad woman with the dangerous husband and the illegitimate children. She will be the woman who became hysterical when she wasn't given any money and made a scene in the court. And at this moment, she doesn't care. Let them say what they like. Soon, none of it will matter. She will keep her children safe and fed for as long as she can, but her life is a fraying piece of rope. It cannot hold much longer.

"Please don't walk away, Lily."

Mae is staring at her, with her long blond hair and her full red lips and the smart dress she has worn throughout the trial so that she will look respectable. It is, Lily remembers, a dress she had sewn for Mae, years ago, although it is looser on her now. Lily can remember running the measuring tape around Mae's waist, under her breasts; she can remember looping it around Mae's neck, laying the lace on her collarbone. Lily had been so close to Mae that she could have leaned forward and pressed her mouth to Mae's.

At any time, over the past two years, Lily could have told Mae how she feels, but she'd never said the words, because she felt sure Mae must know, must understand.

Now, she looks at Mae and realizes she doesn't know her at all. Perhaps she never has.

Mae says, "I didn't understand what would happen. I had no idea what he would say. And then it was too late. I couldn't say anything. They wouldn't have listened to me. But I can help you. Please listen to me now, Lily. You *have* to listen to me." She grabs Lily's arm.

And that is when Lily slaps her. Full across the face. The sound rings through the courtroom and there is a gasp. Lily doesn't stay to see Mae's expression. She turns and strides from the court, trying to quell her sense of growing terror, her certainty that everything will be over soon.

And, over her shoulder, she calls, "I don't have to listen to you at all."

part three

I guess mercy is a muscle like any other. You got
to exercise it, or it just cramp right up.

Esi Edugyan, *Half Blood Blues*

36

Mae, January 1938

Each morning Mae wakes in the new, bigger house, with a heaviness in her chest, the sensation that something has been squatting on her rib cage in the night. She feels bruised. As she watches the new housemaid, Agnes, preparing the dough for the bread, as she buys new coats for the children, new furniture for the living room, new pictures for the walls, she cannot stop imagining that some shadow haunts her, some creature that creeps through the darkness while she is sleeping and takes up residence around her lungs, squeezing them. It is an effort to get up in the mornings, an effort to fix a smile upon her face, but she must, because this is the life she wanted, isn't it? This is the life she paid for.

The new house is near to their old neighborhood. Like the big house they owned before the Crash, it has running water and electricity and an indoor water closet. The walls are clean and bright. The floor gleams. The younger children try to run along the corridors in their excitement, then slip over and smack their heads on the polished stone. They cry and say that they hate this new floor, that they want to go home.

"This is your home now," Mae says, trying to jolly them along.

Still, they refuse to sleep in their separate beds: instead, they pile into one room, or sometimes two. Mae finds them in the mornings, huddled together like animals, their bodies warm and slack with sleep. As soon as she wakes them, their arms and legs tense, as if they are wary of her, as if they are strangers to her.

The child who is most real to her is Robert. When he is not in the hospital, he sleeps in his own room, away from his siblings. He wants to lock the door, but she protests, scared that he will seize on the floor, alone; that he will bite his tongue and choke on his blood; that he will inhale his vomit and she will not find him until the next day, when she will have to ask Leonard to break the door down. The doctors have tried different drugs and therapies: phenobarbital and potassium bromide have left him sleepy and confused. The doctor wants to perform more surgeries, suggesting something called the Montréal procedure, which will involve removing part of Robert's skull while he is awake, then probing his brain, while he tells the surgeon what he feels. The idea horrifies Mae, but Robert, in a passive fashion that is typical of him these days, says he is willing to try it and then, with a rare touch of his old sarcasm, he says, "Really, a bullet would be more effective. That'd stop the seizures for good."

Leonard, who sits in his chair in the big drawing room for hours, staring at the wall, is thinner all the time, as if he is slowly disappearing. Mae had hoped the security of the money and a better house might restore him, but he retreats further into himself each day. Mae can't help feeling that God, or some other force in the universe, is punishing her, somehow, for not speaking out on Lily's behalf, for simply sitting in that courtroom, too paralyzed by indecision to do anything other than watch as the lawyer ripped into Lily. She hadn't known what he was going to do, and then it was too late to stop him. They wouldn't have listened to her, even if she'd tried to speak up. This is what she tells herself. Perhaps if Leonard had been there, if she'd been able to persuade him to speak out for Lily . . . But she knows he wouldn't have said a word.

When Mae says she is worried about Robert, and tries to coax Leonard out of his silence by asking him what they should do, he blinks wearily. "The doctors will fix him. He'll be fine." And he pats her head gently, as if consoling a child.

But Robert is not *fine*. He is growing thinner, the shape of his skull showing beneath his skin, as if his flesh is shrinking on his bones. His eyes have a haunted glitter and his skin is hot, feverish, although he won't let her touch him often, ducking out of reach of her hand. He forgets his siblings' names. Sometimes he looks at Mae as though he doesn't know who she is. And though Mae visits the hospital every few days, demanding more investigations, better treatments, more therapies, she sees the uncertainty in the doctor's expression when he looks at her son and says to her, "Well, we could try more surgery." She doesn't want her child to be an experiment and she feels cheated: the money felt like a promise of something that is slipping away.

At least once a week, Mae walks the distance to Lily's house. She doesn't catch a streetcar or call a cab—during the daytime, at least, Lily's neighborhood doesn't frighten her as it once would have. She looks at the homeless men on the streets, the ragged children playing in puddles of filthy water, and she feels sadness for them, and guilt, but she doesn't feel fear anymore. Always, she carries a bag of food—she took bread at first, but then she realized that the children really wanted candy, so she passes out the sweets as she walks. And she sees the hope and excitement in their eyes. And she doesn't know if this is better or worse than doing nothing at all.

Lily's door is always shut. Mae visits her during the day, when she knows Tony will be at work. At first, when Mae knocked, the day after the court verdict, Lily had opened the door slowly. Her face had been bruised, her lips cracked and puffy. One eye had been swollen shut.

She'd seen Mae, her expression had darkened, and she'd slammed the door in her face. Mae had called apologies in the street, had tried to explain, but the door remained shut, and a crowd gathered, watching.

"Aren't you that Stork Derby lady?" a small boy had asked—he could have been any age from ten to fifteen, his limbs scrawny, his face filthy.

Mae had nodded, smiling at the way his eyes had lit up, as though there was some part of him that his poverty and hopelessness hadn't touched.

"Gimme some money, rich bitch!" he had shouted, and although he'd giggled with the other children, there had been a sudden hard gleam in his eye that had made Mae take a step back. Then the boy had run off with his friends, hooting, and Mae had stood for a moment, undecided and scared, hoping Lily would let her in.

The door stayed shut.

The next time, two days later, Mae was ready, and, when Lily opened the door, she stuck her foot in the crack, the wood bouncing painfully off her boot.

"Please," Mae said. "I want to explain."

Lily's bruises were fading, but there were new dark finger marks on her neck, as if he'd held her by the throat.

"I'm tired of your excuses," Lily said, her voice raspy. "Leave me alone."

"But I need you to understand. I didn't know what the lawyer was going to do, I promise."

"But you didn't *say anything*. Why didn't you stop him? You just *sat* there and watched, while he . . ." Lily's eyes burned into her and Mae had to look away.

"I didn't think the judge would listen to me."

"You didn't try."

"I . . ." Mae swallowed and then admitted, ". . . I needed the money for Robert."

"So you *did* know what the lawyer was going to do? You planned it."

"No! I had no idea. But when he started asking you those questions, I knew they wouldn't listen to me. And I kept thinking about Robert. I'd give up anything for him."

"What about my children?"

"Oh, Lily. If you'd had the money, Tony would just have spent it. But I can give you money now. Without him knowing. I can give you money for food for the children. That's why I came here. I can help you." She dug into her bag and held out a handful of banknotes.

Lily looked at her with such hatred it felt like a slap. And Mae wanted to say to her, *Wouldn't you have done the same? Wouldn't you have done anything to save Sebastian? Would you have spoken out for me, if you knew it would do no good at all, but staying silent would save your child?*

Mae stood with the banknotes in her outstretched hand. "Take them. Please."

Lily's mouth trembled. Behind the closed door, one of the children gave a faint cry. Slowly, Lily reached out and plucked the money from Mae's hand. Mae felt a wash of relief, but Lily's gaze was still hard, her face still set. "Now get out of my doorway," she snarls. "And leave me alone."

"I don't want to leave you like this. I can send the police around for Tony."

Lily gave a bitter laugh. "And what will *they* do? Move your foot."

"Please, Lily—"

"Please *what*? Forgive you? You've taken everything from me, and now you want me to *forgive* you as well?" Her mouth compressed and, for a dreadful moment, Mae thought Lily might spit on her. But then she said, "Get *out* of my doorway and leave me alone."

When Mae didn't move, another hand appeared on

the door—a man's hand—although when he pulled the door back, Mae saw it was Matteo, but taller and broader than she remembered him. His face, too, was bruised. He had a cut above his left eyelid and his cheekbone was the swollen purple of a ripe eggplant.

Oh, God, Mae thought. It's unbearable, what she's done.

"You need to go," he said.

"But—"

"You need to go now." His voice was deep, and there was a threatening rage in the carefully clipped words that made Mae step away from the door and turn her back to walk away.

Every time she returns, she knocks and waits. Lily never answers.

And every time Mae pushes the banknotes under the door. Sometimes, as she turns away, she feels better. The weight in her chest lifts; she can breathe more easily. But the relief doesn't last long. As she walks back through the dirty, noisy neighborhood, with its screaming children, its exhausted, dead-eyed women and angry, hopeless men, Mae feels the load settling back on her rib cage. And by the time she has reached her own clean street, with the big houses, full of people for whom the Crash has meant years of everything becoming easier— cheaper food, affordable clothes, everything within reach—the pressure on Mae's lungs makes it hard to breathe.

The children don't greet her when she returns. Mae checks on Robert, knocking before opening his door a crack. He is lying very still on his bed, with his back to her, pretending to be asleep. Mae stays long enough to reassure herself that he is breathing.

"I love you," she whispers.

He never replies.

Then Mae goes into the drawing room to take Leonard his food on a tray.

"Thank you," he says, and gives her a momentary smile, but as soon as she turns away, the smile is gone, as if she'd imagined it.

When she'd first told Leonard about the judge's decision, when she'd told him how much they'd won, he'd nodded, but hadn't looked relieved or pleased, hadn't said anything at all.

He's in shock, she had told herself at first. *He never imagined winning this much.*

"I'll need to pay the lawyer," Mae said, "and there are the medical bills for Robert. But it's still so much money. We can get a new house. The children won't be hungry anymore. They can go to a good school. And I'm sure the doctors can try different treatments for Robert."

"That's good," he'd said flatly. That smile again. "That's really good."

"You can stop looking for a job because we won't need it."

He'd said nothing and, for a moment, in his eyes, she'd thought she'd seen a flash of anger and it had confused her. Surely he should be relieved. But in the new house, he sits and stares at the wall, just as he did nearly every day in the old house. He doesn't even ask, as he used to, if she has seen Lily.

Now, after she returns from trying to talk to Lily, she gives Leonard his lunch and suggests that he might like to go out somewhere.

"Where?" he says.

"Well, you could meet some of your old friends. People you knew through work."

He stares at her for a moment and his expression is incredulous. "How? They've all either lost everything and are living somewhere in the slums, or they kept everything, and they won't want to know me."

"Of course they'll want to *know* you," she says, but with more certainty than she feels. He looks different from the man who went out to work every day. Older, smaller, his movements more hesitant. "Of course they'll want to," she says again.

"And what would we talk about?" he asks, his voice hard. "Should I ask the friends who've lost everything whether they'd like a game of cards? We can play to win food for their children. Or should I ask the friends who lost nothing—who stayed in their fancy houses—why they didn't bother to see me even once?"

"I . . ." She picks up his plate and unfinished bread roll. She can't bear to throw it away. Perhaps she will eat it herself later, when she doesn't feel so sick.

"I've been humiliated, Mae," Leonard says, his voice still dull and toneless, as if he is tired of explaining. "I'm nothing. In this neighborhood, I'm nothing, and in the place we used to live, I'm nothing."

"That's not true!"

"It is. And it's true for you too. We might have money, but we're a laughingstock."

"We're not!"

"Well, I am." His voice is petulant.

"You're wrong."

The gaze he turns on her is so furious that she takes a step backward. "The problem with you, Mae, is that you don't understand anyone's feelings except your own. You never have. You've never even tried."

Then he closes his eyes, as if he wants to sleep, right there in the chair, but it's just a way of shutting her out. She stands there for a full minute, with his plate in her hands. When he doesn't move, when he doesn't look at her, she turns and walks into the large kitchen, with its bright lights and its shining metal and its polished wooden table.

And she leans against the big stove, with the weight pressing down on her chest, harder than ever, and she cries. But even as she weeps for herself, for Leonard, for Robert, for Lily and for Matteo, she knows she couldn't have done anything differently.

37

Lily, January 1938

The light drops earlier than it used to in Lily's part of the city, in Skid Row, or what is now simply referred to as "the slums." The wind pushes against the walls, funneling down the street and over the roof, so that the loose tiles shift like tiny bones, and whenever Lily looks up from her endless sewing and cooking, cleaning and more sewing, it seems to be night. She knows that it can't be true that the day ends sooner here, knows that the darkness drains from the sky at the same time everywhere, but it seems to her that, whenever she looks up from washing, or cooking, or scrubbing, it is already and always dark.

Perhaps this is because she looks up so rarely when Tony is around. He isn't in the house often—he's there for a short time in the morning, before leaving for work, and most nights to sleep, although he returns later and later, and sometimes not at all. Sometimes, he goes out to work in the morning and she won't see him for days. When he does return, smelling of old alcohol and something darker, something that makes her think of rot, she doesn't ask where he's been.

At first, when she came home from court, Tony had threatened to kill her. He hadn't even seemed angry as he'd said it: he'd held her against the wall by her throat and said, *I should kill you.* His voice flat, his face impassive.

Lily lets the days drift by, giving all the food she can to the children, seeing her own ribs appear from under her skin, feeling her hip bones ache when she lies down on the thin mattress. At night, she sleeps poorly, watching silver moonlight slew in between the thin curtains, or listening to the wind rattling rubbish in the street, or hearing the cries and moans of her neighbors.

The first time Mae knocks on the door, Lily envisages slapping her face, ripping the hair from her head. She's never been violent before, and the intensity of her hatred frightens her. She loathes Mae more because she loved her—or perhaps loves her still, but she won't allow herself to linger on that.

"Go away," she says, fighting to keep her voice calm. After Mae has gone, she breathes more easily, but that night, her dreams are sweat-soaked. She wakes up crying out from a nightmare in which she is Tony, somehow, and Mae has become her. She is pounding Mae's head against a brick wall and then, when Mae is silent and unmoving, she is filled with regret, kissing Mae's bloodied mouth, begging her to come back, though she won't. Lily weeps in the darkness, unable to sleep.

Part of her hates taking the money that Mae stuffs under the door, even as she is grateful for it—even as she loathes the feeling of gratitude. But Lily can't listen to the children crying from hunger anymore. She can't keep boiling down bones to make a stew, then padding out the liquid with old onions and sawdust.

So Lily accepts the money. Each time Mae puts cash under the door, she calls, "I'm sorry," but forgiveness feels impossible.

Rich people, Lily thinks bitterly, accuse the poor of being *a drain on society,* but they're the ones who take everything. They're the ones who shoulder everyone else out of the way, who put their needs first. Mae has won; she owns it all, but she still wants more from Lily. She still wants *forgiveness.* She wants friendship and love, but all Lily can find is anger. Rage keeps her going. Without it, she is frightened that she might just lie down and let Tony kick her into darkness.

Now, a clatter from outside. A footstep. The scrape of a boot, then the thud of a shoulder against the door. *Tony.* Her blood jolts and she hears the children's breathing catch, all of them jerking awake as he stumbles into the room. Only the youngest twins, Roberto and Antonio, drowse on, although they all pretend to be asleep still.

Lily waits, dreading the sensation of the mattress dipping as Tony collapses into bed, but hoping for it at the same time. If he comes to bed, he will leave Matteo in peace. Amorous is better than violent.

Often, Tony will press himself against her, lift her nightdress, and then fall asleep. If he stays awake longer she has to shift her body to accommodate him, has to imagine herself as a jointed figurine, to be moved however he wants. The rules are unspoken and absolute: she cannot wince or cry out in pain. As long as she obeys Tony's demands, it is over quickly, one way or another.

But tonight there is no dip in the mattress. Lily waits, listening to Tony stumbling around, stepping over the younger children. She hears a sharp intake of breath from Elena, in the corner. Perhaps he stepped on her fingers, but Elena, young as she is, knows better than to cry out.

Then Lily hears a thud, a curse, and a smothered gasp, a muted cry.

Matteo! She sits up. In the dim shadows, beyond the spill of moonlight, she can make out Tony's hulking shape over Matteo. She can see her husband's bunched fist at her son's throat as he pulls him upright.

Matteo pushes, Tony stumbles and falls back over eight-year-old Luca, who gives a shout of alarm and pain. Tony struggles to his feet, but Matteo springs past him, dodging his fists, and jumping over the younger children.

At the door, he pauses and looks back at Lily, who is frozen by the bed, her feet halfway into her boots.

"I'm sorry, Mama," Matteo says. And then he stamps into his boots and is gone into the night, running down the street in the ragged old trousers and sweater he sleeps in.

"Matteo!" She pulls on a sweater, grabs a thick shawl, pulls on her boots, and goes to the door.

"Stay there!" Tony says, stepping over the children, reaching out to grab at her arm.

And it only takes a moment, a split-second decision, and she, too, is running down the street in her night things, resisting the painful pull of the cries of the children back in the room, and of Tony's shout, which echoes off the ramshackle houses: "Come back, you bitch!"

She almost stops, then runs on. Tony has never hit the younger children, never done more than threaten them, so they should be safe, just until she can get Matteo back. Because where will he go? He will be beaten or kidnapped or killed. Her imagination spirals as she runs, her heart battering in her chest. She half expects to hear Tony behind her, but the street is empty, the only sound that of barking dogs.

When she gets to the main square on the edge of Skid Row, Lily stops, listening. She can't hear footsteps, and she dares not shout for Matteo. The streets are full of desperate men and women.

But for Lily, terrified as she is, this feels like a moment of freedom, a moment of choice: it reminds her of when she and Matteo ran from Tony all those years ago. It was terrifying and dangerous, but it offered hope; it offered something different from the drudgery and fear of living with him.

Except this time, she and Matteo can't run. This time, she has the cord of nine small lives to tug her back to that house and the darkness it contains.

She walks slowly across the deserted square, toward the church. Sometimes the doors are left open for homeless people to sleep inside, and it's possible Matteo might have thought to come here. Lily brings the children some Sundays, if Tony is in the house and they need a sanctuary. Not because she prays anymore. She has no interest in talking to a God who listens to children begging and crying but won't provide.

The building is cold and dark. The door, when Lily tries it, is locked. She leans back against the wood and blinks out at the still darkness of the streets, straining every sense for some sign of her son. It's freezing. He won't survive long out here. She can't feel her fingers or toes. Her every breath ghosts steam into the air in front of her.

A chill wind lifts dust from the drought-cracked earth and brings with it the stench of shit from a nearby gutter. Three feet away, a rat scuttles past. Lily's stomach jolts, but the rat doesn't pause: it is looking for easier prey.

Lily wipes her cheeks with her sleeve, remembering Sebastian.

She can't allow anything to happen to Matteo, she just can't. She keeps walking, telling herself that she would know if something had happened to her son. She should have made him leave weeks ago, for his own safety, but she couldn't bear the thought of him going.

Lily wonders if her children have any idea of the fierceness of the love she feels for them. They can't possibly understand it, can't possibly know that she would die for them without question, would kill for them without thought. She wonders what else they might not know. She wonders how much they'd heard of the way the

Stork Derby had been reported in the newspapers—the stories that gave the impression that all the mothers were having as many babies as they could in order to win a competition, when she knows that each of her children would have existed anyway. How could they not? She ignores the voice of doubt in her head, the voice that tells her she was purposefully careless with her timings.

You were wanted, she thinks, imagining her children at home, cowering from Tony, who will be waiting, pacing, raging.

Lily walks for another hour, wondering if Matteo might have returned without her—but no, he wouldn't, surely?

It is on a whim that she turns down toward Lake Ontario. Sometimes they come here in the summer, but she rarely walks here if the water is frozen: it brings back vivid memories of Robert falling through the ice, of the horrified expression on Mae's face.

The clasp of her arms around Lily's waist. The longing, which had felt like hunger. The feeling of being known. The relief of being understood.

Tonight, the lake is cold and dark; it is not quite cold enough to have frozen properly. A lace of ice whitens the water just at the shore. And—Lily's heart plummets—there is a dark shape next to the lake, as if someone is lying on the sand.

She starts running before she has time to consider that it might be a vagrant or a drunk or a dead body. And as she reaches him, Matteo turns. His lips are blue and he is shaking violently, but his cheeks are dry. She hasn't seen him cry in the longest time. She puts her hand on his shoulder. "You're freezing!" She tries to wrap her shawl around him, but he shrugs it off.

"I wish I could kill him," he says. "I keep thinking how I could do it. I'd like a gun. I think a gun would work first time. While he was sleeping." He presses his forefinger and middle finger against his own temple.

She reaches out, grabs his hand, and kisses it hard. "You don't mean that."

Although she knows he does. So many times, she's revisited that moment when she let the beam fall onto Tony in Chatsworth, has wished it had hit his head at a different angle. She sits on the cold sand next to him. He lets her take his other hand between her own. His fingers feel like marble.

He gives a shuddering sigh. "I wish you could leave him."

She swallows the painful rising grief, which feels like a stone in her throat. Because there is nothing to say to this: he knows she can't leave Tony without taking the younger children to live on the streets, where they would die. And they both know that Tony would find them anyway. They don't have enough money to travel to another city, and even if they did, they couldn't travel unnoticed with nine other children. And Matteo can't bring himself to leave them behind, even if she tells him to go sometimes.

Lily knows that Matteo understands all of this. He's always been older than his years, has always grasped far more than she ever gave him credit for. All those times when he was a small boy and wouldn't say a word, he was watching, taking everything in; he understood it all.

So now she sits by the lake, holding his hand, and lets him say, *I wish he would die.* She lets him say, *I wish I could kill him.*

She lets him imagine it. She allows herself to envisage a world in which Tony has gone and they can all breathe again. But they both know that the thought of it is still and cold, like the ground beneath them, like the dark lake before them. The dream of freedom is like the ice sculptures she has sometimes seen men making in winter: delicate, filigreed pieces, too fragile to survive.

This dream of freedom can't last, but she lets him hold on to it. Just for a moment.

Soon, she will take his hand. They will stand together and she will embrace him. He will let her hold him as if he is a small boy again, as if she can protect him. They will go back together to the derelict rooms, where the other children wait, anxious for their return.

As they walk, Matteo's words will hang between them, elusive as the fading steam of their breath: *I'll kill him.*

38

Mae, January 1938

Robert is fading fast when Mae insists on bringing him home from the hospital, but the doctors are reluctant to let him go. For weeks, the staff in the expensive clinic have poked and prodded and drugged him. They have tied soft restraints on his wrists and ankles so that he will not fall on the floor when his fits become more frequent and more violent.

They move him to an isolated room at the end of a long corridor, so his groans and glugging gasps for breath will not scare the other patients. Mae visits him every day, sitting at his bedside, fetching him water, bringing him oranges, which have always been his favorite and sit by his bedside, slowly wrinkling, their skins turning jaundiced yellow, then furring green with mold.

Every day, Mae has argued with the doctors, who say they can try other things, he may show signs of improvement, but nothing makes any difference. Robert develops a fear of the door opening, a terror of anyone in a white coat. His arms are covered with dark bruises where they've tried to find a vein. When the nurses come in, bringing a needle and a syringe, Robert moans softly and buries his hands under the covers.

She strokes his hair back from his face. She kisses his burning forehead. She wipes the white scum from the corners of his mouth. And at night she goes home to Leonard and sobs in his arms. He holds her, his body rigid, his arms stiff around her.

Leonard lies next to her in the dark, and she can feel that he's awake, can hear the tension and catch in his breathing when she shifts her weight to turn to him.

"I don't know what to do," she says.

He doesn't answer.

"What do you think we should do?" she asks. She hears him swallow. He smells sour, like an old man. "Don't you care?" she asks. Then, when he still doesn't answer, "You don't, do you? You don't care about anyone's misery except your own."

"Christ, Mae!" he snaps savagely. "Of course I fucking care. He's my *son*, goddamn it. But you need to stop going around thinking that everyone's sadness has to look like yours."

She recoils from the ferocity in his voice, from the glint of his wild eyes and bared teeth in the darkness. Her insides judder, and suddenly she is weeping. And he is holding her, his arms around her, and he is saying, "I'm sorry, Mae. Goddamn it, I'm sorry." He presses his lips against her hair and she falls asleep with her head on his chest.

In the morning, he is back to sitting silently in his

chair. He looks thinner than ever, as if he, too, is being wasted by some disease.

He won't look at her, won't talk about Robert.

Mae needs to talk to someone, to anyone, she thinks. But she knows she doesn't really mean *anyone*. She needs to talk to Lily. Lily, who knows Robert and loves him, too—or did once. Lily, who knows what it means to lose a child.

In the morning, when she approaches Robert's bed, he seems to be asleep, but then he says, without opening his eyes, "If I were a dog, you'd have me shot."

She doesn't flinch—he's said similar things often recently. The words used to make her angry, but now she realizes that his agony is more than she can imagine, and that idea terrifies her. She should be able to take his pain from him, soothe it away, as she used to when he was small. Again, she thinks of that day when Lily had pulled Robert from the freezing lake, had walked home holding him close, rubbing the warmth back into her child's bones.

And she longs for the easy assurance Lily had always had with the children. She'd taught Mae how to mother gently but firmly, how to show love, how to be kind to herself. Lily had pulled them all from a frozen lake on the day she arrived. And Mae is filled with an irrational hope that Lily might be able to help Robert again, or might be able to show Mae what on earth she should do.

Mae looks at Robert's still face, wondering if he is asleep. "You remember Lily?" she says softly.

He nods slightly. And then, as if reading Mae's mind, he says, "She saved me. From the lake. She sews things."

"Yes!" It feels like a sign, that this is the thing Robert remembers. Mae covers her mouth with a hand to stifle her indrawn breath and then, when her voice has steadied, she asks, "Would you like her to visit you?"

At first she thinks he hasn't heard, but then he sighs. "She can measure me for a shroud."

And though he wears his usual bitter smile, a tear creeps out from under his closed eyelid.

She presses her lips to it and says, "I love you."

Wordlessly, he nods.

It is raining that evening, but still Mae walks to Lily's house through the mud-slicked streets, thick with the smoke of rain-quenched barrel fires. The homeless huddle together, backs to the wind, reminding her of sheep or cattle in a field. She thinks of Robert, curled up in the hospital bed, with no one's body near his own—only the white sheets, the metal syringes, the glass bottles of liquids—and she's filled with such fury that she wants to scream, wants to sink to her knees and howl right there in the filthy street.

She has done everything she can, but it still isn't enough. She would have paid anything, given anything, but somehow her son's life isn't hers to buy. She'd thought that money would change it all, that it would be a magical solution, as it was so many years ago, when she first married Leonard and realized she didn't need to be frightened anymore. But it seems that her terror hadn't gone: it was just hidden inside her. Like her love for Lily, and her ability to betray her. Like Robert's cancer, which the doctors can't cure. There are some darknesses, beneath everything else, that remain no matter what.

She knocks harder than usual on Lily's door, and when no one answers, she knocks again, hammering with her fist against the wood until her skin stings.

The door opens suddenly.

Tony. His eyes are glazed and he sways slightly as he looks at her bedraggled hair and muddy clothes. "What d'ya want?" he slurs.

"I need to see Lily."

He leans forward, squinting into the darkness. "It's *you*," he says, and his tone is so venomous that she takes a step back.

"Is Lily here?"

"You're lucky I don't shoot you right here, turning up on my doorstep like this. Swear to God, I could knock you down into the mud and give you the kicking of your life."

"Tony!" Lily is there then, her hand on his chest, but he shakes her off.

"This bitch," he says. "This dumb *bitch*!"

"She's going," Lily says without looking at Mae.

"Please, Lily, I need to tell you—"

"Go *away*, Mae, for God's sake." Lily's voice is high-pitched.

"Swear to God, I'll lay you flat out," says Tony. "If I could find myself a gun, I'd shoot you."

"Robert's dying," says Mae, and her voice cracks.

"What?" Lily turns. "But I thought you paid all those expensive doctors." There is cynicism in her voice, but there is something else too: fear. The same fear that any mother feels when she hears about a sick child. The same dread that will wake her every night and won't allow her to go back to sleep until she has laid a hand on each sleeping child's chest, kissed their warm forehead.

"Is this her kid?" Tony asks. "The kid she wanted the doctors to fix, but now he's dying?" He frowns. Then his expression clears. "Some would say that's God's punishment on you. Me? I just think it's a waste of that money you stole from us."

"Tony!" Lily's voice is horrified, but when he glares at her, she recoils.

"He's at the hospital," says Mae, forcing out the words past the pain in her throat. "I'm going to him now, Lily. I thought you might come. He'd like to see you."

"No," Tony says.

"But. Please. He's my son and he's . . . dying." She chokes on the word. "I know what happened in the court was wrong, but I didn't plan it. And he's my child. I wanted to save him—"

"No," Tony says. "You don't care about our *ill-e-git-i-mate* children." He pronounces every syllable. "So we don't give a damn about you or your kids. Now get off my doorstep, lady, before I kick you into the gutter."

And he slams the door in her face. And from behind the door, over the sound of the rain, Mae hears the sound of a slap and a muffled cry.

Blinded by tears, by the rain, deafened by the wind, Mae doesn't hear the footsteps behind her until a hand has grabbed her and spun her around. Her chest constricts with terror as she waits for a fist or a knife, or Tony, with the gun he'd threatened—but she finds herself face-to-face with Lily.

Rain-drenched and bleeding from her nose, Lily gasps, "How long does he—How long until . . . ?"

Mae shakes her head. "Days, I think." Pain like a stone thudding against her ribs.

"And why do you want me to come?"

"He talked about you. He was thinking about how you pulled him out of the lake. Do you remember, when it was frozen?"

Lily nods, her lips pressed together, and Mae knows what she is thinking: in the court, the lawyer had twisted that day into something else. Mae had never accused Lily of neglecting to look after Robert properly, but somehow the lawyer had turned the story of Lily's bravery against her. And Mae hadn't stopped him.

"So," Mae says quickly, before Lily can reply, "Robert said he wanted to thank you." This isn't entirely true, but Mae rushes on: "And I wanted to thank you, for saving him then. I think . . . I don't think I ever said how grateful I was—I am. You saved him."

She doesn't say, *You saved all of us*, but the words are still there, unspoken.

Lily nods slowly and there are tears on her cheeks. She draws a shaking breath.

Mae can see her wavering. "Please," she says. "I'm so sorry." And she hopes that Lily will understand that she means she is sorry for everything. For not loving her enough; for throwing her out of the house. For letting the lawyer cheat Lily out of the money that should have been hers. She wants Lily to be able to understand the anguish that drove her to do it, but she also knows she wouldn't wish that agony upon anyone.

Lily closes her eyes, something like pain on her face. Then she nods again and begins walking in the direction of the hospital.

Mae pauses, not daring to believe it, and then she follows.

39

Lily, January 1938

It is the thinness of Robert's body that shocks Lily. Under the blankets, he looks shrunken, like a child or a very old man. His shoulders are exposed to the air, the skin on them pale and covered with goose bumps.

"Hello, Robert," she whispers. His eyelids remain closed, but he shivers, and she tugs the blanket up to cover his shoulders. The movement wakes him and his gaze locks on hers. The whites of his eyes are yellow and it seems to her that there is something pained in his blink.

While they were walking here, Mae had warned her that he was rarely lucid enough to make sense.

"But he knows?" Lily had asked. "He understands what's happening?"

"He asked for you this morning. Mostly he asks me to kill him," Mae had said, then clenched her jaw to stop the tears that threatened to fall and blinked very rapidly.

Lily had looked away—there was something indecent in seeing that pain, she felt.

She feels the same now—as if she is looking at something she shouldn't, as if her presence here is an intrusion. Robert barely seems to recognize her—or if he does, he wouldn't want her to see him like this, surely.

She turns to go, but Mae reaches out and touches her arm. "Please," she says.

"I can't. I shouldn't be here."

Mae nods, and her expression is so utterly lost that, in that moment, Lily understands. She isn't here for Robert: she's here for Mae.

Lily glances back at Robert. She can't help imagining Matteo in that bed. Or Ana, nearly full grown and dying nevertheless. Or Sebastian.

But it's not her child here. It's Mae's. And she suddenly understands why Mae would have done anything to help Robert. Lily would have done the same. She would have condemned Mae and all her family to poverty if it would have saved Sebastian.

She reaches for Mae's hand. It is cool and dry; she hardly seems to notice that Lily is holding it.

"Thank you for coming," Mae says eventually. "It's lonely here, you see."

Lily nods. They are all lonely.

Mae gazes at her. She smells different—none of the expensive scent that she used to wear, although Lily wonders why, when she's sure Mae could afford it. Her skin is bare of makeup, too. She looks younger, her face thinner and more vulnerable than Lily can remember seeing it.

Mae pulls out a handkerchief. "Your nose is bleeding again." She dabs the blood away, holding Lily's jaw gently. "You have to leave Tony."

Lily turns away. "I can't."

"Why? Why can't you?"

"You wouldn't understand."

"I'll try." Mae puts her hand on Lily's shoulder, then turns her around and dabs again at the blood under her nose. Her hands are cool, her expression soft.

And perhaps it is this tiny moment of tenderness that makes something inside Lily crumble. The sensation is sudden and alarming, like a dam giving way so that the water comes surging through. She takes a step toward Mae, puts her arms around her waist, and then lays her head upon Mae's shoulder. For a moment, Mae stands entirely still. Then Lily feels her hands around her back, feels Mae's breath, warm against her neck. She can feel the echo of Mae's heart in her own chest.

They hold tightly to each other, as if they are both drowning and can only stay afloat by clinging on. For the first time in months, Lily draws a full breath and allows her body to relax, allows herself to lean upon someone else. And maybe Lily thinks it, or perhaps she imagines Mae saying it, or perhaps Mae really does whisper, "We'll find a way."

After she has left Mae standing next to Robert's bed, Lily walks home. She hopes Tony will have gone out to one of the bars. She hopes he will pass out in the gutter somewhere.

Maybe she should leave the children with Mrs. Palumbi, in case he comes back drunk in the middle of the night.

Along the shores of Lake Ontario, the trees are still green, the water still low. Lily looks south across the cracked-glass surface of the lake, trying to imagine the people and the country on the other side of the water. Perhaps she could escape there, she thinks. She could go to America.

She feels a deep longing, in her blood and bones and every breath, to find a place in the world where being a woman means something different from the person she is here. A place where she won't be that Italian woman or that Stork Derby mother; a place where she won't be measured by her children or her marriages, or by the size of her waist or the curve of her breasts. But perhaps all places are like that. She has felt that way everywhere she has ever been, except in the confines of Mae's arms.

Who is to say that America—or anywhere else—would be different?

And Americans are hungry, too, the newspapers say. For a moment, Lily is filled with a nauseating vertigo: a sense that it won't matter where she goes because the world is crumbling. She's just waiting for her own piece of it to crack and break away forever.

Then she sees them ahead: a moose and her calf. The youngster splashes in the water, butting his nose against his mother's rib cage. She is scrawny, the mother. There's not enough to eat, yet her body will still be making the milk the calf needs. Lily watches the mother nosing at the bare lower branches of the trees: the greener leaves and edible twigs are higher up, far out of the animal's reach.

Without thinking, Lily pulls herself up into the lower branches, stands upright and pulls herself up again, until her head is in the midst of the greenery. It smells clean up here. It smells like life. She picks off as many leaves and twigs as she can, stuffing them into the belt of her skirt, before climbing down. The branches rip at her legs and stockings, and the leaves in her belt scratch her skin, but she ignores the pain.

Once her feet are back on the ground, she crouches down and holds out her hand. The animals see her at once, the calf skittering behind his mother, who blows out nervous gusts of air and eyes Lily warily. But she is too hungry to wait for long. She walks forward, her head low, reaches out and snatches a mouthful of twigs and leaves, before taking a step back and chewing, still watching Lily. The calf comes in close behind her. The mother gives a warning grunt, and for a moment, Lily thinks the creature will charge at her. She would be killed, she knows.

But Lily doesn't move. She won't be intimidated; she won't be scared away. The mother walks forward again, taking another mouthful of leaves, before retreating, but not as far this time. As she returns to take the final mouthful, she stands close to Lily, chewing slowly and watching her with liquid eyes.

Very slowly, Lily reaches out and puts her hand on the creature's nose. The big animal flinches but doesn't run. Lily feels the heat of her, feels the moment of animal kinship with this beast that is strong enough to hurt her but is terrified, nevertheless. Lily can feel her blood thrumming in her ears, her heart thudding in her chest. It is the same terror that grips her every time Tony glares at her, every time he raises his fist. It is the same fear that presses around her whenever she thinks of Mae— her arms around Mae's waist, Mae's head upon her shoulder.

Lily holds her hand steady; she meets the animal's unblinking gaze and she remembers Mae's words.

We'll find a way.

TRAGEDY STRIKES STORK DERBY WINNER!

Mrs. Mae Thébault is grieving the death of her oldest son, Robert Mark Thébault, who passed away earlier this week, at the Hospital for Sick Children. Many of our regular readers will remember that Mrs. Thébault's son had been unwell for some time, but it had been hoped that the financial boon in the form of the Stork Derby winnings would lead to a happy outcome for the Thébault family. However, young Mr. Thébault, who was not yet eighteen, finally succumbed to his illness in the early hours of February 5. Mrs. Thébault was unavailable for comment, but I am sure all our readers will join us in sending our condolences. The funeral date has yet to be announced, but it is understood that it will be a private family event.

40

Lily, February 1938

As she reads and rereads the article, Lily feels nauseated. It sits between a story about a man breaking the world speed-skating record and a review of a new play on Broadway, called *Our Town*. On the opposite page is an article about the man in Germany, Adolf Hitler, who has taken control of the army, and a piece about the rising price of milk across Canada.

Of all the articles, the one about Robert is the smallest.

"Oh, Mae," Lily whispers, her eyes burning with tears. She walks across to Mae's house and knocks on the big door, but there is no reply. When she presses her ear against the wood, Lily can't even hear the sounds of the children playing or chattering inside.

Carefully, Lily rips out the article about Robert, then tears free the word *condolences* and pushes it beneath the door. On the way home, she picks up copies of the newspaper that have been left on benches and thrown into trash cans—the news is old as soon as it is printed.

Later, once the children are asleep, she tears out each one of the articles about Robert and she folds them in on each other, then binds the fragile paper together with careful stitches. By the time she finishes, her fingers are gray with newsprint and she has a bunch of delicate-petaled flowers. Each petal bears the word *condolences*, and the stems are held together with scraps of a ribbon taken from the dress that Lily had worn to court.

She leaves a flower on Mae's doorstep the next morning, and another for the next four mornings. Each time she knocks and each time there is no answer.

Lily collects the newspaper every day, scanning the articles for mention of Mae or Robert, but the reporters have moved on to other things: more ice skating, more about Adolf Hitler, who is banning Jewish people from some jobs, an article about a battle that had been lost and won in Spain. There is no mention of the homeless men and women who still throng Toronto's streets. No mention of anything that might touch their lives.

The price of milk has been rising for months. First six cents a liter, then eight, then nine, twelve, thirteen. Lily has to dilute the children's milk, has to cook their porridge with water.

For a few weeks, she buys milk from Mrs. Palumbi, who says she has found a dairy that will sell for the old price of six cents a liter, but when Mrs. Palumbi is ill, Lily offers to walk to the dairy herself, and discovers that it doesn't exist: Mrs. Palumbi has been buying milk and giving it to Lily for half the price. She thanks the older woman but refuses to buy more from her. Instead, she starts mixing flour into water, to try to fill the children's bellies. None of them will drink it. When Lily tries the mixture, it is gritty and clogs her throat.

One morning, she wakes early to the sound of feet running down the street outside the house. At first, half asleep, Lily thinks it must be Tony, back from the tavern, but he is, for once, snoring on the mattress next to her. The footsteps don't stop at her front door: they continue past, slapping against the stone. As if someone is running toward something or away from it. First one set, then another, then another. The children stir in their sleep and Lily is filled with irritation. She pads to the door and opens it. A boy of fourteen or so is rushing past, his steps hurried.

"What's happening?" she calls. "Where is everyone going?"

"Milk riots," he says, his face bright with excitement.

"Riots?"

He tries to look less excited. "*Protests*. About the price of milk. Everyone's going to the big dairy on King Street."

And then he is gone, half running down the street to catch up with some other boys.

Lily shuts the door and leans her head against the wood. She can't shake the thought of the boy's carefree run, the smile on his face.

A steady stream of people passes the door, chattering to one another and laughing, whooping. They are filled with the excitement of fighting back. Of being *heard*. Lily can't imagine standing in a crowd, shouting. Can't imagine raising her voice and hoping that someone will listen.

Inside, it feels lonely and quiet. The dust stirs and settles with the passing footsteps. Lily wipes up a stain from the floor. The children play quietly, whispering to one another so as not to wake Tony.

A shout outside and more footsteps. Laughter. For a moment, Lily imagines herself among them, imagines standing alongside the other men and women, raising her voice to join the roar.

Tony heaves himself from the mattress, cursing. The children shrink and hold their breath.

He puts his head out of the door and hollers at a passing group of women to keep their voices down. Lily sees their shadows in the window, sees them pause, clustered together. She hears someone explaining about the protests. "You should join," a woman calls to Tony.

"You should mind your own business." He slams the door. "Did you hear that?" he asks. "Protesting about *milk*."

Lily averts her eyes. She'd mentioned the price of milk to Tony on a few occasions when he'd complained about the shortage. She'd asked for more money, but he'd always reacted with anger, and she thinks he's probably picking a fight now.

"I feel like telling them," Tony says, "that if the price of milk has gone up, then they'll just need to spend less." He lights a cigarette.

There is another knock at the door. Tony growls, pushes Lily away, and yanks the door wide.

A young boy of about Matteo's age stands there. Lily has seen him with Matteo—Billy, she thinks his name is, but she can't be certain. He has a pale face, narrow shoulders, and bright red hair. He looks past Tony to Matteo. "They're marching up on King Street. You're coming? Everyone's going."

"Well, Matteo's not," Tony says, and swings the door shut.

But Matteo shoots an apologetic look at Lily, grabs his cap, and barrels past Tony, out of the door and down the street, with the red-haired boy following him.

"That rude little bastard!" Tony exclaims, pulling on trousers and a shirt. "This time, I've had enough." And he takes the knife from the kitchen counter.

"Please, Tony," Lily says, grabbing his arm. "He didn't mean—"

He pushes her off, hard, so that she stumbles backward, hitting her face against the wall. Her cheek throbs and she feels a trickle of blood start from under her nose.

Then he is gone. His hangover will slow him, and Matteo is quick, but still, Lily can imagine Tony catching him. That knife. It is serrated. The blade is four inches long.

She turns to the oldest twins, Julia and Luca, who are ten and a half and terrified. Too little to be looking after so many younger siblings, but that can't be helped. They'll manage: they've been changing diapers and wiping noses since they were four years old.

"Take the others to Mrs. Palumbi's," she says to them. "Stay there until I get back. I won't be long." She dabs at the blood under her nose with her sleeve. And before they can reply, she hugs them close and goes out into the cold.

Half an hour later, she is outside the dairy, surrounded by people holding placards and shouting.

Stop the daylight robbery!

Give our children milk!

Lily shoulders past them, craning her neck to see over the crowd, but she can't catch sight of Matteo or Tony. Perhaps they've found each other already, Lily thinks, panicked.

A red-faced woman with thick arms taps Lily on the shoulder and, without looking at her face, shoves a placard into her hands. It features the words *We Want Milk* in bold capitals, and shows a picture of a crying baby. "Here," the woman says, still not looking at Lily. "Hold this."

Lily pushes it back toward her. "I need to find my son," she says. "Have you seen a tall young man, running? He has dark hair and eyes and he'll be with a red-headed friend."

Even as she asks, Lily knows the description will be useless: she could be talking about so many of the men in the crowd—there is no chance that this stranger will have seen him or noted him.

The woman turns to her and steps back in alarm. "What happened to you?" she asks.

For a moment Lily is confused, but then she remembers her nosebleed and the cut on her cheek from where

Tony shoved her. She forces a smile, but the movement causes a stab of pain and Lily feels the trickle of blood starting again.

The woman's clothes are as faded with age and wear as Lily's. She gives a sympathetic smile. "You need a doctor?"

"No," Lily says. "I just need to find my son. Or," she swallows, "my husband. He's looking for my son too." *He has a knife.*

The woman folds her big arms across her chest, understanding softening her face. "And you need to find the boy first?"

Lily can't speak but manages to nod.

The woman puts a hand on Lily's shoulder. "If I were you," she says, "I'd go to the police, show them your face. Station's just there. I'll come with you." She puts the placard down, but Lily shakes her head.

"Thank you," she says, "but I'll go myself, maybe, once I've found him."

The woman's brow creases with concern. "Sorry I can't help you to look. My own kids are almost grown, but they're here somewhere. I'll need to get them away if this turns nasty." She picks up her placard and begins shouting again.

Stop the daylight robbery!

Lily turns away, looking toward the side streets, where more people are gathering. Perhaps Matteo is there. It's hard not to be angry with him—what good will protesting do? All this shouting changes nothing. It's like screaming at the wind or arguing with the rain.

As she walks past the police station, a number of officers are standing on the steps, watching the crowd, their hands on their batons. A chill runs through Lily. She thinks of the protests in Regina four years ago: people had been marching to Ottawa to argue against the dismal conditions in the government work camps. The protesters had been held in Regina while some of the leaders went to talk to government officials, who accused them of being radicals leading an insurrection. The police had used tear gas and had fired bullets into the crowd again and again. People had died.

Perhaps, Lily thinks, perhaps she can talk to these policemen. Perhaps she can ask if they've seen her son. Perhaps it will remind them that this crowd is mostly women and children.

She walks up to a sandy-haired officer, who looks younger than the others. He is shifting nervously from foot to foot. When he sees Lily staring at him, the hand on his baton tightens.

Lily raises her palms to show that she's unarmed, unthreatening. "I'm not part of the protest. I need help finding my son. He's tall, with dark hair. He will have been running, perhaps with a red-haired boy. He's nothing to do with all this."

The sandy-haired man licks his lips nervously, but the taller, darker, broader man next to him shoves him aside. "We've more important things than lost children, ma'am. Move along."

"He's eighteen, but he's in danger. My husband is chasing him and—"

"Say! What happened to your face?" the younger man asks.

"My husband . . ." Lily touches her cheekbone gently. The wound beats to the rapid rhythm of her pulse, and her fingers come away bloody. She repeats, more loudly, so that all the officers will hear, "My husband did this. And I'm afraid he'll hurt my son now."

Another officer comes to stand next to the others. He is short and broad, with a strangely flattened nose, as if he's been punched too many times. "Your husband did this?"

"Yes." Lily feels stronger now. These men are here to help. They will find Matteo, somehow, or they will find Tony. They will make sure that he can't hurt either of them again. She allows herself to imagine him being tried in court, asked questions as she was. She imagines him being led away and locked up in a dark cell.

"Yes, my husband did this to me."

"I see. And what did *you* do?" the flat-nosed man asks.

"Sorry?"

"What did you do to him, to make him hit you?"

"Nothing, I—"

"You must have done something," he says. "A man doesn't hit his wife for no reason."

The tall man is nodding; the sandy-haired man looks less sure, but stares down at his boots.

"Get on with you, lady," the flat-nosed policeman says. "And go clean yourself up. You look a state."

Lily stares at him for a moment, her throat dry, her legs shaking. Then, slowly, she walks back down the steps. When she gets to the last, she stumbles. One of the policemen says something and the others laugh—even the sandy-haired man gives an uncertain smile.

Lily tries to scan the crowd again, but her vision is clouded by useless tears. She dashes them away, refusing to give the men the satisfaction of watching her cry. Then she begins to walk, away from the crowds, toward the side streets, although she knows she has no hope of finding Matteo. Tony was minutes ahead of her and can run much faster. He will have found her boy. That's why she can't find them: they're not here. Tony will have cornered her son somewhere, beaten him. She doesn't let herself imagine the knife.

She needs help finding him. Or she needs someone who can make the police listen. She remembers the man's words: *What did you do to make him hit you?*

Lily walks faster, scanning the street, wiping away tears and blood with her sleeves, which are stained, as if with rust. There are spots of dried blood on her dress too.

She isn't aware of where her feet have carried her until suddenly she is outside Mae's door. There is nowhere else for her to go.

She knocks loudly. When there is no answer, she knocks again and again and again, pounding on the wood until her knuckles sting.

41

Mae, February 1938

Mae is ready to scold the reporter for hammering on the wood and waking the baby, who is crying, and will need to be given milk to settle, or walked out in the baby carriage, and Mae can't do that because there is yet another protest on the streets outside. She's heard the shouts and chanting all day, and now still more reporters are banging on her door, wanting to ask their ghoulish questions about Robert.

You know my son died, so what do you need me to say? she wants to demand. *Can't you just leave me alone?*

Of course she never says this. She tells the maid to ignore the door and has found that if she sits and waits for long enough, the knocking usually stops.

Mae hadn't even been able to open the door to Lily, although she has promised herself that she will go and see her soon, that she will thank her. On the mantelpiece, a small bunch of paper flowers, held together with a lace ribbon. *Condolences, condolences, condolences.* Sometimes Mae strokes the fragile petals.

The knocking doesn't stop and Mae strides to the door, ready to tell the reporter to leave her alone. But when she pulls the door open, the words die on her lips. Lily is standing there, sobbing, her face covered with blood.

"My God!" Mae tries to pull Lily inside, but she pushes her away.

"You have to help me, Mae. He has a knife and I'm worried he'll kill Matteo, but I don't know where they are and I thought you could—"

"Slow down, please, Lily. Tell it slowly."

And as Lily starts to tell her, Mae pulls on her coat and her shoes; she can't find her hat, but hats be damned. "We're going straight to the police station," she says.

"They won't listen to me."

"They'll listen to me," Mae says gently, the thought clear as a drop of meltwater: she couldn't save Robert, but she can help Matteo. She can help Lily.

"Wait a moment," Mae says, and runs to Betsy's room. The girl is sitting on her bed, knees pulled up to her chest, face pale. She came in here this morning, as soon as the shouting started outside. Mae takes her hands. "My love, I'm sorry to ask you this, but I need you to watch the others. And your papa."

Betsy nods, but then her gaze flicks over Mae's shoulder to where Leonard is standing in the doorway.

"I want you to stay," he says.

Something in the hopelessness in his face and voice reminds her of the old men she used to see on the streets, sleeping in doorways.

"I can't stay. I'm helping Lily," Mae says, walking out of Betsy's room.

Lily is standing in the doorway, her face pinched, anxious and blood-streaked.

"Please, Mae."

"I'm sorry, Leonard. If I'm not back by this evening, please call Millicent to help with the children."

"Mae," he says, reaching for her.

She feels a tug of compassion—she can see the man she loved for years, the man who saved her from her old life, the man who used to sleep with his body pressed against hers.

But then he looks at Lily and says, "You can't go with *her*." And she remembers how, when he'd seen them kissing, years ago, and she'd confessed her feelings for Lily, he'd been horrified, furious. How he'd forced Lily and her family onto the street, even when she'd begged him to let them stay.

"I need you, Mae." And he puts his hand on her arm to pull her back.

Mae feels a crushing pressure around her chest, which threatens to well up in her throat and emerge in a roar of frustration. She has spent *years* being there for Leonard, doing everything for him. It isn't enough. He always wants more from her. He wants her to stay in the house and lie down in his bed and plan his meals and fold his newspaper and lay out his slippers and rub his back and soothe his nerves, as though she is simply a body—not a person with hopes and desires of her own.

He strokes her cheek. "I need you," he repeats.

"I don't need you." As soon as she says the words, she regrets their brutality, their blunt truth. But it is too late to recall them.

He steps backward, as if she has shoved him. He looks small and lost.

She walks past him, slamming the door, and strides down the steps, Lily following.

"Won't he come after you or be angry later?" asks Lily, her voice full of disbelief.

"No," Mae says. "I don't think Leonard feels anything at all." She knows this isn't true, not really, but it feels good to use the words to crush her guilt. It feels good to have made her own decision, to be in charge of her own body.

They walk together toward the end of the street. Mae can hear the shouting crowd and her old terror resurfaces—the memory of the taste of the dirt in her mouth, the men's breath in her ear; the smell of rot in the alleyway.

She adjusts her gloves, hooks her arm through Lily's, and keeps walking.

"They won't hurt you," Lily says.

Mae gives a tight nod and breathes a little more easily. Next to her, Lily is limping slightly.

"You can lean on me," Mae says. "If your leg hurts."

"I'm fine," Lily says, but Mae feels a slight increase of the pressure on her arm as Lily lets her take a little of her weight on each step.

Her heart compresses in her chest. And she thinks of Tony, that brute who is out here somewhere, who has hit his wife, who would beat a child, who is carrying a knife. And she wants to kill him.

Suddenly Lily cranes her neck, squints, points.

"There!" she says.

And before Mae can fully take in the sight of two men fighting in the street, of one man gripping the smaller man—the smaller man who is just a boy, really—and shaking him, Lily has begun to run.

42

Lily, February 1938

Ignoring the ache in her leg, Lily rushes toward them, crying out. Tony has Matteo by the arm and is twisting it behind his back. She can see the back of Matteo's friend as, terrified, he sprints away.

As she runs, Lily can feel her son's pain as if it is her own, can sense the coming *crunch* of ripped tendons and broken bones. Matteo shouts, but Lily can't hear the sound, can't hear anything except her own wordless cry, a sobbing yell that reminds her of the final push of child-birth, when your mind tells you that it's hopeless, all is lost, that you will die here, but your body, your resolute body, turns on itself and fights through pain to produce life.

She isn't aware of covering the distance between her-self and Tony—time sticks and then slips and she is there, her fists raised to batter his skull, his back, to yank at his arms.

She sees the knife in his belt, tries to grab it.

He shoves her off, so that she stumbles, and she hurls herself at him again, with the sensation of throw-ing herself into fast-flowing floodwater and a certain drowning.

Tony lets Matteo go and turns to her—dimly she is aware of Mae's cry: Mae, who is still running, struggling to move fast enough in her fancy shoes. She is also aware, in the moment when Tony raises his fist, that a crowd is gathering, that there are other angry voices, and that Matteo is trying to wrestle Tony off her, that he is trying to take the punch that is meant for her.

Go! she thinks. *Please go!*

Tony's fist hits the side of her skull at the same time as Matteo leaps on him.

Tony, thrown off balance, falls onto Lily. She feels something inside her give, as if part of her has been punctured or broken, and she cannot breathe. But then Tony is grabbing Matteo, and Matteo is pulling him down again. And they are turning, one over the other, and she is trying to gather the breath to scream, but every inhalation is like a blow to her chest.

Mae reaches her side and bends down, just as Lily sees Tony and Matteo rolling near to the streetcar track. And she sees Matteo fighting to get to his feet; she sees him stand. Tony struggles upright and pulls the blade from his belt, just as a streetcar is approaching. As Tony lifts his fist the blade glitters in the sunlight.

Matteo shoves him away. Hard.

Tony falls backward, right under the wheels of the streetcar.

There is a hideous squeal of brakes and someone somewhere is screaming and won't stop. It is only when Mae puts a hand over her mouth that Lily realizes the sound is coming from her.

She struggles to stand, and it is easier now, the pain slackening. She isn't bleeding, just bruised. She hobbles over to Matteo, who is lying on the ground, staring at the stopped streetcar and the body beneath it.

"I didn't mean to," he says. "I didn't mean to."

Time jolts and jars—a string of half-connected moments. Lily holds Matteo, trying to help him to stand, nearly falling herself, the agony in her ribs returning. Mae puts her arms around them, and all three of them stand together.

Then the driver is walking over and shouting at Matteo, and there is a policeman suddenly, too, the sandy-haired man Lily had seen earlier. And Lily notices how young he is, how he appears even younger when he looks under the streetcar and recoils.

There is a terrible silence. All Lily can hear is the beat of her own blood as she remembers how the policemen had looked at her earlier, as though she was some crawling, distasteful creature.

Matteo's hand is in hers and he tries to pull free, but she won't let him go. She won't. Because if she lets him go, he will be swallowed and she will never see him again. There will be a judge and a crowd and newspaper reporters. They will tell his story for him. They will call him a man, even though he is barely more than a boy. They will take his voice, his power to be heard. They will take his life from him and he will not get it back.

So she doesn't let go, but stands, shoulder to shoulder with her son, her boy, and she keeps saying, "He didn't mean it. It was an accident."

There is a suspended moment, a held breath when everyone stares at her, at Matteo, at the policeman.

Then a stranger steps forward from the crowd, a man wearing a battered old hat, and he says, "He didn't do it. Saw the whole thing, and she's right. This boy didn't do a thing."

A woman in a faded flowery dress, a placard in her hand, starts nodding. "He's right. I saw it, too, and the boy didn't do a thing wrong. The man was beating the boy and then he jumped."

An older woman, holding a cracked leather bag, starts nodding. "The boy didn't hurt him. The man jumped. I saw him with my own eyes."

Everyone begins saying it, the whole crowd of strangers: penniless and defeated as they are, they stand by Lily.

"He did himself in, the man," they say. "He jumped."

Her heart lifts and, suddenly, she feels part of something. She feels like she exists.

But it's not enough: the policeman shakes his head and folds his arms.

"I don't see," he says, "why a man who was fighting—and he *was* fighting, I saw that much from up the street—I don't see why he would jump in front of a streetcar."

The people around Lily shift uncomfortably: no one wants to begin inventing a story for a policeman who had seen half the fight. Lily's heart drops. Her mind whirs.

She'll say she was to blame, say she did it. The officer didn't see the actual moment—perhaps he'll believe her when she says that she managed to run and push Tony in front of the streetcar.

She takes a breath.

"The man jumped," Mae says. Her voice is quiet and confident, her gloved hands are clasped in front of her. She looks every inch the respectable lady.

The policeman looks at her, his gaze running over her fine clothes and her perfectly made-up face. "You saw this? You *saw* the man jump?"

Mae nods. "He was drunk. I saw the whole thing. And I can assure you, Officer, that no one else was responsible. I know this boy. He wouldn't hurt anyone."

And Lily feels an overwhelming surge of relief when the officer listens, along with a twinge of envy that Mae can so easily swoop in and rescue her. Still, the officer believes every word Mae says.

"The boy will have to come and answer some questions tomorrow."

"Of course," Mae says.

Then the officer tucks away his notebook and asks the crowd to disperse.

Lily puts her arms around Matteo and lets him weep. She holds him close and whispers, "It's not your fault. You're safe now."

He shudders and says, "I'm sorry."

"Hush. You're safe. We're safe." The words feel like a prayer, an incantation, and Lily doesn't know if they are true. Then Mae steps forward and, very gently, she lays one hand on Matteo's shuddering back, the other on Lily's shoulder. They stand there for a long time.

Mae says, "Come home with me. Please."

"I have to fetch the children."

"I'll do that. You stay with Matteo. He'll need you."

"But—"

"Please, Lily. Please trust me."

Lily hesitates. How is it possible to trust Mae after everything? And yet she can see how Mae is trying—how hard she has tried. Maybe trust, like love, can be earned. Like love, maybe trust can be a choice that you throw out like a rope, time and again, until it snags and holds fast. Until you can cling to it and let it pull you upward.

Lily lets the breath in her chest unfurl. "I trust you."

43

Mae, February 1938

Mae feels terrified as she walks out into the gathering dark, toward Cabbagetown. She has never been out this way during the dark, but she can't wait for the morning. Lily needs her to do this now. She has put on Lily's coat and Lily's boots, which pinch her toes a little, but will be easier to run in than Mae's own high-heeled shoes.

But still the darkness carries a crushing threat. The alleyway. The weight of the men.

They'd laughed when they were finished. One had wiped her blood off himself with her skirts.

She tells herself that it couldn't happen again: she's older, taller, stronger. If she shouted for help now, with her polished accent, people would listen.

Her road is quiet, the expensive houses shuttered and dark, but there are still voices shouting in the square ahead as the rioters argue with the police. Through everything, there is still an electricity of fear.

Two men walk past, laughing, one batting the other over the head with a placard.

Mae moves faster.

The smell of rot. The stench of their breath.

Mae ignores the squeezing terror that tells her to run. She strides along with her head held high, as if the confidence she can feign will be a barrier against harm.

Finally, she reaches Lily's house, knocks on the door, and when Mrs. Palumbi opens it a crack, Mae smiles, keeping her voice bright in front of the gaping children. She explains that Lily and Matteo are safe and that she's taking the children to her house.

Mrs. Palumbi looks at Mae suspiciously. "Tony will be angry."

Mae takes a deep breath, then decides that she can't say it. "Lily wants the children. Tony . . . can't object."

Mrs. Palumbi hears the emphasis and nods slowly. "You're that Stork Derby lady?"

"Yes."

"And you want *more* children?" Mrs. Palumbi shakes her head. "Is this for money?"

Mae is affronted, until she sees that Mrs. Palumbi is smiling, and she forces a small laugh. "No, not more money."

"Good. You should give something to Lily. It is not fair, what happened to her."

Mae doesn't know if Mrs. Palumbi is talking about the money now, or about Tony, or about everything that has befallen Lily. It doesn't much matter: she's right. So much of Lily's life has been unfair, has been Mae's fault.

"I know," Mae says.

"You should make this right."

"I'm trying."

The walk back across the city is both more and less frightening with the children. They huddle close to Mae, the older ones carrying the babies when they squirm away from Mae. The children seem less frightened than she is of the strangers shouting and chanting; when someone smashes a bottle nearby and laughs, Mae jumps, but the children just turn and stare. And when a man comes up to Mae, asking for money, and she ignores him, Julia, the oldest of the twins, frowns at her. "Why don't you give him something?"

"It's dark. It's not safe to give out money."

"Mama isn't rich like you and she always gives money."

Her face burning, Mae scrabbles in her purse and gives the man some coins—not much, but he nods and thanks her, pressing his hands together as if in prayer.

The next time a man comes asking for money, she gives more coins. And then she passes out some of her notes. For a minute, there is a crowd of people around Mae, all holding out their hands. They are close, too close. She empties her purse into their hands; they thank her and turn away.

No one holds a knife to her throat. No one tries to drag her off into an alleyway.

"Thank you, ma'am," they call, as they walk away.

And Mae stares after them. "They were so polite," she says wonderingly.

"Yes," says Julia, her voice so matter-of-fact that she instantly feels shame. What had she expected?

She knows—she does. But that alleyway was so long ago.

The house is warm when Mae returns. Lily's children run to their mother and she wraps her arms around them. Mae's children hang back slightly, looking with suspicion at her shabby borrowed coat and boots. She thinks about how often, over these past two years, she has ignored them because she has been rushing to care for Robert, or going to talk with the lawyer, or looking after Leonard, and she can't help feeling something like grief as she watches Lily. None of the children ask where Tony is and Lily doesn't tell them.

"Where's Leonard?" Mae asks.

Lily doesn't look at her. "He went out just after you left."

Mae hears the meaning beneath the words: he hadn't wanted to be in the house with Lily.

Once the children are all in bed, excited at the prospect of sharing rooms with these half-remembered friends, the older ones helping to settle the younger, Mae goes back downstairs. Leonard still isn't home. She opens the door, gazing out into the foggy night, but can see no sign of him. She hates to think of him out there alone, in the cold and the dark.

His study is empty and his blanket is on his usual chair in the drawing room, but he is nowhere to be found.

She should go and look for him. But how, and where? Outside, it has started to rain. She opens the door and looks out onto the silent street. The pavement glistens.

On the tram tracks, Tony's blood will be washing away. She calls Leonard's name, but there is no reply.

"Do you need to look for him?" Lily appears behind her, a blanket wrapped around her shoulders.

Mae shakes her head, surprised by the sting of tears. She blinks them away, but Lily comes and stands behind her and, as if it is the simplest movement in the world, wraps her arms around her. Mae closes her eyes.

Outside, the rain falls. Upstairs, the children sleep.

Lily's face is so close. Mae stays very still, afraid to break this spell, afraid that she will scare Lily away. Finally, she says, "You can sleep in the spare room. I'll sleep down here, on the chaise."

Lily pulls away slightly and nods, then turns and walks from the room, her blanket trailing behind her. Mae watches her go.

It takes a long time for Mae to feel drowsy. Scenes from the day play over and over in her head: the noise of the tram hitting Tony; Leonard's face as she'd slammed the door; the eager delight of the men as she'd pressed money into their hands. And upstairs, all those children.

And upstairs, Lily.

Twice, Mae rises from the chaise, goes to stand at the bottom of the stairs, and listens.

Nothing but the creaking of the trees outside and the push of the wind against the windows.

Mae goes to lie down on the chaise again. It is hard and she is cold. She fetches Leonard's blanket from the chair. It smells of him. Where is he? Is he with another woman? She feels a twinge of sadness, but no jealousy. She can't remember the last time she felt any desire for him.

A noise in the doorway. A pale shape walking toward her.

Lily.

Mae sits up. "Do you need something?"

"I can't sleep," Lily says, sitting on the chaise. "Did I wake you?"

Mae shakes her head.

She hears Lily swallow. "Could you . . . I'm cold. Up there, alone."

"Do you want a blanket?"

Lily takes Mae's hand and leads her upstairs.

They check each of the children's rooms, listening to their breathing, the sound that is comforting and regular as waves.

The bed in the spare room is still warm from Lily's body. They pull the blankets up and huddle close to each other. Gradually, heat seeps into Mae's limbs, but she can't stop trembling. "I don't want to hurt you," she whispers into the darkness.

She hears Lily turn, feels Lily's lips close to her ear. "Then don't."

It is early in the morning when Mae is woken by hammering on the door.

"Leonard!" she says, climbing out of bed and pulling

a dress over her head. Lily sits up, her eyes full of alarm. "He won't come up to the spare room," Mae says. She can feel the heat in her cheeks as she turns to run down the stairs, buttoning her cardigan. She can't look back at Lily.

She sees two shadows behind the glass in the front door and—absurdly—her first thought is that Leonard has brought a woman home with him. She runs a hand over her hair and her face, then opens the door.

Two policemen in dark uniforms are standing on the step, their expressions grave.

Tony, she thinks. *They're here to ask questions about Tony. Perhaps they'll want to arrest Matteo. Or Lily.*

"Mrs. Thébault?" they say.

She nods, opens the door wider to let them in, and leads them into the drawing room. They sit on the chaise where, only a few hours ago, Lily had sat next to Mae and taken her hand.

The policemen look down at their feet, she notices. They won't look her in the eye. And they haven't asked for Lily or Matteo. Of course she's not thinking clearly: how would the police know they were here?

"Do you know the whereabouts of your husband, Mrs. Thébault?"

Mutely, she shakes her head. A chill is creeping through her limbs.

"I'm afraid," the policeman says, "we have some very bad news."

"Oh?" It's all she can manage.

"I'm sorry."

"Please don't apologize," she says automatically, her mind whirring. What can Leonard have done? Has he been arrested?

"I'm afraid your husband was found in Lake Ontario this morning."

Her mind is a white blank.

"But . . . he can't swim." She has images of Leonard splashing in the water, drunk. Why would he . . . ? What is he thinking, letting her worry like this? She'll never let him hear the end of it.

"A fisherman found him and pulled him out." The policeman pauses. "His body is in the hospital morgue now. I'm sorry."

Mae shakes her head. "His *body*? He's . . . He can't be." But she knows he can. She remembers him begging her not to leave. The fear and abandonment in his face.

Oh, God. How will I tell the children?

"I'm sorry. We'll need you to come and identify him."

"Stop apologizing," she snaps, then immediately feels terrible.

Oh, Leonard. She wonders why she isn't crying, why she hasn't collapsed to the floor. How is her body still upright? There is a dirty scuff on the white wall. Leonard had talked about having it repainted. Mae stands and runs her fingers over the rough mark. Perhaps she can get it off herself, if she scrubs it.

"Sorry, ma'am. You must come with us."

Mae can't go and identify a body in the morgue because she doesn't want to have to look at him, to have to see his face. She doesn't have the time. She has to make sure Lily and the children are all right. She has to send the maid out for flour and tell the cook to make more bread. She will need to take them all to buy new clothes. And they will need new shoes.

She can't go and identify a body.

It won't be him.

And yet it must be.

She doesn't want to see it.

It isn't him.

"Mrs. Thébault?" the policeman says.

"I can't," she whispers. "I'm ever so sorry, but I don't have time today."

And it is only when she sees Lily in the doorway, sees the shock on her face, that Mae allows herself to bend forward, put her face into her hands, and weep.

44

Lily, late February 1938

Leonard's and Tony's funerals have a strange surreal feeling. Leonard's ceremony is held in the big church on Victoria Street, with people spilling out into the road, everyone eager to shake Mae's hand and offer their condolences.

Afterward, Mae says to Lily, "I didn't recognize most of those people. They hadn't seen Leonard in years, not since we lost everything."

Tony's funeral is held in the tiny chapel on the edge of Cabbagetown. Only Lily, Mae, the children, and Mrs. Palumbi are there. Thérèse had offered to come, but she would have had to bring all the children, and Lily told her to stay at home. Mae is buying a bigger house in a better district for Thérèse and Jacques—she can do whatever she wants with the money now, she says, and although she smiles, there's a catch in her voice. Thérèse's children are so excited at the thought of a new home that Lily can't imagine dragging them all into the darkness of Tony's funeral.

Lily wonders about the whereabouts of all of Tony's drinking pals, all the men from the steelworks, who had been happy to spend time with him when he was swigging the money that should have gone toward filling the children's bellies. She doesn't wonder about her other neighbors, those people who had been too scared of Tony to talk to them, or had been jealous or judgmental of Lily going for the Stork Derby winnings, or had been resentful of her visits from *that rich woman*, and of the money and food Mae had left for her. Tony had never liked Lily making friends anyway, and Lily had no energy for conversation.

Except with Mae, where no conversation is needed.

Every night, they share a bed. They sleep holding hands, or with Mae's arm across Lily's chest, or with her face pressed against the warmth of Lily's sleeping back.

If the children think it strange, they don't comment on it, but Lily dreads people noticing and beginning to gossip—she dreads that Mae will want her gone again and then she will be alone.

At Leonard's funeral, Millicent finds her in the churchyard, takes her by the hands, leans in close, and says, "I hear you're living with Mae again."

Lily forces a smile, but a chill runs through her. Somehow, Millicent knows. Has she noticed the way she and Mae look at each other? Or has a neighbor said something, perhaps?

"Yes," Lily says, trying to keep her voice level.

Millicent pulls her furs more closely around her shoulders. "She won't give you the money, you know."

"What?"

"The Stork Derby money. It's hers. It doesn't belong to

you, so don't think you can persuade her to give you some."

"I—I don't," Lily says.

"Of *course* you don't," says Millicent with heavy sarcasm. "Everyone has been saying how *generous* and *selfless* you are, staying in Mae's house, caring for her in her grief."

Lily can feel a blush creeping across her chest, but at the same time she feels a wash of relief. No one suspects. But then, as she looks around at the other faces in the churchyard, at the people making small talk among the gravestones, looking toward her and then Mae and whispering, Lily knows it will be only a matter of time.

That night, in the dark, after the children are asleep, Mae shifts across the bed toward Lily and takes her hand. Lily stays rigid.

"What's wrong?" Mae asks.

"I have to leave," Lily says, and repeats what Millicent had said.

"I don't care what Millicent thinks," Mae says. "I don't care what anyone thinks. And if you're worried, then we can say you're helping me with the children, just like years ago."

"And what about after the children have left?" Lily asks. "What will people say?"

Mae presses a kiss into Lily's cheek and says, "Why does it matter?"

Lily blinks up at the ceiling in the darkness and feels, for a moment, as though she's floating. As though something has shifted and she's been cut free. *Why does it matter?* She can't remember ever thinking this before. There's never been a moment when she hasn't been worried about how she might seem, what people might think of her, how they look at her, what her husband might want or expect of her.

Does it matter?

Lily drifts into sleep, her fingers entwined with Mae's.

In the morning, Lily wakes early to find a note on the pillow next to her, in Mae's handwriting, saying, *In the garden.* She creeps downstairs. It is a strange thought that if the children wake there is a maid and a nanny to care for them.

The grass is chill and damp under Lily's feet, the light an orange rumor behind the trees. Mae is sitting on the bench at the end of the garden, a blanket around her shoulders. She turns when she hears Lily, her expression bright, her cheeks flushed from the cold.

Lily's heart lifts, as it does every time Mae smiles. "I didn't hear you get up."

"No. I . . . I fetched this for you yesterday." She is holding out a large folder. She looks nervous.

"What is it?"

"It's from the lawyer."

"Which lawyer?"

"The lawyer who was dealing with the Stork Derby. He gave me this for you—"

"No!" Lily says. "No, I'm not going to court again."

"You won't have to." Mae's tone is still light, but there's an anxious tension around her eyes. "I asked the

426

lawyer to speak to the judge. There's some money left over from the will, to pay the court expenses. And the judge has decided that the money can go to you. It's not so much, only about ten thousand dollars—"

"What? No! Mae, that's madness. Why would he give the money to me?"

"To stop the court case being opened up again."

"I don't understand. Why would that happen?"

Mae's smile is smug. "Because I threatened to do it. I said that if you weren't given some share in the money, I would ask my lawyer to petition to have the case opened again, which would be expensive and embarrassing for the court."

"How? Why would they open the case again?"

"I asked my lawyer to hunt out all the paperwork he could. He found the birth certificates for your children. If the court had had them during the trial, the judge wouldn't have dismissed your case so easily. It means the whole trial was unfair."

"Why couldn't the lawyer find them before?"

Mae blushes. "He called it an *administrative error*."

Lily takes a moment to absorb this. "And the judge will accept my claim now? He'll agree that my children are legitimate?"

"Well, he might not agree, but they'd lose money if the case was opened again, and they want to avoid a scandal. They'll pay you so that you don't make a fuss about your missing paperwork." Her gaze is steady. "You were cheated, Lily. The lawyer cheated you. And the judge let it happen, and I . . ." She clears her throat, her eyes shining. ". . . I let it happen. I should have stopped it. I'm sorry. But this is yours. You can do whatever you want with it. You can . . . If you want to, you can go anywhere you like . . ." She trails off and Lily can hear the nervousness in her voice, can read the question in her eyes.

Where do you want to be?

"But this is too much. It's . . ." Mae is right: it's enough to do anything she wants. She could buy her own house, move away from Toronto. She could go anywhere.

Mae holds out the folder. She offers it freely, still smiling, still nervous.

Safety. Freedom. A future. A choice. Many choices.

Whatever you want. Anywhere you want.

"Take it, Lily," Mae says gently. "It's yours."

Lily reaches out. It is surprisingly light, for a folder that contains a new life. "Thank you," she whispers.

"Where . . ." Mae clears her throat again. "Where do you want to go?"

"Can I . . . can I stay here?"

"Oh!" Mae reaches out and places her hands on Lily's cheeks, cupping her face, then runs her fingers over her lips, as if committing every line of her to memory, her voice almost cracking as she says, "Oh, love, yes."

45

Mae and Lily, late March 1938

They sleep curled into each other or apart and with the curtains open so that the light spills in early and they might have a chance of some time together before the children are up. Sometimes, Mae wakes with the sun in her eyes and Lily's lips on hers. Sometimes, she stirs with her face buried in Lily's hair or her arm slung across her waist. She rouses from the darkness of sleep, stretches, and feels herself surfacing.

Dawn in March. Light sings across the tops of the pines outside the window. Mae watches Lily sleeping, traces but doesn't touch the contours of her face the fine lines around her eyes, the glints of silver in her dark hair. She has gained weight since she has been living with Mae and her face is softer; her eyes have lost some of their watchfulness. She smiles more often, laughs aloud more freely. Mae is gentle with her: at first, she had been alarmed by the way Lily froze if a door banged. Once, after Mae had snapped at her children, she'd not been able to find Lily anywhere. Eventually, she opened the door to the pantry and found Lily standing behind it, rigid and trembling. Mae took her in her arms. "I would never hurt you."

Lily had nodded. "I know."

"I love you."

"I love you too."

They say it often, many times each day, and yet the words are never worn out. They say it before they fall asleep and when they wake in the morning. They say the words after they argue. Sometimes, Mae will walk into the kitchen, her arms laden with washing, and Lily will look up from drying the dishes and say softly, "I love you," and Mae will feel uplifted by a tide of contentment so strong that it brings tears to her eyes.

I love you. Which means, so often, *I choose you.* Because sometimes love is a choice, one you never thought you'd be lucky enough to make. Day after day, the same choice, each day fresh with the choosing. The choice a privilege. The choice an effort, sometimes. The choice a gift.

One of the things Lily loves most about Mae's house is the way that her children's laughter echoes in the big corridors. After they had moved in, it took them some time to play: at first, they didn't seem to know how, but sat and watched as Mae's children rolled marbles in the hallway or ran races in the garden. Matteo, in particular, stayed close to Lily, as if he was guarding her, or as if he was still the frightened, silent boy who had traveled from Chatsworth with her.

But then Alfred asked Matteo to walk to the blacksmith with him to get a saucepan mended, and they returned hours later, Matteo flushed and smiling, as he told Lily that he'd helped the blacksmith with the bellows because his apprentice was *out slacking*, and Matteo had been so attentive and polite, and quick to pick up the skills, that the blacksmith had offered him an apprenticeship, if he wanted it.

"Can I, Mama?" he asked Lily.

She smiled, managing to hide her sadness that he still felt he had to ask. "You're old enough to decide, but of course, you have my blessing."

"You should have seen him!" exclaimed Alfred. "He watched the blacksmith working and he knew what to do even before the fellow asked. I don't know how he did it."

Lily kept smiling, but she knew that living with Tony and the constant threat of fist and boot had made Matteo an expert in reading facial expressions and gestures. Matteo was helpful and obedient because he'd had to be. "I'm proud of you, my love," she said to Matteo.

The younger children will be starting at a good school in a month. Lily had been worried that they'd be behind and that they'd be mocked she remembered her own miserable experiences in school so Mae has employed an ex-schoolmistress to come to the house every weekday. Mrs. White is small, gray-haired, and always seems to be smiling, but the children hang on her every word.

Thérèse sometimes visits and the women sit in the garden together. At first, Lily had been worried that Thérèse would comment on her and Mae living together again, or that she would catch some glance or gesture between them. When Thérèse had first come to the house, Lily had sat as far from Mae as possible and had kept her attention on Thérèse or the children.

On her third visit, they were watching the children

playing leapfrog in the garden, and Mae got up to fetch more tea.

Thérèse said, without looking at Lily, "At least you won't have more children. And two mothers is better than the fathers they've had."

Lily had felt suddenly breathless. "Pardon?"

Thérèse kept staring at the trees. "It's none of my business. Do you know why I love Jacques?"

Lily blinked. "No."

"Exactly. It's none of your business. I can't stand people prying."

"Thank you," Lily managed.

Thérèse smiled. "You're happy, aren't you?"

Happy didn't describe the sense of peace and relief Lily woke up with every day.

"Then it's no one else's concern."

Mae, who must have been listening at the door, came and set the tea on the table and gently pressed her lips to the top of Lily's head.

Thérèse, still looking out into the garden, nodded to herself. "Being happy is the thing."

One late-March day dawns brighter than the rest and Mae wakes early, expecting warmth. But when she looks out of the window, the world is frozen. Frost lattices the windows and feathers the trees in the garden.

Lily is still asleep next to her, but then as Mae reaches out and traces the filigree of ice on the windowpane, Lily murmurs, "I think we should walk to the lake today."

"I'd like that," Mae says, as Lily presses her body

against hers, their curves and planes so familiar that, even half-asleep, they shift to fit each other.

They walk together, the children sweeping frost from the walls and hurling fragments of ice at one another. Some homeless, jobless men watch them go past, women and children crowding behind them. As they always do, Mae and Lily bring a purse each and give out the coins until they're all gone. Each week, Lily sends money to Mrs. Palumbi. They also give a monthly amount to the soup kitchen on Yorke Street, and a larger amount to a new shelter that has been set up to support unmarried mothers.

Sometimes giving the money makes Lily feel less guilty for all that she has. And then she feels guilty all over again, at her sense of relief, at her knowledge that it isn't enough.

Once they are past the hungry crowd, Lily says, "I think about them sometimes all the other mothers who could have gotten money in the Stork Derby but didn't know how to submit their papers or didn't qualify. It seems so cruel."

"I know," Mae says. "We can give more."

"We can," Lily says, nodding, "but then I think that the children need new clothes, and I need to pay for their schooling, and I'd like to show them other places in the world. One day, I'd like to take them to Italy. But then I think that's probably selfish."

Mae takes Lily's hand. "We do what we can. And that has to be enough."

They are nearing the lake now. The edges are lined with frost, and every time the water moves, it pushes the ice against itself, so that the banks are piled with glittering splinters. From a distance, they could be knives or broken glass. Tomorrow they will be gone.

All their moments, piled up together, layered like the translucent shards of shattered ice at the edge of the half-frozen lake. And above it all, the sun and the geese, tugged into flight by some ancestral urge that they can't deny.

Mae waits, watching Lily's face. She turns toward the weak winter sunlight, closing her eyes, and she looks so vulnerable at that moment, so trusting. Mae feels such tenderness toward her. She wants to hold her, but she waits, holding her breath, for Lily to open her eyes.

Lily has had to make so many decisions to run for the sake of her life, or to leave because she has been thrown out, or to stay for the good of her children, or to stand under the gaze of a hostile courtroom and be judged. Now every day is hers for the choosing.

Later, they will look out of the window together and watch the sky peeling into night, revealing smudges of far-off bands of stars, like smears of spilled milk the stars that sometimes can't be seen, that are sometimes obscured by other things but are always there nevertheless. Just as the earth is turning, even though Lily can't sense it, just as her heartbeat is there, even though she can't feel it. Just as Mae has been there all along. Just as they have chosen each other, again and again, returning to that unseen, irresistible pull.

Now Lily inhales, listening to the lake, the ice. The cries of the children, mingling with the calls of the geese overhead—the geese that are companions for life and return time after time to the place they know as home. She reaches for Mae's outstretched hand.

Author's Note

The Great Stork Derby was a real event that took place in Toronto between 1926 and 1936, in the ten years after the death of the lawyer Charles Vance Millar, although really the seeds were sown long before those ten years, and the echoes resounded long after, not least in the court case of 1937.

Millar was rich, had no descendants, and had a penchant for practical jokes. It has been speculated that he'd intended the most divisive clause of his outrageous will to act as a social commentary on the need for contraception, but in reality, his offer of money in return for children came at a time of financial and social instability. Arguably, it was the interpretation of the will that was crueller than the will itself: the court's decision to refuse to award money to women who'd had stillborn children, or to women who'd had children outside wedlock, or whose births weren't properly registered meant that some who should have been given a share in the winnings were excluded and that, in many cases, this became an issue of class, in the midst of a brutal media circus.

Mae and Lily are fictitious characters, as are their husbands and children. I'm always drawn to fascinating stories, but like most writers, I struggle with the knotty question of which stories I have the "right" to tell. I'm deeply uncomfortable with the idea of misrepresenting real people's lives although almost every piece of narrative writing (including biographies) is, arguably, a work of fiction, in that it is a feat of the imagination. Still, I have tried to remain true to the spirit of the story: the effect of men's decisions and choices on the lives of women who had no choice at all.

While I enjoy researching the period and the place about which I'm writing, I often invent for the purposes of fiction: the earthquake I describe in 1927 was based on an event in 1929 and the epicenter was farther north than the quake I have fictionalized here. There was no sudden drop in temperature on the morning of the Wall Street crash. Both the national outcry around the Stork Derby itself and the milk riots actually happened, although I have taken a writer's license with the timings.

In the Stork Derby trial, there really was a baby who had died from rat bites; women really were asked to talk about their stillbirths in a court full of strangers; the judge really did express contempt for the whole enterprise and cast doubt on the women's motivations, although many of the women involved already had large families and were adamant that all their children would have been born regardless of the competition.

Along with the uncomfortable exploration of how money grants autonomy and makes voices more audible, I wanted to consider the ways in which the Stork Derby trial exposed difficult truths about motherhood and the role and choices of women, many of which are still relevant today. For many women, domesticity and motherhood subsume the self; it is easy to become lost in family life, to become no more (and no less) than "mother," a role that is endlessly challenging and multidimensional, but is often reduced to stereotype. I wanted to write about the ways in which motherhood can coexist with desire; the ways in which longing and duty are the dual forces that are a point of conflict within so many women. I wanted to talk about the choices women have, and the ways in which, sometimes, they have very few choices at all.

I also wanted to present the idea of the Stork Derby as metaphor: for the ways in which women are often on unofficial public trial for the decisions they make in private. It's a strange dichotomy that women's domestic lives are often ignored (and that fictional presentations of these lives are often dismissed or trivialized). And yet these are some of the lives that are most harshly judged by the media: for stepping outside the unspoken constraints of the domestic ideal, women are often ruthlessly condemned.

Perhaps this is changing, but not quickly enough. Nearly a century after the start of the Stork Derby, women's lives and bodies and decisions are still often a matter of public scrutiny and, in some instances, public control: in Hungary, where the birth rate has been consistently falling over a number of years, the government offers large financial incentives to couples who have three or more children within a requisite time period. Loans are offered to heterosexual families intending to have children and, after the birth of each child, repayments are deferred. If the couple have three children or more, the loan is written off. However, couples who divorce or are found to be infertile have to repay the loan within 120 days. One woman recounted how, after her child was stillborn at seven months, she had to repay the loan.

Many of these policies are set against fearmongering around rising immigration, with politicians citing that the native population must have children because they are "facing extinction" and saying that "For us, migration is surrender."

Italy, Poland, Greece, and Russia also offer "baby bonuses" to families. In many ways, it is wonderful to see families with young children being offered financial support, but, as in 1936, the pressure to produce children, and the appropriation of female bodies, remains disturbing and raises the question as to exactly how equal gender roles are, when women are viewed as being more valid because they are fertile, and when their contribution to society is via procreation. For some women, motherhood is a choice (indeed, for others, it is a choice that is unavailable for various biological or financial reasons). But for many, motherhood becomes a manifold appropriation of women's bodies and involves the limitation or removal of many other options. I would be very happy if, in some small way, this book contributed to an ongoing and complex debate about women's bodies, ownership and choices.

Acknowledgements

This book would not exist without my wonderful, inspirational, relentless agent, Nelle Andrew, who shot down six of my ideas in the space of five minutes and then, when I said, in a fit of pique, "Well, *you* tell me what to write then," suggested I go away and find out about The Great Stork Derby because it sounded like exactly what I wanted to write. The idea consumed me for the next two years and even though the book is long-since finished, I haven't stopped thinking about those women and what they must have gone through. To the descendants of those women: I hope I have done justice to the story.

Thank you to my brilliant, gifted, insightful editor, Jill Taylor, who consistently pushes me to find the heart of the story and to write more compassionate, more complex and more emotional books than I ever think is possible. Her belief in my writing is unerring; I couldn't ask for a more enthusiastic champion of my work.

Huge thanks to my fantastic team at Penguin, Michael Joseph: Sriya Varadharajan, Courtney Barclay, Emma Plater, Hazel Orme, Bea McIntyre—I'm so lucky to have all of you behind my books.

The wonderful team at HarperCollins in the United States deserve endless thanks for their dedication to this novel. Thank you to the excellent Erin Wicks, Emma Kupor, and all the people at Harper who have put their time and love into my stories.

Enormous thanks to my early readers: Bill Gurney (and Nettie, of course), Luisa Cheshire, Bert Ward-Penny, Emma Ritson, Adele Kenny, my lovely sister Annabelle Flambard and my mum, Sue Lea. I'm so grateful to you for giving up your time and energy and being brave enough to offer advice. Criticism is the test of every relationship and now we'll never speak again. Thank you. ☺

Thank you to the lovely friends who offered emotional support and listened to me talking about writing this book: Luisa Cheshire (I can't overstate how grateful I am), Cathy Thompson, Penny Clarke, Andrea Docherty, Sachin Choithramani, Adele Kenny, Laura Baxter, Nicky Leamy, Alison Hall, Jane Guest, Sophie Pooler, Pamela Lyddon (Nana!), Kat Reay, Harriet Gott, Jenny Mitchell-Hilton, Claire Revell, Liz and Doug Day, Sarah Richardson, Luke Moore, Anna Hardman, Bansi Kara, Emma Swift, Phil Tuck, Sarah Lewsey, Claire Williams.

Thank you to the booksellers who have championed my books, particularly Mog and Pauline at Warwick Books and Tamsin, Judy, and Charlotte at Kenilworth Books. My huge gratitude to all the staff at Waterstones, particularly in Scotland for championing *The Metal Heart*. I hope you love this book just as much. Thanks, too, to all the book bloggers and readers who put time and passion into passing on their enthusiasm for my work.

The biggest thanks and the most love to the people who have to live with me and my stories, and to whom this book is dedicated. To Roger: the kindest, funniest, most interesting, and thoughtful man I know. And to Arthur and Rupert, my lovely, brilliant boys. I love you all more than words can possibly express.

READ MORE FROM CARLONE LEA!

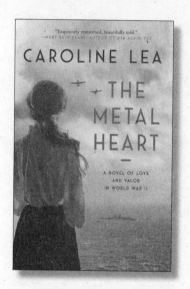

"The story of true innocents caught up in the machinery of war. Exquisitely researched, beautifully told, this tiny corner of Scotland came alive for me in all of my senses and I found myself rooting for the central characters with all my heart."

—MARY BETH KEANE,
author of *Ask Again, Yes*

"Memorable and compelling. A novel about what haunts us— and what should."

—SARAH MOSS,
author of *Ghost Wall*

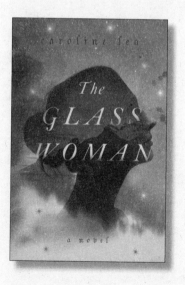